JEFFREY ARCHER

A MATTER
OF HONOR

To Will

A MATTER OF HONOR

Copyright © 1986 by Jeffrey Archer.

Cover photo © Vine-London.

For information address St. Martin's Press, 175 Fifth Avenue, New York, NY 10010.

ISBN: 0-312-93354-1
EAN: 80312-93354-8

Printed in the United States of America

Pocket Books edition published 1987
HarperPaperbacks edition / December 1993
St. Martin's Paperbacks edition / January 2005

St. Martin's Paperbacks are published by St. Martin's Press, 175 Fifth Avenue, New York, NY 10010.

10 9 8 7 6 5 4

PRAISE FOR
JEFFREY ARCHER
AND HIS BESTSELLING NOVELS

"Archer is a master entertainer."   —*Time*

"One of the top ten storytellers in the world"
—*Los Angeles Times*

"There isn't a better storyteller alive."   —Larry King

"Archer is one of the most captivating storytellers writing today. His novels are dramatic, fast-moving, totally entertaining—and almost impossible to put down."
—*Pittsburgh Press*

"Cunning plots, silken style...Archer plays a cat-and-mouse game with the reader."   —*The New York Times*

"A storyteller in the class of Alexandre Dumas... Unsurpassed skill...making the reader wonder intensely what will happen next."   —*The Washington Post*

A TWIST IN THE TALE

"Archer is a smoothly accomplished writer, able to produce a touching pause as well as a snappy pace."
—*Cosmopolitan*

"Archer's talent as a raconteur is evident...[His] straightforward style actually enhances each concluding jolt. Archer's understanding of human nature and his talent for surprise endings make this volume a must."
—*Publishers Weekly*

FIRST AMONG EQUALS

"A dramatic plot...An absorbing read."
—*Detroit Free Press*

MORE...

"This engrossing, well-spun tale of ambition and will-to-power is a pick-hit in the summer sweepstakes. Archer received his usual high marks for readability and gives his novel a pleasing sense of substance."

—*Publishers Weekly*

"Not since Gore Vidal's *1876* has there been such a cliff-hanger aspect to an election and to the selection of a head of government…At the conclusion, Archer brings the reader to a moment of truth…a surprising finish."

—*The San Diego Union-Tribune*

THE PRODIGAL DAUGHTER

"Chalk up another smash hit for Jeffrey Archer…An exceptional storyteller." —*John Barkham Reviews*

"Fast-moving and compelling." —*Library Journal*

KANE & ABEL

"A smashing good read!" —*The Des Moines Register*

"I defy anyone not to enjoy this book, which is one of the best novels I have ever read." —Otto Preminger

"A sprawling blockbuster!" —*Publishers Weekly*

"Grips the reader from the first page to the last. A smash hit." —*John Barkham Reviews*

AS THE CROW FLIES

"A certified page-turner." —*New York Daily News*

"Archer…has an extraordinary talent for turning notoriety into gold, and telling fast-moving stories." —*The Philadelphia Inquirer*

"An endearing story." —*The Wall Street Journal*

"Archer plots with skill, and keeps you turning the pages."
—*The Boston Globe*

"Top flight...Mr. Archer tells a story to keep you turning those pages."
—*The Washington Post*

"Great fun!"
—*Kirkus Reviews*

THE FOURTH ESTATE

"Telling...Triumphant...Proceeds in bursts of energy, like automatic fire."
—*London Times*

"Well-crafted and accomplished."
—*The Spectator*

HONOR AMONG THIEVES

"The action is furious."
—*Los Angeles Times Book Review*

"Outrageous and top-notch terror."
—*Vogue*

"Witty, action-filled...Archer's masterful narrative provides thrills and surprises."
—*Publishers Weekly*

"A taut, international political thriller, professionally crafted and plotted. The action and dialogue move forward seamlessly with no loose ends...*Honor Among Thieves* has excitement, currency and humor, and is expertly constructed. It will be another in the string of wildly successful novels by Jeffrey Archer."
—*The Milwaukee Journal Sentinel*

A QUIVER FULL OF ARROWS

"Exciting...Archer offers versatility, laughter, inventive plotting and a gift for characterization...*A Quiver Full of Arrows* is everything a reader could want."
—*Baltimore Sun*

"Amusing...Poignant."
—*The New York Times*

ALSO BY JEFFREY ARCHER

NOVELS
A Prisoner of Birth
False Impression
Not a Penny More, Not a Penny Less
Shall We Tell the President?
Kane & Abel
First Among Equals
The Prodigal Daughter
As the Crow Flies
Honor Among Thieves
The Fourth Estate
The Eleventh Commandment
Sons of Fortune

SHORT STORIES
Cat O' Nine Tales
A Quiver Full of Arrows
A Twist in the Tale
Twelve Red Herrings
To Cut a Long Story Short
The Collected Short Stories

PLAYS
Beyond Reasonable Doubt
Exclusive
The Accused

PRISON DIARIES
Volume One: Hell
Volume Two: Purgatory
Volume Three: Heaven

SCREENPLAYS
Mallory: Walking Off the Map
False Impression

PART I

THE KREMLIN

MOSCOW
May 19, 1966

CHAPTER ONE

THE KREMLIN
MAY 19, 1966

"IT'S A FAKE," said the Russian leader, staring down at the small exquisite painting he held in his hands.

"That can't be possible," replied his Politburo colleague. "The Czar's icon of Saint George and the dragon has been in the Winter Palace at Leningrad under heavy guard for over fifty years."

"True, Comrade Zaborski," said the old man, "but for fifty years we've been guarding a fake. The Czar must have removed the original sometime before the Red Army entered Petrograd and overran the Winter Palace."

The head of state security moved restlessly in his chair as the cat-and-mouse game continued. Yuri Zaborski knew after years of running the KGB who had been cast as the mouse the moment his phone had rung at four that morning to say that the General Secretary required him to report to the Kremlin office—immediately.

"How can you be so sure it's a fake, Leonid Ilyich?" the diminutive figure inquired.

"Because, my dear Zaborski, during the past eighteen months the age of all the treasures in the Winter Palace has been tested by carbon dating, the modern scientific process that does not call for a second opinion," said Brezhnev, displaying his newfound knowledge. "And what we have always thought to be one of the nation's masterpieces," he continued, "turns out to have been painted five hundred years after Rublev's original."

"But by whom and for what purpose?" asked the Chairman of the Committee for State Security, his voice incredulous.

"The experts tell me it was probably a court painter," replied the Russian leader, "who must have been commissioned to execute the copy only months before the Revolution took place. It has always worried the curator at the Winter Palace that the Czar's traditional silver crown was not attached to the back of the frame, as it was to all his other masterpieces," added Brezhnev.

"But I always thought that the silver crown had been removed by a souvenir hunter even before we had entered Petrograd."

"No," said the General Secretary dryly, his bushy eyebrows rising every time he completed a statement. "It wasn't the Czar's silver crown that had been removed, but the painting itself."

"Then what can the Czar have done with the original?" the Chairman said, almost as if he were asking himself the question.

"That is exactly what I want to know, Comrade," said Brezhnev, resting his hands on the desk and dwarfing the little painting that remained in front of him. "And you are the one who has been chosen to come up with the answer," he added.

For the first time the Chairman of the KGB looked unsure of himself.

"Do you have anything for me to go on?"

"Very little," admitted the General Secretary, flicking

open a file that he removed from the top drawer of his desk. He stared down at the closely typed notes headed, "The Significance of the Icon in Russian History." Someone had been up all through the night preparing a ten-page report that the leader had only found time to scan. Brezhnev's real interest began on page four. He quickly turned over the first three pages before reading aloud: " 'At the time of the Revolution, Czar Nikolai II obviously saw Rublev's masterpiece as his passport to freedom in the West. He must have had a copy made, which he then left on his study wall, where the original had previously hung.' " The Russian leader looked up. "Beyond that we have little to go on."

The head of the KGB looked perplexed. He remained puzzled as to why his leader should want state security involved in the theft of a minor masterpiece. "And how important is it that we find the original?" he asked, trying to pick up a further clue.

Leonid Brezhnev stared down at his Kremlin colleague.

"Nothing could be more important, Comrade," came back the reply. "And I shall grant you any resources you may consider necessary in terms of people and finance in your quest to discover the whereabouts of the Czar's icon."

"But if I were to take you at your word, Comrade General Secretary," said the head of the KGB, trying to disguise his disbelief, "I could so easily end up spending far more than the painting is worth."

"That would not be possible," said Brezhnev, pausing for effect, "because it's not the icon itself that I'm after." He turned his back on the Chairman for State Security and stared out of the window. He had always disliked not being able to see over the Kremlin wall and into Red Square. He waited for some moments before he proclaimed, "The money the Czar might have raised from selling such a masterpiece would only have kept Nikolai in his accustomed life-style for a matter of months, perhaps a year at the most. No, it's what we feel certain that the Czar had secreted *inside* the icon that would have guaranteed security for himself and his family for the rest of their days."

A little circle of condensation formed on the windowpane in front of the General Secretary.

"What could possibly be that valuable?" asked the Chairman.

"Do you remember, Comrade, what the Czar promised Lenin in exchange for his life?"

"Yes, but it turned out to be a bluff because no such document was hidden. . . ." He stopped himself just before saying "in the icon."

Zaborski stood silently, unable to witness Brezhnev's triumphant smile.

"You have caught up with me at last, Comrade. You see, the document was hidden in the icon all the time. We just had the wrong icon."

The Russian leader waited for some time before he turned back and passed over to his colleague a single sheet of paper. "This is the Czar's testimony indicating what we would find in the icon of Saint George and the dragon. At the time, nothing was discovered in the icon, which only convinced Lenin that it had been a pathetic bluff by the Czar to save his family from execution."

Yuri Efimovich Zaborski slowly read the hand-written testimony that had been signed by the Czar hours before his execution. Zaborski's hands began to tremble, and a bead of sweat appeared on his forehead long before he had reached the last paragraph. He looked across at the tiny painting, no larger than a book, which remained in the center of the Chairman's desk.

"Not since the death of Lenin," continued Brezhnev, "has anyone believed the Czar's claim, but now there can be little doubt that if we are able to locate the genuine masterpiece, we will undoubtedly also be in possession of the promised document."

"And with the authority of those who signed that document no one could question our legal claim," said Zaborski.

"That would undoubtedly prove to be the case, Comrade Chairman," replied the Russian leader, "and I also feel confident that we would receive the backing of the United Nations and the World Court if the Americans tried to deny us our right. But I fear time is now against us."

"Why?"

"Look at the completion date on the Czar's testimony, and you will see how much time we have left to honor our part of the agreement," said Brezhnev.

Zaborski stared down at the date, June 20, 1966. He handed back the testimony as he considered the enormity of the task with which his leader had entrusted him. Leonid Ilyich Brezhnev continued his monologue.

"So you can see, Comrade Zaborski, we have one month before the deadline, but if you can discover the whereabouts of the original icon, President Johnson's defense strategy would be rendered virtually useless, and the United States would then become a pawn on the Russian chessboard."

CHAPTER
TWO

APPLESHAW, HAMPSHIRE, ENGLAND
JUNE 1966

" 'AND TO MY dearly beloved son, Captain Adam Scott, M.C., I bequeath the sum of five hundred pounds.' "

Although Adam had anticipated the amount would be pitiful, he nevertheless remained bolt upright in his chair as the solicitor glanced over his half-moon spectacles.

The old lawyer who was seated behind the large partner's desk raised his head and blinked at the handsome young man before him. Adam put a hand nervously through his thick black hair, suddenly conscious of the lawyer's stare. Then Mr. Holbrooke's eyes returned to the papers in front of him.

" 'And to my dearly beloved daughter, Margaret Scott, I bequeath the sum of four hundred pounds.' " Adam was unable to prevent a small grin spreading across his face. Even in the minutiae of his final act, father had remained a chauvinist.

"'To the Hampshire County Cricket Club,'" droned on Mr. Holbrooke, unperturbed by Miss Scott's relative misfortunes, "'twenty-five pounds, life membership, finally paid up. To the Old Contemptibles, fifteen pounds. And to the Appleshaw Parish Church, ten pounds.'" Death membership, thought Adam. "'To Wilf Proudfoot, our loyal gardener part-time, ten pounds, and to Mrs. Mavis Cox, our daily help, five pounds.

"'And finally, to my dearly beloved wife Susan, our marital home, and the remainder of my estate.'" This pronouncement made Adam want to laugh out loud because he doubted if the remainder of Pa's estate, even if they sold his premium bonds and the prewar golf clubs, amounted to more than another thousand pounds.

But Mother was a daughter of the regiment and wouldn't complain, she never did. If God ever announced the saints, as opposed to some Pope in Rome, Saint Susan of Appleshaw would be up there with Mary and Elizabeth. All through his life Pa, as Adam always thought of his father, had set such high standards for the family to live up to. Perhaps that was why Adam continued to admire him above all men. He only hoped that if he ever had a son those standards would be passed on to another generation. Sometimes the very thought made him feel strangely out of place in the swinging sixties.

Adam began to shift in his chair, assuming that the proceedings were now drawing to a close. The sooner they were all out of this cold, drab little office the better, he felt.

Mr. Holbrooke looked up once more and cleared his throat, as if he were about to announce who was to be left the Goya or the Hapsburg diamonds. He pushed his half-moon spectacles farther up the bridge of his nose and stared back down at the last paragraphs of his late client's testament. The three surviving members of the Scott family sat in silence. What could he have to add? thought Adam.

Whatever it was, the solicitor had obviously pondered the final bequest several times, because he delivered the words like a well-versed actor, his eyes returning to the script only once.

"'And I also leave to my son,'" Mr. Holbrooke paused, "'the enclosed envelope,'" he said, holding it up, "'which I can only hope will bring him greater happiness than it did me. Should he decide to open the envelope, it must be on the condition that he will never divulge its contents to any other living person.'" Adam caught his sister's eye, but she only shook her head slightly, obviously as puzzled as he was. He glanced toward his mother, who looked shocked; was it fear or was it distress? Adam couldn't decide.

Without another word, Mr. Holbrooke passed the yellowed envelope over to the colonel's only son.

Everyone in the room remained seated, not quite sure what to do next. Mr. Holbrooke finally closed the thin file marked Col. Gerald Scott, D.S.O., O.B.E., M.C., pushed back his chair, and walked slowly over to the widow. They shook hands and she said, "Thank you," a faintly ridiculous courtesy, Adam felt, as the only person in the room who had made any sort of profit on this particular transaction had been Mr. Holbrooke, and that on behalf of Holbrooke, Holbrooke and Gascoigne.

He rose and went quickly by his mother's side.

"You'll join us for tea, Mr. Holbrooke?" she was asking.

"I fear not, dear lady," the lawyer began, but Adam didn't bother to listen further. Obviously the fee hadn't been large enough to cover Holbrooke taking time off for tea.

Once they had left the office and Adam had ensured his mother and sister were seated comfortably in the back of the family Morris Minor, he took his place behind the steering wheel. He had parked outside Mr. Holbrooke's office in the middle of High Street. No yellow lines in the streets of Appleshaw—yet, he thought. Even before he had switched on the ignition his mother had offered matter-of-factly, "We'll have to get rid of this, you know. I can't afford to run it now, not with petrol at six shillings a gallon."

"Don't let's worry about that today," said Margaret consolingly, but in a voice that accepted that her mother was right.

"I wonder what can be in that envelope, Adam," she added, wanting to change the subject.

"Detailed instructions on how to invest my five hundred pounds, no doubt," said her brother, attempting to lighten their mood.

"Don't be disrespectful of the dead," said his mother, the same look of fear returning to her face. "I begged your father to destroy that envelope," she added in a voice that was barely a whisper.

Adam's lips pursed when he realized this must be *the* envelope his father had referred to all those years ago when Adam had witnessed the one row he would ever see his parents have. Adam still remembered his father's raised voice and angry words just a few days after he had returned from Germany.

"I have to open it, don't you understand?" Pa had insisted.

"Never," his mother had replied. "After all the sacrifices I have made, you at least owe me that."

Over twenty years had passed since that confrontation, and he had never heard the subject referred to again, and the only time Adam ever mentioned it to his sister she could throw no light on what it might have been over.

Adam pressed his foot on the brake as they reached a crossroads at the end of High Street. He turned right and continued to drive out of the village for a mile or so down a winding country lane before bringing the old Morris Minor to a halt. Adam leapt out and opened the trellised gate, whose path led through a neat lawn to a little thatched cottage.

"I'm sure you ought to be getting back to London," were his mother's first words as she entered the drawing room.

"I'm in no hurry, Mother. There's nothing that can't wait until tomorrow."

"Just as you wish, my dear, but you don't have to worry yourself over me," his mother continued. She stared up at the tall young man who reminded her so much of Gerald. He would have been as good-looking as her husband if it weren't for the slight break in his nose. The same dark hair and deep brown eyes, the same open honest face, even the same gentle approach to everyone he came across. But most of all the same high standards of morality that had brought them to their present sad state. "And in any case I've always got Margaret to take care of me," she added. Adam looked across at his sister and wondered how she would now cope with Saint Susan of Appleshaw.

Margaret had recently become engaged to a London stockbroker, and although the marriage had been postponed, she would soon be wanting to start a life of her own. Thank God her fiancé had already put a down payment on a little house only fourteen miles away.

After tea and a sad uninterrupted monologue from their mother on the virtues and misfortunes of their father, Margaret cleared away and left the two of them alone. They had both loved him in such different ways, although Adam felt that he had never let Pa really know how much he appreciated him.

"Now that you're no longer in the army, my dear, I do hope you'll be able to find a worthwhile job," his mother said uneasily, as she recalled how difficult that had proved to be for his father.

"I'm sure everything will be just fine, Mother," he replied. "The Foreign Office has asked to see me again," he added, hoping to reassure her.

"Still, now that you've got five hundred pounds of your own," she said, "that should make things a little easier for you." Adam smiled fondly at her, wondering when she had last spent a day in London. His share of the Chelsea flat alone was four pounds a week, and he still had to eat occasionally. She raised her eyes and, looking up at the clock on the mantelpiece, said, "You'd better be getting along, my dear, I don't like the thought of you on that motorbike after dark."

Adam bent down to kiss her on the cheek. "I'll give you a call tomorrow," he said. On his way out, he stuck his head around the kitchen door and shouted, to his sister, "I'm off. I'll be sending you a check for fifty pounds."

"Why?" asked Margaret, looking up from the sink.

"Just let's say it's my blow for women's rights." He shut the kitchen door smartly to avoid the dishcloth that was hurled in his direction. Adam revved up his BSA and drove down the A303 through Andover and on toward London. As most of the traffic was coming west out of the city, he was able to make good time on his way back to the flat on Ifield Road.

Adam had decided to wait until he had reached the privacy of his own room before he opened the envelope. Lately the excitement in his life had not been such that he felt he could be blasé about the little ceremony. After all, in a way, he had waited most of his life to discover what could possibly be in the envelope he had now inherited.

Adam had been told the story of the family tragedy by his father a thousand times—"It's all a matter of honor, old chap," his father would repeat, lifting his chin and squaring his shoulders. Adam's father had not realized he had spent a lifetime overhearing the snide comments of lesser men and suffering the sidelong glances from those officers who had made sure they were not seen too regularly in his company. Petty men with petty minds. Adam knew his father far too well to believe, even for a moment, that he could have been involved in such treachery as was whispered. Adam took one hand off the handle bars and fingered the envelope in his inside pocket like a schoolboy the day before his birthday feeling the shape of a present in the hope of discovering some clue as to its contents. He felt certain that whatever it contained would not be to anyone's advantage now his father was dead, but it did not lessen his curiosity.

He tried to piece together the few facts he had been told over the years. In 1946, within a year of his fiftieth birthday, his father had resigned his commission from the army. The *Times* had described Pa as a brilliant tactical officer with a courageous war record. His resignation had been a decision that had surprised the *Times* correspondent, astonished his immediate family and shocked his regiment, as it had been assumed by all who knew him that it was only a matter of months before crossed swords and a baton would have been sewn on to his epaulette.

Because of the colonel's sudden and unexplained departure from the regiment, fact was augmented by fiction. When asked, all the colonel would offer was that he had had enough of war and felt the time had come to make a little money on which Susan and he could retire before it was too late. Even at the time few people found his story credible, and that credibility was not helped when the only job the colonel managed to secure for himself was as secretary of the local golf club.

It was only through the generosity of Adam's late grandfather, Gen. Sir Pelham Westlake, that he had been able to remain at Wellington College and thereby be given the opportunity to continue the family tradition and pursue a military career.

After leaving school Adam was offered a place at the Royal Military Academy, Sandhurst. During his days at the RMA, Adam was to be found diligently studying military history, tactics, and battle procedure, while on weekends he concentrated on rugby and squash. But his greatest success came whenever he ran cross-country races. For two years panting cadets from Cranwell and Dartmouth only saw his mud-spattered back as Adam went on to become the Inter-Services champion. He also became the middleweight boxing champion despite a Nigerian cadet's breaking his nose in the first round of the final. The Nigerian made the mistake of assuming the fight was already over.

When Adam graduated Sandhurst in August 1956, he managed ninth place in the academic order of merit, but his leadership and example outside the classroom was such that no one was surprised when he was awarded the Sword of Honor. Adam never doubted from that moment he would follow his father and command the regiment.

The Royal Wessex Regiment accepted the colonel's son soon after he had been awarded his regular commission. Adam quickly gained the respect of the soldiers and was popular with those officers whose currency was not to deal in rumor. As a tactical officer he had no equal, and when it came to combat duty it was clear he had inherited his father's courage. Yet, when six years later, the War Office published in the *London Gazette* the names of those subalterns who had been promoted to captain, Lt. Adam Scott was not to be found on the list. His contemporaries were genuinely surprised, while senior officers of the regiment remained tightlipped. To Adam it was becoming abundantly clear that he was not to be allowed to atone for whatever it was his father was thought to have done.

Eventually Adam was promoted to captain, but not before he had distinguished himself in the Malayan jungle in hand-to-hand fighting against the never-ending waves of Chinese soldiers. Having been captured and held prisoner by the Communists, he endured solitude and torture of the kind that no amount of training could have prepared him for. He escaped eight months after his incarceration only to discover on returning to the front line that he had been awarded a posthumous Military Cross. When, at the age of twenty-nine, Captain Scott passed his staff exam but still failed to be offered a regimental place at the staff college, he finally accepted he could never hope to command the regiment. He resigned his commission a few weeks later; there was no need to suggest that the reason he had done so was because he needed to earn more money.

While he was serving out his last few months with the regiment, Adam learned from his mother that Pa only had weeks to live. Adam made the decision not to inform his father of his resignation. He knew Pa would only blame himself, and he was at least thankful that he had died without being aware of the stigma that had become part of his son's daily life.

The sight of the outskirts of London made Adam's thoughts return, as they had so often lately, to the pressing problem of finding himself gainful employment. In the seven weeks he had been out of work he had already had more interviews with his bank manager than with prospective employers. It was true that he had another meeting lined up with the Foreign Office, but he had been impressed by the standard of the other candidates he had encountered on the way, and Adam was only too aware of his lack of a university qualification. However, he felt the first interview had gone well, and he had been quickly made aware of how many ex-officers had joined the service. When he discovered that the chairman of the selection board had a Military Cross, Adam assumed he wasn't being considered for desk work.

As he swung the motorbike into King's Road Adam once again fingered the envelope in his inside jacket pocket hoping, uncharitably, that Lawrence would not yet have returned from the bank. Not that he could complain: his old school friend had been extremely generous in offering him such a pleasant room in his spacious flat for only four pounds a week.

"You can start paying more when they make you an ambassador," Lawrence had told him.

"You're beginning to sound like a slumlord," Adam had retorted, grinning at the man he had so admired during their days at Wellington. For Lawrence—in direct contrast to Adam—everything seemed to come so easily—exams, jobs, sports and women, especially women. When he had won his place at Balliol and then gone on to take a first in Politics, Philosophy and Economics, no one was surprised. But when Lawrence chose banking as a profession, his contemporaries could not hide their disbelief. It seemed to be the first time he had embarked on anything that might be described as mundane.

Adam parked his motorbike just off Ifield Road, aware that like his mother's old Morris it would have to be sold if the Foreign Office job didn't materialize. As he strolled toward the flat a girl who passed gave him a second look; he didn't notice. He took the stairs in threes and had reached the fifth floor and was pushing his Yale key into the lock when a voice from inside shouted, "It's on the latch."

"Damn," said Adam under his breath.

"How did it go?" were Lawrence's first words as Adam entered the drawing room.

"Very well, considering," Adam replied, not quite sure what else he could say as he smiled at his flatmate. Lawrence had already changed from his city clothes into a blazer and gray flannels. He was slightly shorter and stockier than Adam with a head of wavy fair hair and gray thoughtful eyes that always seemed to be inquiring.

"I admired your father so much," he added. "He always assumed one had the same standards as he did." Adam could still remember nervously introducing Lawrence to his father one Speech Day. They had become friends immediately. But then Lawrence was not a man who dealt in rumors.

"Able to retire on the family fortune, are we?" asked Lawrence in a lighter vein.

"Only if that dubious bank you work for has found a way of converting five hundred pounds into five thousand in a matter of days."

"Can't manage it at the present time, old chum—not now that Harold Wilson has announced a standstill in wages and prices."

Adam smiled as he looked across at his friend. Although taller than Lawrence now, he could still recall those days when Lawrence seemed like a giant.

"Late again, Scott," he would say as Adam scampered past him in the corridor. Adam had looked forward to the day when he could do everything in the same relaxed superior style, or was it just that Lawrence was superior? His suits always seemed to be well pressed, his shoes always shone, and he never had a hair out of place. Adam still hadn't mastered how he did it all so effortlessly.

Adam heard the bathroom door open. He glanced interrogatively toward Lawrence.

"It's Carolyn," whispered Lawrence. "She'll be staying the night . . . I think."

When Carolyn entered the room Adam smiled shyly at the tall, beautiful woman. Her long, blond hair bounced on her shoulders as she walked toward them, but it was the faultless figure that most men couldn't take their eyes off. How did Lawrence manage it?

"Care to join us for a meal?" asked Lawrence, putting his arm round Carolyn's shoulder, his voice suddenly sounding a little too enthusiastic. "I've discovered this Italian restaurant that's just opened on Fulham Road."

"I might join you later," said Adam, "but I still have one or two papers left over from this afternoon that I ought to check through."

"Forget the finer details of your inheritance, my boy. Why not join us and spend the entire windfall in one wild spaghetti fling?"

"Oh, have you been left lots of lovely lolly?" asked Carolyn, in a voice so shrill and high-pitched that nobody would have been surprised to learn that she had recently been Deb of the Year.

"Not," said Adam, "when considered against my present overdraft."

Lawrence laughed. "Well, come along later if you discover there's enough left over for a plate of pasta." He winked at Adam—his customary sign for "Be sure you're out of the flat by the time when we get back. Or at least stay in your own room and pretend to be asleep."

"Yes, do come," cooed Carolyn, sounding as if she meant it—her hazel eyes remained fixed on Adam as Lawrence guided her firmly toward the door.

Adam didn't move until he was sure he could no longer hear her penetrating voice echoing on the staircase. Satisfied, he retreated to his bedroom and locked himself in. Adam sat down on the one comfortable chair he possessed and pulled his father's envelope out of his inside pocket. It was the heavy, expensive type of stationery Pa had always used, purchasing it at Smythson of Bond Street for almost twice the price he could have obtained it for at the local W. H. Smith's. "Captain Adam Scott, M.C." was written in his father's copperplate hand.

Adam opened the envelope carefully, his hand shaking slightly, and extracted the contents: a letter in his father's unmistakable hand and a smaller envelope that was clearly old, as it was faded with time. Written on the old envelope in an unfamiliar hand were the words "Colonel Gerald Scott" in faded ink of indeterminate color. Adam placed the old envelope on the little table by his side and, unfolding his father's letter, began to read. It was undated.

My dear Adam,

Over the years, you will have heard many explanations for my sudden departure from the regiment. Most of them will have been farcical, and a few of them slanderous, but I always considered it better for all concerned to keep my own counsel. I feel, however, that I owe you a fuller explanation, and that is what this letter will set out to do.

As you know, my last posting before I resigned my commission was at Nuremberg from February 1945 to October 1946. After four years of almost continuous action in the field I was given the task of commanding the British section that had responsibility for those senior-ranking Nazis who were awaiting trial for war crimes. Although the Americans had overall responsibility, I came to know the imprisoned officers quite well, and after a year or so I had even grown to tolerate some of them, Hess, Doenitz and Speer in particular, and I often wondered how the Germans would have treated us had the situation been reversed. Such views were considered unacceptable at the time. "Fraternization" was often on the lips of those men who are never given to second thoughts.

Among the senior Nazis with whom I came into daily contact was Reichsmarschall Hermann Goering, but unlike the three other officers I have previously mentioned, here was a man I detested from the first moment I came across him. I found him arrogant, overbearing and totally without shame about the barbaric role he had played in the war. And I never once found any reason to change my opinion of him. In fact

I sometimes wondered how I didn't end up on several occasions hitting him.

The night before Goering was due to be executed, he requested a private meeting with me. It was a Monday, and I can still recall every detail of that encounter as if it were only yesterday. I received the request when I took over the Russian watch from Major Vladimir Kosky. In fact Kosky personally handed me the written request. As soon as I had inspected the guard and dealt with the usual paperwork I went along with the duty corporal to see the Reichsmarschall in his cell. Goering stood to attention by his small low bed and saluted as I entered the room. The sparse, gray-painted brick cell always made me shudder.

"You asked to see me?" I said. I never could get myself to address him by his name or rank.

"Yes," he replied. "It was kind of you to come in person, Colonel. I simply wish to make the last request of a man condemned to death. Would it be possible for the corporal to leave us?"

Imagining it was something highly personal, I asked the corporal to wait outside. I confess I had no idea what could be so private when the man only had hours to live, but as the door closed he saluted again and then passed over the envelope you now have in your possession. As I took it all he said was, "Would you be kind enough not to open this until after my execution tomorrow." He then added, "I can only hope it will compensate for any blame that might later be placed on your shoulders." I had no idea what he could be alluding to at the time and presumed some form of mental instability had overtaken him. Many of the prisoners confided in me during their last few days, and toward the end some of them were undoubtedly on the verge of madness.

Adam stopped to consider what he would have done in the same circumstances, and decided to read on to discover whether father and son would have taken the same course.

However, Goering's final words to me as I left his cell seemed hardly those of a madman. He said quite simply: "Be assured it is a masterpiece; do not underestimate its value." Then he lit up a cigar as if he was relaxing at his club after a rather good dinner. We all had different theories as to who smuggled the cigars in for him, and equally wondered what might also have been smuggled out from time to time.

I placed the envelope in my jacket pocket and left him to join the corporal in the corridor. We then checked the other cells to see that all the prisoners were locked up for the night. The inspection completed, I returned to my office. As I was satisfied that there were no more immediate duties, I settled down to make out my report. I left the envelope in the jacket pocket of my uniform with every intention of opening it immediately after Goering's execution had been carried out the following morning. I was checking over the orders of the day when the corporal rushed into my office without knocking. "It's Goering, sir, it's Goering," he said frantically. From the panic on the man's face, I didn't need to ask for any details. We both ran all the way back to the Reichsmarschall's cell.

I found Goering lying face downward on his bunk. I turned him over to find he was already dead. In the commotion that immediately followed I quite forgot Goering's letter. An autopsy a few days later showed that he had died from poisoning; the court came to the conclusion that the cyanide capsule that had been found in his body must have been implanted in one of his cigars.

As I had been the last to see him alone, it took only a few whispers before my name was linked with his death. There was, of course, no truth in the accusation; indeed I never doubted for one moment that the court had delivered the correct verdict in his case and that he justly deserved to be hanged for the part he had played in the war.

So stung was I by the continual behind-the-back accusations that I might have helped Goering to an easy death by smuggling in the cigars that I felt the only thing to do in the circumstances was to resign my commission immediately for fear of bringing further dishonor to the regiment. When I returned to England later that year and finally decided to throw out my old uniform I came across the envelope again. When I explained to your mother the details of the incident she begged me to destroy the envelope, as she considered it had brought enough dishonor to our family already, and even if it did point to whoever had been responsible for helping Goering to his suicide, in her opinion such knowledge could no longer do anyone any good. I agreed to comply with her wishes, and although I never opened the envelope I could never get myself to destroy it, remembering that last sentence Goering had uttered about it being a masterpiece. And so finally I hid it among my personal papers.

However, since the imagined sins of the father are inevitably visited upon the next generation I feel no such qualms should influence you. If there is therefore anything to be gained from the contents of this envelope, I make only one request, namely that your mother should be the first to benefit from it without ever being allowed to know how such good fortune came about.

Over the years I have watched your progress with considerable pride and feel confident that I can leave you to make the correct decision.

If you are left in doubt about opening the envelope yourself, destroy it without further consideration. But if you open it only to discover its purpose is to involve you in some dishonorable enterprise, be rid of it without a second thought.

May God be with you.
Your loving father,

Gerald Scott

Adam read the letter over once again, realizing how much trust his father had placed in him. His heart thumped in his chest as he considered how Pa's life had been wasted by the murmurings and innuendos of lesser men. The same men who had succeeded in bringing his own career to a premature halt. When he had finished reading the missive for a third time he folded it up neatly and slipped it back into its envelope.

He then picked up the second envelope from the side table. The words "Colonel Gerald Scott" were written in a faded bold script across it.

Adam removed a comb from his inside pocket and wedged it into the corner of the envelope. Slowly he began to slit it open. He hesitated for a moment before extracting two pieces of paper, both yellowed with age. One appeared to be a letter while the other seemed to be a document of some sort. The crest of the Third Reich was embossed at the head of the letter paper above the printed name of Reichsmarschall Hermann Goering. Adam's hands began to tremble as he read the first line.

It began, *Sehr geehrter Herr Oberst Scott:*

CHAPTER
THREE

As the Black Chaika limousine drove out under the Spasskaya Bashnya and on to Red Square, two Kremlin guards in khaki uniforms sprang to attention and presented arms. A shrill whistle sounded, which ensured that Yuri Efimovich Zaborski would experience no delays on his route back to Dzerzhinsky Square.

Zaborski touched the corner of his black felt hat in automatic acknowledgment of the salute although his thoughts were elsewhere. As the car rumbled over the cobbled stones, he didn't even glance at the long snakelike line that stretched from Lenin's Tomb to the edge of Red Square. The first decision he had to make would undoubtedly be the most important. Which of his senior operatives should be charged with the task of heading the team to find the Czar's icon? He continued to ponder the problem as his driver took him across Red Square, passing the gray facade of the GUM department store away to his left before driving along Neitsa Kuibysheva.

Within moments of leaving his leader, the Chairman of State Security had formed in his own mind a shortlist of two, but which of those two, Valchek or Romanov, should be given the nod still taxed him. In normal circumstances he would have spent at least a week making such a decision, but the General Secretary's deadline of June 20 left him with no such freedom. He knew he would have to make the choice even before he reached his office. The driver cruised through another green light past the Ministry of Culture and into Cherkasski Bolshoi Pereulok, lined with its imposing blocklike, gray buildings. The car remained in the special inside lane that could be used only by senior party officials. In England, he was amused to learn, they had plans for such a traffic lane—but it would only be for the use of buses.

The car came to an abrupt halt outside KGB headquarters. It hadn't helped that they had been able to cover the three-kilometer journey in less than four minutes. The driver ran around and opened the back door to allow his master to step out, but Zaborski didn't move. The man who rarely changed his mind had already done so twice on the route back to Dzerzhinsky Square. He knew he could call on any number of bureaucrats and academics to do the spade work, but someone with flair was going to have to lead them and be responsible for reporting back to him.

His professional intuition told him to select Yuri Valchek, who had proved over the years to be a trusty and reliable servant of the State. He was also one of the Chairman's longest-serving heads of department. Slow, methodical and reliable, he had completed a full ten years as an agent in the field before confining himself to largely a desk job.

In contrast, Alex Romanov, who had only recently become head of his own section, had shown flashes of brilliance in the field, but they had been so often outweighed by a lack of personal judgment. At twenty-nine, he was the youngest and without question the most ambitious of the Chairman's select team.

Zaborski stepped out on to the pavement and walked toward another door held open for him. He strode across the marble floor and stopped only when he reached the lift gates. Several silent men and women had also been waiting for the lift, but when it returned to the ground floor and the Chairman stepped in to the little cage, none of them made any attempt to join him. Zaborski traveled slowly up toward his office, never failing to compare it unfavorably with the speed of the one American elevator he had experienced. They could launch their rockets before you could get to your office, his predecessor had warned him. By the time Zaborski had reached the top floor and the gates had been pulled back for him, he had made up his mind. It would be Valchek.

A secretary helped him off with his long black coat and took his hat. Zaborski walked quickly to his desk. The two files he had asked for were awaiting him. He sat down and began to pore over Valchek's file. When he had completed it he barked out an order to his hovering secretary: "Find Romanov."

Comrade Romanov lay flat on his back, his left arm behind his head and his opponent's right over his throat, preparing for a double knee-thrust. The coach executed it perfectly, and Romanov groaned as he hit the floor with a thud.

An attendant came rushing over to them and bent down to whisper in the coach's ear. The coach reluctantly released his pupil, who rose slowly as if in a daze, bowed to the coach, and then in one movement of right arm and left leg took the legs from under him and left him flat on the gymnasium floor before making his way quickly to the off-the-hook phone in the office.

Romanov didn't notice the girl who handed him the phone. "I'll be with him as soon as I have had a shower," was all she heard him say. The girl who had taken the call had often wondered what Romanov looked like in the shower. She, like all the other girls in the office, had seen him in the gymnasium a hundred times. Six feet tall with that long, flowing blond hair—he resembled a Western film star. And those eyes, "piercing blue," the friend who shared her desk described them.

"He's got a scar on his . . ." the friend confided.

"How do you know that?" she had asked, but her friend had only giggled in reply.

The Chairman meanwhile had opened Romanov's personal file for a second time and was still perusing the details. He began to read the different entries that made up a candid character assessment that Romanov would never see unless he became Chairman:

Alexander Petrovich Romanov. Born Leningrad,
12 March 1937.
Elected full party member 1958.
Father: Petr Nikolayevich Romanov, served on the
Eastern Front in 1942. On returning to Russia in 1945
refused to join Communist party. After several
reports of anti-state activities supplied by his son he
was sentenced to ten years in prison. Died in jail 20
October 1948.

Zaborski looked up and smiled—a child of the State.

Grandfather: Nikolai Alexandrovich Romanov,
merchant, and one of the wealthiest landowners in
Petrograd. Shot and killed on 11 May 1918, while
attempting to escape from the forces of the Red
Army.

The revolution had taken place between the princely grandfather and the reluctant Comrade father.

Alex, as he preferred to be known, had nevertheless inherited the Romanov ambition, so he enrolled for the party's Pioneer organization at the age of nine. By the age of eleven, he had been offered a place at a special school at Smolensk—to the disgust of some of the lesser party workers, who considered such privileges should be reserved for the sons of loyal party officials, not the sons of those in jail. Romanov immediately excelled in the classroom, much to the dismay of the director, who had been hoping to disprove any Darwinian theories. And at fourteen he was selected as one of the party's elite and made a member of the Komsomol.

By the age of sixteen, Romanov had won the Lenin language medal and the junior gymnastics prize, and despite the director's attempts to undermine young Alex's achievements, most members of the school board recognized Romanov's potential and ensured that he was still allowed to take a place at a university. As an undergraduate he continued to excel in languages, specializing in English, French, and German. Natural flair and hard work kept him near the top of every subject he specialized in.

Zaborski picked up the phone by his side. "I asked to see Romanov," he said curtly.

"He was completing his morning workout at the gymnasium, Comrade Chairman," replied the secretary. "But he left to change the moment he heard you wanted to see him."

The Chairman replaced the phone, and his eyes returned to the file in front of him. That Romanov could be found in the gymnasium at all hours came as no surprise: the man's athletic prowess had been acknowledged far beyond the service.

During his first year as a student, Romanov had diligently continued with his gymnastics and even gone on to represent the State side until the university coach had written in bold letters across one of his reports, "This student is too tall to be considered for senior Olympic competition." Romanov heeded the coach's advice and took up judo. Within two years, he had been selected for the 1958 Eastern Bloc games in Budapest, and within a further two years found that other competitors preferred not to be drawn against him on his inevitable route to the final. After his victory at the Second Soviet Games in Moscow the Western press crudely described him as "The Axe." Those who were already planning his long-term future felt it prudent not to enter him for the Olympics.

Once Romanov had completed his fifth year at the university and obtained his diploma (with distinction) he remained in Moscow and joined the diplomatic service.

Zaborski had now reached the point in the file at which he had first come across the self-confident young man. Each year the KGB was able to choose for assignment from the diplomatic service any person it considered to be of exceptional talent. Romanov was an obvious candidate. Zaborski's rule, however, was not to enlist anyone who didn't consider the KGB to be the elite. Unwilling candidates never made good operatives and sometimes even ended up working for the other side. Romanov showed no such doubt. He had always wanted to be an officer of the KGB. During the next six years he carried out tours at Soviet embassies in Paris, London, Prague, and Lagos. By the time he had returned to Moscow to join the headquarters staff he was a sophisticated operative who was as comfortable at an ambassadorial cocktail party as he was in the gymnasium.

Zaborski began to read some of the comments he himself had added to the report during the last four years—in particular how much Romanov had changed during his time on the Chairman's personal staff. As an operative he had reached the rank of major, having served successfully in the field before being appointed head of a department. Two red dots—indicating successful missions—were placed by his name: a defecting violinist attempting to leave Prague and a general who had thought he was going to be the next head of a small African state. What impressed Zaborski most about his protégé's efforts was that the Western press thought the Czechs were responsible for the first and the Americans for the second. Romanov's most significant achievement, however, had been the recruitment of an agent from the British Foreign Office, whose parallel rise had only assisted Romanov's career. Romanov's appointment as head of a department had surprised no one, Romanov included, although it soon became clear to Zaborski that he missed the raw excitement of fieldwork.

The Chairman turned to the last page, a character assessment, in which the majority of contributors were in accord: ambitious, sophisticated, ruthless, arrogant but not always reliable were the words that appeared with regularity in almost every summation.

There was an assertive rap on the door. Zaborski closed the file and pressed a button under his desk. The doors clicked open to allow Alexander Petrovich Romanov to enter the room.

"Good morning, Comrade Chairman," said the elegant young man who now stood at attention in front of him. Zaborski looked up and felt a little envy that the gods had bestowed so much on one so young. Still, it was he who understood how to use such a man to the State's best advantage.

He continued to stare into those clear blue eyes and considered that if Romanov had been born in Hollywood he would not have found it hard to make a living. His suit looked as if it had been tailored in Savile Row—and probably had been. Zaborski chose to ignore such irregularities although he was tempted to ask the young man where he had his shirts made.

"You called for me," said Romanov.

The Chairman nodded. "I have just returned from the Kremlin," he said. "The General Secretary has entrusted us with a particularly sensitive project of great importance to the State." Zaborski paused. "So sensitive in fact that you will report only to me. You can hand-select your own team, and no resources will be denied you."

"I am honored," said Romanov, sounding unusually sincere.

"You will be," replied the Chairman, "if you succeed in discovering the whereabouts of the Czar's icon."

"But I thought . . ." began Romanov.

CHAPTER
FOUR

ADAM WALKED OVER to the side of his bed and removed from the bookshelf the Bible his mother had given him as a Confirmation present. As he opened it a layer of dust rose from the top of the gold leaf-edged pages. He placed the envelope in Revelations and returned the Bible to the shelf.

Adam strolled through to the kitchen, fried himself an egg and warmed up the other half of the previous day's tinned beans. He placed the unwholesome meal on the kitchen table, unable to put out of his mind the one Lawrence and Carolyn must now be enjoying at the new Italian restaurant. After Adam had finished and cleared his plate away, he returned to his room and lay on the bed thinking. Would the contents of the faded envelope finally prove his father's innocence?

When the grandfather clock in the hall chimed ten times, Adam lifted his long legs over the end of the bed and pulled the Bible back out of the bookshelf. With some apprehension Adam removed the envelope. Next, he switched on the reading light by the side of the small writing desk, unfolded the two pieces of paper, and placed them in front of him.

One appeared to be a personal letter from Goering to Adam's father, while the other had the look of an older, more official document. Adam placed this second document to one side and began to go over the letter line by line. It didn't help.

He tore a blank piece of paper from a notepad that he found on Lawrence's desk and started to copy down the text of Goering's letter. He left out only the greeting and what he assumed to be a valediction, *hochachtungsvoll,* followed by the Reichsmarschall's large, bold signature. He checked over the copy carefully before replacing the original back in its faded envelope. He had just begun the same process with the official document, using a separate sheet of paper, when he heard a key turning, followed by voices at the front door. Both Lawrence and Carolyn sounded as if they had drunk more than the promised bottle of wine, and Carolyn's voice in particular had ascended into little more than a series of high-pitched giggles.

Adam sighed and switched off the light by the side of the desk so they wouldn't know he was still awake. In the darkness he became more sensitive to their every sound. One of them headed toward the kitchen, because he heard the refrigerator door squelch close and, a few seconds later, the sound of a cork being extracted—he presumed from his last bottle of white wine, as they were unlikely to be so drunk they had started on the vinegar.

Reluctantly he rose from his chair and, circling his arms in front of him, he made his way back to bed. He touched the corner of the bedstead and quietly lowered himself onto the mattress, then waited impatiently for Lawrence's bedroom door to close.

He must have fallen asleep because the next thing he remembered was the tick of the hall clock. Adam licked his fingers and rubbed them over his eyes as he tried to get accustomed to the dark. He checked the little luminous dial on his alarm clock: ten past three. He eased himself off the bed gingerly, feeling more than a little crumpled and weary.

Slowly he groped his way back toward the desk, banging his knee on the corner of a chest of drawers during his travels. He couldn't stop himself cursing. He fumbled for the light switch, and when the bulb first glowed it made him blink several times. The faded envelope looked so insignificant—and perhaps it was. The official document was still laid out on the center of the table alongside the first few lines of his handwritten duplicate.

Adam yawned as he began to study the words once more. The document was not as simple to copy out as the letter had been, because this time the hand was spidery and cramped, as if the writer had considered paper an expensive commodity. Adam left out the address on the top right-hand corner and reversed the eight-digit number underlined at the head of the text. Otherwise he ended up with a faithful transcript of the original.

The work was painstaking and took a surprisingly long time. He wrote out each word in block capitals, and when he wasn't certain of the spelling he put down the possible alternative letters below; he wanted to be sure of any translation the first time.

"My, you do work late," whispered a voice from behind him.

Adam spun round, feeling like a burglar who had been caught with his hands on the family silver.

"You needn't look so nervous. It's only me," said Carolyn, standing by the bedroom door.

Adam stared up at the tall blonde who was even more attractive clad only in Lawrence's large unbuttoned pajamas and floppy slippers than she had been fully dressed. Her long, fair hair now dropped untidily over her shoulders, and he began to understand what Lawrence had meant when he had once described her as someone who could turn a matchstick into a Cuban cigar.

"The bathroom is at the end of the corridor," said Adam, a little feebly.

"It wasn't the bathroom I was looking for, silly." She giggled. "I don't seem able to wake Lawrence. After all that wine he's passed out like a defeated heavyweight boxer." She

sighed. "And long before round fifteen. I don't think anything will rouse him again until morning." She took a step
toward him.

Adam stammered something about feeling rather beat
himself. He made sure his back shielded her from any sight
of the papers on the desk.

"Oh, God," said Carolyn, "you're not a queer, are you?"

"Certainly not," said Adam, a little pompously.

"Just don't fancy me?" she asked.

"Not that exactly," said Adam.

"But Lawrence is your chum," she said. Adam didn't reply.

"My God, this is the sixties, Adam. Share and share
alike."

"It's just that . . ." began Adam.

"What a waste," said Carolyn, "perhaps another time." She
tiptoed to the door and slipped back into the corridor, unaware of her German rival.

The first action Romanov took on leaving the Chairman's
office that morning was to return to his alma mater and
hand-pick a team of twelve researchers. From the moment
they had been briefed they proceeded to study in pairs on
four-hour shifts, so that the work could continue night and
day.

The early information had come in almost by the hour,
and the researchers had quickly been able to establish that
the Czar's icon had remained in his private quarters at the
Winter Palace in Petrograd until as late as December 1914.
Romanov studied religiously a photo of the small delicate
painting of Saint George and the dragon—Saint George in a
tiny mosaic pattern of blue and gold while the dragon was in
red and yellow. Although he had never shown any interest in
art, Romanov could well understand why people could be
moved by the little masterpiece. He continued to read details of the icon's history but still couldn't work out why it
was so important to the State. He wondered if Zaborski even
knew the reason.

A royal servant who had testified before the People's Court three years after the Revolution claimed that the Czar's icon had disappeared for a few days in 1915 after the visit of Ernst Ludwig, Grand Duke of Hesse. At the time, the inquisitors had taken scant interest in the misplaced icon because it was still on the wall of the Czar's study when they had stormed the Winter Palace. What concerned the court more was why, in the middle of a fierce war with the Kaiser's Germany, the Grand Duke of Hesse should want to visit the Czar at all.

The professor of history at the university had immediately been asked for his opinion. The great academic was puzzled by the request, as the KGB had never shown any interest in the nation's past history before. Nevertheless he briefed Romanov on everything that was known of the incident. Romanov pored over his report once again. The Grand Duke, it was thought, had been on a secret visit to his sister Alexandra, the Czarina. Historians now believed that it had been his intention to secure a cease-fire between Germany and Russia, in the hope that Germany could then concentrate her war efforts on the British and the French.

There was no proof that the Czar made any promises on behalf of his people, but the Grand Duke, it seemed, did not return to Germany empty-handed. As the reports of the proceedings of the People's Court showed, another palace servant had been instructed to wrap up the Czar's icon and pack it with the Grand Duke's belongings. However, no one on the palace staff could properly explain to the court how a few days later the icon reappeared in its rightful place on the wall of the Czar's study.

Romanov's chief researcher, Prof. Oleg Konstantinov, having studied the professor's notes and the other researchers' contributions, had underlined his own conclusion in red ink.

"The Czar must have replaced the original painting with a brilliant copy, having handed over the real icon for safekeeping to his brother-in-law, the Grand Duke."

"But why," asked Romanov, "when the Czar had a palace

full of Goyas, El Grecos, Titians, and Rubenses did he bother to smuggle out one icon, and why does Brezhnev want it back so badly?"

Romanov instructed the professor and his twenty-four researchers to turn their talents to the Royal House of Hesse in the hope of tracing what had then happened to the Czar's icon. Within ten days, they possessed between them more information about the Grand Duke and his family than any professor at any university had managed to gather in a lifetime. As each file appeared on his desk Romanov labored through the night, checking every scrap of information that might give him a lead to the whereabouts of the original painting. Romanov came to a dead end when after the Grand Duke's death the painting had been left to his brother, who was tragically killed in a plane crash. Nothing had been seen or heard of the icon after that day.

By the beginning of the third week, Romanov had reluctantly reached the conclusion that there was nothing new on the whereabouts of the icon to be discovered. He was preparing his final report for the Chairman of the KGB when one researcher, Comrade Petrova, whose mind did not work in parallel lines, stumbled across an article in the *London Times* of Wednesday, 17 November 1937. Petrova bypassed the research leader and handed the relevant photocopy to Romanov personally, who, over the next few hours, read the news item so often that he came to know it by heart.

In keeping with the paper's tradition, the foreign correspondent remained anonymous. The article carried the dateline "Ostend, 16 November 1937." It read:

Grand Duke George of Hesse and four members of his family were tragically killed this morning when a Sabena aircraft carrying them from Darmstadt to London crashed in thick fog over the Belgian countryside.

The Grand Duke had been on his way to England to attend the wedding of his younger brother, Prince Louis, to the Hon. Joanna Geddes. The younger brother had been waiting at Croydon Airport to greet his family when the news was broken to him. He immediately cancelled his original wedding plans and announced they would be rescheduled with a small private service in the Chapel at Windsor.

The *Times* went on: "Prince Louis, who succeeds his brother as the Grand Duke of Hesse, will leave for Ostend with his bride later today in order that they can accompany the five coffins on their journey back to Germany. The funerals will all take place in Darmstadt on 23 November."

It was the next paragraph that the researcher had circled boldly.

"Some of the late Grand Duke's personal belongings, including several wedding presents for Prince Louis and his bride, were scattered for miles in the vicinity of the crashed aircraft. The German government announced this morning that a senior German general has been appointed to lead a team of salvage experts to ensure the recovery of any family possessions that still belong to the Grand Duke's successor."

Romanov immediately called for the young researcher. When Anna Petrova arrived a few minutes later she gave no impression of being overawed by her head of department. She accepted that it would be hard to make any impression on him with the clothes she could afford. However, she had put on the smartest outfit she possessed and cut her hair in the style of an American actress called Mia Farrow, whom she had seen in one of the few films not banned by the authorities. She hoped Romanov would notice.

"I want you to scour the *Times* every day from 17 November 1937 to six months later, and also check the German and Belgian press during the same period in case you come across anything that would show what the salvage experts had discovered." He dismissed her with a smile.

Within twenty-four hours Comrade Petrova barged back into Romanov's office without even bothering to knock. Romanov merely raised his eyebrows at the discourtesy before devouring an article she had discovered in the *Berlin Zeitung* of Saturday, 29 January 1938.

> The investigation into the crash last November of the Sabena aircraft that was carrying the Hesse royal family to London has now been concluded. All personal possessions belonging to the family that were discovered in the vicinity of the wreckage have been returned to the Grand Duke. Prince Louis, it is understood, was particularly saddened by the loss of a family heirloom that was to have been a wedding gift from his brother, the late Grand Duke. The gift, a painting known as the "Czar's Icon," had once belonged to his uncle, Czar Nikolai II. The icon of Saint George and the dragon, although only a copy of Rublev's masterpiece, was considered to be one of the finest examples of early twentieth-century craftsmanship to come out of Russia since the Revolution.

Romanov looked up at the researcher. "Twentieth century be damned," he said. "It was the fifteenth-century original, and none of them realized it at the time—perhaps not even the old Grand Duke himself. No doubt the Czar had plans for the icon had he managed to escape."

Romanov dreaded having to tell Zaborski that he could now prove conclusively that the original Czar's icon had been destroyed in a plane crash some thirty years before. Such news would not ensure promotion for its messenger, as he remained convinced that there was something far more important than the icon at stake for Zaborski to be so involved.

He stared down at the photograph above the *Zeitung* report. The young Grand Duke was shaking hands with the general in charge of the salvage team that had been successful in returning so many of the Prince's family possessions. "But did he return them all?" Romanov said out loud.

"What do you mean?" asked the young researcher. Romanov waved his hand as he continued to stare at the pre-war, faded photograph of the two men. Although the general was unnamed, every schoolboy in Germany would have recognized the large, impassive, heavy-jowled face with the chilling eyes that would become famous to the Allied powers.

Romanov looked up at the researcher. "You can forget the Grand Duke from now on, Comrade Petrova. Concentrate your efforts on Reichsmarschall Hermann Goering."

When Adam woke his first thoughts were of Carolyn. His yawn turned into a grin as he considered her invitation of the night before. Then he remembered. He jumped out of bed and walked over to his desk: everything was in place exactly as he had left it. He yawned for a second time.

It was ten to seven. Although he felt as fit as he had been the day he left the army some seven weeks before, he still completed a punishing routine of exercise every morning. He intended to be at his peak when the Foreign Office put him through a physical. In moments he was dressed in a sweatshirt and a pair of running shorts. He pulled on an old army tracksuit and finally tied up his gym shoes.

Adam tiptoed out of the flat, not wanting to wake Lawrence or Carolyn, although he suspected she was wide awake, waiting impatiently. For the next thirty-four minutes he pounded the pavement down to the Embankment, across Albert Bridge and through Battersea Park, to return by way of Chelsea Bridge. Only one thought was going through his mind. After twenty years of gossip and innuendo this was going to be the one chance to clear his father's name. The moment he arrived back at the flat Adam checked his pulse: 150 beats a minute. Sixty seconds later it was down to 100, in another minute 70, and before the fourth minute was up it was back to a steady 58. It's your recovery that proves fitness, not your speed, his old Physical Training Instructor at Aldershot had drummed into him.

As Adam walked back through to his room, there was still

no sign of Carolyn. Lawrence, smart in a gray pinstriped suit, was preparing breakfast in the kitchen while glancing at the cricket scores in the *Daily Telegraph*.

"The West Indies made 526," he informed Adam forlornly.

"Have we begun our innings?" shouted Adam from the bathroom.

"No, bad light stopped play."

Adam groaned as he stripped for the shower. He was ready for his morning game of finding out how long he could last under the freezing jets. The forty-eight needles of ice-cold water beat down on his back and chest, which made him take several deep breaths. Once you survive the first thirty seconds, you could stay under forever, the instructor had assured them. Adam emerged three minutes later, satisfied but still damning the PTI, from whose influence he felt he would never escape.

Once he had toweled himself down Adam walked back to his bedroom. A moment later he had thrown on his dressing gown and joined his friend in the kitchen for breakfast. Lawrence was now seated at the kitchen table concentrating hard on a bowl of cornflakes, while running a finger down the foreign exchange rates in the *Financial Times*.

Adam checked his watch: already ten past eight. "Won't you be late for the office?" he asked.

"Dear boy," said Lawrence, "I am not a lackey who works at the kind of bank where the customers keep shop hours."

Adam laughed.

"But I will, however, have to be shackled to my desk in London by nine-thirty," Lawrence admitted. "They don't send a driver for me nowadays," he explained. "In this traffic, I told them it's so much quicker by tube."

Adam started to make himself breakfast.

"I could give you a lift on my motorbike."

"Can you imagine a man in my position arriving at the headquarters of Barclays Bank on a motorbike? The chairman would have a fit," he added, as he folded the *Financial Times*.

Adam cracked a second egg into the frying pan.

"See you tonight, then, glorious, unwashed, and unemployed," declared Lawrence as he collected his rolled umbrella from the hat stand.

Adam cleared away and washed up, happy to act as housewife while he was still unemployed. Despite years of being taken care of by an orderly, he knew exactly what was expected of him. All he had planned before his interview with the Foreign Office that afternoon was a long bath and a slow shave. Then he remembered that Reichsmarschall Goering was still resting on the table in the bedroom.

"Have you come up with anything that would indicate Goering might have kept the icon for himself?" asked Romanov, turning hopefully to the researcher.

"Only the obvious," Anna Petrova replied in an offhand manner.

Romanov considered reprimanding the young girl for such insolence but said nothing on this occasion. After all, Comrade Petrova had proved to be far the most innovative of his team of researchers.

"And what was so obvious?" inquired Romanov.

"It's common knowledge that Hitler put Goering in charge of all the art treasures captured on behalf of the Third Reich. But as the Führer had such fixed personal opinions as to what constituted quality, many of the world's masterpieces were judged as 'depraved' and therefore unworthy to be put on public view for the delectation of the master race."

"So what happened to them?"

"Hitler ordered them to be destroyed. Among those works condemned to death by burning were such masters as Van Gogh, Manet, Monet—and especially the young Picasso, who was considered unworthy of the blue-blooded Aryan race. Hitler was grooming to rule the world."

"You are not suggesting Goering could have stolen the Czar's icon," asked Romanov staring up at the ceiling, "only then to burn it?"

"No, no. Goering was not that stupid. As we now know, he didn't always obey the Führer's every word."

"Goering failed to carry out Hitler's orders?" said Romanov in disbelief.

"Depends from which standpoint you view it," Petrova replied. "Was he to behave as his lunatic master demanded or turn a blind eye and use his own common sense?"

"Stick to the facts," said Romanov, his voice suddenly sharp.

"Yes, Comrade Major," said the young researcher in a tone that suggested she believed herself to be indispensable, at least for the time being.

"When it came to it," Petrova continued, "Goering did not destroy any of the denounced masterpieces. He held some public burnings in Berlin and Düsseldorf of lesser-known German artists, who would never have fetched more than a few hundred marks on the open market in the first place. But the masterpieces, the real works of genius, were moved discreetly over the border and deposited in the vaults of Swiss banks."

"So there's still an outside chance that having found the icon . . ."

"He then had it placed in a Swiss bank," added Petrova. "I wish it were that simple, Comrade Major," said the researcher, "but unfortunately Goering wasn't quite as naive as the newspaper cartoonists of the time made him out to be. I think he deposited the paintings and antiques in several Swiss banks, and to date no one has ever been able to discover which banks or the aliases he used."

"Then *we* shall have to do so," said Romanov. "Where do you suggest we start?"

"Well, since the end of the war many of the paintings have been found and restored to their rightful owners, including the galleries of the German Democratic Republic. Others, however, have appeared on walls as far-flung as the Getty Museum in California and the Gotoh in Tokyo, sometimes without a fully satisfactory explanation. In fact, one of Renoir's major works can currently be seen hanging on the walls of the Metropolitan Museum in New York. It undoubtedly passed through Goering's hands, although the curator of the Museum has never been willing to explain how the gallery came into possession of it."

"Have all the missing pictures now been found?" asked Romanov anxiously.

"Over seventy percent, but there are still many more to be accounted for. Some may even have been lost or destroyed, but my guess is that there are still a large number that remain lodged in Swiss banks."

"How can you be so certain?" demanded Romanov, fearful that his last avenue might be closing.

"Because the Swiss banks always return valuables when they can be certain of a nation's or individual's right of possession. In the case of the Grand Duke of Hesse and the Czar's icon there was no proof of ownership, as the last official owner was Czar Nikolai II, and he, as every good Russian knows, Comrade, had no successors."

"Then I must do exactly what Goering did and retrace his steps by going direct to the banks. What has been their policy to date?" asked Romanov.

"That differs from establishment to establishment," said Petrova. "Some banks wait for twenty years or more and then try either by extensive research or advertising to contact the owner or their next of kin. In the case of the Jews who lost their lives under the Nazi regime, it has often proved impossible to trace a legitimate owner. Although I have been unable to prove it, I suspect they kept the rewards and split the proceeds among themselves," said Petrova. "Typical capitalists."

"That is neither fair nor accurate, Comrade," said Romanov, glad to show that he had also been doing some research. "Because that is another of the great myths perpetrated by the poor. In fact, when the banks have been unable to discover the rightful owner of any treasures left with them they have handed them over to the Swiss Red Cross to auction."

"But if the Czar's icon had ever been auctioned wouldn't we have heard about it through one of our agents?"

"Precisely," said Romanov. "And we've already checked through the inventory of the Red Cross: four icons have been disposed of but none of them is of Saint George and the dragon."

"Then that can only mean some unscrupulous bankers have disposed of the icon privately once they felt sure no one was going to make a claim."

"Another false premise, I suspect, Comrade Petrova."

"How can you be so certain?" the young researcher asked.

"For one simple reason, Comrade. The Swiss banking families all know each other intimately and have never shown in the past any propensity for breaking the law. Swiss justice, in our experience, is as tough on corrupt bankers as it is on murderers, which is precisely why the Mafia was never happy about laundering its money through the established banks. The truth is that Swiss bankers make so much money dealing with honest people that it has never been in their best interests to become involved with crooks. There are remarkably few exceptions to this rule, which is the reason so many people are willing to do business with the Swiss."

"So if Goering stole the Czar's icon and deposited it in a Swiss bank vault, it could be anywhere in the world by now," said Petrova.

"I doubt it."

"Why?" sighed Petrova, a little peeved that her deductions were now proving wide of the mark.

"Because for the past three weeks I have had heaven knows how many operatives combing Europe for the Czar's icon. They have spoken to nearly every major curator, keeper, dealer, and crook in the art world, and yet they still haven't come up with a single lead. And why not? Because the only people who have seen the icon since 1917 were the Hesses and Goering, which leaves me with only one hope if it was not destroyed when the Grand Duke's plane crashed," said Romanov.

"Namely?" asked Petrova.

"That while the rest of the world is under the illusion that the original still hangs in the Winter Palace, it has for the past twenty years been lodged in a Swiss bank waiting for someone to claim it."

"A long shot," said the researcher.

"I am quite aware of that," said Romanov sharply, "but don't forget that many Swiss banks have a twenty-five-year rule before disclosure, some even thirty. One or two even have no deadline at all as long as enough money has been deposited to cover the housing of the treasure."

"Heaven knows how many banks there might be who fall into that category," sighed Petrova.

"Heaven knows," agreed Romanov, "and so will you by nine o'clock tomorrow morning. And then it will be necessary for me to pay a visit to the one man in this country who knows everything about banking."

"Am I expected to start straight away, Comrade Major?" the researcher asked coyly.

Romanov smiled and looked down into the girl's green eyes. Dressed in the dull gray uniform of her trade, no one would have given her a second look. But in the nude she was quite magnificent. He leaned over until their lips nearly met.

"You'll have to rise very early, Anna, but for now, just turn out the light."

CHAPTER FIVE

IT TOOK ADAM only a few more minutes before he had checked over both documents. He put the original back in the faded envelope and replaced it in the Bible on his book shelf. Finally he folded his duplicate copy of Goering's letter into three horizontal pieces and cut it carefully into three separate strips, which he placed in a clean envelope and left on his bedside table. Adam's next problem was how to obtain a translation of the document and Goering's letter without arousing unnecessary curiosity. Years of army training had taught him to be cautious when faced with an unknown situation. He quickly dismissed the German embassy, the German Tourist Board, and the German press agency, as all three were too official and therefore likely to ask unwanted questions. Once he was dressed he went to the hall and began to flick through the pages in the London E-K directory until his finger reached the column he had been searching for.

German Broadcasting

German Cultural Institute
German Federal Railway
German Hospital
German Old People's Home

His eye passed over "German Technical Translations" and stopped at a more promising entry. The address was given as Bayswater House, 35 Craven Terrace, W2. He checked his watch.

Adam left the flat a few minutes before ten, the three pieces of the letter now safely lodged in the inside pocket of his blazer. He strolled down Edith Grove and onto King's Road, enjoying the morning sun. The street had been transformed from the one he had known as a young subaltern. Boutiques had taken the place of antiquarian bookshops. Record shops had replaced the local cobbler, and Dolcis had given way to Mary Quant. Take a fortnight's holiday, and you couldn't be sure anything would still be there when you returned, he reflected ruefully.

Crowds of people spilled out from the pavement onto the road, staring or hoping to be stared at, according to their age. As Adam passed the first of the record shops, he had no choice but to listen to "I Wanna Hold Your Hand," as it blared into the ears of everyone within shouting distance.

By the time Adam reached Sloane Square the world had almost returned to normal—Peter Jones, W. H. Smith's and the London underground. The words his mother had sung so often over the kitchen sink came back to him every time he walked into the square.

> And you're giving a treat (penny ice and cold meat)
> To a party of friends and relations,
> They're a ravenous horde, and they all came aboard
> At Sloane Square and South Kensington stations.

He paid a shilling and threepence for a ticket to Paddington and, installed in a half-empty carriage, once again went over his plan. When he emerged into the open air at Paddington he checked the street name, and once he was sure of his bearings walked down to Craven Road until he came to the first available newsagent and then asked the directions for Craven Terrace.

"Fourth road on the right, mate," said the shopkeeper, not bothering to look up from a pile of *Radio Times* on which he was penciling names. Adam thanked him and a few minutes later found himself standing at the end of a short drive, looking up at the bold green-and-yellow sign: The German Young Men's Christian Association.

He opened the gate, walked up the drive, and strode confidently through the front door. He was stopped by a porter standing in the hallway.

"Can I help you, guv'nor?"

Adam put on an exaggerated military accent and explained that he was looking for a young man called Hans Kramer.

"Never 'eard of 'im, sir," said the porter, almost standing to attention when he recognized the regimental tie. He turned to a book that lay open on the desk. " 'e isn't registered," he added, a Woodbine-stained thumb running down the list of names in front of him. "Why don't you try the lounge or the games room?" he suggested, gesturing with the thumb to a door on the right.

"Thank you," said Adam, not dropping the plummy tones. He walked smartly across the hall and through the swinging doors—which from the lack of paint on the base looked as if they had been kicked more often than they had been pushed. He glanced around the room. Several students were lounging about reading German papers and magazines. He wasn't sure where to start until he spotted a studious-looking girl on her own in a corner, poring over a copy of *Time* magazine. Brezhnev's face stared out from the cover. Adam strolled over and took the empty seat beside her. She glanced sideways at him and couldn't hide her surprise at his formal dress. He waited for her to put the paper down before asking, "I wonder if you could assist me?"

"How?" inquired the girl, sounding a little apprehensive.

"I just need something translated."

She looked relieved. "I will see if I can help. Have you brought something with you?"

"Yes I have, I hope it isn't too difficult," he said. Adam took the envelope from his inside pocket and extracted the first paragraph of Goering's letter. Then he put the envelope back in his pocket, took out a little notebook, and waited expectantly. He felt like a cub reporter.

She read the paragraph over two or three times, then seemed to hesitate.

"Is anything wrong?"

"Not exactly," she replied, still concentrating on the words in front of her. "It's just that it's a little bit old-fashioned, so that I might not be able to give you the exact sense."

Adam breathed a sigh of relief.

She repeated each sentence slowly, first in German and then in English as if wanting to feel the meaning as well as just translating the words.

"Over the last . . . past year we have come to know . . . each other somewhat . . . no, no," she said, "quite well." Adam wrote each word down as the girl translated them.

"You have never disguised—perhaps a better meaning is 'hidden,' " she added, "your distaste for the National Socialist Party."

She raised her head and stared at Adam. "It's only out of a book," he assured her. She didn't look convinced but nevertheless continued. "But you have at every time . . . no, at all times, behaved with the courtesy of an officer and a gentleman."

The girl looked up, even more puzzled, as she had now reached the last word.

"Is that all?" she asked. "It doesn't make sense. There has to be more."

"No, that's it," said Adam, quickly taking back the sheet of paper. "Thank you," he added. "It was most kind of you to help." He left the girl and was relieved to see her shrug resignedly and return to her copy of *Time*. Adam went in search of the games room.

When he swung the door open he found a young man in a World Cup T-shirt and brown suede shorts. He was tapping a table-tennis ball up and down listlessly.

"Care for a game?" said the boy, not looking at all hopeful.

"Sure," said Adam, removing his jacket and picking up the table-tennis racket at his end of the table. For twenty minutes Adam had to go all out to make sure he lost 18–21, 21–12, 17–21. As he replaced his jacket and congratulated his opponent, he felt sure he had gained the young man's confidence.

"You put up a good fight," said the German. "Give me good game."

Adam joined him at his end of the table. "I wonder if you could help me with something?" he said.

"Your backhand?" said the young man.

"No, thank you," said Adam, "I just need a paragraph of German translated." He handed over the middle paragraph of the letter. Once again, the would-be translator looked puzzled.

"It's from a book, so it may seem a little out of context," Adam said unconvincingly.

"Okay, I try." As the boy began to study the paragraph, the girl who had already translated the first section came into the games room. She made her way toward them.

"This hard to make out, I am not good translation for," the young man said. "My girlfriend better, I think. I ask her. *Liebling, kannst du dies für den Herrn auf Englisch?*" Without looking at Adam he passed the second paragraph over to the girl who immediately said, "I knew there was more."

"No, no, don't bother," said Adam, and grabbed the piece of paper away from the girl. He turned back to the boy and said, "Thank you for the game. Sorry to have bothered you," and walked hurriedly out into the corridor, heading for the front door.

"Did you find 'im, sir?"

"Find him?" said Adam.

"Hans Kramer," said the porter.

"Oh, yes, thank you," said Adam. As he turned to leave, he

saw the young boy and his girlfriend were following close behind.

Adam ran down the drive and hailed a passing taxi.

"Where to?" said the cabbie.

"The Royal Lancaster Hotel."

"But that's only just round the corner."

"I know," said Adam, "but I'm already late."

"Suit yourself, guv," said the cabbie, "it's your money."

As the cab moved off Adam peered out of the back window to see his table-tennis opponent in conversation with the porter. The girl stood alongside them, pointing at the taxi.

Adam relaxed when the cab turned the corner and they were out of sight.

In less than a minute the taxi had drawn up outside the Royal Lancaster. Adam handed the cabbie half a crown and waited for the change. Then he pushed through the revolving doors of the hotel and hung around in the foyer for a few moments before returning to the pavement again. He checked his watch: twelve-thirty. Easily enough time for lunch, he thought, before going on to his interview with the Foreign Office. He headed across Bayswater Road into the park at a brisk pace, knowing he couldn't hope to find a pub until he reached Knightsbridge.

Adam recalled the table-tennis match. Damn, he thought. I should have thrashed him. At least that would have given him something else to think about.

Romanov's eye ran down the list of the fourteen banks. There was still an outside chance that one of them might be in possession of the Czar's icon, but the names meant nothing to him. It was another world, and he knew he would now have to seek advice from an expert.

He unlocked the top drawer of his desk and flicked through the red book held only by the most senior-ranking officers in the KGB. Many names had been scratched out or overwritten as regimes came and went, but Alexei Andreyevich Poskonov had remained in his present position as Chairman of the National Bank for nearly a decade. Only Gromyko, the Foreign Secretary, had served in any office longer. Romanov dialed a number on his private line and asked to be put through to the chairman of Gosbank. It was some considerable time before another voice came on the line.

"Comrade Romanov, what can I do for you?"

"I urgently need to see you," said Romanov.

"Really?" The gravelly tones that came from the other end of the line sounded distinctly unimpressed. Romanov could hear pages being flicked over. "I could manage Tuesday, say eleven-thirty?"

"I said it was urgent," repeated Romanov. "It concerns a State matter that can't wait."

"We are the nation's bankers and do have one or two problems of our own, you might be surprised to hear," came back the unrepentant voice. Romanov checked himself and waited. There was more flicking of pages. "Well, I suppose I could fit you in at three forty-five today, for fifteen minutes," said the banker. "But I must warn you that I have a long-standing engagement at four."

"Three forty-five it is, then," said Romanov.

"In my office," said Poskonov. The phone went dead.

Romanov cursed out loud. Why did everyone feel obliged to prove their manhood with the KGB? He began to write down the questions he needed answered in order to put his plan into operation. He couldn't afford to waste even a minute of his fifteen. An hour later he asked to see the Chairman of the KGB. This time he was not kept waiting.

"Trying to play the capitalists at their own game, are we?" said Zaborski, once Romanov had outlined his intentions. "Be careful. They've been at it a lot longer than we have."

"I realize that," said Romanov. "But if the icon is in the West, I'm left with little choice but to use their methods to get my hands on it."

"Perhaps," said the Chairman. "But with your name such an approach could be misunderstood."

Romanov knew better than to interrupt the brief silence that ensued. "Don't worry, I'll give you all the backing you need—although I've never had a request quite like this one before."

"Am I allowed to know why the icon is so important?" Romanov inquired.

The Chairman of the KGB frowned. "I do not have the authority to answer that question, but as Comrade Brezhnev's enthusiasm for the arts is well known, you must have been able to work out that it is not the painting itself that we are after."

What secret can the painting hold? thought Romanov, and decided to press on. "I wonder if . . ."

The Chairman of the KGB shook his head firmly.

Bugs don't have eyes, thought Romanov, but you know what that something is, don't you?

The Chairman rose from his desk and walked over to the wall and tore another page from the calendar. "Only ten days left to find the damn thing," he said. "The General Secretary has taken to phoning me at one o'clock every morning."

"One o'clock in the morning?" said Romanov, joining in the game.

"Yes, the poor man can't sleep, they tell me," said the Chairman, returning to his desk. "It comes to all of us in time—perhaps even you, Romanov, and maybe earlier than you expect if you don't stop asking questions." He gave his young colleague a wry smile.

Romanov left the Chairman a few minutes later and returned to his office to go over the questions that did need to be answered by the chairman of Gosbank. He couldn't help becoming distracted by thoughts of what could possibly be the significance of such a small painting, but accepted he must concentrate his efforts on finding it and then perhaps the secret it contained would become obvious.

* * *

Romanov reached the steps of Neglinnaya 12 at three-thirty because he knew he needed more than the fifteen minutes he had been allocated if he was to get all his questions answered. He only hoped Poskonov would agree to see him immediately.

After announcing himself at the reception desk he was accompanied by a uniformed guard up the wide marble staircase to the first floor, where Poskonov's secretary was waiting to greet him. Romanov was led to an anteroom. "I will inform the chairman of the bank that you have arrived, Comrade Romanov," the secretary said and then disappeared back into his own office. Romanov paced up and down the small anteroom impatiently, but the secretary did not return until the hands on the clock were in a straight line. At three-fifty, Romanov was ushered into the chairman's room.

The young major was momentarily taken aback by the sheer opulence of the room. The long red velvet curtains, the marble floor, and the delicate French furniture wouldn't, he imagined, have been out of place in the governor's rooms at the Bank of England. Romanov was reminded not for the first time that money still remained the most important commodity in the world—even in the Communist world. He stared at the old stooped man with the thinning gray hair and bushy walrus mustache who controlled the nation's money. The man of whom it was said that he knew of one skeleton in everyone's closet. Everyone's except mine, thought Romanov. The old man's checked suit might have been made before the Revolution and would once again be considered "with it" on London's King's Road.

"What can I do for you, Comrade Romanov?" inquired the banker with a sigh, as if addressing a tiresome customer who was seeking a small loan.

"I require one hundred million American dollars in gold bullion immediately," he announced evenly.

The chairman's bored expression suddenly changed. He went scarlet and fell into his chair. He took several short, sharp breaths before pulling open a drawer, taking out a square box, and extracting a large white pill from it. It took fully a minute before he seemed calm again.

"Have you gone out of your mind, Comrade?" the old man inquired. "You ask for an appointment without giving a reason, you then charge into my office and demand that I hand over one hundred million American dollars in gold without any explanation. For what reason do you make such a preposterous suggestion?"

"That is the business of the State," said Romanov. "But since you have inquired, I intend to deposit equal amounts in a series of numbered accounts across Switzerland."

"And on whose authority do you make such a request?" the banker asked in a level tone.

"The General Secretary of the Party."

"Strange," said Poskonov. "I see Leonid Ilyich at least once a week, and he has not mentioned this to me," the chairman looked down at the pad in the middle of his desk, "that a Major Romanov, a middle-ranking"—he stressed the words—"officer from the KGB would be making such an exorbitant demand."

Romanov stepped forward, picked up the phone by Poskonov's side, and held it out to him. "Why don't you ask Leonid Ilyich yourself and save us all a lot of time?" He pushed the phone defiantly toward the banker. Poskonov stared back at him, took the phone, and placed it to his ear. Romanov sensed the sort of tension he only felt in the field.

A voice came on the line. "You called, Comrade Chairman?"

"Yes," replied the old man. "Cancel my four o'clock appointment and see that I am not disturbed until Major Romanov leaves."

"Yes, Comrade Chairman."

Poskonov replaced the phone and without another word rose from behind his desk and walked around to Romanov's side. He ushered the young man into a comfortable chair on the far side of the room below a bay window and took the seat opposite him.

"I knew your grandfather," he said in a calm, matter-of-fact tone. "I was a junior commodity clerk when I first met him. I had just left school, and he was very kind to me, but he was just as impatient as you are. Which was why he was the best fur trader in Russia and thought to be the worst poker player."

Romanov laughed. He had never known his grandfather, and the few books that referred to him had long ago been destroyed. His father talked openly of his wealth and position, which had only given the authorities ammunition to destroy him.

"You'll forgive my curiosity, Major, but if I am to hand over one hundred million dollars in gold I should like to know what it is to be spent on. I thought only the CIA put in receipts for those sort of expenses without explanation."

Romanov laughed again and explained to the chairman how they had discovered that the Czar's icon was a fake and he had been set the task of recovering the original. When he had completed his story he handed over the names of the fourteen banks. The banker studied the list closely while Romanov outlined the course of action he proposed to take, showing how the money would be returned intact as soon as he had located the missing icon.

"But how can one small icon possibly be that important to the State?" Poskonov asked out loud, almost as if Romanov were no longer in the room.

"I have no idea," replied Romanov truthfully and then briefed him on the results of his research.

There was an exasperated grunt from the other chair when Romanov had finished. "May I be permitted to suggest an alternative to your plan?"

"Please do," said Romanov, relieved to be gaining the older man's cooperation.

"Do you smoke?" asked the banker, taking a pack of Dunhill cigarettes from his coat pocket.

"No," said Romanov, his eyebrows lifting slightly at the sight of the red box.

The old man paused as he lit a cigarette. "That suit was not tailored in Moscow either, Major," the banker said, pointing at Romanov with his cigarette. "Now, to business—and do not hesitate to correct me if I have misunderstood any of your requirements. You suspect that lodged in one of these fourteen Swiss banks"—the chairman tapped the list with his index finger—"is the original Czar's icon. You therefore want me to deposit large amounts of gold with each bank in the hope that it will give you immediate access to the head of the family, or chairman. You will then offer the chairmen the chance to control the entire hundred million if they promise to cooperate with you?"

"Yes," said Romanov. "Bribery is surely something the West has always understood."

"I would have said 'naive' if I hadn't known your grandfather; it was he who ended up making millions of rubles, not me. Nevertheless, how much do you imagine is a lot of money to a major Swiss bank?"

Romanov considered the question. "Ten million, twenty million?"

"To the Moscow Narodny Bank perhaps," said Poskonov. "But every one of the banks you hope to deal with will have several customers with deposits of over a hundred million each."

Romanov was unable to hide his disbelief.

"I confess," continued the chairman, "that our revered General Secretary showed no less incredulity when I informed him of these facts some years ago."

"Then I will need a billion?" asked Romanov.

"No, no, no. We must approach the problem from a different standpoint. You do not catch a poacher by offering him a rabbit."

"But if the Swiss are not moved by the offer of vast amounts of money, what *will* move them?"

"The simple suggestion that their bank has been used for criminal activity," said the chairman.

"But how . . ." began Romanov.

"Let me explain. You say that the Czar's icon hanging in the Winter Palace is not the original but a copy. A good copy, painted by a twentieth-century court painter, but nevertheless a copy. Therefore why not explain to each of the fourteen banks privately that, after extensive research, we have reason to believe that one of the nation's most valuable treasures has been substituted with a copy and the original is thought to have been deposited in their bank? And rather than cause a diplomatic incident—the one thing every Swiss banker wishes to avoid at any cost—perhaps they would in the interests of good relationships consider checking in their vaults items that have not been claimed for over twenty years."

Romanov looked straight at the old man, realizing why he had survived several purges. "I owe you an apology, Comrade Poskonov."

"No, no, we each have our own little skills. I am sure I would be as lost in your world as you appear to be in mine. Now, if you will allow me to contact each of the chairmen on this list and tell them no more than the truth—a commodity I am always obliged to trade in although I imagine your counterparts are not so familiar with—namely that I suspect the Czar's icon is in *their* bank, most of them will be disinclined to hold on to the masterpiece if they believe in so doing a crime has been perpetrated against a sovereign state."

"I cannot overstress the urgency," said Romanov.

"Just like your grandfather," Poskonov repeated. "So be it. If they can be tracked down, I shall speak to every one of them today. At least that's one of the advantages of the rest of the world waking up after us. Be assured I shall be in touch with you the moment I have any news."

"Thank you," said Romanov, rising to leave. "You have been most helpful." He was about to add, as he normally did in such circumstances, I shall so inform my chairman, but he checked himself, realizing the old man wouldn't have given a damn.

The chairman of the Gosbank closed the door behind him and then walked over to the bay window and watched Romanov run down the steps of the bank to a waiting car.

I couldn't have supplied you with the one hundred million in gold bullion at this particular time, even if the General Secretary had ordered me to, he thought to himself. I doubt if I have ten million dollars' worth of gold left in the vaults at this moment. The General Secretary has already ordered me to fly every available ounce to the Bank of New York—so cleverly was his ploy disguised that the CIA had been informed about the deposit within an hour of its arrival. It's hard to hide over seven hundred million dollars in gold, even in America. I tried to tell him. The chairman watched Romanov's car drive away. Of course if, like your grandfather, you read the *Washington Post* as well as *Pravda*, you would already have known this. He returned to his desk and checked the names of the fourteen banks.

He knew instantly which of the fourteen had to be phoned.

Adam stepped out of Tattersall's Tavern on the corner of Knightsbridge Green and headed past the Hyde Park Hotel toward the Royal Thames Yacht Club in Knightsbridge. It seemed a strange place for the Foreign Office to hold an interview, but so far everything connected with the application had been somewhat mysterious.

He arrived a few minutes early and asked the ex-Royal Marines sergeant at the door where the interviews were taking place.

"Sixth floor, sir. Take the lift in the corner," he pointed ahead of him, "and announce yourself at reception."

Adam pressed a button and waited for the lift. The doors opened immediately and Adam stepped in. A rather overweight, bespectacled man of roughly his own age who looked as if he never turned down the third course of any meal joined him. Adam touched the sixth button, but neither man spoke on their journey up to the sixth floor. The large man stepped out of the lift in front of Adam.

"Wainwright's the name," he informed the girl on the reception desk.

"Yes, sir," said the girl, "you're a little early, but do have a seat over there." She gestured toward a chair in the corner; then her eyes moved on to Adam, and she smiled.

"Scott," he informed her.

"Yes, sir," she repeated. "Could you join the other gentleman? They will be seeing you next." Adam went over and picked up a copy of *Punch* before settling down next to Wainwright, who was already filling in the *Telegraph* crossword.

Adam soon became bored with flicking through endless issues of *Punch* and took a more careful look at Wainwright. "Do you by any chance speak German?" Adam asked suddenly, turning to face the other interviewee.

"German, French, Italian, and Spanish," Wainwright replied, looking up. "I assumed that was how I managed to get this far," he added somewhat smugly.

"Then perhaps you could translate a paragraph from a German letter for me?"

"Delighted, old fellow," said Adam's companion, who proceeded to remove the pair of thick-lensed glasses from his nose and waited for Adam to extract the middle paragraph of the letter from his envelope.

"Now, let me see," Wainwright said, taking the little slip of paper and replacing the glasses. "Quite a challenge. I say, old fellow, you're not part of the interviewing team by any chance?"

"No, no," said Adam, smiling. "I'm in exactly the same position as you—except I don't speak German, French, Italian, or Spanish."

Wainwright seemed to relax. "Now let me see," he repeated, as Adam took out the small notebook from his inside pocket.

" 'During the past year you cannot have failed to . . . notice that I have been receiving from one of the guards a regular, regular . . . regular supply,' " he said suddenly, "yes, 'supply of Havana cigars. One of the few pleasures I have been allocated'—no, 'allowed,' better still, 'permitted'—'despite my . . . incarceration.' That's the nearest I can get," Wainwright added. "'The cigars themselves have also served another purpose,'" Wainwright continued, obviously enjoying himself, "'as they contained tiny capsules . . .'"

"Mr. Scott."

"Yes," said Adam, jumping up obediently.

"The board will see you now," said the receptionist.

"Do you want me to finish it off while they're finishing you off, old chap?" said Wainwright.

"Thank you," Adam replied, "if it's not too much trouble."

"Far easier than the crossword," Wainwright added, leaving on one side the little unfilled half-matrix of squares.

Alex Romanov was not a patient man at the best of times, and with the General Secretary now ringing up his chief twice a day, these were not the best of times.

While he waited for results of the chairman of Gosbank's inquiries he reread the research papers that had been left on his desk and checked any new intelligence that had been sent back by his agents in the field. Romanov resented the scraps of information the chairman of Gosbank must have been receiving by the hour, but he made no attempt to pester the old man despite his time problem.

Then the chairman of the bank called.

On this occasion Romanov was driven straight over to the State Bank and ushered up to the finely furnished room without a moment's delay. Poskonov, dressed in another of those suits with an even larger check, was standing to greet him at the door.

"You must have wondered if I had forgotten you," were Poskonov's opening words as he ushered Romanov to the comfortable chair. "But I wanted to have some positive news to give you rather than waste your time. You don't smoke, if I remember correctly," he added, taking out his pack of Dunhill cigarettes.

"No, thank you," Romanov said, wondering if the chairman's doctor realized how much the old man smoked.

The chairman's secretary entered the room and placed two empty glasses, a frosted flask, and a plate of caviar in front of them.

Romanov waited in silence.

"I have, over the past two days, managed to talk to the chairmen of twelve of the banks on your original list," Poskonov began, as he poured two vodkas, "but I have avoided making contact with the remaining two."

"Avoided?" repeated Romanov.

"Patience, Comrade," said Poskonov, sounding like a benevolent uncle. "You have longer to live than I, so if there is any time to be wasted it must be yours."

Romanov lowered his eyes.

"I avoided one of the chairmen," Poskonov continued, "because he is in Mexico showing President Ordaz how not to repay their loan to Chase Manhattan while at the same time borrowing even more dollars from the Bank of America. If he pulls that off, I shall have to recommend to the General Secretary of the party that he is offered my job when I retire. The second gentleman I have avoided because he is officially in Chicago, closing a major Eurobond deal with Continental Illinois, while in fact he is booked in at the Saint Francis Hotel in San Francisco with his mistress. I feel certain you would agree, Comrade Major, that it would not advance our cause to disturb either of these gentlemen at this precise moment. The first has enough problems to be going on with for the rest of the week, while the second may well have his phone tapped—and we wouldn't want the Americans to discover what we are searching for, would we?"

"Agreed, Comrade," said Romanov.

"Good. Anyway as they both return to Switzerland early next week, we have quite enough to be going on with for now."

"Yes, but what—" Romanov began.

"It will please you to know," continued Poskonov, "that of the twelve remaining chairmen all have agreed to cooperate with us, and five have already phoned back. Four to say they have run a thorough check on the possessions of customers who have been out of contact with the bank for over twenty years, but have come up with nothing that remotely resembles an icon. In fact, one of them opened a deposit box in the presence of three other directors that had not been touched since 1931 only to discover it contained nothing but a cork from a 1929 bottle of Taylor's port."

"Only a cork?" said Romanov.

"Well, 1929 was a vintage year," admitted the chairman.

"And the fifth?" inquired Romanov.

"Now that, I suspect, may be our first breakthrough," continued Poskonov, referring to the file in front of him. He adjusted his spectacles with the forefinger of his right hand before continuing. "Herr Dieter Bischoff of Bischoff et Cie"—he looked up at his guest, as if Romanov might have recognized the name—"an honorable man, whom I have dealt with many times in the past—honorable, that is, by Western standards of course, Comrade," added the chairman, obviously enjoying himself. "Bischoff has come up with something that was left with the bank in 1938. It is unquestionably an icon, but he has no way of knowing if it is the one we are looking for."

Romanov leaped up from his seat in excitement. "Then I had better go and see for myself," said Romanov. "I could fly out today," he added. The chairman waved him back into his chair.

"The plane you require does not leave Sheremetyevo Airport until four thirty-five. In any case, I have already booked two seats on it for you."

"Two?" inquired Romanov.

"You will obviously need an expert to accompany you, unless you know considerably more about icons than you do about banking," Poskonov added. "I also took the liberty of booking you on the Swissair flight. One should never fly Aeroflot if it can be avoided. It has managed only one aviation record consistently every year since its inception, namely that of losing the most passengers per miles flown, and a banker never believes in going against known odds. I have fixed an appointment for you to see Herr Bischoff at ten o'clock tomorrow morning—unless, of course, you have something more pressing to keep you in Moscow, Comrade?"

Romanov smiled.

"I note from your file that you have never served in Switzerland," said the old man, showing off, "so may I also recommend that you stay at the Saint Gothard while you are in Zurich. Jacques Pontin will take excellent care of you. Nationality has never been a problem for the Swiss, only currency. And so that brings my little investigation up to date, and I shall be in touch again as soon as the two itinerant chairmen return to Switzerland next Monday. All I can do for the moment, however, is wish you luck in Zurich."

"Thank you," said Romanov. "May I be permitted to add how much I appreciate your thoroughness."

"My pleasure, Comrade. Let's just say that I still owe your grandfather a favor, and perhaps one day you will find you owe me one, and leave it at that."

Romanov tried to fathom the meaning of the old man's words. There was no clue to be found in Poskonov's expression, and so he left without another word. But as Romanov walked down the wide marble staircase, he considered the banker's sentiment again and again because throwaway lines were never delivered to an officer of the KGB.

By the time Romanov had returned to Dzerzhinsky Square his secretary informed him that Herr Bischoff's assistant had telephoned from Zurich to confirm his appointment with the chairman at ten o'clock the following morning. Romanov asked him to call the manager at the Saint Gothard Hotel and book two rooms. "Oh, and confirm my flight on Swissair," he added before walking up two floors to see the Chairman for State Security and brief him on the meeting he had had with the head of the National Bank.

"Thank God for that," were Zaborski's first words. "With only nine days left, at least you've given me something to discuss with the General Secretary when he calls me at one tomorrow morning."

Romanov smiled.

"Good luck, Comrade. Our embassy will be alerted to your every need. Let us fervently hope that you will be able to return the masterpiece to the walls of the Winter Palace."

"If it is in that bank, it will be in your hands by tomorrow night," said Romanov, and left the Chairman smiling.

When he walked into his own office he found Petrova waiting for him.

"You called for me, Comrade?"

"Yes, we're going to Zurich." Romanov looked at his watch. "In three hours' time. The flight and the rooms are already booked."

"In the names of Herr and Frau Schmidt, no doubt," said his lover.

CHAPTER SIX

WHEN ADAM EMERGED from the interview he felt quietly confident. The chairman's final words had been to ask him if he would be available for a thorough physical in a week's time. Adam had told them he could think of nothing that would stop him attending. He looked forward to the opportunity of serving in the British Foreign Service.

Back in the waiting room Wainwright looked up and handed him back his piece of paper.

"Thank you very much," said Adam, trying to look casual by slipping it in his inside pocket without looking at the results.

"What was it like, old chap?" his companion asked cautiously.

"No trouble for a man who has German, French, Spanish, and Italian as part of his armory," Adam assured him. "Best of luck, anyway."

"Mr. Wainwright," said the secretary, "the board will see you now."

Adam took the lift to the ground floor and decided to

walk home, stopping on the corner of Wilton Place to buy a bag of apples from a pushcart boy who seemed to spend most of his time on the lookout for the police. Adam moved on, going over in his mind the board's questions and his answers—a pointless exercise, he decided, although he still felt confident the interview had gone well. He came to such a sudden halt that the pedestrian behind only just stopped himself bumping into Adam. What had attracted his attention was a sign that read: The German Food Centre. An attractive girl with a cheerful smile and laughing eyes was sitting at the cash register by the doorway. Adam strode into the shop and went straight over to her.

"You have not bought anything?" she inquired with a slight accent.

"No, I'm just about to," Adam assured her, "but I wondered, do you speak German?"

"Most girls from Mainz do," she replied, grinning.

"Yes, I suppose they would," said Adam, looking at the girl more carefully. She must have been in her early twenties, Adam decided, and he was immediately attracted by her friendly smile and manner. Her shiny, dark hair was done up in a ponytail with a big red bow. Her white sweater and neat pleated skirt would have made any man take a second look. Her slim legs were tucked under the chair. "I wonder if you would be kind enough to translate a short paragraph for me?"

"I try," she said, still smiling.

Adam took the envelope containing the final section of the letter out of his pocket and handed it over to her.

"The style is a bit old-fashioned," she said, looking serious. "It may take a little time."

"I'll go and do some shopping," he told her, and started walking slowly around the long stacked shelves. He selected a little salami, frankfurters, bacon, and some German mustard, looking up now and then to see how the girl was progressing. From what he could make out, she was only able to translate a few words at a time, as she was continually interrupted by customers. Nearly twenty minutes passed before he saw her put the piece of paper to one side. Adam immediately went over to the cash register and placed his purchases on the counter.

"One pound, two shillings and sixpence," she said. Adam handed over two pounds, and she returned his change and the little piece of paper.

"This I consider a rough translation, but I think the meaning is clear."

"I don't know how to thank you," said Adam, as an elderly woman joined him in the line.

"You could invite me to share with you your frankfurters," she laughed.

"What a nice idea," said Adam. "Why don't you join me for dinner tonight?"

"I was not serious," she said.

"I was," said Adam, smiling. Another person joined the line, and the old lady immediately behind him began to look restive.

Adam grabbed a leaflet from the counter, retreated toward the back of the store, and began to scribble down his name, address, and phone number. He waited for the two customers in front of him to pay, then handed over to her a "once-in-a-lifetime" Tide offer.

"What's this?" the girl asked innocently.

"I've put my name and address on the center page," Adam said. "I will expect you for dinner at about eight this evening. At least you know what's on the menu."

She looked uncertain. "I really was only joking."

"I won't eat you," said Adam. "Only the sausages."

She looked at the leaflet in her hand and laughed. "I'll think about it."

Adam strolled out on to the road whistling. A bad morning, a good afternoon, and—perhaps—an even better evening.

He was back at the flat in time to watch the five forty-five news. Mrs. Gandhi, as the new Prime Minister of India, was facing an open revolt in her cabinet and Adam wondered if Britain could ever have a woman Prime Minister. England was 117 for 7 in its first innings, with the West Indies still well on top. He groaned and turned off the television. Once he had put the food in the refrigerator he went into his bedroom to assemble the full text of the Goering letter. After he had read through all the little slips of paper he took out his notepad and began to copy out the translations in order: first, the paragraph supplied by the girl from the YMCA; then Wainwright's handwritten words from the notepad; and finally the section of the letter translated by the lovely girl from Mainz. He read the completed draft through slowly a second time.

Nuremberg
15 October 1946

Dear Colonel,

Over the past year, we have come to know each other quite well. You have never disguised your distaste for the National Socialist party, but you have at all times behaved with the courtesy of an officer and a gentleman.

During the year you cannot have failed to notice that I have been receiving from one of the guards a regular supply of Havana cigars—one of the few pleasures I have been permitted, despite my incarceration. The cigars themselves have also served another purpose, as each one contained a capsule with a small amount of poison. Enough to allow me to survive my trial, while ensuring that I shall cheat the executioner.

My only regret is that you, as the officer in charge of the watch during the period when I am most likely to die, may be held responsible for something to which you were never a party. To make amends for this I enclose a document in the name of one Emmanuel Rosenbaum which should help with any financial difficulties you face in the near future.

All that will be required of you . . .

"Anyone at home?" shouted Lawrence. Adam folded up the pieces of paper, walked quickly over to the bookcase, and inserted them alongside the original letter in the Bible seconds before Lawrence put his head around the door.

"Bloody traffic," said Lawrence cheerfully. "I can't wait to be appointed chairman of the bank and be given that luxury flat on the top floor, not to mention the chauffeur and the company car."

Adam laughed. "Had another hard day at the office, darling?" he mimicked, before joining him in the kitchen. Adam started removing food from the refrigerator.

"Guess who's coming to dinner?" said Lawrence as each new delicacy appeared.

"A rather attractive German girl, I hope," said Adam.

"What do you mean, 'hope'?"

"Well, it could hardly have been described as a formal invitation, so I'm not certain she'll turn up."

"If that's the situation, I may as well hang around in case she gives you the elbow and you need someone to help you eat that lot."

"Thanks for the vote of confidence, but I think you'll find it's your turn to be missing, presumed dead. Anyway, what about Carolyn?" said Adam.

"Carolyn was yesterday's girl, to quote the esteemed Harold Wilson. How did you come across your *gnädiges Fräulein?*"

"She was working at a food store in Knightsbridge."

"I see. We're down to shop assistants now."

"I have no idea what she is or even what her name is, come to that," said Adam. "But I am hoping to find out tonight. As I said, your turn to disappear."

"*Natürlich.* As you see, you can rely on me to provide a helping hand if you need anything translated."

"Just put the wine in the fridge and set the table."

"Are there no serious jobs for a man of my accomplishments to be entrusted with?" said Lawrence with a chuckle.

When eight o'clock chimed, the table was set, and Adam had everything ready on the boil. By eight-thirty both of them stopped pretending and Adam served up two plates of frankfurters, salami and lettuce with a baked potato and sauerkraut. He then hung up his Marx Brothers apron behind the kitchen door and took the chair opposite Lawrence, who had begun pouring the wine.

"Oh, *mein liebes Mädchen*, you look ravishing in that Harris tweed jacket," said Lawrence, raising his glass.

Adam was just about to retaliate with the vegetable spoon when there was a loud knock on the front door. The two men stared at each other before Adam leaped up to open it. Standing in the doorway was a man well over six foot with shoulders like a professional bouncer's. By his side, dwarfed by him, was the girl that Adam had invited to dinner.

"This is my brother, Jochen," she explained. Adam was immediately struck by how beautiful she looked in a dark blue patterned blouse and pleated blue skirt that fell just below the knee. Her long dark hair, now hanging loose, looked as if it had just been washed and shone even under the forty-watt light bulb that hung in the hall.

"Welcome," said Adam, more than a little taken aback.

"Jochen is just dropping me off."

"Yes, of course," said Adam. "Do come in and have a drink, Jochen."

"No, I thank you. I have a date as well, but I will pick up Heidi at eleven o'clock, if all right by you?"

"Fine by me," said Adam, at last learning her name.

The giant bent down and kissed his sister on both cheeks. He then shook hands with Adam before leaving them both on the doorstep.

"I am sorry to be late," said Heidi. "My brother did not get back from work until after seven."

"It was no problem," said Adam, leading her into the flat. "If you had come any earlier, I wouldn't have been ready for you. By the way, this is my flatmate, Lawrence Pemberton."

"In England the men also need a chaperone?" said Heidi.

Both men laughed. "No, no," said Lawrence. "I was just on my way out. Like your brother, I already have a date. As you can see, the table is only laid for two. I'll be back around eleven, Adam, just to make sure you're safe." He smiled at Heidi, put on his coat, and closed the door behind him before either could object.

"I hope I don't drive him away," said Heidi.

"No, no," said Adam, as she took Lawrence's place at the

table. "He's already late for his girlfriend. Charming girl called Carolyn, a social worker." He quickly topped up her wine, pretending it hadn't already been poured.

"So I am going to eat my own sausages, after all," she said, laughing. And the laughter didn't stop for the rest of the evening, as Adam learned about Heidi's life in Germany, her family, and the holiday job she had taken while on vacation from Mainz University.

"My parents only allow me to come to England because my brother is already in London; it is to help my languages course. But now, Adam, I would like to know what you are doing when you are not picking up girls in food stores."

"I was in the army for nine years, and I'm now hoping to join the Foreign Office."

"In what capacity, if that is the right expression?" Heidi asked.

"It's the right expression, but I'm not sure I know the right answer," said Adam.

"When someone says that about the Foreign Service it usually means they are a spy."

"I don't know what it means, to be honest, but they're going to tell me next week. In any case, I don't think I'd make a very good spy. But what are you going to do when you return to Germany?"

"Complete my final year at Mainz, and then I hope to find a job as a television news researcher."

"What about Jochen?" asked Adam.

"He will join my father's law practice as soon as he is arriving home."

"So how long will you be in London?" he found himself asking.

"Another two months," she said. "If I can stand the job."

"Why do you carry on with it if it's that bad?"

"There is no better way to test your English than impatient shoppers who speak all accents."

"I hope you stay the full two months," said Adam.

"So do I," she replied, smiling.

When Jochen arrived back punctually at eleven, he found Adam and Heidi doing the dishes.

"Thank you for a most interesting evening," she said, wiping her hands.

"Not a good word," reprimanded Jochen. "Not interesting, I think. Lovely, happy, delightful, enjoyable, perhaps, but not interesting."

"It was all those things," said Adam, "but it was also interesting."

She smiled.

"May I come and buy some more sausages tomorrow?"

"I would like that," said Heidi, "but don't hold up any sour old women this time with translation demands. By the way, you never tell me why you needed the strange paragraph translated. I have been wondering who is this Rosenbaum and what it is he left to someone."

"Next time, perhaps," said Adam, looking a little embarrassed.

"And next time you can bring my sister home yourself," said Jochen, as he shook Adam's hand firmly.

After Heidi had left, Adam sat down and finished off the last glass of wine, aware that he hadn't spent such a lovely, happy, delightful, enjoyable, and interesting evening for a long time.

A black limousine with dark windows and unlit license plates remained parked in the VIP area of Zurich Kloten. Fastidious Swiss policemen had twice gone up to the car and checked the driver's credentials before Major Romanov and Anna Petrova emerged from the customs hall and took their places in the back of the car.

It was already dark as the driver moved off toward the neon glow of the city. When the car drew up outside the Saint Gothard Hotel the only words that passed between Romanov and the driver were, "I shall return to Moscow on the Tuesday morning flight."

Jacques Pontin, the manager of the hotel, was stationed at

the door waiting to greet the new arrivals; he introduced himself immediately, and as soon as he had checked them in he banged a little bell with the palm of his hand to summon a porter to assist the guests with their bags. A moment later a young man in his early twenties, dressed in green livery, appeared.

"Suite seventy-three and room seventy-four," Jacques instructed before turning back to Romanov. "I do hope your stay will prove to be worthwhile, Herr Romanov," he said. "Please do not hesitate to call upon me if there is anything you need."

"Thank you," said Romanov as he turned to join the porter, who stood sentinel-like by the door of an open lift. Romanov stood to one side to allow Anna to go in first. The lift stopped at the seventh floor, and the porter led the way down a long corridor to a corner suite. He turned the key in the lock and invited the two guests to go in ahead of him. The suite was as Romanov had expected, in a different league from the finest hotels he had ever experienced in either Moscow or Leningrad. When he saw the array of gadgets in the marble bathroom he reflected that even prosperous travelers to Russia, if seasoned visitors, brought their own bath drains with them.

"Your room is through here, madame," the porter informed the researcher and unlocked an adjoining door. Although smaller in size, it maintained the same unassuming elegance. The porter returned to Romanov, handed him his key, and asked if there would be anything else he would require. Romanov assured him there was nothing and passed over a five-franc note.

Once again the porter gave a slight bow and, closing the door behind him, left Romanov to unpack while Anna Petrova went to her room.

Romanov started to undress and then disappeared into the bathroom. He studied himself in the mirror. Although he was vain about his looks, he was even vainer about the state of his physique. At twenty-nine, despite being six feet, he still only weighed 165 pounds on western scales, and his muscles remained hard and taut.

By the time Romanov had returned to the bedroom, he could hear the shower beating down in the adjoining bathroom. He crept over to the door and edged it open. He could see quite clearly the outline of Anna standing in the shower. He smiled and noiselessly moved back across the thick carpet, slipped under the sheets and into the researcher's bed. He waited for her to turn off the steaming shower.

Adam stepped out of the freezing shower. Within minutes he was dressed and joined Lawrence in the kitchen for breakfast.

"Still unable to charge you for hot water, am I?" Lawrence said as Adam peered over his flatmate's shoulder. "Sorry, can't stay and chatter with the unemployed," he said, picking up his briefcase. "The Shah of Iran wants to discuss his financial problems with me. Sorry to rush off before you've had your cornflakes, but I can't afford to keep His Imperial Majesty waiting."

Left on his own, Adam boiled himself an egg and burned some toast before he turned to the newspaper to learn of the latest casualties in Vietnam and President Johnson's proposed tour of the Far East. At this rate he decided he wasn't going to win the *Daily Mail*'s "Housewife of the Year" competition. He eventually cleared away in the kitchen, made his bed, and tidied up behind Lawrence—nine years of self-discipline wasn't going to change old habits that quickly—then he settled down to plan another day.

He realized he could no longer avoid making a decision. He sat once again at his desk and began to consider how to get the official document translated without arousing further suspicion.

Almost absentmindedly he removed the Bible from the bookshelf and extracted the letter he had read the night before. The final paragraph still puzzled him. He considered Heidi's translation once again.

All that will be required of you is to present yourself
at the address printed on the top right-hand corner of
the enclosed document, with some proof that you are
Colonel Gerald Scott. A passport should prove
sufficient. You will then be given a bequest that I
have left to you in the name of Emmanuel
Rosenbaum.

I hope it will bring you good fortune.

Adam turned his attention back to the document. He was
still quite unable to discern what the bequest could possibly
be, let alone whether it was of any value. Adam mused over
the fact that such an evil man could involve himself in an act
of kindness hours before he knew he was going to die.

An act that now left him with no choice about his own
involvement.

Romanov gathered the blankets together and in one
movement hurled them on to the floor to expose Anna
curled up like a child, knees almost touching her exposed
breasts. Anna's hand groped for a corner of the sheet to
cover her naked body.

"Breakfast in bed?" she murmured hopefully.

"Dressed in ten minutes, or no breakfast at all," came back
the reply. Anna lowered her feet gingerly on to the thick carpet and waited for the room to stop going round in circles
before heading off toward the bathroom. Romanov heard
the shower burst forth its jets. "Ahhh," came the pitiful cry.
Romanov smiled when he remembered that he had left the
indicator locked on dark blue.

During breakfast in the dining room they mulled over the
approach he intended to take with the bank if Petrova were
able to confirm that the icon was in fact Rublev's original
masterpiece. He kept looking up from the table and then
suddenly, without warning, said, "Let's go."

"Why?" Anna asked, as she bit into another slice of toast.
Romanov rose from the table and without bothering to offer

an explanation strode out of the room and headed straight for the lift. Petrova caught up with her boss only moments before the lift gate closed. "Why?" she asked again, but Romanov did not speak until they were both back in his suite. He then threw open the large window that overlooked the railway station.

"Ah, it's outside your room," he said, looking to his right, and quickly walked through to the adjoining bedroom. He marched past the disheveled double bed, jerked open the nearest window, and climbed outside. Petrova stared down from the seventh floor and felt giddy. Once Romanov had reached the bottom rung of the fire escape, he ran to a passing streetcar. Petrova would never have made it if she hadn't been lifted bodily onto the tram by Romanov's sheer strength.

"What's going on?" she asked, still puzzled.

"I can't be sure," said Romanov, looking out of the back of the streetcar. "All I do know for certain is what the local CIA agent looks like."

The researcher looked back in the direction of the hotel, but all she could see was a mass of anonymous people walking up and down the pavement.

Romanov remained on the streetcar for about a mile before he jumped off and hailed a passing taxi going in the opposite direction.

"Bischoff et Cie," he said as he waited for his puffing assistant to join him.

The cab headed back in the direction of the hotel, winding in and out of the morning traffic, until it came to a halt in front of a large brown granite building that filled the entire block. Romanov paid off the driver and stood in front of imposing double doors made of thick glass and covered in wrought iron welded to look like the branches on a tree. By the side of the door, carved inconspicuously into the stone and inlaid with gilt, were the words "Bischoff et Cie." There was no other clue as to what kind of establishment lay within.

Romanov turned the heavy wrought-iron knob, and the two Russians stepped into a spacious hall. On the left-hand side of the hall stood a solitary desk behind which a smartly dressed young man was seated.

"*Guten morgen, mein Herr,*" he said.

"Good morning," said Romanov in German. "We have an appointment with Herr Dieter Bischoff."

"Yes, Herr Romanov," said the receptionist, checking the list of names in front of him. "Will you please take the lift to the fifth floor, where you will be met by Herr Bischoff's secretary." When the two of them stepped out of the lift they were greeted by a lady in a neat plain suit. "Will you please follow me," she said, without any trace of accent. The two Russians were escorted along a picture-lined corridor to a comfortable room that more resembled the reception room of a country house than a bank.

"Herr Bischoff will be with you in a moment," the lady said, withdrawing. Romanov remained standing while he took in the room. Three black-and-white framed photographs of somber old men in gray suits, trying to look like somber old men in gray suits, took up most of the far wall, while on the other walls were discreet but pleasant oils of town and country scenes of nineteenth-century Switzerland. A magnificent oval Louis XIV table with eight carved mahogany chairs surrounding it dominated the center of the room. Romanov felt a twinge of envy at the thought that he could never hope to live in such style.

The door opened and a man in his mid-sixties, followed by three other men in dark gray suits, entered the room. One look at Herr Bischoff, and Romanov knew whose photograph would eventually join that of the other three gray, somber men.

"What an honor for our little bank, Mr. Romanov," were Bischoff's first words as he bowed and shook the Russian by the hand. Romanov nodded and introduced his assistant, who received the same courteous bow and handshake. "May I in turn present my son and two of my partners, Herr Muller and Herr Weizkopf." The three men bowed in unison, but remained standing while Bischoff took his seat at the head of the table.

At his gesture both Romanov and Anna sat down beside him.

"I wonder if I might be permitted to check your passport?" asked Bischoff, as if to show that the formal business had begun. Romanov took out the little blue passport with a soft cover from his inside pocket and handed it over. Bischoff studied it closely, as a philatelist might check an old stamp, and decided it was mint. "Thank you," he said, as he returned it to its owner.

Bischoff then raised his hand, and one of the partners immediately left them. "It will only take a moment for my son to fetch the icon we have in safekeeping," he confided. "Meanwhile perhaps a little coffee—Russian," he added.

Coffee appeared within moments, borne by yet another smartly dressed lady.

"Thank you," said Petrova, clearly a little overawed, but Romanov didn't speak again until Herr Bischoff's son reappeared with a small box and handed it over to his father.

"You will understand that I have to treat this matter with the utmost delicacy," the old man confided. "The icon may not turn out to be the one your government is searching for."

"I understand," said Romanov.

"This magnificent example of Russian art has been in our possession since 1938 and was deposited with the bank on behalf of a Mr. Emmanuel Rosenbaum."

Both visitors looked shocked.

"*Nevozmozhno*," said Anna, turning to her master. "He would never . . ."

"I suspect that's exactly why the name was chosen in the first place," Romanov said curtly to Anna, annoyed at her indiscretion. "Can't you see? It makes perfect sense. May I see the icon now?" said Romanov, turning back toward the bank's chairman.

Herr Bischoff placed the box in the center of the table. The three men in gray suits each took a pace forward. Romanov looked up. "Under Swiss law we must have three witnesses when opening a box in someone else's name," explained the old man.

Romanov nodded curtly.

Herr Bischoff proceeded to unlock the metal box with a key he produced from his pocket, while his son leaned over and undid a second lock with a different key. The little ceremony completed, Herr Bischoff pushed up the lid of the box and turned it round to face his guests. Romanov placed his hands into the box like an expectant child does with a Christmas stocking and drew out the icon. He stared at the beautiful painting. A small wooden rectangle that was covered in tiny pieces of red, gold, and blue making up the mosaic of a man who looked as if he had all the worries of the world on his shoulders. The face, although sad, still evoked a feeling of serenity. The painting Romanov held in his hand was quite magnificent, as fine as any he had seen at the Winter Palace. No one in the room was quite sure what would happen next as Romanov offered no opinion.

It was Anna who finally spoke.

"A masterpiece it is," she said, "and undoubtedly fifteenth century, but as you can see it's not Saint George and the dragon."

Romanov nodded his agreement, still unable to let go of the little painting. "But do you know the origin of this particular icon?" Romanov asked.

"Yes," Anna replied, glad to be appreciated for the first time. "It is the icon of Saint Peter, you see he holds the keys . . . painted by Dionisiy in 1471, and although it is undoubtedly one of the finest examples of his work, it is not the Czar's icon."

"But does it belong to the Russian people?" asked Romanov, still hopeful of some reward for all his trouble.

"No, Comrade Major," said the researcher emphatically. "It belongs to the Munich Gallery, from where it has been missing since the day Hitler was appointed Reichschancellor."

Herr Bischoff scribbled a note on a piece of paper in front of him. At least one bank in Munich was going to be happy to do business with him in the future.

Romanov reluctantly handed back the icon to Herr Bischoff, only just managing to say, "Thank you."

"Not at all," said Herr Bischoff imperturbably, replacing

the icon in the box and turning his key in his lock. His son completed the same routine with his own key and then departed with the unclaimed treasure. Romanov rose, as he considered nothing more could be gained from the meeting—although he believed he had discovered Goering's alias, or one of them.

"I wonder if I might be permitted to have a word with you in private, Herr Romanov?" asked the elderly banker.

"Of course."

"It is rather a delicate matter I wish to put to you," said Herr Bischoff, "so I thought you might prefer your associate to leave us."

"That won't be necessary," said Romanov, unable to think of anything Bischoff might have to say that he wouldn't later need to discuss with Petrova.

"As you wish," said Bischoff. "I am curious to discover whether there was any other reason behind your request to see me."

"I don't understand what you mean," said Romanov.

"I felt perhaps I knew the real reason you had selected this bank in particular to start your inquiry."

"I didn't select you," said Romanov. "You were only one of—" he stopped himself.

"I see," said Bischoff, himself now looking somewhat bemused. "Then may I be permitted to ask you a few questions?"

"Yes, if you must," said Romanov, now impatient to get away.

"You are Alexander Petrovich Romanov?"

"You must already believe that or we would not have proceeded this far."

"The only son of Petr Nikolayevich Romanov?"

"Yes."

"And grandson of Count Nikolai Alexandrovich Romanov?"

"Is this to be a history lesson on my family tree?" asked Romanov, making his irritation visible.

"No, I just wanted to be sure of my facts, as I am even

more convinced it would be wise for your associate to leave
us for a moment," the old man diffidently suggested.

"Certainly not," said Romanov. "In the Soviet Union we
are all equal," he added pompously.

"Yes, of course," said Bischoff, glancing quickly at Anna
before continuing. "Did your father die in 1948?"

"Yes. He did," said Romanov, beginning to feel distinctly
uncomfortable.

"And you are the only surviving child?"

"I am," confirmed Romanov proudly.

"In which case this bank is in possession . . ." Bischoff hesitated as a file was put in front of him by one of the men in
gray. He placed a pair of gold, half-moon spectacles on his
nose, taking as long as he could over the little exercise.

"Don't say anything more," said Romanov quietly.

Bischoff looked up. "I'm sorry, but I was given every reason to believe your visit had been planned."

Petrova was now sitting on the edge of her seat, enjoying
every moment of the unfolding drama. She had already anticipated exactly what was going to happen and was disappointed when Romanov turned to speak to her.

"You will wait outside," was all he said. Petrova pouted and
rose reluctantly to leave them, closing the door behind her.

Bischoff waited until he was certain the door was closed,
then slid the file across the table. Romanov opened it gingerly. On the top of the first page was his grandfather's name
underlined three times. Below the name were printed row
upon row of incomprehensible figures.

"I think you will find that we have carried out your grandfather's instructions in maintaining a conservative portfolio
of investments with his funds." Bischoff leaned across and
pointed to a figure showing that the bank had achieved an
average increase of 6.7 percent per annum over the previous
forty-nine years.

"What does this figure at the foot of the page represent?"
asked Romanov.

"The total value of your stocks, bonds, and cash at nine
o'clock this morning. It has been updated every Monday

since your grandfather opened an account with this bank in 1916." The old man looked up proudly at the three pictures on the wall.

"*Bozhe Moi,*" said Romanov, as he took in the final figure. "But what currency is it in?"

"Your grandfather only showed faith in the American dollar," said Herr Bischoff.

"*Bozhe Moi,*" Romanov repeated.

"May I presume from your comment that you are not displeased with our stewardship?"

Romanov was speechless.

"It may also interest you to know that we are in possession of several boxes, the contents of which we have no knowledge. Your father also visited us on one occasion soon after the war. He appeared satisfied and assured me that he would return, but we never heard from him again. We were saddened to learn of his death. You might also prefer in the circumstances to return and investigate the boxes at another time," the banker continued.

"Yes," said Romanov quietly. "Perhaps I could come back this afternoon?"

"The bank will always be at your service, Your Excellency," replied Herr Bischoff.

No one had addressed a Romanov by his title since the Revolution. He sat in silence for some time.

Eventually he rose and shook hands with Herr Bischoff. "I will return this afternoon," he repeated before joining his companion in the corridor.

Neither uttered a word until they were back on the street outside the bank. Romanov was still so overcome by what he had learned that he failed to notice that the man he had so deftly avoided at the hotel was now standing in a streetcar line on the far side of the road.

CHAPTER SEVEN

🙚 ❧

THE PASTOR SAT at the table studying the document but didn't offer an opinion for some considerable time. When he had heard Adam's request he had invited the young man into the privacy of his little office at the back of the German Lutheran church.

It turned out to be a stark room dominated by a wooden table and several wooden chairs that didn't match. A small black crucifix was the only ornament on the whitewashed walls. Two of the unmatching chairs were now occupied by Adam and the pastor. Adam sat bolt upright while the man of God, clad from head to toe in a black cassock, elbows on the table and head in hands, stared down at the copy of the document.

After some considerable time, without raising his eyes he offered, "This is a receipt, if I am not mistaken. Although I have little knowledge of such things, but I am fairly confident that Roget et Cie, who must be Swiss bankers based in Geneva, have in their possession an object described herein as 'the Czar's icon,' of which, if I remember my history correctly, the original can be viewed somewhere in Moscow. It appears," he continued, his eyes still fixed on the document, "that if the holder of this receipt presents himself in Geneva, he will be able to claim the aforementioned icon of Saint George and the dragon, deposited there by a Mr. Emmanuel Rosenbaum. I confess," said the pastor, looking up for the first time, "that I've never seen anything like it before." He folded up the copy of the document and handed it back to Adam.

"Thank you," said Adam. "That has been most helpful."

"I am only sorry that my superior the bishop is away on his annual retreat because I feel sure he would have been able to throw more light on the matter than I have."

"You have told me everything I need to know," said Adam, but couldn't resist asking, "Are icons at all valuable?"

"Once again, I must confess that I am not the best man from whom to seek such an opinion. All I can tell you is that, as with all art, the value of any object can vary from one extreme to the other without any satisfactory explanation to us normal mortals."

"Then there is no way of knowing the value of this particular icon?" asked Adam.

"I wouldn't venture an opinion, but no doubt the art auctioneers Sotheby's or Christie's might be willing to do so. After all, they claim in their advertisements that they have an expert in every field waiting to advise you."

"Then I shall put their claim to the test," said Adam, "and pay them a visit." Adam rose from his chair, shook hands with the pastor, and said, "You have been most kind."

"Not at all," said the pastor. "I was only too pleased to assist you. It makes a change from Frau Gerber's marital problems and the size of the church warden's marrows."

Adam took a bus up to Hyde Park Corner and jumped off as it turned left into Knightsbridge. He walked through the subway and continued briskly down Piccadilly toward the Ritz. He had read somewhere that Sotheby's was on Bond Street, although he couldn't remember having ever seen it.

He walked another hundred yards before turning left, where he shortened his stride to check all the signs on both sides of the road. He passed Gucci's, Cartier's, Asprey's, and was beginning to wonder if his memory had failed him and whether he should check in the telephone directory. He continued on past the Irish Tourist Board and Celine's before he finally spotted the gold lettering above a little newspaper kiosk on the far side of the road.

He crossed the one-way street and entered the front door by the side of the kiosk. He felt like a boy on his first day at a new school unsure of his surroundings and not certain to whom he should turn for advice. Most of the people who passed him went straight up the stairs, and he was just about to follow them when he heard a voice say, "Up the stairs and straight through, madam. The auction is due to start in a few minutes."

Adam turned and saw a man in a long, green coat. The name "Sotheby" was embroidered over his lefthand pocket.

"Where do I go if I want something valued?" Adam asked.

"Straight along the passage, sir, as far as you can go, and you'll see a girl on the left-hand side in reception," barked his informant. Adam thanked him, presuming that the guide's former place of work could only have been on an Aldershot drill square. He walked along to the reception area. An old lady was explaining to one of the girls behind the counter that her grandmother had left the vase to her several years before and she wondered what it might be worth.

The girl only glanced at the heirloom before asking, "Can you come back in about fifteen minutes? By then our Mr. Makepeace will have had time to look at it and give you an estimate."

"Thank you, my dear," said the old lady expectantly. The girl picked up the large ornate vase and carried it to a room in the back. She returned a few moments later to be faced with Adam waiting.

"May I help you, sir?"

"I'm not sure," began Adam. "I need some advice concerning an icon."

"Have you brought the piece with you, sir?"

"No, it's still abroad at the moment."

"Do you have any details?"

"Details?"

"Artist's name, date, size. Or better still, do you have a photograph of the piece?"

"No," said Adam sheepishly. "I only know its title, but I do have some documentation," he added, handing over the receipt he had shown the pastor.

"Not a lot to go on," said the girl, studying the German transcript. "But I'll ask Mr. Sedgwick, the head of our Russian and Greek icon department, if he can help you."

"Thank you," said Adam, as the girl picked up the phone.

"Is Mr. Sedgwick able to advise a customer?" the girl inquired. She listened for a moment, then replaced the phone.

"Mr. Sedgwick will be down in a few moments, if you would care to wait."

"Certainly," said Adam, feeling something of a fraud. While the girl attended to the next customer Adam waited for Mr. Sedgwick and studied the pictures on the wall. There were several photos of items that had come under the auctioneer's hammer in recent sales. A large painting by Picasso called *Trois Baigneuses* had been sold for fourteen thousand pounds. As far as Adam could make out the brightly colored oil was of three women on a beach. He felt confident they were women because they had breasts, even if these weren't in the middle of their chests. Next to the Picasso was a Degas of a girl at a ballet lesson; this time there was no doubt it was a girl. But the painting that most caught Adam's eye was a large oil by an artist he had never heard of called Jackson Pollock that had come under the hammer for eleven thousand pounds. Adam wondered what sort of people could afford to spend such sums on works of art.

"Wonderful example of the artist's brushwork," said a voice behind him. Adam turned to face a tall, cadaverous figure with a ginger mustache and thinning red hair. His suit hung on him as if from a coathanger. "My name is Sedgwick," he announced in a donnish voice.

"Scott," said Adam, offering his hand.

"Well, Mr. Scott, why don't we sit over here, and then you can let me know how I can help you."

"I'm not sure you can," admitted Adam, taking the seat opposite him. "It's just that I have been left an icon in a will, and I was hoping it might turn out to be valuable."

"A good start," said Sedgwick, unfolding a pair of spectacles, which he had removed from his top pocket.

"It may not be," said Adam, "because I know nothing about paintings and I wouldn't want to waste your time."

"You won't be wasting my time," Sedgwick assured Adam. "We sell many items for less than ten pounds, you know." Adam hadn't known, and Sedgwick's gentle voice made him feel less apprehensive. "Now am I to understand you do not have a photograph of this particular icon?"

"That's right," said Adam. "The icon is still abroad, and to be honest I've never laid eyes on it."

"I see," said Sedgwick, folding up his glasses. "But can you tell me anything of its provenance?"

"A little. It is known as 'the Czar's icon,' and the subject is Saint George and the dragon."

"How strange," said Sedgwick. "Someone else was inquiring after that particular painting only last week, but he wouldn't leave his name."

"Someone else wanted to know about the Czar's icon?" said Adam.

"Yes, a Russian gentleman, if I wasn't mistaken." Sedgwick tapped his glasses on his knee. "I checked on it extensively for him but found little that wasn't already well documented. The man wondered if it had ever passed through our hands, or even if we had heard of it. I was able to explain to him that the great work by Rublev remains in the Winter Palace for all to see. One can always be certain that it's an original from the Winter Palace because the Czar's silver crown will be embedded in the back of the frame. Since the fifteenth century many copies of Rublev's masterpiece have been made, and they vary greatly in quality and value; but the one he seemed interested in was a copy made for Czar Nikolai by a court painter circa 1914. I was unable to find any trace of such an icon in any of the standard works on the subject. Do you have any documentation on your icon?" Sedgwick inquired.

"Not a lot," said Adam. "Although I do have a copy of the receipt that was left to me in the will," he added, and handed it over.

Mr. Sedgwick once again unfolded his glasses before studying the paper for several moments. "Excellent, quite excellent," he said eventually. "It seems to me that, as long as Roget et Cie will release it, a copy of the Czar's icon painted by the court painter of the time belongs to you. But you will have to go and pick it up yourself, that's for certain."

"But is it worth all that trouble?" asked Adam. "Can you give me any idea of its value?"

"Hard to be precise without actually seeing it," Sedgwick said, returning the document.

"So what is the lowest figure I might expect to get for it?"

The older man frowned. "Ten," he said, after considerable thought. "Perhaps fifteen, but with an absolute top of twenty."

"Twenty pounds," said Adam, unable to hide his disappointment. "I'm sorry to have wasted your time, Mr. Sedgwick."

"No, no, no, Mr. Scott, you misunderstand me. I meant twenty *thousand* pounds."

CHAPTER EIGHT

"A LITTLE MORE caviar, Comrade?" inquired Petrova across the lunch table.

Romanov frowned. His pretense at "strictly confidential information" only to be passed on at the highest level had merely elicited a knowing smile from his companion, who was also not inclined to believe that her boss had a pressing appointment at the consulate that afternoon, an appointment that he had forgotten to mention to her before.

Anna held out a spoon brimming with caviar and pushed it toward Romanov as if to feed a reluctant baby.

"Thank you—*no,*" said Romanov firmly.

"Suit yourself," said the young woman before it disappeared down her own throat. Romanov called for the bill. When he was presented with the slip of paper he couldn't help thinking that for that price he could have fed a Russian family for a month. He paid without comment.

"I will see you back in the hotel later," he said curtly.

"Of course," said Petrova, still lingering over her coffee. "What time shall I expect you?"

Romanov frowned again. "Not before seven," he replied.

"And do you have any plans for me this afternoon, Comrade Major?"

"You may do as you please," said Romanov, and left the table without further word. Once on the street, he set off in the opposite direction to the bank, but he doubted he had fooled the researcher, who was still eyeing him suspiciously through the restaurant window, or the agent, who had waited patiently on the far side of the road for nearly two hours.

By three o'clock Romanov was once again seated in the private room on the fifth floor looked down on by the three photographs of the Herr Bischoffs, and with the fourth Herr Bischoff sitting opposite him and the fifth Herr Bischoff standing behind him.

"We are in possession of," began Herr Bischoff, in the same deliberate, formal way that had dictated the pace of the morning session, "five boxes which have remained unopened since your father visited us in 1945. Should it be your desire to inspect the contents . . ."

"Why else would I have returned?" asked Romanov, already made impatient by the measured voice and studied ritual.

"Indeed," said Herr Bischoff, seemingly unaware of any discourtesy. "Then all we now require is that you sign a disclaimer in order to legalize the situation under Swiss law." Romanov looked apprehensive. "It is only a formality." The Russian still didn't speak. "You can rest assured, Your Excellency, that you are not the only one of your countrymen who from time to time sits in that chair."

Herr Bischoff slid a sheet of paper across the table. There were over twenty clauses of German, all in small print. Romanov scrawled his signature between the two x's with the proffered gold pen. He made no attempt to discover what he was signing. If they hadn't stolen his grandfather's heritage already, why should they be bothering to try now? he thought.

"Perhaps you will be kind enough to accompany me," said Herr Bischoff, quickly passing the sheet of paper to his son, who left immediately. He rose and led Romanov silently back to the corridor. But on this occasion they traveled down in the chairman's private lift all the way to the basement.

When the doors opened Romanov might have thought they had entered a jail had the bars not been made of highly polished steel. A man who was seated behind a desk on the far side of the bars jumped up the moment he saw the chairman and turned the lock on the steel door with a long-shafted key. Romanov followed Herr Bischoff through the open door, then waited until they were both locked inside. The guard preceded them down a corridor, not unlike that of a wine cellar with temperature and humidity gauges every few yards. The light was barely bright enough to ensure that they did not lose their footing. At the end of the corridor, they found Herr Bischoff's son waiting in front of a vast circular steel door. The old man nodded, and the younger Herr Bischoff placed a key in a lock and turned it. Then the chairman stepped forward and undid a second lock. Father and son pushed open the nine-inch-thick door, but neither made any attempt to enter the vault.

"You are in possession of five boxes. Numbers 1721, 1722, 1723, 1724—"

"And 1725, no doubt," interrupted Romanov.

"Precisely," said Herr Bischoff, as he removed a small package from his pocket and added, "This is your envelope, and the key inside it will open all five boxes." Romanov took the envelope and turned toward the open cavern. "But we must open the bank's lock first before you proceed," said Herr Bischoff. "Will you be kind enough to follow us?" Romanov nodded and both Herr Bischoffs proceeded into the vault. Romanov ducked his head and stepped in after them. Young Mr. Bischoff opened the upper lock of the five boxes, three small ones above two larger ones, making a perfect cube. "Once we have left, Your Excellency," said the old man, "we shall pull the door closed, and when you require it to be opened you have only to press the red button on the side wall to alert us. But I must warn you that at five o'clock the vault locks itself automatically, and it cannot be reopened until nine the following morning. However, a warning alarm will sound at four forty-five." Romanov checked the clock on the wall: three-seventeen. He couldn't believe he would need close to two hours to find out what was in the five boxes. The two Herr Bischoffs bowed and left.

Romanov waited impatiently for the vast door to close behind him. Once alone in Aladdin's cave he looked around the room and estimated there must have been two or three thousand boxes filling the four walls, giving them the appearance of a library of safes. He suspected there was more private wealth in that one vault than most countries on earth could call on. He checked the numbers of his own boxes and stood waiting like an orphan who has been told there will be second helpings.

He decided to start with one of the small boxes. He turned the key and heard the lock click before pulling out the stiff drawer to discover it was full of papers. He flicked through them to find they were title deeds to many large tracts of land in Bohemia and Bulgaria—once worth millions, now controlled by Socialist states. As he checked each document, the old saying "not worth the paper they were written on" sprang to mind. Romanov moved to the second box, which he discovered contained the bond certificates of companies once managed by His Excellency Count Nikolai Alexandrovich Romanov. The last time they had declared a profit was 1914. He cursed the system he had been born under as he moved on to the third box, which contained only one document, his grandfather's will. It took only moments to discover that all had been left to his father and therefore he was the lawful owner of everything—and nothing.

Dismayed, Romanov knelt down to study the two larger boxes, both of which looked big enough to hold a cello. He hesitated before placing his key in the lock, turning it and pulling out the vast container.

He stared down in anticipation.

It was empty. He could only presume that it had been that

way for over fifty years unless his father had removed everything, and there was no reason to believe that. He quickly unlocked the fifth box and in desperation pulled it open.

The box was split into twelve equal compartments. He raised the lid of the first compartment, and stared down in wonder. Before him lay precious stones of such size, variety, and color that would have made anyone who was not royal gasp. Gingerly he lifted the lid off the second compartment, to find it contained pearls of such quality that one single string of them would have transformed a plain girl into a society beauty. As he opened the third box, his amazement did not lessen, and he understood for the first time why his grandfather had been considered one of the most enterprising merchants of the century. And now it all belonged to Alex Romanov, an impecunious government official, who was already wondering how he could possibly enjoy such riches.

It took Romanov a further hour to go through the contents of the remaining nine compartments. When he reached the last one—almost an anticlimax, in that it contained nothing but gold coins—he felt thoroughly exhausted. He checked the clock on the wall: four-thirty. He began to replace the lids on each of the compartments, but during the treasure hunt he had come across one object of such magnificence that he could not resist removing it. He paused as he held up the long heavy gold chain weighted by a medallion, also made of solid gold, that hung from it. On one side was an engraved picture of his grandfather—Count Nikolai Alexandrovich Romanov, a proud, handsome man—while on the other was a profile of his grandmother, so beautiful that she surely could have worn any of the jewelry in that treasure trove with distinction.

For some time, Romanov held the chain in his hand before finally placing it over his head and letting the medallion fall from his neck. He gave the piece one last look before tucking it under his shirt. When he had replaced the lid on the last compartment he slid the box back into place and locked it.

For the second time that day Romanov's thoughts turned to his father and the decision he must have made when faced with such a fortune. He had gone back to Russia with his secret. Had he planned to rescue Alex from the life of drudgery that was all he could look forward to? What had been his plans, and had they included Alex? His father had always assured him that he had an exciting future but that there were secrets he was too young to share, and he, in turn, had passed that information on to the authorities. His reward had been a place at the Komasol. But his father must have taken that secret to the grave, because Alex would never have learned of the fortune if it had not been for . . . Poskonov.

His mind turned to the old banker. Had he known all along, or was it a coincidence that he had been sent to this bank first? Members of his chosen profession didn't survive if they believed in coincidence.

A false move and the State would not hesitate to send him to the same grave as his father and grandfather. He would have to be at his most skillful when he next came into contact with the old banker, otherwise he might not live to choose between power in his homeland or wealth in the West.

"After I have found the Czar's icon I will return," he said quite audibly. He turned suddenly as the alarm bell's piercing sound rang out. He checked the clock on the wall and was surprised by how much time he had spent in the locked room. He walked toward the vault door and on reaching it pressed the red button without looking back. The great door swung open to reveal two anxious-looking Herr Bischoffs. The son stepped quickly into the vault, walked over to the five boxes, and made safe the bank's locks.

"We were beginning to get quite worried about the time," said the old man. "I do hope you found everything to your satisfaction."

"Entirely," said Romanov. "But what happens if I am unable to return for some considerable time?"

"It's of no importance," Herr Bischoff replied. "The boxes

will not be touched again until you come back, and as they are all hermetically sealed, your possessions will remain in perfect condition."

"What temperature are the boxes kept at?"

"Fifty degrees Fahrenheit," said Herr Bischoff, somewhat puzzled.

"Are they airtight?"

"Certainly," replied the banker. "And watertight, not that the basement has ever been flooded," he added quite seriously.

"So anything left in them is totally safe from any investigation?"

"You are only the second person to look inside those boxes in fifty years," came back the firm response.

"Excellent," said Romanov, looking down at Herr Bischoff. "Because there is just a possibility that I shall want to return tomorrow morning, with a package of my own to deposit."

"Can you put me through to Mr. Pemberton, please?" said Adam.

There was a long pause. "We don't have a Mr. Pemberton working here, sir."

"That is Barclays International in London, isn't it?"

"Yes, sir."

"Mr. Lawrence Pemberton. I feel certain I've got the right branch."

The silence was even longer this time. "Ah, yes," came back the eventual reply. "Now I can see which department he works in. I'll see if he's in." Adam heard a phone ringing in the background.

"He doesn't seem to be at his desk at the moment, sir, would you like to leave a message?"

"No, thank you," said Adam, and replaced the receiver. He sat alone, thinking, not bothering to switch on the light as the day grew darker. If he was to carry through the idea, he needed some information that Lawrence as a banker should find easy to supply.

A key turned in the door, and Adam watched Lawrence enter and switch the light on. He looked startled when he saw Adam seated in front of him.

"How does one open a Swiss bank account?" were Adam's first words.

"I can't imagine one would find it that easy if all you have to offer is next week's unemployment check," said Lawrence. "Mind you, they usually keep a code name for English customers," he added, as he put his copy of the *Evening News* on the table. "Yours could be 'pauper.'"

"It may surprise you to learn that it was a serious question," said Adam.

"Well," said Lawrence, taking the question seriously, "in truth, anyone can open a Swiss bank account as long as they have a worthwhile sum to deposit. And by worthwhile I mean at least ten thousand pounds."

"Yes, but how would you go about getting the money back out?"

"That can be done over the phone or in person, and in that way Swiss banks don't differ greatly from any bank in England. Few customers, however, would risk the phone, unless they're resident in a country where there are no tax laws to break. In which case why would they need the gnomes of Zurich in the first place?"

"What happens when a customer dies and the bank can't be sure who the rightful owner of the assets is?"

"They would do nothing, but a claimant would have to prove that he was the person entitled to inherit any deposits the bank held. That's not a problem if you're in possession of the correct documentation such as a will and proof of identity. We deal with such matters every day."

"But you just admitted that it's illegal!"

"Not for those clients resident overseas, or when it becomes necessary to balance our gold deposits, not to mention the bank's books. But the Bank of England keeps a strict watch over every penny that goes in and out of the country."

"So, if I were entitled to a million pounds' worth of gold left to me by an Argentinian uncle deposited in a Swiss bank, and I was in possession of the right legal documents to prove I was the beneficiary, all I would have to do is go and claim it?"

"Nothing to stop you," said Lawrence. "Although under the law as it currently stands, you would have to bring it back to this country and sell the gold to the Bank of England for the sum they deemed correct, and then pay death duty on that sum." Adam remained silent. "If you do have an Argentinian uncle who has left you all that gold in Switzerland, your best bet would be to leave it where it is. Under this government, if you fulfilled the letter of the law, you would end up with about seventeen and a half percent of its true value."

"Pity I haven't got an Argentinian uncle," said Adam.

"He doesn't have to be Argentinian," said Lawrence, watching his friend's every reaction closely.

"Thanks for the information," said Adam and disappeared into the bedroom.

The last pieces of the jigsaw were beginning to fit into place. He was in possession of Roget's receipt of the icon originally meant for his father; all he needed now was a copy of the will to show that the document had been left to him. He could then prove that he was the owner of a worthless/priceless—he still had no way of being sure which—copy of the Czar's icon. He lay awake that night recalling the words in his father's letter. "If there is anything to be gained from the contents of this envelope, I make only one request of you, namely that your mother should be the first to benefit from it without ever being told how such good fortune came about."

When Romanov returned to the hotel, via the Russian consulate, he found Petrova in her room dressed in jeans and a bright pink jersey, sitting in a corner reading, her legs dangling over the side of the chair.

"I hope you had a fruitful afternoon?" he inquired, politely.

"I certainly did," Anna replied. "The galleries in Zurich are well worthy of a visit. But tell me about *your* afternoon: did it also turn out to be fruitful?"

"It was a revelation, my little one, nothing less. Why don't we have a quiet supper in my room so I can tell you all about it while we celebrate in style?"

"What a magnificent idea," said the researcher. "And may I be responsible for ordering dinner?"

"Certainly," said Romanov.

Petrova dropped her book on the floor and began to concentrate on the extensive à la carte menu that had been left by Romanov's bedside table. She spent a considerable time selecting each dish for their banquet, and even Romanov was impressed when it finally appeared.

Anna had chosen as an entrée slivers of Gravlax edged with dill sauce. Accompanying it was a half-bottle of Premier Cru Chablis 1958. Between mouthfuls Romanov told her of the contents of his family inheritance, and as he described each new treasure the researcher's eyes grew larger and larger.

Romanov's monologue was only once interrupted, by a waiter who wheeled in a trolley on which sat a silver salver. The waiter lifted the salver to reveal a rack of lamb surrounded by courgettes and tiny new potatoes. To accompany this particular dish, the hotel had provided a Gevrey-Chambertin.

The final course, a fluffy raspberry soufflé, required in the researcher's view only the finest Château d'Yquem. She had selected the '49, which only made her lapse into singing Russian folk songs, which, Romanov felt, given the circumstances, was somewhat inappropriate.

As she drained the last drop of wine in her glass Petrova rose and slightly unsteady, said, "To Alex, the man I love."

Romanov nodded his acknowledgment and suggested it might be time for them to go to bed, as they had to catch the first flight back to Moscow the following morning. He wheeled the trolley out into the corridor and placed a Do Not Disturb sign over the doorknob.

"A memorable evening," smiled the researcher, as she

flicked off her shoes. Romanov stopped to admire her as she began to remove her clothes, but when he unbuttoned his shirt the researcher stopped undressing and let out a gasp of surprise.

"It's magnificent," she said in awe. Romanov held up the gold medallion.

"A bauble compared with the treasures I left behind," he assured her.

"Comrade lover," Anna said in a childlike voice, pulling him toward the bed, "you realize how much I adore, admire, and respect you?"

"Um," said Romanov.

"And you also know," she continued, "that I have never asked you for any favor in the past."

"But I have a feeling you are about to now," said Romanov as she lifted back the sheet.

"Only that if the gold chain is nothing more than a mere bauble, perhaps you might allow me to wear it occasionally?"

"Occasionally?" said Romanov, staring into Anna's eyes. "Why occasionally? Why not permanently, my darling?" and without another word he removed the gold chain from around his neck and placed it over the young woman's head. Anna sighed as she fingered the thick gold rings that made up the chain that Romanov didn't let go of.

"You're hurting me, Alex," she said with a little laugh. "Please let go." But Romanov only pulled the chain a little tighter. Tears began to run down her cheeks as the metal began to bite into her skin. "I can't breathe properly," gasped the researcher. "Please stop teasing." Romanov continued to tighten the chain against her throat until Anna's face began to turn red as it filled with blood.

"You wouldn't tell anyone about my windfall, would you, my little one?"

"No, never, Alex. No one, you can rely on me," she choked out desperately.

"Can I feel certain?" he asked with an edge of menace in his voice.

"Yes, yes, of course, but please stop now," she piped, her

delicate hands clutching desperately at her master's blond hair, but Romanov only continued to squeeze and squeeze the heavy gold chain around her neck like a rack and pinion, tighter and tighter.

Romanov was not aware of the girl's hands clinging so desperately to his hair as he twisted the chain a final time. "I'm sure you understand that I must be absolutely certain that you wouldn't share our secret—with anyone," he explained to her. But she did not hear his plea because the vertebrae in her neck had already snapped.

On his morning run along the Embankment, Adam mulled over the task that still needed to be carried out.

If he took the morning flight out of Heathrow on Wednesday, he could be back in London by the same evening, or Thursday at the latest. But there were several things that had to be completed before he could leave for Geneva.

He stopped on the pavement outside his block and checked his pulse, before climbing the stairs to the flat.

"Three letters for you," said Lawrence. "None for me. Mind you," he added as his flatmate joined him in the kitchen, "two of them are in buff envelopes." Adam picked up the letters and left them on the end of his bed en route to the shower. He survived five minutes of ice-cold water before toweling down. Once he was dressed he opened the letters. He began with the white one, which turned out to be a note from Heidi thanking him for dinner and hoping she would be seeing him again sometime. He smiled and tore open the first of the buff envelopes, which was yet another missive from the Foreign Office Coordination Staff.

Captain Scott—the rank already seemed out of place—was requested to attend a medical at 122 Harley Street at three o'clock on the following Monday, to be conducted by Dr. John Vance.

Finally he opened the other brown envelope and pulled out a letter from Lloyds, Cox and King's branch on Pall Mall, informing Dear Sir/Madam that they had been in receipt of a check for five hundred pounds from Holbrooke, Holbrooke and Gascoigne, and that his current account at the close of business the previous day was in credit to the sum of £272.18.4d. When Adam checked through the account it showed that at one point he had, for the first time in his life, run up a debt—a situation that he knew would have been frowned upon had he still been in the army, for as little as twenty years before it was in some regiments a court-martial offense for an officer to be overdrawn.

What would his brother officers have said if he told them he was about to remove two hundred pounds from the account with no real guarantee of a return?

Once Adam had finished dressing, he rejoined Lawrence in the kitchen.

"How was the Shah of Iran?" he asked.

"Oh, very reasonable really," said Lawrence, turning a page of the *Daily Telegraph*, "considering the circumstances. Promised he would do what he could about his current financial embarrassment, but he was a bit pushed until the West allowed him to raise the price of oil from four pounds a barrel."

"Where did you eventually take him to lunch?" asked Adam, enjoying the game.

"I offered him a shepherd's pie at the Green Man, but the bloody fellow became quite snotty. It seems he and the empress had to pop along to Harrods to be measured up for a new throne. Would have gone along with him, of course, but my boss wanted his wastepaper basket emptied, so I missed out on the Harrods deal as well."

"So what are you up to today?"

"I shouldn't let you in on this," said Lawrence, peering at the photograph of Ted Dexter, the defeated English cricket captain, "but the governor of the Bank of England wants my views on whether we should devalue the pound from $2.80 to $2.40."

"And what are your views?"

"I've already explained to the fellow that the only two-forty I know is the bus that runs between Golders Green and

Edgware, and if I don't get a move on, I'll miss my beloved 14," said Lawrence, checking his watch. Adam laughed as he watched his friend slam his briefcase shut and disappear out of the door.

Lawrence had changed considerably over the years since he had left Wellington. Perhaps it was that Adam could only remember him as school captain and then leaving with the top classics scholarship to Balliol. He had seemed so serious in those days and certainly destined for greater things. No one would have thought it possible he would end up as an investment analyst at Barclays District and Commonwealth Office. At Oxford contemporaries had half-joked about him being a cabinet minister. Was it possible that one always expected too much of those idols who were only a couple of years older than oneself? On leaving school their friendship had grown, and when Adam was posted to Malaya, Lawrence never accepted the army report that said his friend was missing, presumed dead. And when Adam announced that he was leaving the army, Lawrence asked for no explanation and couldn't have been kinder about his unemployment problem. Adam hoped that he would be given the chance to repay such friendship.

Adam fried himself an egg and a couple of rashers of bacon, as there wasn't much more he could do before nine-thirty, although he did find time to scribble a note to his sister, enclosing a check for fifty pounds.

At nine-thirty he made a phone call. Mr. Holbrooke—Adam wondered if he actually had a Christian name—couldn't hide his surprise at receiving a call from young Mr. Scott. Now that my father is dead, I must be old Mr. Scott, Adam wanted to tell him. And Holbrooke sounded even more surprised by his request. "No doubt connected in some way with that envelope," he muttered, but agreed to put a copy of his father's will in the post that afternoon.

Adam's other requirements could not be carried out over the phone, so he locked up the flat and jumped on a bus heading up King's Road. He left the doubledecker at Hyde

Park Corner and made his way to Lloyds Bank on Pall Mall, where he joined a line at the foreign exchange counter.

"May I help you?" asked a polite assistant when he finally reached the front.

"Yes," said Adam. "I would like fifty pounds in Swiss francs, fifty pounds in cash, and a hundred pounds in traveler's checks."

"What is your name?" she inquired.

"Adam Scott."

The girl entered some calculations on a large desktop machine before cranking the handle round several times. She looked at the result, then disappeared for a few moments to return with a copy of the bank statement Adam had received in the morning post.

"The total cost, including our charges, will be £202.1s.8d. That would leave your account in credit with £70.16s.4d.," she informed him.

"Yes," said Adam, but didn't add that in truth it would only be £20.16s.4d the moment his sister presented her check. He began to hope that the Foreign Office paid by the week; otherwise it would have to be another frugal month. Unless of course . . .

Adam signed the tops of the ten traveler's checks in the cashier's presence, and she then handed over five hundred and ninety-four Swiss francs and fifty pounds in cash. It was the largest sum of money Adam had ever taken out at one time.

Another bus journey took him to the British European Airways terminal on Cromwell Road, where he asked the girl to book him a round-trip ticket to Geneva.

"First class or economy?" she asked.

"Economy," said Adam, amused by the thought that anyone might think he would want to go first class.

"That will be thirty-one pounds please, sir." Adam paid in cash and placed the ticket in his inside pocket, before returning to the flat for a light lunch. During the afternoon, he called Heidi, who had agreed to join him for dinner at the Chelsea Kitchen at eight o'clock. There was one more thing

Adam needed to be certain about before he joined Heidi for dinner.

Romanov was woken by the ringing of the phone.

"Yes," he said.

"Good morning, Comrade Romanov, it's Melinac, the second secretary at the embassy."

"Good morning, Comrade, what can I do for you?"

"It's about Comrade Petrova." Romanov smiled at the thought of her now lying in the bath. "Have you come across the girl since you reported her missing?"

"No," replied Romanov. "And she didn't sleep in her bed last night."

"I see," said the second secretary. "Then your suspicions that she might have defected are beginning to look like a serious possibility."

"I fear so," said Romanov, "and I shall have to make a full report of the situation to my superiors the moment I get back to Moscow."

"Yes, of course, Comrade Major."

"I shall also point out that you have done everything possible to assist me with this problem, Comrade Second Secretary."

"Thank you, Comrade Major."

"And brief me the moment you come up with any information that might lead us to where she is."

"Of course, Comrade Major." Romanov replaced the phone and walked across to the bathroom in the adjoining room. He stared down at the body hunched up in the bath. Anna's eyes were bulging in their sockets, her face contorted, and the skin already gray. After throwing a towel over the dead researcher's head and locking the door, he went into his own bathroom for an unusually long shower.

He returned and sat on his side of the bed, only a towel around his waist, and picked up the phone. He ordered breakfast, which arrived fifteen minutes later, by which time he had dressed. Once he had finished orange juice and croissants he returned to the phone trying to recall the name of the hotel's manager. It came back to him just as the receptionist said, *"Guten morgen, Mein Herr."*

"Jacques, please," was all Romanov said. A moment later he heard the manager's voice, "Good morning, Herr Romanov."

"I have a delicate problem that I was hoping you might be able to help me with."

"I shall certainly try, sir," came back the reply.

"I am in possession of a rather valuable object that I wish to deposit with my bank, and I wouldn't want . . ."

"I understand your dilemma entirely," said the manager. "And how can I be of assistance?"

"I require a large container in which to place the object."

"Would a laundry basket be large enough?"

"Ideal, but does it have a secure lid?"

"Oh, yes," replied Jacques. "We often have to drop them off down lift shafts."

"Perfect," said Romanov.

"Then it will be with you in a matter of moments," said Jacques. "And I shall send a porter to assist you. May I also suggest that it is taken down in the freight elevator at the rear of the hotel, thus ensuring that no one will see you leaving?"

"Very considerate," said Romanov.

"Will a car be calling to collect you?"

"No," said Romanov. "I—"

"Then I shall arrange for a taxi to be waiting. When will you require it?"

"In no more than half an hour."

"You will find it parked outside the freight entrance in twenty minutes' time."

"You have been most helpful," said Romanov, before adding, "the chairman of the State Bank did not exaggerate his praise of you."

"You are too kind, Herr Romanov," said the voice. "Will there be anything else?"

"Perhaps you would be good enough to have my account prepared so that there will be no holdup."

"Certainly."

Romanov put the phone down, wishing he could export such service to Moscow. He only waited a moment before he dialed the first of two local numbers. On both occasions his wishes were immediately granted. As he replaced the phone for the third time there was a gentle tap on the door. Romanov went quickly over to answer it. A young porter stood in the corridor, a large laundry basket by his side. He smiled politely. Romanov merely nodded and pulled in the basket. "Please return as soon as the taxi has arrived," said Romanov. The porter bowed slightly but said nothing.

As soon as the porter had left, Romanov locked the door and put the chain in place before wheeling the laundry basket into the main bedroom and leaving it by the side of the bed. He undid the tough leather straps and threw open the lid.

Next he unlocked the bathroom door and lifted Petrova's stiff body in his arms before trying to cram it into the basket. Rigor mortis had already gripped the body; the legs refused to bend, and the researcher didn't quite fit in. Romanov placed the naked Petrova on the floor. He held his fingers out straight and suddenly brought them down with such force on the right leg that it broke like a branch in a storm. He repeated the action on her left leg. Like the guillotine, it didn't require a second attempt. He then tucked the legs under her body. It amused Romanov to consider that, had it been he who had been murdered, Anna Petrova would never have been able to get him in the basket, whatever she had tried to break. Romanov then wheeled the trolley into the researcher's bedroom and, after emptying all her drawers, including Anna's clothes, clean and dirty, her shoes, her toilet bag, toothbrush, and even an old photograph of himself he hadn't realized she possessed, he threw them in the basket on top of her. Once he had removed the gold medallion from around her neck and was certain that there was nothing of the researcher's personal belongings left, he covered up the body with a hotel bath towel and sprayed it with a liberal amount of Chanel No. 5 that had been left courtesy of the hotel.

Finally he strapped the lid down securely, wheeled the creaking basket out, and left it by the outer door.

Romanov began to pack his own suitcase, but there was a knock on the door before he had finished.

"Wait," he said firmly. There was a muffled reply of "*Ja, mein Herr.*" A few moments later Romanov opened the door. The porter entered, nodded to him, and began to tug at the laundry basket, but it took a firm shove from Romanov's foot before it got moving. The porter sweated his way down the corridor as Romanov walked by the side of the basket, carrying his suitcase. When they reached the rear of the hotel Romanov watched as the basket was wheeled safely into the freight elevator before he stepped in himself.

When the ground-floor doors opened Romanov was relieved to be greeted by Jacques, who was standing by a large Mercedes waiting for him with the trunk already open. The taxi driver and the porter lifted up the laundry basket and placed it into the trunk, but Romanov's suitcase could not be fitted in as well, so it had to be put in the front of the car alongside the driver's seat.

"Shall we forward your bill to the consulate, *mein Herr?*" asked Jacques.

"Yes, that would be helpful . . ."

"I do hope everything has worked out to your satisfaction," said Jacques, as he held open the back door of the Mercedes for his departing guest.

"Entirely," said Romanov.

"Good, good. And will your young colleague be joining you?" asked the manager, looking back over his shoulder toward the hotel.

"No, she won't," said Romanov. "She has already gone on to the airport ahead of me."

"Of course," said Jacques, "but I am sorry to have missed her. Do please pass on my best wishes."

"I certainly will," said Romanov, "and I look forward to returning to your hotel in the near future."

"Thank you, sir," the manager said as Romanov slipped into the backseat, leaving Jacques to close the door behind him and wave as the car moved off.

When Romanov arrived at the Swissair office his suitcase was checked in, and he waited only moments before continuing on to the bank. Herr Bischoff's son, accompanied by another man, also clad in a gray suit, were waiting by in the hall to greet him.

"How pleasant to see you again so soon," volunteered the young Herr Bischoff. His deep voice took Romanov by surprise. The taxi driver waited by the open trunk while Herr Bischoff's companion, a man of at least six foot four and heavily built, lifted out the laundry basket as if it were a sponge cake. Romanov paid the fare and followed Herr Bischoff into the far lift.

"We are fully prepared for your deposition following your phone call," said Herr Bischoff. "My father was only sorry not to be present personally. He had a long-standing engagement with another customer and only hopes that you will understand." Romanov waved his hand.

The lift traveled straight to the ground floor, where the guard, on seeing young Herr Bischoff, unlocked the massive steel cage. Romanov and the banker proceeded at a leisurely pace down the corridor, while the giant carried the basket in their wake.

Standing with folded arms by the vault door was another of the partners Romanov recognized from the previous day. Herr Bischoff nodded, and the partner placed his key in the top lock of the vault door without a word. Herr Bischoff then turned the second lock, and together they pushed open the great steel door. Herr Bischoff and his partner walked in ahead of Romanov and opened the top lock of all five of his boxes, while the guard placed the laundry basket on the floor beside them.

"Will you require any assistance?" asked Herr Bischoff as he handed his Russian client a personal sealed envelope.

"No, thank you," Romanov assured him but did not relax until he had seen the vast door close behind him and all four of his Swiss helpers left invisibly on the other side.

Once he felt certain he was alone, he stared down at the one large box he knew to be empty: it was smaller than he had recalled. Beads of sweat appeared on his forehead as he unlocked it, pulled it out, and raised the airtight lid. It was going to be a tight fit. Romanov unstrapped the laundry basket and removed everything except the body. He stared down at the contorted face; the deep marks in the skin around the neck were now a dark blue. He bent over and lifted the researcher up by her waist, but as no part of the body moved other than her broken legs, he had to drop her into the box headfirst. Even then he had to adjust her various limbs in order that the box could be shut: had Anna been even an inch taller the exercise would have proved pointless. He then stuffed the girl's belongings down at the sides of her body, leaving only the Chanel-covered towel behind in the laundry basket.

Romanov proceeded to replace the lid on the airtight box before pushing it back securely in place and locking it. He then double-checked that it could not be opened without his own personal key. He was relieved to find he could not budge it. He hesitated for a moment, glancing at the second large box, but accepted that this was not the time to indulge himself: that would have to wait for another occasion. Satisfied that everything was back in place, he closed and strapped down the lid of the laundry basket and wheeled it back to the entrance of the vault. He pressed the little red button.

"I do hope you found everything in order," said the young Herr Bischoff once he had returned from locking the five boxes.

"Yes, thank you," said Romanov. "But would it be possible for someone to return the laundry basket to the Saint Gothard Hotel?"

"Of course," said the banker, who nodded toward the large man.

"And I can be assured that the boxes will not be touched in my absence?" he asked as they walked down the corridor.

"Naturally, Your Excellency," said Herr Bischoff, looking somewhat aggrieved at such a suggestion. "When you return," he continued, "you will find everything exactly as you left it."

Well, not exactly, Romanov thought to himself.

When they stepped out of the lift on the ground floor, Romanov spotted Herr Bischoff's father with another customer.

A Rolls-Royce accompanied by a police motorcycle whisked the Shah of Iran quickly away, and the chairman discreetly waved his farewell.

When they reached the entrance to the bank, the young Herr Bischoff bowed. "We shall look forward to seeing you again when you are next in Zurich, Your Excellency," he said.

"Thank you," said Romanov, who shook hands with the young man and walked out on to the pavement to find the anonymous black car waiting to take him to the airport.

He cursed. This time he did spot the agent he had seen earlier in the hotel.

CHAPTER
NINE

"KILL HIM, SIR," the corporal whispered in Adam's ear.

"Not much hope of that," muttered Adam as he bounced into the center of the ring.

The lean muscle-bound instructor stood waiting for him. "Let's have a few rounds and see how you make out, sir." Adam bobbed and weaved around the Physical Training Instructor, looking for an opening.

Adam led with a left and received a tap on the nose for his trouble. "Keep your guard up," said the sergeant major. Adam led again, catching the instructor a full blow on the chest, but was punished with a sharp left jab into the side of his head. He wobbled and his ear tingled, but this time he managed to keep his guard up when a right and left followed. "You're feeble, sir, that's your problem. You couldn't knock the skin off a rice pudding." Adam feinted with his right and then swung a left with such force that when it caught the sergeant major full on the chin he staggered and fell.

The corporal standing by the side of the ring smirked as the instructor remained on the floor. Eventually he managed to get back on his feet.

"I'm sorry," said Adam, his guard up and ready.

"Don't be sorry, you bloody fool . . . sir. You landed a bloody good punch. A technical knockout, to be accurate, so I'll have to wait for a day or two to seek my revenge." Adam breathed a sigh of relief and lowered his guard. "But that doesn't mean you're off the hook. It's weight training for you now, sir. Beam work and floor exercises."

For the next hour the sergeant major chased, kicked, harried, and badgered Adam until he finally collapsed in a heap on the floor, incapable of lifting an evening paper.

"Not bad, sir. I feel sure the Foreign Office will find some niche for you. Mind you," he added, "as most of that lot are about as wet as a dishcloth even you'll have a chance to shine."

"You are most flattering, sergeant major," said Adam from a supine position.

"Up, sir," the instructor bellowed. Adam unwillingly got to his feet as quickly as his tired body would allow.

"Don't tell me, Sergeant Major."

"It's the recovery that proves fitness, not the speed," they said in unison.

"Sad day when you left the army," said the instructor to Adam once they were back in the Queen's Club changing room. "Can't name a lot of officers who have put me on the floor." The instructor touched his chin tenderly. "That will teach me to underestimate a man who survived nine months of Chink food. And let's hope the Foreign Office doesn't underestimate you as well."

The sergeant major rose from the bench by his locker. "Same time Wednesday?"

"Can't make it Wednesday, Sergeant Major. I may not be back from a trip to Geneva."

"Swanning around Europe nowadays, are we?"

"I could manage Thursday morning if that suits you," Adam said, ignoring the jibe.

"Your checkup with the quack is next Monday afternoon, if I remember correctly."

"Right."

"Thursday at ten then, it will give you a little longer to think about my right hook."

The Chairman of the KGB studied the report on the desk in front of him: something didn't ring true. He looked up at Romanov. "Your reason for visiting Bischoff et Cie was because they claimed to be in possession of a fifteenth-century icon that might have fitted the description of the one we are searching for?"

"That is correct, Comrade, and the chairman of Gosbank will confirm that he personally arranged the meeting."

"But the icon turned out to be of Saint Peter and not of Saint George and the dragon."

"Also confirmed by Comrade Petrova in her report."

"Ah, yes, Comrade Petrova," said Zaborski, his eyes returning to the sheet of paper in front of him.

"Yes, Comrade."

"And later that evening Comrade Petrova mysteriously failed to keep an appointment with you?"

"Inexplicably," said Romanov.

"But which you reported to Comrade Melinac at the embassy." He paused. "You were responsible for selecting Petrova yourself, were you not?"

"That is correct, Comrade Chairman."

"Does that not reveal a certain lack of judgment on your part?"

Romanov made no attempt to reply.

The Chairman's eyes returned to the file. "When you awoke the next morning, there was still no sign of the girl?"

"She also failed to turn up for breakfast as arranged," said Romanov, "and when I went to her room all her personal belongings were gone."

"Which convinced you she had defected."

"Yes, sir," said Romanov.

"But the Swiss police can find no trace of her," said Zaborski. "So I keep asking myself why would she defect? Her husband and her immediate family live in Moscow. They are all employed by the State, and it is not as if this were Comrade Petrova's first visit to the West."

Romanov didn't offer an opinion.

"Perhaps Petrova disappeared because she might have been able to tell us something you didn't want us to hear."

Still Romanov said nothing.

The Chairman's gaze once again returned to the file. "I wonder what it was that young Petrova wanted to tell us? Who else you were sleeping with that night, perhaps?"

Romanov felt a shiver of fear as he wondered how much Zaborski really knew. Zaborski paused and pretended to check something else in the report. "Perhaps she could tell us why you felt it necessary to return to Bischoff et Cie a second time." Once again Zaborski paused. "I think I may have to open an inquiry into the disappearance of Comrade Petrova. Because, Comrade Romanov, by the time you returned to the bank a third time," said the Chairman, his voice rising with each word, "every second-rate spy from here to Istanbul knew that we were searching for something." The Chairman paused. Romanov was still desperate to find out if Zaborski had any real evidence. Neither spoke for some time. "You have always been a loner, Major Romanov, and I do not deny that at times your results have allowed me to overlook certain indiscretions. But I am not a loner, Comrade. I am a desk man, no longer allowed your freedom of action." He fiddled with the paperweight of Luna Nine on the desk in front of him.

"I am a file man, a paper man. I make reports in triplicate, I answer questions in quadruplicate, explain decisions in quintuplicate. Now I will have to explain the circumstances of Petrova's strange disappearance to the Politburo in multiplicate."

Romanov remained silent, something the KGB had taken several years to instill into him. He began to feel confident that Zaborski was only guessing. If he had suspected the truth, the interview would have taken place in the basement where a less intellectual approach to questioning was carried out.

"In the USSR," continued Zaborski, now rising from his chair, "despite our image in the Western world, we investigate a suspicious death"—he paused—"or defection more scrupulously than any other nation on earth. You, Comrade Romanov, would have found your chosen profession easier to follow had you been born in Africa, South America, or even Los Angeles."

Still Romanov did not venture an opinion.

"The General Secretary informed me at one o'clock this morning that he is not impressed by your latest efforts, distinctly unimpressed were the exact words he used, especially after your excellent start. All he is interested in, however, is finding the Czar's icon, and so, for the time being, Comrade, he has decided there will be no investigation. But if you ever act in such an irresponsible way again it will not be an inquiry you are facing, but a tribunal, and we all know what happened to the last Romanov that faced a tribunal."

He closed the file. "Against my better judgment and because we are left with less than a week, the General Secretary has allowed you a second chance in the belief that you will indeed come up with the Czar's icon. Do I make myself clear, Comrade?" he barked.

"Very clear, Comrade Chairman," said Romanov and, turning smartly on his heel, quickly left the room.

The Chairman of the KGB waited for the door to close before his eyes settled back on the file. What was Romanov up to, Zaborski needed to know suddenly realizing that his own career might now be on the line. He flicked down a switch on the little console by his side. "Find Major Valchek," he ordered.

"I've never actually had champagne and caviar," admitted Adam, as he looked up at the beautiful girl who sat opposite him across the table. He loved the way she tied her hair, the way she dressed and the way she laughed, but most of all the way she smiled.

"Well, don't get frightened, because I can't imagine caviar will ever find its place on this particular menu," teased Heidi. "But perhaps soon when you are the proud owner of the Czar's icon, that is, if Mr. Rosenbau . . ."

Adam put a finger to his lips. "No one else knows about that, not even Lawrence."

"That may be wise," Heidi whispered. "He will only expect you to invest all the money you make from the sale in his boring bank."

"What makes you think I'd sell it?" asked Adam, trying to discover how much she had worked out.

"If you own a Rolls-Royce and you are out of work you do not then go and hire a chauffeur."

"But I've only got a motorbike."

"And you'll have to sell that as well if the icon turns out to be worthless," she said, laughing.

"Would you like a coffee to follow?" asked the waiter, who was already clearing their table in the hope of fitting in two more customers before the night was out.

"Yes, please. Two cappuccinos," said Adam. He turned his gaze back to Heidi. "Funnily enough," he continued as the waiter retreated, "the only time I've ever rung Lawrence at the bank the operator couldn't immediately locate him."

"What's so surprising about that?" asked Heidi.

"It was as if they had never heard of him," said Adam, "but perhaps I was imagining it."

"A bank that size must have over a thousand employees. You could go years without knowing everyone who worked there."

"I suppose you're right," Adam said, as two coffees were placed in front of them.

"When do you plan on going to Geneva?" Heidi asked, after she had tried a sip of the coffee and found it too hot.

"First thing Wednesday morning. I hope to be back the same evening."

"Considerate."

"What do you mean?" asked Adam.

"To choose my one day off to fly away," she said. "Not very romantic."

"Then why not come with me?" he asked, leaning across the table to take her hand.

"That might turn out to be more significant than sharing your sausages."

"I would hope so, and in any case, you could be most useful."

"You do have a way with words," said Heidi.

"You know, I didn't mean it that way. It's simply that I don't speak German or French, and I've never been to Switzerland other than on a school skiing trip—and then I kept falling over." Heidi tried her coffee again.

"Well?" said Adam, not letting go of her hand.

"The Swiss speak perfect English," she said eventually, "and should you have any problem with the bank, you can always get in touch with Lawrence."

"It would only be for the day," said Adam.

"And a waste of your money."

"Not very romantic," said Adam.

"Touché."

"Think about it," said Adam. "After the cost of your round-trip flight I will be left with only £19,969. I don't know how I'll get by."

"You really mean it, don't you?" said Heidi, sounding serious for the first time. "But women are not impulsive creatures."

"You could always bring Jochen along with you."

Heidi laughed. "He wouldn't fit on the plane."

"Do say you'll come," said Adam.

"On one condition," said Heidi thoughtfully.

"Separate planes?" said Adam grinning.

"No, but if the icon turns out to be worthless, you will let me refund the price of my ticket."

"It couldn't be worth less than thirty-one pounds, so I agree to your terms," said Adam. He leaned over and kissed

Heidi on the lips. "Perhaps it will take more than one day," he said. "Then what would you say?"

"I would demand separate hotels," replied Heidi, "if it wasn't for the high cost of the Swiss franc," she added.

"You are always so reliable, Comrade Romanov. You fulfill the primary qualification for a successful banker." Romanov studied the old man carefully, looking for a hint that he knew exactly what had been awaiting him at the bank.

"And you are always so efficient, Comrade Poskonov," he said, then paused, "the only qualification necessary in my chosen profession."

"Good heavens, we are beginning to sound like a couple of aging commissars at an annual reunion. How was Zurich?" he asked as he lit a cigarette.

"Like a Polish tractor. The bits that worked were fine."

"From that I assume the bits that didn't work failed to produce the Czar's icon," the chairman said.

"Correct, but Bischoff turned out to be most helpful, as was Jacques. My every need was catered for."

"Your every need?"

"Yes," replied Romanov.

"Good man, Bischoff," said the banker, "that's why I sent you to him first." The old man slumped down into his chair.

"Was there any other reason you sent me to him first?" asked Romanov.

"Five other reasons," said Poskonov, "but we'll not bother with any of them until you have found your icon."

"Perhaps I'd like to bother now," said Romanov firmly.

"I've outlived two generations of Romanovs," said the old man raising his eyes. "I wouldn't want to outlive a third. Let's leave it at that for now. I'm sure we can come to an understanding when the spotlight is no longer on you."

Romanov nodded.

"Well, you will be pleased to learn that I have not been idle in your absence. But I fear my results also resemble a Polish tractor."

The banker waved Romanov to a seat before he reopened his file, which had grown in size since he had last seen it. "Originally," the chairman began, "you presented me with a list of fourteen banks, eleven of which have now confirmed that they are not in possession of the Czar's icon."

"I have been wondering about that—is their word to be taken at face value?" asked Romanov.

"Not necessarily," said the banker. "But on balance the Swiss prefer not to become involved rather than tell a deliberate lie. In time the liar is always found out, and I still, from this office, control the cash flow of eight nations. I may not wield what they would call financial clout, but I can still put the odd spoke into the wheel of the capitalist monetary system."

"That still leaves us with three banks?" said Romanov.

"Correct, Comrade. The first is Bischoff et Cie, whom you have already visited. But the other two have refused to cooperate in any way."

"Why is it your influence does not extend to them?"

"The most obvious of reasons," replied Poskonov. "Other interests exert a stronger influence. If, for example, your major source of income emanates from the leading Jewish families, or alternatively the Americans, no amount of pressure will ever allow you to deal with the Soviet Union." Romanov nodded his understanding. "That being the case," continued Poskonov, "there still has to be an outside chance that one of these two banks is in possession of the Czar's icon, and as they are never going to admit as much to Mother Russia, I am not sure what I can recommend you do next."

The banker sat back and waited for Romanov to take in his news.

"You are unusually silent," Poskonov ventured, after he had lit another cigarette.

"You have given me an idea," said Romanov. "I think the Americans would describe it as a 'long shot.' But if I'm right, it will be the Russians who will get the home run."

"Baseball is a game that I've never understood, but I am

glad, however, to have been of some use today. Although I suspect you will still need this, whatever your long shot." Poskonov removed a single piece of paper from his file and handed it over to Romanov. On it were the words:

DAUMIER ET CIE, ZURICH *(refused)*
ROGET ET CIE, GENEVA *(refused)*.

"No doubt you will be returning to Switzerland very soon."

Romanov stared directly at the banker.

"I wouldn't recommend you visit Bischoff et Cie on this trip, Alex. There will be time enough for that in the future."

Romanov straightened his fingers.

The old man returned his stare. "You won't find me as easy to get rid of as Anna Petrova," he added.

CHAPTER
TEN

THE ELDERLY LOOKING man took his place at the back of
the taxi line. It was hard to estimate his height because he
looked so bent and frail. A large overcoat that might have
been even older than its wearer reached almost to the
ground, and the fingers that could only just be seen peeping
through the sleeves were covered in gray woollen mittens.
One hand clung on to a little leather suitcase, with the ini-
tials E. R. in black, looking so worn that it might have belonged to his grandfather.

One would have had to bend down or be very short to see
the old man's face—a face that was dominated by a nose that
would have flattered Cyrano de Bergerac's. He shuffled forward slowly until it was his turn to climb into a taxi. The
operation was a slow one, and the driver was already drumming his fingers against the wheel when his passenger told
him in guttural tones that he wanted to be taken to the bankers, Daumier et Cie. The driver moved off without asking for
further directions. Swiss taxi drivers know the way to the

banks in the same way as London cabbies can always find a theater and New York's cabs a West Side bar.

When the old man arrived at his destination he took some time sorting out with which coins to pay. He then pushed himself slowly out on to the pavement and stood gazing at the marble building. Its solidity made him feel safe. He was about to touch the door when a man in a smart blue uniform opened it.

"I have come to see—" he began in stilted German, but the doorman only pointed to the girl behind the reception desk. He shuffled over to her and then repeated, "I have come to see Herr Daumier. My name is Emmanuel Rosenbaum."

"Do you have an appointment?" she asked.

"I fear not."

"Herr Daumier is in conference at the moment," said the girl, "but I will find out if there is another partner available to see you." After a phone conversation in German she said, "Can you take the lift to the third floor?" Mr. Rosenbaum nodded with obvious signs of reluctance, but did as he was bid. When he stepped out of the lift, only just before the door closed on him, another young woman was standing there ready to greet him. She asked him if he would be kind enough to wait in what he would have described as a cloak-room with two chairs. Some time passed before anyone came to see him, and the old man was unable to hide his surprise by the age of the boy who eventually appeared.

"I am Welfherd Praeger," said the young man, "a partner of the bank."

"Sit down, sit down," said Mr. Rosenbaum. "I cannot stare up at you for so long." The young partner complied.

"My name is Emmanuel Rosenbaum. I left a package with you in 1938, and I have returned to collect it."

"Yes, of course," said the junior partner, the tone of his voice changing. "Do you have any proof of your identity, or any documentation from the bank?"

"Oh, yes," came back the reply, and the old man handed over his passport and a receipt that had been folded and un-folded so many times it was now almost in pieces.

The young man studied both documents carefully. He recognized the Israeli passport immediately. Everything seemed to be in order, and the bank's receipt, too, although issued in the year of his birth, appeared authentic.

"May I leave you for a moment, sir?"

"Of course," said the old man, "after twenty-eight years I think I can wait for a few more minutes."

Shortly after the young man had left the woman returned and invited Mr. Rosenbaum to move to another room. This time it was larger and comfortably furnished. Within minutes the junior partner returned with another man, whom he introduced as Herr Daumier.

"I don't think we have ever met, Herr Rosenbaum," said the chairman courteously. "You must have dealt with my father."

"No, no," said Mr. Rosenbaum. "I dealt only with your grandfather, Helmut."

A look of respect came into Herr Daumier's eyes.

"I saw your father only on the one occasion and was sad to learn of his premature death," added Rosenbaum. "He was always so considerate. You do not wear a rose in your lapel as he did."

"No, sir, a tiny rebellion."

Rosenbaum tried to laugh but only coughed.

"I wonder if you have any further proof of identity other than your passport?" Herr Daumier asked politely.

Emmanuel Rosenbaum raised his head and, giving Herr Daumier a tired look, turned his wrist so that it faced upward. The number 712910 was tattooed along the inside.

"I apologize," said Daumier, visibly embarrassed. "It will take me only a few minutes to bring your box up, if you will be kind enough to wait."

Mr. Rosenbaum's eyes blinked as if he were too tired even to nod his agreement. The two men left him alone. They returned a few minutes later with a flat box about two feet square and placed it on the table in the center of the room. Herr Daumier unlocked the top lock while the other partner acted as a witness. He then handed over a key to Rosenbaum saying, "We will now leave you, sir. Just press the button underneath the table when you wish us to return."

"Thank you," said Rosenbaum, and waited for the door to close behind them. He turned the key in the lock and pushed up the lid. Inside the box was a package in the shape of a picture, about eighteen by twelve inches, covered in muslin and tied securely. Rosenbaum placed the package carefully in his old suitcase. He then shut the box and locked it. He pressed the button under the table, and within seconds Herr Daumier and the junior partner returned.

"I do hope everything was as you left it, Herr Rosenbaum," said the chairman, "it has been some considerable time."

"Yes, thank you." This time the old gentleman did manage a nod.

"May I mention a matter of no great consequence?" asked Herr Daumier.

"Pray do so," said the old man.

"Is it your intention to continue with the use of the box? Because the funds you left to cover the cost have recently run out."

"No, I have no need for it any longer."

"It's just that there was a small charge outstanding. But in the circumstances, Herr Rosenbaum, we are happy to waive it."

"You are most kind." Herr Daumier bowed, and the junior partner accompanied their client to the front door, helped him into a taxi, and instructed the driver to take Mr. Rosenbaum to Zurich airport.

At the airport, the old man took his time reaching the check-in desk, because he appeared to be frightened of the escalator, and with the suitcase now quite heavy the flight of steps was difficult to negotiate.

At the desk he produced his ticket for the girl to check and was pleased to find that the passenger lounge was almost empty. He shuffled over toward the corner and collapsed on to a comfortable sofa. He checked to be sure he was out of sight of the other passengers in the lounge.

He flicked back the little knobs on the old suitcase, and the springs rose reluctantly. He pushed up the lid, pulled out the parcel, and held it to his chest. His fingers wrestled with the knots for some time before they became loose. He then removed the muslin to check his prize. Mr. Rosenbaum stared down at the masterpiece *Man Gathering in Corn* by Van Gogh—which he had no way of knowing had been missing from the Vienna National Gallery since 1938.

Emmanuel Rosenbaum swore, which was out of character. He packed the picture safely up and returned it to his case. He then shuffled over to the girl at the Swissair sales desk and asked her to book him on the first available flight to Geneva. With luck he could still reach Roget et Cie before they closed.

The BEA Viscount landed at Geneva airport at eleven twenty-five local time that morning, a few minutes later than scheduled. The stewardess advised passengers to put their watches forward one hour to Central European Time.

"Perfect," said Adam. "We shall be in Geneva well in time for lunch, a visit to the bank, and then back to the airport for the five-past-five flight home."

"You're treating the whole thing like a military exercise," said Heidi, laughing.

"All except the last part," said Adam.

"The last part?" she queried.

"Our celebration dinner."

"At the Chelsea Kitchen again, no doubt."

"Wrong," said Adam. "I've booked a table for two at eight o'clock at the Coq d'Or just off Piccadilly."

"Counting your chickens before they're hatched, aren't you?" said Heidi.

"Oh, very droll," said Adam.

"Droll? I do not understand."

"I'll explain it to you when we have that dinner tonight."

"I was hoping we wouldn't make it," said Heidi.

"Why?" asked Adam.

"All I have to look forward to tomorrow is the checkout counter at the German Food Centre."

"That's not as bad as a workout with the sergeant major at

ten," groaned Adam. "And by ten past I shall be flat on my back regretting I ever left Geneva."

"That will teach you to knock him out," said Heidi, "so perhaps we ought to stay put after all," she added, taking him by the arm. Adam leaned down and kissed her gently on the cheek as they stood in the gangway waiting to be let off the plane. A light drizzle was falling out on the aircraft steps. Adam unbuttoned his raincoat and attempted to shelter Heidi beneath it as they ran across the tarmac to the Immigration Hall.

"Good thing I remembered this," he said.

"Not so much a raincoat, more a tent," said Heidi.

"It's my old army trench coat," he assured her, opening it up again. "It can hold maps, compasses, even an overnight kit."

"Adam, we're just going to stroll around Geneva in the middle of the summer, not get lost in the Black Forest in the middle of winter."

He laughed. "I'll remember your sarcasm whenever it pours."

The airport bus that traveled to and from the city took only twenty minutes to reach the center of Geneva.

The short journey took them through the outskirts of the city until they reached the magnificent still lake nestled in the hills. The bus continued alongside the lake until it came to a halt opposite the massive single-spouting fountain that shot over four hundred feet into the air.

"I'm beginning to feel like a day tripper," said Heidi, as they stepped out of the bus, pleased to find the light rain had stopped.

Both of them were immediately struck by how clean the city was as they walked along the wide litter-free pavement that ran alongside the lake. On the other side of the road neat hotels, shops, and banks seemed in equal preponderance.

"First we must find out where our bank is so that we can have lunch nearby before going to pick up the booty."

"How does a military man go about such a demanding exercise?" asked Heidi.

"Simple. We drop in at the first bank we see and ask them to direct us to Roget et Cie."

"I'll bet your little arm must have been covered in initiative badges when you were a Boy Scout."

Adam burst out laughing. "Am I that bad?"

"Worse," said Heidi. "But you personify every German's image of the perfect English gentleman." Adam turned, touched her hair gently and leaning down, kissed her on the lips.

Heidi was suddenly conscious of the stares from passing strangers. "I don't think the Swiss approve of that sort of thing in public," she said. "In fact, I'm told some of them don't approve of it in private."

"Shall I go and kiss that old prune over there who is still glaring at us?" said Adam.

"Don't do that, Adam, you might turn into a frog. No, let's put your plan of campaign into action," she said, pointing to the Banque Populaire on the far side of the avenue.

When they had crossed the road Heidi inquired of the doorman the way to Roget et Cie. They followed his directions, once again admiring the great single-spouted fountain as they continued on toward the center of the city.

Roget et Cie was not that easy to pinpoint, and they walked past it twice before Heidi spotted the discreet sign chiseled in stone by the side of a high wrought-iron-and-plate-glass door.

"Looks impressive," said Adam, "even when it's closed for lunch."

"What were you expecting—a small branch in the country? I know you English don't like to admit it, but this is the center of the banking world."

"Let's find that restaurant before our entente cordiale breaks down," said Adam. They retraced their steps toward the fountain, and as the sun was trying to find gaps between the clouds, they chose a pavement café overlooking the lake. Both selected a cheese salad and shared a half bottle of white wine. Adam was enjoying Heidi's company so much that he began to tell her stories of his army days. She had to stop him and point out that it was nearly two. He reluctantly called for the bill. "The time has now come to discover if the Czar's icon really exists," he said.

When they had returned to the entrance of the bank Adam pushed open the heavy door, took a step inside, and stared around the gloomy hall.

"Over there," said Heidi, pointing to a woman who was seated behind a desk.

"Good morning. My name is Adam Scott. I have come to collect something that has been left to me in a will."

The woman smiled. "Have you made an appointment with anyone in particular?" she asked, with only the slightest trace of accent.

"No," said Adam. "I didn't realize that I had to."

"I'm sure it will be all right," said the lady. She picked up a phone, dialed a single number, and held a short conversation in French. Replacing the phone, she asked them both to go to the fourth floor.

As Adam walked out of the lift, he was surprised to be met by someone of his own age.

"Good afternoon, my name is Pierre Neffe, and I am a partner of the bank," said the young man in perfect English.

"I did warn you that I would be redundant," whispered Heidi.

"Don't speak too soon," replied Adam. "We haven't even begun to explain our problem yet."

M. Neffe led them to a small, exquisitely furnished room.

"I could settle down here," said Adam, taking off his coat, "without any trouble."

"We do like to make our customers feel at home," said M. Neffe condescendingly.

"You obviously haven't seen my home," said Adam. M. Neffe did not laugh.

"How can I help you?" was all the young partner offered by way of reply.

"My father," began Adam, "died last month and left me in

his will a receipt for something I think you have had in your safekeeping since 1938. It was a gift given to him by one of your customers." Adam hesitated. "A Mr. Emmanuel Rosenbaum."

"Do you have any documentation relating to this gift?" inquired M. Neffe.

"Oh, yes," said Adam, digging into the map pocket of his trench coat. He passed over the Roget et Cie receipt to the young banker. M. Neffe studied it and nodded. "May I be permitted to see your passport, M. Scott?"

"Certainly," said Adam, delving back into his trench coat and passing it to M. Neffe.

"If you will excuse me for one moment." M. Neffe rose and left them on their own.

"What do you imagine they are up to now?" said Heidi.

"Checking first if they still have the icon, and second if my receipt is authentic. Nineteen thirty-eight was rather a long time ago."

As the minutes ticked by, Adam started to feel disappointed, then depressed, and finally began to believe it was all going to turn out to be a complete waste of time.

"You could always take one of the pictures off the wall and put it in your trench coat," teased Heidi. "I'm sure it would fetch a good price in London. Perhaps even more than your beloved icon."

"Too late," said Adam as M. Neffe reappeared with another banker, whom he introduced as M. Roget.

"Good morning," said M. Roget. "I am sorry that my father is not here to meet you, M. Scott, but he has been held up in Chicago on business." He shook hands with both Adam and Heidi. "We have on file a letter from M. Rosenbaum giving clear instructions to the bank that the box is not to be opened by anyone other than"—he looked at the piece of paper he had brought with him—"Colonel Gerald Scott, D.S.O., O.B.E., M.C."

"My father," said Adam. "But as I explained to M. Neffe, he died last month and left me the gift in his will."

"I would be happy to accept what you say," said M. Roget,

"if I might be allowed sight of a copy of the death certificate and of the will itself."

Adam smiled at his own foresight and once more searched in his trench coat before removing a large brown envelope with the words "Holbrooke, Holbrooke and Gascoigne" printed in heavy black letters across the top. He took out copies of his father's death certificate, the will and a letter marked "To Whom It May Concern" and passed them to M. Roget, who read all three documents slowly, then handed them to his senior partner, who after he had read them whispered in his chairman's ear.

"Would you object to us phoning M. Holbrooke in your presence?" asked M. Roget.

"No," said Adam simply. "But I must warn you that he is rather curmudgeonly."

"Curmudgeonly?" said the banker. "A word I am not familiar with, but I think I can sense its meaning." He turned and spoke to M. Neffe, who swiftly left the room, only to return a minute later with a copy of the *English Society Register*, 1966.

Adam was impressed by the bank's thoroughness as M. Roget checked that the number and address on the letterhead corresponded with the number and address in the yearbook. "I don't think it will be necessary to call M. Holbrooke," said M. Roget, "but we have encountered one small problem, M. Scott."

"And what is that?" asked Adam, nervously.

"M. Rosenbaum's position is somewhat overdrawn, and the bank's rule is that an account must be cleared before any box can be opened."

Adam's pulse raced, as he assumed that he hadn't brought enough money to cover this eventuality.

"The account is only 120 francs in debit," continued M. Roget, "which is the charge for housing the box over the past two years since M. Rosenbaum's deposit ran out."

Adam breathed a sigh of relief. He took out his wallet and signed a traveler's check and handed it over.

"And finally," said M. Roget, "we will need you to sign a form of indemnity for the bank."

M. Roget passed over a long form containing clause after clause in tightly printed French, at which Adam only glanced before passing it over to Heidi. She studied each clause carefully. M. Roget used the time to explain to Adam that it was a standard disclaimer clearing the bank of any liability concerning what might be in the box and Adam's legal claim to it.

Heidi looked up and nodded her agreement.

Adam signed on the dotted line with a flourish.

"Excellent," said the banker. "All we have to do now is go and retrieve your box."

"I suppose it could be empty," said Adam once the two of them were left alone again.

"And it could be jam-packed with gold doubloons, you old pessimist," said Heidi.

When both men returned a few minutes later, M. Neffe was carrying a flat metal box about one foot by nine inches, and some three inches deep.

Adam was disappointed by its modest size but didn't show his feelings. M. Roget proceeded to undo the top lock with the bank's key and then handed Adam a small faded envelope with signatures scrawled across the waxed seal. "Whatever is in the box belongs to you, M. Scott. When you have finished, perhaps you would be kind enough to let us know. Until then we shall remain outside in the corridor."

Both men left the room.

"Come on," said Heidi, "I can't wait." Adam opened the envelope and a key fell out. He fumbled with the lock, which clicked, and then at last he pushed up the lid. Inside the box was a small flat package wrapped in muslin and tied tightly with string. The knots took some untying, and then finally an impatient Adam tore off the string before slowly removing the muslin. They both stared at the masterpiece in disbelief.

The simple beauty of the golds, reds, and blues left them both speechless. Neither of them had expected the icon to be so breathtaking. Saint George towered over the dragon, a massive sword in hand on the point of plunging it into the heart of the beast. The fire that belched from the dragon's jaw was a deep red and made a startling contrast to the gold cloak that seemed to envelop the saint.

"It's magnificent," said Heidi, eventually finding her voice.

Adam continued to hold the tiny painting in his hand.

"Say something," said Heidi.

"I wish my father had seen it; perhaps it would have changed his whole life."

"Don't forget he wanted it to change yours," said Heidi.

Adam finally turned the icon over to find on the back a small silver crown inlaid in the wood. He stared at it, trying to recall what Mr. Sedgwick of Sotheby's had said that proved.

"I wish my father had opened the letter," said Adam, turning the icon back over and once again admiring Saint George's triumph. "Because it was his by right."

Heidi checked there was nothing else left inside the box. She then flicked down the lid, and Adam locked it again with his key. He then tucked the muslin round the masterpiece, tied it up firmly, and zippered the little painting into the map pocket of his trench coat.

Heidi smiled. "I knew you'd prove you needed that coat even if it didn't rain."

Adam walked over to the door and opened it. The two bankers immediately returned.

"I hope you found what you had been promised," said M. Roget.

"Yes, indeed," said Adam. "But I shall have no further need of the box," he added, returning the key.

"As you wish," said M. Roget, bowing, "and here is the change from your traveler's check, sir," he said, passing over some Swiss notes to Adam. "If you will excuse me, I will now take my leave of you. M. Neffe will show you out." He shook hands with Adam, bowed slightly to Heidi, and added with a faint smile, "I do hope you didn't find us too cur—mud—geonly." They both laughed.

"I also hope that you will enjoy a pleasant stay in our city," said M. Neffe as the lift took its leisurely pace down.

"It will have to be very quick," said Adam. "We must be back at the airport in just over an hour."

The lift stopped at the ground floor and M. Neffe accompanied Adam and Heidi to the door. The door was held open for them, but they both stood aside to allow an old man to shuffle past. Although most people would have stared at his nose Adam was more struck by his penetrating blue eyes.

When the old man eventually reached the woman at the reception desk, he announced, "I have come to see M. Roget."

"I'm afraid he's in Chicago at the moment, sir, but I'll see if his son is available. What name shall I tell him?"

"Emmanuel Rosenbaum." The woman picked up the phone and held another conversation in French. When she had replaced it she asked, "Would you go to the fourth floor, M. Rosenbaum?"

Once again he had to take the fearsome lift, and once again he only just got out before its great teeth sprang back on him. Another middle-aged woman accompanied him to the waiting room. He politely declined her offer of coffee, thumping his heart with his right hand.

"M. Roget will be with you shortly," she assured the old man.

He did not have to wait long before a smiling M. Roget appeared.

"How nice to make your acquaintance, M. Rosenbaum, but I'm afraid you have just missed M. Scott."

"M. Scott?" the old man uttered in surprise.

"Yes. He left only a few minutes ago, but we carried out the instructions as per your letter."

"My letter?" said M. Rosenbaum.

"Yes," said the banker, opening for the second time that morning a file that had remained untouched for over twenty years.

He handed a letter to the old man.

Emmanuel Rosenbaum removed a pair of glasses from his inside pocket, unfolded them slowly, and proceeded to read a hand that he recognized. It was a bold hand written in thick black ink.

> Forsthaus Haarhot
> Amsberg 14
> Vosswinnel
> Sachsen
> Germany
> 12 September 1945

Dear M. Roget,

I have left in your safe keeping a small icon of Saint George and the dragon in my box 718. I am transferring the ownership of that painting to a British army officer, Colonel Gerald Scott, D.S.O., O.B.E., M.C. If Colonel Scott should come to claim the icon at any time please ensure that he receives my key without delay.

My thanks to you for your help in this matter, and I am only sorry we have never met in person.

> Yours sincerely,
> Emmanuel Rosenbaum

"And you say that Colonel Scott came to collect the contents of the box earlier today?"

"No, no, M. Rosenbaum. The colonel died quite recently and left the contents of the box to his son, Adam Scott. M. Neffe and I checked all the documents including the death certificate and the will, and we were left in no doubt that they were both authentic and that everything was in order. He was also in possession of your receipt." The young banker hesitated. "I do hope we did the right thing, M. Rosenbaum?"

"You certainly did," said the old man. "I came only to check that my wishes had been carried out."

M. Roget smiled in relief. "I feel I ought also to mention that your account had run into a small deficit."

"How much do I owe you?" asked the old man, fumbling in his breast pocket.

"Nothing," said M. Roget. "Nothing at all. M. Scott dealt with it."

"I am in debt to M. Scott. Are you able to tell me the amount?"

"One hundred and twenty francs," said M. Roget.

"Then I must repay the sum immediately," said the old man. "Do you by any chance have an address at which I can contact him?"

"No, I'm sorry I am unable to help you there," said M. Roget. "I have no idea where he is staying in Geneva." A hand touched M. Roget's elbow, and M. Neffe bent down and whispered in his ear.

"It appears," said M. Roget, "that M. Scott was planning to return to England shortly because he had to check in at Geneva airport by five."

The old man lifted himself up. "You have been most helpful, M. Roget, and I will not take up any more of your time."

"It's flight BE 171, and your seats are 14A and B," the man behind the BEA check-in counter told them. "The plane's on time so you should be boarding at gate number nine in about twenty minutes."

"Thank you," said Adam.

"Do you have any luggage that needs checking in?"

"No," said Adam. "We only spent the day in Geneva."

"Then have a good flight, sir," said the man, handing over their boarding passes. Adam and Heidi started walking toward the escalator that would take them to the departure lounge.

"I have seven hundred and seventy Swiss francs left," said Adam, thumbing through some notes, "and while we're here I must get my mother a box of decent liqueur chocolates. When I was a boy I used to give her a minute box every Christmas. I swore when I grew up if I ever got to Switzerland I would find her the finest box available." Heidi pointed to a counter that displayed row upon row of ornate boxes. Adam selected a large, gold-wrapped box of Lindt chocolates, which the girl behind the counter gift-wrapped and placed in a carrier bag.

"Why are you frowning?" asked Adam after collecting his change.

"She's just reminded me that I have to be back behind a till tomorrow morning," said Heidi.

"Well, at least we've got the Coq d'Or to look forward to tonight," said Adam. He checked his watch. "Not much else we can do now except perhaps pick up some wine at the duty-free."

"I'd like to find a copy of *Der Spiegel* before we go through customs."

"Fine," said Adam. "Why don't we try the paper shop over in the corner."

"A call for Mr. Adam Scott. Will Mr. Adam Scott please return to the BEA desk on the ground floor," came booming out over the public-address system.

Adam and Heidi stared at each other. "Must have given us the wrong seat allocation, I suppose," said Adam, shrugging. "Let's go back and find out."

They returned downstairs and walked over to the man who had handed them their boarding passes. "I think you put a call out for me," said Adam. "My name is Scott."

"Oh, yes," said the man. "There's an urgent message for you," he said, reading from a pad in front of him. "Please call M. Roget at Roget et Cie on Geneva 271279." He ripped off the piece of paper and handed it over. "The phones are over there in the far corner behind the KLM desk, and you'll need twenty centimes."

"Thank you," said Adam, studying the message, but it gave no clue as to why M. Roget should need to speak to him.

"I wonder what he can want," said Heidi. "It's a bit late to ask for the icon back."

"Well, there's only one way I'm going to find out," said Adam, passing over the bag to her. "Hang on to that, and I'll be back in a moment."

"I'll try and pick up my magazine at the same time, if I can find a stand on this floor," said Heidi as she gripped the brightly colored bag that contained the chocolates.

"Right," said Adam. "Meet you back here in a couple of minutes."

"Roget et Cie. *Est-ce que je puis vous aider?*"

"I am returning Mr. Roget's call," said Adam, making no attempt to answer in French.

"Yes, sir. Whom shall I say is calling?" asked the telephonist, immediately switching to English.

"Adam Scott."

"I'll find out if he's available, sir."

Adam swung round to see if Heidi had returned to the BEA counter, but as there was no sign of her he assumed she must still be looking for a newspaper. Then he noticed an old man shuffling across the hall. He could have sworn he had seen him somewhere before.

"Mr. Scott?" Adam leaned back into the box.

"Yes, M. Roget, I am returning your call."

"Returning my call?" said the banker, sounding puzzled. "I don't understand."

"There was a message left at the BEA counter asking me to phone you. Urgent."

"There must be somē mistake, I didn't leave any message. But now that you have rung, it might interest you to know that just as you were leaving Mr. Emmanuel Rosenbaum visited us."

"Emmanuel Rosenbaum?" said Adam, "but I assumed he was . . ."

"Could you assist me, please, young lady?" Heidi looked up at the old man who had addressed her in English, but with such a strong mid-European accent. She wondered why he had taken for granted that she spoke English but decided it must be the only language he felt confident conversing in.

"I am trying to find a taxi and I am already late, but I fear my eyesight is not what it used to be."

Heidi replaced the copy of *Der Spiegel* back on the shelf and said, "They're just through the double doors in the center. Let me show you."

"How kind," he said. "But I do hope I am not putting you to too much trouble."

"Not at all," said Heidi, taking the old man by the arm and guiding him back toward the door marked "Taxi et Autobus."

"Are you sure it was Rosenbaum?" said Adam anxiously.

"I'm certain," replied the banker.

"And he seemed happy about me keeping the icon?"

"Oh, yes. That was not the problem. His only concern was to return your 120 francs. I think he may try and get in touch with you."

"BEA announce the departure of their flight BE 171 to London Heathrow from gate number nine."

"I must leave," said Adam. "My plane takes off in a few minutes."

"Have a good flight," said the banker.

"Thank you, M. Roget," said Adam and replaced the receiver. He turned toward the BEA counter and was surprised to find that Heidi had not yet returned. His eyes began to search the ground floor for a newspaper shop as he feared she might well not have heard the departure announcement. Then he spotted her walking out through the double door, helping the old man he had noticed earlier.

Adam called out and quickened his pace. Something didn't feel quite right. When he reached the automatic door he had to check his stride to allow it to slide back. He could now see Heidi standing on the pavement in front of him, opening a taxi door for the old man.

"Heidi," he shouted. The old gentleman suddenly turned and once again Adam found himself staring at the man he could have sworn he had seen at the bank. "Mr. Rosenbaum?" he questioned. Then with a movement of his arm that was so fast and powerful it took Adam by surprise, the old man threw Heidi into the back of the taxi, jumped in beside her and, pulling the taxi door closed, hollered at the top of his voice, "*Allez, vite.*"

For a moment Adam was stunned, but then he dashed to the side of the taxi and only just managed to touch the handle as it accelerated away from the curb. The car's sudden momentum knocked Adam backward on to the pavement, but not before he saw the petrified look on Heidi's face. He stared at the license plate of the departing car: B712—was all he could catch, but at least he recognized it was a blue Mercedes. Desperately he looked around for another taxi, but the only one in sight was already being filled up with luggage.

A Volkswagen beetle drew up on the far side of the concourse. A woman stepped out of the driver's seat and walked to the front to open the trunk. A man joined her from the passenger's side and lifted out a suitcase before she slammed the trunk back into place.

On the curb, the two of them embraced. As they did so, Adam sprinted across the road and, opening the passenger door of the Volkswagen, leaped inside and slid into the driver's seat. The key was still in the ignition. He turned it on, threw the car into gear, slammed his foot on the accelerator, and shot backward. The embracing couple stared at him in bafflement. Adam jerked the gear lever out of reverse into what he hoped was first. The engine turned over slowly, but just fast enough for him to escape the pursuing man. It must be third, he thought, and changed down as he began to follow the signs to the center of Geneva.

By the time he reached the first traffic circle he had mastered the gears but had to concentrate hard on remaining on the right-hand side of the road. "B712 . . . B712," he repeated to himself again and again, to be sure it was fixed in his memory. He checked the license plate and the passengers of every blue taxi he passed. After a dozen or so, he began to wonder if Heidi's taxi might have left the highway for a minor road. He pressed the accelerator even harder—90,

100, 110, 120 kilometers an hour. He passed three more taxis, but there was still no sign of Heidi.

Then he saw a Mercedes in the outside lane some considerable distance ahead of him, its lights full on and traveling well above the speed limit. He felt confident that the Volkswagen was powerful enough to catch the Mercedes, especially if it had a diesel engine. Meter by meter he began to narrow the gap as he tried to fathom why the old man would want to kidnap Heidi in the first place. Could it be Rosenbaum? But he had wanted him to keep the icon, or so the banker had assured him. None of it made sense, and he drove on wondering if at any moment he was going to wake up.

When they reached the outskirts of the city Adam hadn't woken up as he followed carefully the taxi's chosen route. By the next traffic circle only three cars divided them. "A red light, I need a red light," Adam shouted, but the first three traffic lights into the city remained stubbornly green. And when one finally turned red, a van suddenly pulled in front of him, lengthening the gap between them. Adam cursed as he leaped out of the car and started running toward the taxi, but the light changed back to green just before he could reach it, and the Mercedes sped away. Adam sprinted back to the Volkswagen and only just managed to drive the car across the junction as the light turned red. His decision to get out of the car had lost him several crucial seconds, and when he looked anxiously ahead he could only just spot the taxi in the distance.

When they reached the Avenue de France, running parallel with the west side of the lake, both cars weaved in and out of the traffic, until the Mercedes suddenly turned left and climbed up a slight hill. Adam threw his steering wheel over to follow it, and for several yards careened up the wrong side of the road, narrowly missing a mail truck meandering down toward him. He watched carefully as the taxi turned left again, and in order to keep in contact, veered in front of a bus so sharply that it was forced to jam on its brakes. Several passengers, thrown from their seats, waved their fists at him as the bus's horn blared.

The taxi was now only a couple of hundred yards ahead. Once again Adam began to pick up some ground, when suddenly it swerved to the curbside and screeched to a halt. Nothing seemed to happen for the next few seconds as Adam weaved his way toward the stationary taxi, skidding directly behind it. He then leaped out of the car and ran toward the parked vehicle. But without warning, the old man jumped out of the taxi on the far side of the car and sprinted off up a side street carrying with him Heidi's airport shopping bag and a small suitcase.

Adam pulled the back door open and stared at the beautiful girl, who sat motionless. "Are you all right, are you all right?" he shouted, suddenly realizing how much she meant to him. Heidi did not move a muscle and made no reply. Adam put his arms on her shoulders and looked into her eyes, but they showed no response. He began to stroke her hair, and her head fell limply on to his shoulder like a rag doll's, and a small trickle of blood started to run from the corner of her mouth. Adam felt cold and sick and began to tremble uncontrollably. He looked up at the taxi driver. His arms were loose by his sides, and his body slumped over the wheel. There was no sign of life in the middle-aged face.

He refused to accept they were dead.

Adam kept holding on to Heidi as he stared beyond her: the old man had reached the top of the hill.

Why did he still think of him as an old man? He was obviously not old at all, but young and very fit. Suddenly Adam's fear turned to anger. He had a split second to make a decision. He let go of Heidi, jumped out of the car, and started to sprint up the hill and after her killer. Two or three onlookers had already gathered on the curbside and were now staring at Adam and the two cars. He had to catch the man, who was still running. Adam moved as fast as he could, but the trench coat he was wearing slowed him down, and by the time he too had reached the top of the hill the killer was a clear hundred yards ahead of him, weaving his way through the main thoroughfare. Adam tried to lengthen his stride as he watched the man leap on to a passing streetcar, but he was too far behind to make any gain on him and could only watch the streetcar moving inexorably into the distance.

The man stood on the streetcar steps and stared back at Adam. He held up the shopping bag defiantly with one hand. The back was no longer hunched, the figure no longer frail, and even at that distance, Adam could sense the triumph in the man's stance. Adam stood for several seconds in the middle of the road, helplessly watching the streetcar as it disappeared from sight.

He tried to gather his thoughts. He realized that there was little hope of picking up a taxi during the rush hour. Behind him he could hear sirens of what he presumed were ambulances trying to rush to the scene of the accident. "Accident," said Adam. "They will soon discover it was murder." He tried to start sorting out in his mind the madness of the last half hour. None of it made sense. He would surely find it was all a mistake. . . . Then, he touched the side of his coat pocket and felt the package that held the Czar's icon. The killer hadn't gone to all that trouble for twenty thousand pounds—murdering two innocent people who happened to have got in his way—why, why, *why*, was the icon that important? What had the Sotheby's expert said? "A Russian gentleman had inquired after the piece." Adam's mind began to whirl. If it was Emmanuel Rosenbaum, and that was what he had killed for, all he had ended up with was a large box of Swiss liqueur chocolates.

When Adam heard the whistle behind him he felt relieved that help was at hand, but as he turned he saw two officers with guns out of their holsters pointing toward him. He instinctively turned his jog into a run, and looking over his shoulder he saw that several police were now giving chase. He lengthened his stride again and, despite the trench coat, doubted if there were a member of the Swiss force who could hope to keep up the pace he set for more than a quarter of a mile. He turned into the first alley he came to and speeded up. It was narrow—not wide enough for even two bicycles to pass. Once he was beyond the alley he selected a one-way street. It was crammed with cars, and he was able swiftly and safely to move in and out of the slow-moving oncoming traffic.

In a matter of minutes he had lost the pursuing police, but he still ran on, continually switching direction until he felt he had covered at least two miles. He turned into a quiet street and halfway down saw a fluorescent sign advertising the Hotel Monarche. It didn't look much more than a guest house, and certainly wouldn't have qualified under the description of a hotel. He stopped in the shadows and waited, taking in great gulps of air. After about three minutes his breathing was back to normal, and he marched straight into the hotel.

Chapter Eleven

He stood naked, staring at the image of Emmanuel Rosenbaum in the hotel mirror. He didn't like what he saw. First he removed the teeth, then began to click his own up and down: he had been warned that the gums would ache for days. Then painstakingly he shed each layer of his bulbous nose, admiring the skill and artistry that had gone into creating such a monstrosity. It will be too conspicuous, he had told them. They will remember nothing else, had come back the experts' reply.

When the last layer had been removed, the aristocratic one that took its place looked ridiculous in the center of such a face. Next he began on the lined forehead that even moved when he frowned. As the lines disappeared, so the years receded. Next the flaccid red cheeks, and finally the two chins. The Swiss bankers would have been amazed at how easily the sharp rubbing of a pumice stone removed the indelible number on the inside of his arm. Once more he studied himself in the mirror. The hair, short and graying, would take nature longer. When they had cut his hair short and smeared that thick mudlike concoction all over his scalp, it made him feel like a deloused animal. Moments later he stood under a warm shower, his fingers massaging deep into the roots of his hair. Black treacly water started to run down his face and body before finally disappearing down the drain. It took half a bottle of shampoo before his hair had returned to its normal color, but he realized that it would take considerably longer before he stopped looking like one of these moronic staff sergeants in the United States Marines.

In a corner of the room lay the long baggy coat, shiny shapeless suit, black tie, off-white shirt, woollen mittens, and the Israeli passport. Days of preparation discarded in a matter of minutes. He longed to burn them all, but instead left them in a heap. He returned to the main room and stretched himself out on the bed like a yawning cat. His back still ached from all the bending and crouching. He stood up, then touched his toes and threw his arms high above his head fifty times. He rested for one minute before completing fifty sit-ups.

He returned to the bathroom and had a second shower—cold. He was beginning to feel like a human being again. He then changed into a freshly ironed cream silk shirt and a new double-breasted suit.

Before making one phone call to London and two more to Moscow, he ordered dinner in his room so that no one would see him—he had no desire to explain how the man who checked in was thirty years older than the man eating alone in his room. Like a hungry animal he tore at the steak and gulped the wine.

He stared at the colorful carrier bag but felt no desire to finish off the meal with one of Scott's liqueur chocolates. Once again he felt anger at the thought of the Englishman getting the better of him.

His eyes then rested on the little leather suitcase that lay on the floor by the side of his bed. He opened it and took out the copy of the icon that Zaborski had ordered he should always have with him so that there could be no doubt when he came across the original of Saint George and the dragon.

At a little after eleven he switched on the late-night news. They had no photograph of the suspect, only one of that stupid taxi driver who had driven so slowly it had cost the fool his life, and the pretty German girl who had tried to fight back. It had been pathetic; one firm clean strike and her neck was broken. The television announcer said the police were searching for an unnamed Englishman. Romanov smiled at the thought of police searching for Scott while he was eating steak in a luxury hotel. Although the Swiss police had no photograph of the murderer, Romanov didn't need one. It was a face he would never forget. In any case his contact in England had already told him a lot more about Captain Scott in one phone call than the Swiss police could hope to discover for another couple of days.

When Romanov was told the details of Scott's military career and decoration for bravery he considered it would be a pleasure to kill such a man.

Lying motionless on a mean little bed, Adam tried to make sense of all the pieces that made up a black jigsaw. If Goering had left the icon to his father, and his alias had been Emmanuel Rosenbaum, then a real-life Emmanuel Rosenbaum didn't exist. But he *did* exist: he had even killed twice in his attempt to get his hands on the Czar's icon. Adam leaned over, switched on the bedside light, then pulled the small package out of the pocket of his trench coat. He unwrapped it carefully before holding the icon under the light. Saint George stared back at him—no longer looking magnificent, it seemed to Adam, but more accusing. Adam would have handed the icon over to Rosenbaum without a second thought if it would have stopped Heidi from sacrificing her life.

By midnight Adam had decided what had to be done, but he didn't stir from that tiny room until a few minutes after three. He lifted himself quietly off the bed, opened the door, checked the corridor, and then locked the door noiselessly behind him before creeping down the stairs. When he reached the bottom step he waited and listened. The night porter had nodded off in front of a television that now let out a dim, monotonous hum. A silver dot remained in the center of the screen. Adam took nearly two minutes to reach the front door, stepping on a noisy floorboard once, but the porter's snores had been enough to cover that. Outside, Adam checked up and down the street, but there was no sign of any movement. He didn't want to go far, so he stayed in the shadows by the side of the road, moving at a pace unfamiliar to him. When he reached the corner he saw what he had been searching for and it was still about a hundred yards away.

There was still no one to be seen, so he quickly made his way to the phone booth. He pressed a twenty-centime coin into the phone and waited. A voice said, *"Est-ce que je puis vous aider?"* Adam uttered only one word, "International." A moment later another voice asked the same question.

"I want to make a reverse charge call to London," said Adam firmly. He had no desire to repeat himself.

"Yes," said the voice. "And what is your name?"

"George Cromer," replied Adam.

"And the number you are speaking from?"

"Geneva 271982." He reversed the last three digits: he felt the police could well be listening in on all calls to England that night. He then told the girl the number in London he required.

"Can you wait for a moment, please?"

"Yes," said Adam as his eyes checked up and down the street once again, still looking for any unfamiliar movement. Only the occasional early-morning car sped by. He remained absolutely motionless in the corner of the box.

He could hear the connection being put through. Please wake up, his lips mouthed. At last the ringing stopped, and Adam recognized the familiar voice which answered.

"Who is this?" Lawrence asked, sounding irritated but perfectly awake.

"Will you accept a reverse charge call from a Mr. George Cromer in Geneva?"

"George Cromer, Lord Cromer, the Governor of the Bank of Eng—? Yes, I will," he said.

"It's me, Lawrence," said Adam.

"Thank God. Where are you?"

"I'm still in Geneva, but I'm not sure you're going to believe what I'm about to tell you. While we were waiting to board our plane home a man pulled Heidi into a taxi and later murdered her before I could catch up with them. And the trouble is that the Swiss police think I'm the killer."

"Now just relax, Adam. I know that much. It's been on the evening news, and the police have already been around to interview me. It seems Heidi's brother identified you."

"What do you mean *identified* me? I didn't do it. You know I couldn't do it. It was a man called Rosenbaum, not me, Lawrence."

"Rosenbaum? Adam, who is Rosenbaum?"

Adam tried to sound calm. "Heidi and I came to Geneva this morning to pick up a gift from a Swiss bank that Pa had left me in his will. It turned out to be a painting. Then when we returned to the airport, this Rosenbaum grabbed Heidi, thinking she had got the painting, which didn't make any sense because the damned icon's only worth twenty thousand pounds."

"Icon?" said Lawrence.

"Yes, an icon of Saint George and the dragon," said Adam. "That's not important. What's important is that . . ."

"Now listen and listen carefully," interrupted Lawrence, "because I'm not going to repeat myself. Keep out of sight until the morning and then give yourself up at our consulate. Just see you get there in one piece, and I'll make sure that the consul will be expecting you. Don't arrive until eleven because London is an hour behind Geneva, and I'll need every minute to arrange matters and see that the consul staff is properly organized."

Adam found himself smiling for the first time in twelve hours.

"Did the killer get what he was after?" Lawrence asked.

"No, he didn't," said Adam, "he only got my mother's chocolates . . ."

"Thank God for that," said Lawrence, "and be sure to keep out of sight of the Swiss police because they are convinced it was you who killed Heidi."

"But . . ." began Adam.

"No explanations. Just be at the consulate at eleven. Now you'd better get off the line," said Lawrence. "Eleven, and don't be late."

"Right," said Adam, "and . . ." but the phone had already been put down. Thank God for Lawrence, he thought. The Lawrence of old, the Lawrence of old who didn't need to ask any questions because he already knew the answers. Christ, what had he got himself involved in? Adam checked the street once again. Still no one in sight. He quickly stole the two hundred yards back to the hotel. The front door remained unlocked, the porter asleep, the television screen still faintly humming, the silver dot in place. Adam was back on his bed by four-oh-five. He didn't sleep. Rosenbaum, Heidi, the taxi driver, the Russian gentleman at Sotheby's. So many pieces of a jigsaw, none of them fitting into place.

But the one thing that worried him most was the conversation with Lawrence—the Lawrence of old?

The two policemen arrived at the Hotel Monarche at twenty past seven that Thursday morning. They were tired, discontent, and hungry. Since midnight they had visited forty-three hotels on the west side of the city, on each occasion with no success. They had checked over a thousand registration cards and woken seven innocent Englishmen who had not come anywhere near fitting the description of Adam Scott.

At eight they would be off duty and could go home to their wives and breakfasts; but they still had three more hotels to check before then. When the landlady saw them coming into the hall she waddled as quickly as possible from the inner office toward them. She loathed the police and was willing to believe anyone who told her that the Swiss pigs were even worse than the Germans. Twice in the last year she had been fined and once even threatened with jail over her failure to register every guest. If they caught her once more, she knew they would take her license away and with it her living. Her slow mind tried to recall who had booked in the previous evening. Eight people had registered, but only two had paid cash—the Englishman who hardly opened his mouth, Mr. Pemberton was the name he had filled in on the missing card, and Maurice, who always turned up with a different girl whenever he was in Geneva. She had destroyed both their cards and pocketed the money. Maurice and the girl had left by seven, and she had already made up their bed, but the Englishman was still asleep in his room.

"We need to check your registration cards for last night, madame."

"Certainly, monsieur," she replied with a warm smile, and gathered together the six remaining cards: two Frenchmen, one Italian, two nationals from Zurich, and one from Basle.

"Did an Englishman stay here last night?"

"No," said the landlady firmly. "I haven't had an Englishman," she added helpfully, "for at least a month. Would you like to see the cards for last week?"

"No, that won't be necessary," said the policeman. The landlady grunted with satisfaction. "But we will still need to check your unoccupied rooms. I see from the certificate that there are twelve guest bedrooms in the hotel," the policeman continued. "So there must be six that should be empty."

"There's no one in them," said the landlady. "I've already checked them once this morning."

"We still need to see for ourselves," the other officer insisted.

The landlady picked up her pass key and waddled toward the stairs, which she proceeded to climb as if they were the final summit of Everest. She opened bedrooms five, seven, nine, ten, and eleven. Maurice's room had been remade within minutes of his leaving but the old lady knew she would lose her license the moment they entered twelve. She just stopped herself from knocking on the door before she turned the key in the lock. The two policemen walked in ahead of her while she remained in the corridor, just in case there was any trouble. Not for the first time that day she cursed the efficiency of Swiss police.

"Thank you, madame," said the first policeman as he stepped back into the corridor. "We are sorry to have troubled you," he added. He put a tick on his list next to the Hotel Monarche.

As the two policemen made their way downstairs, the landlady walked into room number twelve, mystified. The bed was undisturbed, as if it had not been slept in, and there was no other sign of anyone having spent the night there. She called on her tired memory. She hadn't drunk that much the previous night—she touched the fifty francs in her pocket as if to prove the point. "I wonder where he is," she muttered.

For the past hour Adam had been crouching behind a derelict coach in a railway goods yard less than half a mile from the hotel. He had a clear view for a hundred yards in every direction. He had watched the early-morning commuters flooding in on every train. By twenty past eight Adam judged they were at their peak. He checked that the icon was in place and left his hideout to join the flood as they headed to work. He stopped at the kiosk to purchase a newspaper. The only English paper on sale at that time in the morning was the *Herald Tribune*; the London papers didn't arrive until the first plane could land, but Adam had seen the *Herald Tribune* come in on the train from Paris. He made two other purchases at the station kiosk before rejoining the scurrying crowds: a city map of Geneva and a large bar of Nestlé's chocolate.

There were still over two hours to kill before he could present himself at the consulate. Although it was some way in the distance, he could already see the building he had marked out as his next place of sanctuary. He steered a route toward it that allowed him to stay in contact with the largest number of people. When he arrived in the square he continued under the shop awnings round the longest route, clinging to the wall, always avoiding the open spaces. It took a considerable time, but his judgment was perfect. He reached the front door as hundreds of worshippers were leaving after the early-morning Communion service.

Once inside, he felt safe. Saint Peter's was set out like most of the great cathedrals of the world, and Adam found his bearings in a matter of moments. He made his way slowly down the side aisle toward the Lady Chapel, dropped some coins in one of the collection boxes, lit a candle, and placed it in a vacant holder below a statue of the Virgin Mother. He then fell on his knees, but his eyes never closed. A lapsed Catholic, he found he no longer believed in God—except when he was ill, frightened, or in an airplane. After about twenty minutes had passed Adam was distressed to see that there were now only a handful of people left in the cathedral. Some old ladies dressed in black filled a front pew, moving their rosary beads methodically and chanting, *"Ave Maria, gratia plena ..."* A few tourists were craning their necks to admire the King beam roof, their eyes only looking upward.

Adam rose slowly, his eyes darting from side to side. He stretched his legs and walked over to a confessional box partly hidden behind a pillar. A small sign on the wooden support showed that the box was not in use. Adam slipped in, sat down, and pulled the curtain closed.

First he took out the *Herald Tribune* from his trench coat pocket, and then the bar of chocolate. He tore the silver paper from the chocolate and began to munch greedily. Next he searched for the story. Only one or two items of English news were on the front page, as most of the articles were devoted to what was happening in America. "The Pound Still Too High at $2.80?" one headline suggested. Adam's eyes passed over the smaller headlines until he saw the paragraph he was looking for. It was in the bottom left-hand corner: "Englishman Sought after German Girl and

Swiss Taxi Driver Murdered." Adam read the story and only began to tremble when he discovered they knew his name.

"Captain Adam Scott, who recently resigned his commission from the Royal Wessex Regiment, is wanted . . . please turn to page fifteen." Adam began to turn the large pages. It was not easy in the restricted space of a confessional. ". . . for questioning by the Geneva police in connection with . . ."

"Au nom du Père, du Fils et du Saint-Esprit."

Adam looked up from the paper, startled, and considered making a dash for it. But he allowed his long-ago training to take hold, and he found himself saying automatically, "Father, bless me, for I have sinned and wish to confess."

"Good, my son, and what form has this sin taken?" asked the priest in accented but clear English.

Adam thought quickly, I must give him no clue as to who I am. He looked out through the gap in the curtain and was alarmed to see two policemen questioning another priest by the west door. He drew the curtains tight and turned to the only accent he could ever imitate with conviction.

"I'm over from Dublin, Father, and last night I picked up this local girl in a bar and took her back to my hotel."

"Yes, my son."

"Well, one thing led to another, Father."

"Another what, my son?"

"Well, I took her up to my room."

"Yes, my son?"

"And she started to undress."

"And then what happened?"

"She started to undress me."

"Did you try to resist, my son?"

"Yes, Father, but it got harder."

"And did intercourse take place?" asked the priest.

"I'm afraid so, Father, I couldn't stop myself. She was very beautiful," Adam added.

"And is it your intention to marry this girl, my son?"

"Oh, no, Father, I'm already married and have two lovely children, Seamus and Maureen."

"It is a night you must forever put behind you."

"I'd like to, Father."

"Has this happened before?"

"No, Father, it's the first time I've been abroad on my own. I swear to it."

"Then let it be a lesson to you, my son, and may the Lord find it in his mercy to forgive you this abominable sin, and now you must make your act of contrition."

"Oh, my God. . . ."

When Adam had completed the act of contrition the priest pronounced absolution and told him he must as penance say three decades of the Rosary.

"And one more thing."

"Yes, Father?"

"You will tell your wife everything the moment you return to Ireland, or you cannot hope for atonement. You must promise me that, my son."

"When I see my wife I will tell her everything that happened last night, Father," Adam promised, as he once again checked through the curtains. The police were no longer anywhere to be seen.

"Good, and continue to pray to our Blessed Lady to keep you from the evils of temptation."

Adam folded up his paper, pushed it in the trench coat, and bolted from the little box and took a seat on the end of a pew. He lowered his head and began to whisper the Lord's Prayer as he opened the map of Geneva and began to study the road plan. He had located the British consulate on the far side of a large garden square by the time he reached, "Deliver us from evil." He estimated that it was just over a mile away from the cathedral, but seven streets and a bridge had to be negotiated before he would be safe. He returned to the Lady Chapel and his knees. Adam checked his watch. It was too early to leave Saint Peter's, so he remained head in hands for another thirty minutes going over the route again and again. He watched a party of tourists being conducted through the cathedral. His eyes never left them as they began to move nearer and nearer to the great door at the west end of the aisle. He needed to time it to perfection.

Suddenly Adam rose and walked quickly down the side aisle reaching the porch only a yard behind the party of tourists. They shielded him out on to the square. Adam ducked under a shop awning at the side of the road, then walked round three sides of the square to avoid the one policeman on duty by the north corner. He crossed the first road as the light turned red and headed up a one-way street. He kept on the inside of the pavement, knowing he had to turn left at the end of the road. Two uniformed policemen came round the corner and walked straight toward him. He jumped into the first shop without looking and turned his back on the pavement.

"Bonjour, monsieur," said a young lady to Adam. "Vous désirez quelque chose?" Adam looked around him. Lissome dummies in panties and bras with garters and fasteners and long black nylon stockings stood all around him.

"I'm looking for a present for my wife."

The girl smiled. "Perhaps a slip?" she suggested.

"Yes," said Adam, "definitely a slip. Do you have one in burgundy?" he asked, as he half turned to watch the policemen stroll past.

"Yes, I think so, but I'll have to check in the stock room."

Adam had reached the next streetcorner long before she had returned with "just the thing."

He managed the next three crossings without incident, and with only two hundred yards to go could already feel his heart thumping as if it were trying to escape from his body. On the final corner there was only one policeman in sight, and he seemed intent on directing traffic. Adam kept his back to the officer. He could now see the garden square that had only shown up on the map as a tiny green blob. On the far side of the road he spotted a Union Jack hanging above a blue door.

Never run the last few yards, especially when it's open ground, his sergeant had told him many times when on patrol in the Malayan jungle. He crossed the road and stood on the edge of the small park, only fifty yards away from safety. A policeman was patrolling aimlessly up the road, but Adam suspected that was only because there were several consulates standing adjacent to one another. He watched the officer carefully. It took the man two minutes to reach the French consulate before he turned and continued his leisurely walk back. Adam ducked behind a tree in the corner of the little park and selected another tree on the far side of the road only yards from the consulate front door that would shield him from the oncoming policeman. He estimated that by walking at a speed that wouldn't attract attention he could cover the last thirty yards in under ten seconds. He waited for the policeman to reach his farthest point.

He checked the consulate door again, relieved to see a girl go in and a man carrying a briefcase come out on to the street. There seemed to be no guard in sight as the door remained half open. He looked up at the bay window on the first floor. He could see two men staring out at the park as if waiting expectantly for someone to arrive. Lawrence had succeeded. In moments he would be home. Adam pulled up the collar of his trench coat and set off as the cathedral clock behind him struck eleven. The policeman was now a few paces from reaching his farthest point but still walking in the opposite direction. Adam crossed the road at a measured stride. When he reached the streetcar lines in the center he had to stop suddenly to let a car pass by. The policeman turned to start his journey back.

For several seconds Adam remained motionless between the streetcar lines as he stared at the tree he had selected to shield him if the policeman turned before he could reach the front door. He took a confident pace toward the consulate. A tall man of athletic build, his head covered in a stubble of short fair hair, stepped out to greet him.

Adam would not have recognized him but for the eyes.

PART II

10 DOWNING STREET

LONDON S.W.1
June 16, 1966

CHAPTER
TWELVE

❦～❦

10 DOWNING STREET
JUNE 16, 1966

WHEN SIR MORRIS Youngfield left the Prime Minister he still was unable to work out why the possession of any icon could be that important.

Leaving Number Ten behind him, Sir Morris marched quickly into the Foreign Office courtyard and within moments was stepping out of the lift on the seventh floor. When he walked into his office, Tessa, his secretary, was sorting out some papers for him.

"I want a D4 assembled immediately," he said to the woman who had served him so loyally for fourteen years. "And ask Commander Busch to join the team."

Tessa raised her eyebrows, but Sir Morris ignored her silent comment as he knew he couldn't hope to get to the bottom of this one without the cooperation of the Americans. Once more Sir Morris considered the Prime Minister's instructions. Harold Wilson hadn't needed to explain that he didn't get that many transatlantic calls from Lyndon Johnson seeking his help. But why a Russian icon of an English saint?

As Romanov moved toward him, Adam took a pace backward from the streetcar lines to allow the streetcar to pass between them. When the streetcar had passed Adam was no longer to be seen. Romanov snarled at such an amateur trick, sprinted the twenty yards necessary to catch up with the streetcar, and to the astonishment of the passengers, leaped on. He began checking over the faces row by row.

Adam waited for the streetcar to travel another twenty yards before he emerged from behind a tree on the far side of the road. He felt confident he could reach the safety of the consulate door long before Heidi's killer could hope to return. He checked the other side of the road and swore under his breath. The policeman patrolling was now only a few paces from the consulate and heading relentlessly toward it. Adam looked back at the streetcar, which had just been passed by another, which was heading toward him. To his dismay, he saw his adversary leap from one platform to the other with the agility of a top-class gymnast. With the policeman only yards from the consulate door Adam was left with no choice but to turn and sprint back up the one-way street. After fifty yards he glanced over his shoulder. The man he knew only as Rosenbaum couldn't have looked less like a helpless old man as he started running toward him.

Adam jumped between the cars and buses and dodged around the milling pedestrians as he tried to lengthen the fifty yards' distance between them. At the first crossroad he saw a plump lady coming out of a phone booth a few yards away. He changed direction quickly and leaped into the empty box, crouching into the far corner. The door slowly squelched shut. Rosenbaum came hurtling round the corner and was twenty yards past the booth before he realized that Adam had shot back out and down the road in the opposite direction. Adam knew he had at least five seconds before Rosenbaum could hope to see which direction he had chosen. One, two, three, four, and five he counted as he ran along the road. He then checked right, before mounting three steps and pushing through some swinging doors. He found himself in front of a small counter behind which sat a young woman holding a small wad of tickets.

"*Deux francs, monsieur,*" said the girl. Adam looked at the little box, quickly took out two francs, and made his way down the long dark passage and through another set of swinging doors. He stood at the back waiting for his eyes to become accustomed to the dark. It was the first performance of the day, and the cinema was nearly empty. Adam chose a seat on the end of a row that was an equal distance from both exits.

He stared at the screen, thankful that the movie had just begun, because he needed some time to formulate a plan. Whenever the screen was bright enough he checked the little red road on the map, and then using the top of his thumb as a one-inch ruler, he was able to estimate that the nearest border into France was only eight miles away at Ferney-Voltaire. From there he could travel to Paris via Dijon and be back home almost as quickly as it would take him to sit through *Exodus* a second time. Having decided on his route, the next problem for Adam was how to travel. He dismissed all forms of public transport and settled on renting a car. He remained in his seat during the interval to double-check the routes. The moment Paul Newman reappeared on the screen, he folded up the map and left the cinema by the exit that had been least used during the past four hours.

When Sir Morris entered the room for the meeting of the Northern Department, he found the rest of the D4 already assembled and familiarizing themselves with the files that had been presented to them only an hour before.

He glanced around the table at the specially selected D4, all handpicked men, but only one of them did he consider his equal. And it wasn't the old war-horse Alec Snell, who had served at the Foreign Office longer than any of them, and was touching his mustache nervously as he waited for Sir

Morris to take his seat. Next to him sat Brian Matthews, known in the department as the "well-balanced man": a grammar school boy with high honors and a chip on both shoulders. Opposite him was Commander Ralph Busch, the CIA representative with a short fuse, who, after five years attached to the embassy in Grosvenor Square considered himself more British than the British and even imitated the Foreign Office style of dress to prove it. At the far end of the table was Sir Morris's second in command, who some said was a little too young, although everyone except Tessa had forgotten that Sir Morris had held his job at the same age.

The four members of the committee stopped talking once Sir Morris had settled in his seat at the head of the table.

"Gentlemen," he began—the only lady present being the long-suffering Tessa, whose existence he rarely acknowledged—"the Prime Minister has given this D4 his full blessing. And, he requires detailed reports to be sent to him every twelve hours, wherever he is, and at any time of the night or day should there be some unexpected development. So, as you can see, there is no time to waste. This particular D4 has co-opted as part of its team a liaison officer from the CIA, Commander Ralph Busch. I have worked with Commander Busch several times over the last five years, and I am delighted that the American embassy has chosen him to represent them."

The man seated on Sir Morris's right bowed slightly. At five feet nine inches, with broad, muscular shoulders and a neat black beard, he looked every inch the sailor whom Player's cigarettes were always trying to please. Indeed, a sailor wouldn't have been a bad guess because Busch had been a commander of PT boats during the Second World War.

"From the latest reports I have received," Sir Morris continued, opening the file in front of him, "it appears that Scott never reached the consulate this morning, despite our request for the police to have no more than a token force on duty within two hundred yards of the park.

"Since our sketchy information yesterday BEA has confirmed," said Sir Morris, consulting a note in front of him, "that Scott received a call from Roget et Cie while he was at the airport. After considerable pressure from our ambassador and Interpol we have learned from Mr. Roget that the purpose of Scott's visit to the bank was to pick up an unknown bequest from a Mr. Emmanuel Rosenbaum. Further checking shows that a Mr. Rosenbaum arrived in Zurich yesterday morning and traveled on to Geneva in the afternoon. He left his hotel first thing this morning and has subsequently vanished from the face of the earth. None of this would be of any great significance if Mr. Rosenbaum had not boarded the airplane to Zurich from"—Sir Morris couldn't resist a short dramatic pause—"Moscow. I think it is not unreasonable therefore to assume that Mr. Rosenbaum, whoever he is, works directly or indirectly for the KGB.

"The KGB, as we know to our cost, is well serviced in Geneva, by a large number of East Europeans working under the guise of the United Nations for the ILO and the WHO, all with the diplomatic status they need to carry out undercover work. What still remains a mystery is why Mr. Rosenbaum should be willing to kill two innocent people for a relatively obscure icon. That brings me up to date, but have you come up with anything in the last few hours?" asked Sir Morris turning to his number two.

Lawrence Pemberton looked up from his end of the table. "Since our meeting this morning, Sir Morris," he began, "I have spoken to Scott's sister, his mother, and a firm of solicitors in Appleshaw who administered his father's will. It transpires that Scott was left with nothing of any real importance in the will apart from an envelope, which his mother says contained a letter from Reichsmarschall Hermann Goering." There was an immediate buzz around the table until Sir Morris tapped his knuckle on the desk.

"Do we have any idea of the contents of Goering's letter?" asked Sir Morris.

"The whole letter, no, sir. But one of our examination entrants, a Nicholas Wainwright, was asked by Scott to translate what we now believe was a paragraph from it because later Wainwright asked the examination board if it was part of his test." Lawrence extracted a piece of paper from the file in front of him and read out the paragraph:

> During the year you cannot have failed to notice that I have been receiving from one of the guards a regular supply of Havana cigars—one of the few pleasures I have been permitted, despite my incarceration. The cigars themselves have also served another purpose, as each one contained a capsule with a small amount of poison. Enough to allow me to survive my trial, while ensuring that I shall cheat the executioner.

"That's it?" said Sir Morris.

"Yes," said Lawrence, "but I believe it confirms what Scott explained last night was his reason for traveling to Geneva. There is no doubt in my mind that the package contained the icon of Saint George and the dragon."

"Saint George and the Dragon," said Matthews interrupting, "but that's the icon that half of the KGB has been searching for during the past two weeks, and my department has been trying to find out why."

"And what have you come up with?" asked Sir Morris.

"Very little," admitted Matthews. "But we had assumed it must be a decoy because the Czar's icon of Saint George and the dragon hangs in the Winter Palace at Leningrad and has done so for three hundred years."

"Anything else?" asked Sir Morris.

"Only that the section leader in search of the icon is Alex Romanov," said Matthews.

Snell gave out a low whistle. "Well, at least we know we're dealing with the A-list," he said.

There was a long silence before Sir Morris offered, "One thing is clear. We have to get to Scott first and must also assume that it's Romanov we're up against. So what are we doing about it?"

"As much as we can get away with," said Lawrence. "Along

with the Americans we have seventeen operatives in Geneva, all of them trying to find Scott."

"The Swiss police have a thousand trying to do the same job, though heaven knows whose side they imagine they're on," added Snell.

Lawrence chimed back in. "And it's been almost impossible to convince them that Scott is not in any way responsible for the two murders. So we may have to get him out without relying on their cooperation."

"But what do you consider would be the outcome if Romanov or this Rosenbaum, who must also be part of the KGB, manages to get to Scott before we do?" asked Matthews.

"A civilian against one of the Russians' most ruthless agents. That's all we need," said Commander Busch.

Lawrence inclined his head toward the American. "I've known Adam for most of my life. The irony of his particular predicament is that it was I who, without his knowledge, recommended that he should be interviewed for a place in the Northern Department. It was my intention that he should join us as soon as he had completed his course as a trainee. If Romanov or any of his cohorts come face to face with Scott, they'd better remember that he was awarded a Military Cross for facing a thousand Chinese."

"But if it turned out to be Romanov," asked Snell, "would Scott be able to kill him?"

"I would have said no before Rosenbaum murdered his girlfriend," said Lawrence.

"I still wouldn't be confident of his chances even then," said Busch.

"Neither would I," added Matthews.

"That's because you don't know Adam Scott," Lawrence retorted.

Matthews lowered his eyes in order to avoid a clash with his boss. His boss. Ten years his junior. A shortlist of two, and they had chosen another Oxbridge man to be under secretary. Matthews knew that as far as the Foreign Office was concerned, he had gone to the wrong school and the wrong university. He should have taken his father's advice and joined the police force. There were no class barriers there, and he would probably have been a chief superintendent by now.

Sir Morris ignored the little outburst, which had become fairly common since he had selected Pemberton to leapfrog the older man.

"Are we allowed to know," interrupted Snell, looking straight at Busch, "why a relatively obscure icon is of such disproportionate importance to both Russia and the United States?"

"We are as mystified as you," said the American. "All we can add to your current information is that two weeks ago the Russians deposited gold bullion in New York to the value of over seven hundred million dollars without any explanation. We are, of course, not certain at the moment that there is any connection."

"Seven hundred million dollars?" said Sir Morris. "You could buy half the countries in the United Nations for that."

"And every icon that has ever been painted," said Matthews.

"Let's get down to what we actually know, and stop guessing at what might be," Sir Morris said, turning back to his number two again. "What's the exact I.A. position?"

Lawrence undid a folder with a red band around it, the words "Immediate Action" printed across the top in black. He did not need to refer to it, but still glanced down from time to time to check he had not forgotten anything. "As I have already briefed you, we have seventeen agents in the field, and the Americans are flying a further twelve into Geneva today. With the Russians and the Swiss roaming the city like knights of the Round Table in search of the Holy Grail, I can only believe that someone will come across Scott fairly soon. One of our biggest problems, as I explained, is that the Swiss are not willing to cooperate. As far as they are concerned, Scott is a common criminal on the run, and should they get to him first they have made it clear they will not allow him diplomatic immunity.

"We, as well as the Swiss police and undoubtedly the Russians," continued Lawrence, "have started checking out all the obvious places: hotels, guest houses, restaurants, airports, car hire companies, even lavatories, and we remain in constant touch with every one of our agents on the ground. So if Scott suddenly appears out of nowhere, we should be able to go to his aid at a moment's notice." Lawrence looked up to observe one of the team was taking down all the details. "Added to that, the Post Office is intercepting every call made to Barclays DCO from Geneva. If Scott does try to get in contact with me again at the bank or at my flat, it will be put through to this office automatically," he said.

"Is he aware that you work for the Service?" asked Snell, putting a hand through his dark hair.

"No. Like my dear mother, he still thinks I'm a bank official in the International Department of Barclays DCO. But it won't be long before he works out that that's only a front. Unlike my mother, he doesn't always believe everything I tell him, and after our conversation this morning he is bound to have become suspicious."

"Do we have anything else to go on?" Sir Morris asked, looking up at Lawrence.

"Not a lot more at the moment, sir. We are doing everything possible, remembering this is not a home match; but I still anticipate that the exercise will be over one way or another within twenty-four hours. Because of that I have requested overnight facilities to be set up in the building. When you return after dinner you will find beds already made up in your offices."

"No one will be going out to dinner tonight," said Sir Morris.

The cinema door opened on to the busy pavement, and Adam slipped into the mainstream of commuters, who were now returning home for dinner. As he kept walking he made certain of as little head movement as possible, but his eyes never stayed still, checking everything within 180 degrees. After he had covered three blocks, he spotted a red Avis sign swinging in the afternoon breeze on the far side of the road. He safely reconnoitered the crowded crossing, but once his foot touched the far pavement he froze on the spot. Just ahead of him in the fast, jostling crowd stood a man in a raincoat. He was continually looking around while making no attempt to walk in either direction. Was he one of Rosenbaum's men, the police, or even British? There was no way of telling whose side he was on. Adam's eyes didn't leave the man as he took out an intercom and, putting it to his mouth, whispered into it. "Nothing to report, sir. Still no sign of our man, and I haven't seen any of the KGB either."

Adam, unable to hear the words, turned into a side road and almost knocked over a boy selling papers. *"Le soldat anglais toujours à Genève"* the headline blared. Quickly he crossed another road, where he came to a stop again, this time behind a marble statue in the center of a small patch of grass. He stared at the building in front of him, but he knew there would be no point in his trying to hide there. He started to move away as an empty large touring coach drew up and parked in front of the block. Smart blue lettering along the side of the coach proclaimed The Royal Philharmonic Orchestra. Adam watched as some musicians walked out of the front door and climbed onto the coach carrying their instrument cases of assorted lengths and widths. One was even lugging a large kettle drum, which he deposited in the trunk of the coach. As the musicians continued to stream out of the hotel, Adam decided he wouldn't get a better opportunity. When the next group came through the double doors he walked quickly forward and stepped into the middle of them before anyone could have spotted him. He then continued on past them through the open hotel door. The first thing he spotted in the crowded lobby was a double bass leaning against the wall. He glanced at the label around the neck of the unwieldy case. "Robin Beresford."

Adam walked over to the counter and gestured to the clerk. "I need my room key quickly—I've left my bow upstairs, and now I'm holding everyone up."

"Yes, sir. What room number?" asked the clerk.

"I think it's 312, or was that yesterday?" said Adam.

"What name, sir?"

"Beresford—Robin Beresford."

The clerk handed him key 612. His only comment was: "You were three floors off."

"Thank you," said Adam. As he left the counter, he turned to check that the receptionist was already dealing with another customer. He walked smartly over to the lift, which was disgorging still more musicians. Once it had emptied he stepped in, pressed the button for the sixth floor, and waited. He felt exhilarated as the lift doors eventually slid across, and he was alone for the first time in several hours. When the doors opened again he was relieved to find there was no one standing in the corridor. He made his way quickly along the passage to room 612.

As he turned the key and opened the door he said firmly in as good a French accent as he could manage, "Room service," but no one responded, he stepped in and locked the door behind him. An unopened suitcase had been left in one corner. Adam checked the label. Obviously Mr. Beresford hadn't even had time to unpack. Adam checked the room, but there was no other sign of the hotel guest apart from a piece of paper on the side table. It was a typed itinerary:

European Tour: Geneva, Frankfurt, Berlin, Amsterdam, London.

Geneva, bus 5.00 to concert hall rehearsal 6.00, concert performance 7.30, encores 10.00.

Program: Mozart's Horn Concerto, No. 1, Brahms's Second Symphony, Schubert's "Unfinished Symphony."

Adam looked at his watch: by the time Robin Beresford had completed the "Unfinished Symphony," he would be over the border; but he still felt safe to remain in room 612 until it was dark.

He picked up the phone by the bed and dialed room service. "Beresford, 612," he announced, and ordered himself some dinner before going into the bathroom. On the side of the basin was propped a little plastic bag with the words "Compliments of the Management" printed across it. Inside Adam found soap, a tiny toothbrush, toothpaste, and a plastic razor.

He had just finished shaving when he heard a knock on the door and someone calling, "Room service." Adam quickly covered his face with lather again and put on a hotel dressing gown before he opened the door. The waiter set up a table without giving Adam a second look.

When he had finished his task he inquired, "Will you sign the bill, please, sir?"

He handed Adam a slip of paper. He signed it "Robin Beresford" and added a fifteen percent tip.

"Thank you," said the waiter and left. As soon as the door closed behind him Adam's eyes settled on the feast of onion soup, rump steak with green beans and potatoes and finally a raspberry sorbet. A bottle of house wine had been uncorked and needed only to be poured. He suddenly didn't feel that hungry.

He still couldn't accept what he had gone through. If only he hadn't pressed Heidi into joining him on this unnecessary journey. A week before she hadn't even known him, and now he was responsible for her death. He would have to explain to her parents what had happened to their only daughter. But before Adam could face them he had to come up with some explanation for the things he hadn't yet begun to understand. Not least the unimportant icon. Unimportant?

Adam lay down on the bed and began to consider what had happened in the last twenty-four hours.

"Antarctic is in possession of an icon of Saint George and the dragon. But we know from our files of that period that that particular icon was destroyed when the Grand Duke of Hesse's plane crashed over Belgium in 1937."

"That's what is written in your files in Washington," said the man on the other end of the phone. "But what if your information is wrong and the icon was found by Goering and not returned to the Grand Duke?"

"But Stalin confirmed at Yalta that the icon and its contents had been destroyed in the plane crash. He agreed to make no protest while he was not in possession of the original document. After all, that was the reason Roosevelt appeared to be gaining so little while Stalin was getting so much in return. Can't you remember the fuss Churchill made?"

"I certainly can, because he had worked out that it wasn't Britain who was going to benefit from such a decision."

"But if the Russians have now discovered the original icon?"

"Are you suggesting they might have the original document?"

"Precisely. So you must be sure to get to Antarctic before the Russians do, or, for that matter, the Foreign Office."

"But I'm part of the Foreign Office team."

"And that's precisely what we want the Foreign Office to go on believing."

"And who's been sleeping in my bed, said Mother Bear."

Adam woke with a start. Looking down at him was a girl who held a double bass firmly by the neck with one hand and a bow in the other. She was nearly six feet and certainly weighed considerably more than Adam. She had long, gleaming red hair that was in such contrast to the rest of her that it was as if the Maker had started at the top and then quickly lost interest. She wore a white blouse and a black flowing skirt that stopped an inch above the ground.

"Who are you?" asked Adam, startled.

"I'm not Goldilocks, that's for sure," parried the girl. "More to the point, who are you?"

Adam hesitated. "If I told you, you wouldn't believe me."

"I can't imagine why not," she said. "You don't look like Prince Charles or Elvis Presley to me, so go on, try me."

"I'm Adam Scott."

"Am I meant to swoon and run to your side, or scream and run away?" she inquired.

Adam suddenly realized that the girl couldn't have watched television or read a paper for at least two days. He switched tactics. "I thought my friend Robin Beresford was meant to be staying in this room," he said confidently.

"And so did I until I saw you on my bed."

"You're Robin Beresford?"

"You're quite sharp for someone who has just woken up."

"But Robin?"

"It's not my fault my father wanted a boy," she said. "And you still haven't explained what you're doing on my bed."

"Is there any hope of you listening to me for five minutes without continually interrupting?" asked Adam.

"Yes, but don't bother with any more fairy stories," said Robin. "My father was a born liar, and by the time I was twelve I could see through him like a pane of glass."

"I should have a seat if I were you," said Adam. "This may take longer than the average double bass accompaniment."

"I'll remain on my feet, if you don't mind," said Robin. "At least until the first lie."

"Suit yourself. What would you like first? The good news or the bad news?"

"Try me on the bad news," said Robin.

"The Swiss police want to arrest me and . . ."

"What for?" interrupted Robin.

"Murder," said Scott.

"What's the good news?" she asked.

"I'm innocent."

Romanov stood in the ambassador's office and rested his fingers on the table. "I blame myself," he said very quietly, "even more than I blame any of you. I underestimated the Englishman. He's good, and if any of you are hoping to kill him before I get to him you'll have to be *very* good." No one assembled in the ambassador's office that night was disposed to disagree with the Comrade Major. Romanov paused to study the group of men who had been flown in from several Eastern satellites at short notice. All with long records of service to the State, but only one of them, Valchek, was known to Romanov, and he worked too closely with Zaborski to be trusted. Romanov had already faced the fact that only a few of them were acquainted with Geneva. He could only pray that the British and Americans were suffering from the same problem.

His eyes swept around the room. The Swiss police had the best chance of finding Scott, and they weren't being at all helpful, he thought ruefully. However, Romanov had been pleased to learn from their head man stationed in Geneva that the Swiss had also refused to cooperate with the British or Americans.

"Comrades," he said, the moment they had all settled, "there is no need to remind you that we have been entrusted with a vital assignment for the Motherland." He paused to check if any of the faces registered the slightest suggestion of cynicism. Satisfied, he continued. "We will therefore maintain a tight surveillance over Geneva in case Scott is still holed up somewhere in the city. My own guess is that, like any amateur, he would be, and will wait until it's dark, perhaps even first light, before he makes a run for the nearest border. The French border will be his most obvious choice. Despite going to war against the Germans twice in the past fifty years, the English have never bothered to master the German language, although a few of them can manage to speak passable French. So he's more likely to feel safe in that country. It also offers him the opportunity to cross only one border before reaching the coast.

"If he's stupid enough to try and leave by plane, he will find we have the airport covered; if by train, we have the stations manned. But my guess is still that he will try to escape by motor vehicle.

"I shall therefore take five men to the French border with me while Major Valchek will take another five to Basle to cover the German crossing point. The rest of you will remain on surveillance in Geneva. Those of you who have just arrived will relieve those agents who are in the field already. And don't expect Scott to be roaming around looking like a tourist on holiday. Study your picture of the Englishman carefully and even be prepared for him to try and get away with some amateur disguise."

Romanov paused for effect. "The man who brings me the Czar's icon need have no fear for his future prosperity when we return home." Hopeful expressions appeared on their faces for the first time as Romanov pulled out the duplicate icon from his coat pocket and held it high above his head for all to see.

"When you find the original of this your task will be completed. Study it carefully, Comrades, because no photographs are being issued. And remember," Romanov added, "the only difference between this and Scott's icon is that his has a small silver crown embedded in the back of the frame. Once you see the crown you will know that you have found the missing masterpiece."

Romanov put the icon back in his pocket and looked down at the silent men.

"Remember that Scott is good, but he's not that good."

CHAPTER
THIRTEEN

"YOU'RE NOT BAD, Scott, not bad at all," said Robin, who had remained standing by the double bass throughout Adam's story. "Either you're one hell of a liar, or I've lost my touch." Adam smiled up at the massive girl, who made the bow she was holding in her right hand look like a toothpick.

"Am I permitted to see this icon, or am I supposed just to take your word for it?"

Adam jumped off the bed and pulled out the package containing the Czar's icon from the map pocket of his trench coat. Robin put her double bass up against the wall and, leaving the bow propped against it, lowered herself into the only chair in the room.

Adam handed the icon over to her. For some time she stared at the face of Saint George without making any comment. "It's magnificent," she said at last, "and I can understand anyone wanting to possess it. But no painting could be worth the tragedy and trouble you've had to go through."

"I agree it's inexplicable," said Adam. "But Rosenbaum or

whatever his real name is has been willing to kill twice to get his hands on the piece, and he's already convinced me that as long as I am in possession of the icon I'll be the next in line."

Robin continued to stare at the tiny pieces of gold, blue, and yellow that made up Saint George and the Dragon.

"No other clues?" she asked, looking up.

"Only the letter given to my father by Goering."

Robin turned the painting over. "What does that mean?" she asked, pointing to the tiny silver crown embedded in the wood.

"That proves it was once owned by a czar, according to the man from Sotheby's. And greatly enhances its value, he assured me."

"Still, couldn't be worth killing for," said Robin. She handed the icon back to Adam. "So what other secret is Saint George keeping to himself?"

Adam shrugged and frowned, having asked himself the same question again and again since Heidi's death. He returned the silent saint to his trench coat.

"What was to have been your plan if you had stayed awake?" asked Robin. "Other than making the bed?"

Adam smiled. "I hoped to call Lawrence again once I could be sure he had returned home and check if he had any more news for me. If he wasn't back or couldn't help, I was going to hire a car and try to get across the Swiss border to France and then on to England. I·felt sure that between Rosenbaum and his men and the Swiss police they would have had all the airports and stations fully covered."

"No doubt Rosenbaum will have also thought that much out as well, if he's half as good as you claim," said Robin. "So we'd better try and get in touch with your friend Lawrence and see if he's come up with any bright ideas." She pushed herself up out of the chair and walked across to the phone.

"You don't have to get yourself involved," said Adam hesitantly.

"I am involved," said Robin. "And I can tell you it's far more exciting than Schubert's 'Unfinished.' Once I've got your friend on the line I'll pass him over to you, and then no one will realize who's phoning." Adam told her the number of the flat, and she asked the girl on the switchboard to connect her.

Adam checked his watch: eleven-forty. Surely Lawrence would be home by now? The phone didn't complete its first two rings before Robin heard a man's voice on the line. She immediately handed the receiver over.

"Hello, who is that?" asked the voice. Adam was reminded how strange he always found it that Lawrence never announced his name.

"Lawrence, it's me."

"Where are you?"

"I'm still in Geneva."

"My clients were waiting for you at eleven o'clock this morning."

"So was Rosenbaum."

"Who is Rosenbaum?"

"A six-foot, fair-haired, blue-eyed monster, who seems determined to kill me."

Lawrence did not speak for some time. "And are you still in possession of our patron saint?"

"Yes, I am," said Adam. "But what can be so important about—"

"Put the phone down and ring me back again in three minutes."

The line went dead. Adam couldn't fathom the sudden change in his old friend's manner. What had he missed during those months he had lodged with him? He tried to recall details that he had previously considered unimportant and that Lawrence had so skillfully disguised.

"Is everything all right?" asked Robin, breaking into his thoughts.

"I think so," said Adam, a little mystified. "He wants me to ring back in three minutes. Will that be all right with you?"

"This tour's already lost eight thousand pounds of the taxpayers' money, so what difference can a few international calls make?" she said.

Three minutes later, Robin picked up the receiver and repeated the number. In one ring Lawrence was back on the line.

"Only answer my questions," said Lawrence.

"No, I will not answer your questions," said Adam, becoming increasingly annoyed with Lawrence's manner. "I want one or two of my own answered before you get anything more out of me. Do I make myself clear?"

"Yes," said a more gentle-sounding Lawrence.

"Who is Rosenbaum?"

Lawrence didn't immediately reply.

"You'll get nothing further from me until you start telling the truth," said Adam.

"From your description I have every reason to believe Rosenbaum is a Russian agent whose real name is Alex Romanov."

"A Russian agent? But why should a Russian agent want to get his hands on my icon?"

"I don't know," said Lawrence. "We were rather hoping you might be able to tell us."

"Who's we?"

Another long silence.

"Who's we?" repeated Adam. "You can't really expect me to go on believing you work for Barclays DCO."

"I work at the Foreign Office," said Lawrence.

"In what capacity?"

"I am not at liberty . . ."

"Stop being so pompous, Lawrence. In what capacity?"

"I'm the number two in a small section that deals in . . ." Lawrence hesitated.

"Espionage I think is the current jargon we laymen are using," said Adam, "and if you want my icon that badly you had better get me out of this mess alive because Romanov is willing to kill me for it, as I am sure you know."

"Where are you?"

"The Richmond Hotel."

"In a public phone booth?" asked Lawrence, sounding incredulous.

"No, in a private room."

"But not registered in your name?"

"No, in the name of a friend. A girlfriend."

"Is she with you now?" asked Lawrence.

"Yes," said Adam.

"Damn," said Lawrence. "Right. Don't leave that room until seven A.M., then phone on this number again. That will give me enough time to get everything in place."

"Is that the best you can do?" said Adam, but the phone had already gone dead. "It looks as if I'm stuck with you for the night," he told Robin as he replaced the phone.

"On the contrary, it is I who am stuck with you," said Robin, and disappeared into the bathroom. Adam paced around the room several times before he tested the sofa. Either he had to rest his head on a cushion, balanced on the thin wooden arm, or he had to let his legs dangle over the far end. By the time Robin had come back out clad in a pair of sky-blue pajamas, he had selected the floor as his resting place.

"Not much of a chair, is it?" said Robin. "But then British Intelligence didn't warn me to book a double room." She climbed into the bed and turned out the light. "Very comfortable," were the last words she uttered.

Adam lay down flat on the bedroom floor, using the cushion from the chair as a pillow and a hotel dressing gown as a blanket. He slept intermittently, his mind switching between why the icon could be that important, how Lawrence knew so much about it and, most immediately, how the hell were they going to get him out of the hotel alive?

Romanov waited patiently for the phone to be picked up.

"Yes," said a voice that he recognized immediately.

"Where is he?" were the only words Romanov uttered. Four words were all he received from Mentor in reply before the phone went dead.

* * *

Adam woke with a start an hour before he was due to phone Lawrence back. For nearly forty minutes he lay on the floor with only Robin's steady breathing to remind him he was not alone. Suddenly he became aware of a strange sound coming from the corridor outside—two or three steps, a pause, then *whoosh*, two or three steps, a pause, another *whoosh*. Adam raised himself up silently from the floor and crept to the door. The rhythm of Robin's breathing never faltered. *Whoosh*, it now sounded closer. He picked up a heavy wooden coat hanger from the table by the door. He gripped it firmly in his right hand, raised it above his head, and waited. *Whoosh*—and a newspaper shot under the door and the steps moved on. He didn't have to bend down to see that it was his photograph that dominated the front page of the international edition of the *Herald Tribune*.

Adam took the paper into the bathroom, closed the door silently, switched on the light, and read the lead article. It was yesterday's story with guarded comments from his old commanding officer and embarrassed silence from his mother. He felt helpless.

He crept up to Robin, hoping she wouldn't wake. He stood over her, but she didn't stir. He silently picked up the phone and dragged it to the bathroom. He could only just manage to close the door behind him. He dialed the operator and repeated the number.

When the ringing stopped, he immediately said, "Is that you, Lawrence?"

"Yes," came back the reply.

"Things have become much worse now. I'm still holed up in the hotel, but my picture is on the front page of every paper."

"I know," said Lawrence. "We tried to prevent it, but yet again the Swiss wouldn't cooperate."

"Then I may as well give myself up to the Swiss," said Adam. "Damn it all, I am innocent."

"No, Adam, in Switzerland you're guilty until proven innocent, and you must have worked out by now that you're involved in something far more important than a double murder."

"What could be more important than a double murder when the rest of the world thinks you're the murderer?" asked Adam angrily.

"I can understand exactly how you feel, but your only chance now is to carry out my instructions to the letter and treat every other person you come in contact with with suspicion."

"I'm listening," said Adam.

"Just remember everything I say because I am only going to tell you once. The Royal Philharmonic Orchestra is staying in the same hotel as you. They are going on to Frankfurt at ten o'clock this morning. Leave your room at five to ten, join the orchestra in the lobby, and then make your way to the front door, where you'll find their coach parked. We will have a car waiting for you on the far side of the road. The car is a black Mercedes, and you will see a man in gray chauffeur's uniform holding the door open for you. We have already arranged that no other car will be able to park on that side of the road between nine-thirty and ten-thirty, so you can't mistake it. Just get into the back and wait. There will be another man in the back with you, and you will then be driven to the safety of our consulate. Do you need me to repeat any of that?"

"No," said Adam, "but . . ."

"Good luck," said Lawrence, and the phone went dead.

By seven he had showered and shaved, while Robin remained unrepentant in a deep sleep. He envied her; only a twig had to break outside and Adam was wide awake. Two years of living in the Malayan jungle, never knowing when the Chinese would strike, never being able to sleep for more than two or three hours at a time if one wanted to stay alive, still kept its hold on him.

Robin did not stir for another thirty minutes, during which time Adam sat on the sofa and went over Lawrence's plan in his mind. At ten to eight she finally woke, even then taking several minutes before she was fully conscious. Robin blinked at Adam, and a large grin appeared on her face.

"So you didn't murder me while I slept," she said.

"I don't think you'd have noticed if I had," said Adam.

"When your father is a habitual drunk and comes home at all hours of the night, you learn to sleep through anything," she explained, placing both feet firmly on the carpet. "Aren't you meant to have phoned London by now?"

"I already have."

"And what is the master plan to be?" she asked, rubbing her eyes on her way to the bathroom.

"I will be leaving with you," said Adam.

"Most of my one-night stands don't bother to stay that long," she remarked as she closed the bathroom door behind her. He tried to read the paper while the bath was filling up.

"Does that mean we're sharing a room in Frankfurt as well?" she asked a few minutes later when the bathroom door reopened, as if the conversation had never been interrupted.

"No, as soon as we're clear of the hotel I leave you at the coach and make my own way to a car on the far side of the road."

"That sounds more like the men in my life," she said. "But at least we can have a farewell breakfast," she added, picking up the phone. "I'm nuts about kippers. How about you?"

Adam didn't answer. He had begun looking at his watch every few moments. The waiter arrived with breakfast about fifteen minutes later; Adam waited in the bathroom. When he reappeared he showed no interest in the food, so Robin ate four kippers and most of the toast. Nine o'clock passed; a porter took away the breakfast trolley, and Robin began to pack. The phone rang and Adam jumped nervously as Robin picked it up.

"Yes, Stephen," she said. "No, I won't need any help with my luggage. Not this time." She put the phone down. "We depart for Frankfurt at ten."

"I know," said Adam.

"We ought to make Lawrence the orchestra manager. He seems to know everything even before it's been decided."

Adam had been thinking the same thing. "Well, at least I've found someone to help with my luggage for a change," added Robin cheerfully.

"I'll carry the double bass for you if you like," offered Adam.

"I'd like to see you try," said Robin. Adam walked over to the large instrument that was propped up in its case against the wall. He tried the double bass from all angles but couldn't manage to do better than hold it off the floor for a few moments. Robin joined him, and with one flick she had the stem on her shoulder and the instrument balanced perfectly. She walked up and down the bedroom demonstrating her prowess.

"It's a matter of skill, my puny friend," she said. "And to think I believed all those stories last night about your outrunning half the Swiss police force to spend a night with me."

Adam tried to laugh. He picked up his trench coat, checking that the icon was secure. But he couldn't stop himself shaking from a combination of fear and anticipation.

Robin looked at him. "Don't worry," she said gently. "It will be all over in a few minutes' time." Then she saw the paper on the floor. "I should sue them if I were you."

"Why?" asked Adam.

"You're a lot better-looking than that." Adam smiled and just managed to get his arms around her to give her a hug.

"Thanks for everything," he said. "But now we have to go."

"You're sounding more like one of my lovers all the time," said Robin mournfully.

Adam picked up her suitcase while Robin jerked up the stem of the double bass onto her shoulder. She opened the door and checked the corridor. Two of her colleagues from the RPO were waiting by the lift; otherwise there was nobody else in sight. Robin and Adam joined the two musicians and after "good mornings" no one spoke until the lift doors slid open. Once the doors were closed, Robin's colleagues couldn't resist taking a closer look at Adam. At first Adam was anxious they had recognized him from the newspaper. Then he realized that it was who Robin had spent the night with that fascinated them. Robin gave him a lewd wink, as if she fully intended to live off this one for a long time. For his part Adam ducked behind the double bass and remained in the corner breathing deeply as the lift trundled down toward the ground floor. The doors sprung open and Robin waited for her two colleagues to leave before she shielded Adam as best she could all the way across the foyer. His eyes were now fixed on the front door. He could see the bus taking up most of the road, and several members of the orchestra were already clambering on. One more minute, and he should be safely away. He watched as the drums were packed carefully in the large trunk.

"Oh, God, I forgot," said Robin. "I meant to put this in the trunk at the back of the bus."

"Do it later," said Adam sharply. "Just keep going until you reach the coach door." Then he saw the car on the far side of the road. He felt light with relief, almost dizzy. The car door was being held open for him. Another man was seated in the back, just as Lawrence had promised. Ten o'clock struck somewhere in the distance. The man dressed in a chauffeur's uniform, hat pulled down over his forehead, stood by the open door. He turned toward the hotel in anticipation. Adam stared toward him as the man's eyes scanned the hotel entrance.

The uniform wasn't a good fit.

"Into the bus," hissed Adam.

"With this thing? They'll kill me," said Robin.

"If you don't, he'll kill me."

Robin obeyed, despite the adverse comments as she lumbered down the aisle with her double bass screening Adam from the gaze of anyone on the far side of the road.

Adam slumped into the seat next to Robin with the double bass between them. He wanted to be sick.

"Which one?" she whispered.

"In the chauffeur's uniform."

Robin glanced out of the window. "He may be evil, but he's damned good-looking," she said, inconsequentially.

Adam looked disbelieving. Robin smiled apologetically.

"Everybody's in," called a man from the front of the bus. "And I've double-checked, and we seem to have one extra."

Oh, my God, thought Adam, he's going to throw me off the bus.

"My brother," shouted Robin from the back. "He's only traveling with us for part of the journey."

"Oh, that's okay then," said the manager. "Well, let's be on our way." He turned to the driver.

"He's started looking at the bus," said Robin. "But I don't think he can see you. No, you're all right, he's now turned his gaze back to the hotel entrance."

"I didn't realize you had a brother," said the manager, who was suddenly standing beside them. The coach moved slowly out of the square.

"Neither did I until this morning," mumbled Robin, still looking out of the window. She turned to face her boss. "Yes, I forgot to mention to you that he might be in Switzerland at the same time as the orchestra. I do hope it's not going to cause a problem."

"Not at all," said the manager.

"Adam, this is Stephen Grieg, who, as you will already have gathered, is the orchestra's manager."

"Are you a musician as well?" asked Stephen as he shook Adam's hand.

"No, I can truthfully say that I have never been able to master any instrument," said Adam.

"He's tone deaf," butted in Robin. "Takes after my father. He's in magazines, actually," she continued, enjoying herself.

"Oh, really. Do you publish them or sell them?" inquired Stephen.

"I'm with *Playboy*," said Adam, mentioning the first magazine that came into his head.

"*Playboy*, the magazine that produces those fabulous calendars?"

"What's so special about their calendars?" asked Robin innocently. "I'm sure Adam can get you one."

"Oh, that would be great," said Stephen. "I hope it won't put you to too much trouble."

"No trouble at all," said Robin, leaning over Adam conspiratorially. "Actually, to let you in on a little family secret, there is a rumor at H.Q. that Adam will soon be joining the main board. The youngest member in the publishing company's history, you know."

"How impressive," said the manager, taking a closer look at the orchestra's latest recruit.

"Where shall I send the calendar?" bleated out Adam.

"Oh, direct to the RPO. No need to tell you the address, is there?"

"In a brown paper envelope, no doubt," said Robin. "And don't worry about the year. It's not the dates that he gets worked up about."

"What time are we expecting to reach Frankfurt, Stephen?" shouted a voice from the front.

"Must leave you now," said the manager. "Thanks for the promise of a calendar. Robin's right, of course—any year will do."

"Who taught you to spin a yarn like that?" asked Adam, as soon as he was out of earshot.

"My father," said Robin. "You should have heard him at his best. In a class of his own. The problem was my mother still believed every word."

"He would have been proud of you today."

"Now we've found out what you do for a living," said Robin, "may we learn what's next on the agenda for the youngest director of *Playboy*?"

Adam smiled. "I've started trying to reason like Rosenbaum, and I think he'll stay in Geneva for at least an hour, two at the most, so with luck I'll get a fifty-mile start on him." He unfolded the map across the two seats.

His finger ran along the road the bus was traveling on, and it was Robin who spoke first.

"That means you could make Zurich airport before he has any chance of catching up with you."

"Perhaps," said Adam, "but that would be too much of a

risk. Whoever Rosenbaum is," he went on, abiding by Lawrence's request to be cautious by not letting Robin into his secret, "we now know for certain that he has a professional organization behind him, so I must expect the airports to be the first place he will have covered. And don't forget the Swiss police are still on the lookout for me as well."

"So why don't you come on to Frankfurt with us?" asked Robin. "I can't believe you'll have any trouble from Stephen."

"I've thought about that already but discounted it also as too great a risk," said Adam.

"Why?"

"Because, when Rosenbaum has had time to think about it," said Adam, "the one thing he'll remember is this bus. Once he's found out the direction we're heading in he's sure to come after us."

Robin's eyes returned to the map. "So you'll need to decide where and when to get off."

"Exactly," whispered Adam. "I can risk sixty to seventy miles, but not a lot further."

Robin's finger ran along the little road. "About here," she said, her finger stopping on a little town called Solothurn.

"Looks about the right distance."

"But once you're off the bus, what will you do for transport?"

"I've little choice but to walk or thumb lifts—unless I pinch another car."

"With your luck, Rosenbaum will be the one person who stops to pick you up."

"Yes, I've thought about that as well," said Adam. "I would have to find a long stretch of road where I can see without being seen for about one hundred yards, and then thumb lifts only from British cars or cars with British license plates."

"They taught you a trick or two in the army, didn't they?" said Robin. "But how do you intend to cross the frontier with your passport?"

"That's one of the many problems I haven't yet come up with a solution for."

"If you decide to stay with us," said Robin, "it wouldn't be a problem."

"Why?" asked Adam.

"Because whenever we cross a border they only count the number of people on the bus and the number of passports, and as long as they tally, the customs officials don't bother to check everyone individually. After all, why should they? The RPO is not exactly an unknown quantity. All I would have to do is add your passport to the bundle and mention it to the manager."

"It's a clever idea, but it's not on. If Rosenbaum caught up with me while I'm still on this bus, then I would be left with no escape route."

Robin was silent for a moment. "Once you're on your own, will you contact Lawrence again?"

"Yes. I've got to let him know what happened this morning, because whoever he's dealing with must have a direct line to Rosenbaum."

"Could it be Lawrence himself?"

"Never," said Adam.

"Your loyalty is touching," said Robin, turning to look at him, "but what you actually mean is you don't want to believe it could be Lawrence."

"What are you getting at?"

"Like my mother didn't want to believe that my father was a liar and a drunk. So she turned a blind eye to his little foibles. You know, even when he dropped dead of cirrhosis of the liver, her only words were, 'strange for a man who never drank.'"

Adam thought about his relationship with Lawrence and wondered if you could know someone for twenty years and really not know him at all.

"Just be wary how much you let him know," advised Robin.

They sat in silence as Adam checked the map and went over all the different possible routes he could take once he had left the bus. He decided to aim for the German border and take the long route back to England, from Hamburg or

Bremerhaven, rather than the shorter, more obvious route via Calais or Ostend.

"Got it," said Robin suddenly.

"Got what?" said Adam, looking up from the map.

"How we solve your passport problem," she murmured.

Adam glanced at her hopefully. "If you let me have your passport," she explained, "I'll substitute it for the member of the orchestra who most resembles you. No one will notice anything strange at our end until we're back home in Britain on Sunday night."

"Not a bad idea, if there is anyone who remotely resembles me."

"We'll have to see what we can do," said Robin. She sat bolt upright, her eyes moving slowly from person to person. By the time she had scanned all those in the bus from front to back, a small smile appeared on her face. "There are two of our lot who bear a passable resemblance to you. One is about five years older, and the other is four inches shorter, but you go on working out the safest way of escape while I carry out some sleight of hand. Let me have your passport," she said. Adam handed it over and then watched Robin walk up to the front and sit next to the manager. He was chatting to the driver about the most convenient place to stop for lunch.

"I need to check something in my passport," Robin broke in. "Sorry to bother you."

"No bother. You'll find them all under my seat in a plastic bag," he said, and continued his conversation with the driver.

Robin bent down and started to shuffle through the passports as if searching for her own. She picked out the two she had considered as possible substitutes and compared the photographs. The shorter man's photo looked nothing like Adam. The older man's was at least five years out of date but could have passed for Adam as long as the officials didn't study the date of birth too carefully. She bundled up the passports, placing Adam's in the middle. She then put them back in the plastic bag and returned the bag under the manager's seat.

Robin made her way back to her seat. "Take a look at yourself," she said, slipping the passport over to Adam. He studied the photo.

"Other than the mustache, not a bad likeness, and it's certainly my best chance in the circumstances. But what will happen when you return to London and they find out my passport has been substituted?"

"You'll be back in England long before us," said Robin. "So put this one in an envelope with the calendar and send it direct to the RPO on Wigmore Street, W1, and I'll see that they return yours." Adam vowed to himself that if he ever got back to London, he would become a life subscriber to the Friends of the Royal Philharmonic.

"That seems to have solved one of your problems."

"For the moment at least," said Adam. "I only wish I could take you with me for the rest of the trip."

Robin smiled. "Frankfurt, Berlin, Amsterdam, just in case you get bored. I wouldn't mind meeting up with Rosenbaum. But this time face to face."

"He might just be meeting his match," said Adam.

"Can I have a last look at the icon?" Robin asked, ignoring the comment.

Adam bent down to retrieve his trench coat and slipped the painting out of his map pocket, careful to shield it from anyone else's view. Robin stared into the eyes of Saint George before she spoke again. "When I lay awake last night waiting for you to ravish me, I passed the time trying to fathom out what secret the icon held."

"I thought you were asleep," said Adam, smiling. "When all along, we were both doing the same thing. Anyway, did you come up with any worthwhile conclusions?"

"First, I decided your taste was for male double bass players," said Robin, "or how else could you have resisted me?"

"But what about Saint George and the dragon?" asked Adam, grinning.

"To begin with I wondered if the little pieces of mosaic

made up a code. But the picture is so magnificently executed that the code would have to have been worked out afterward. And that didn't seem credible."

"Good thinking, Batman."

"No, you're Batman. So I wondered if there was another painting underneath. I remembered from my schooldays that Rembrandt and Constable often painted on the top of their paintings, either because they didn't care for their original effort or because, in the case of Rembrandt, he couldn't afford another canvas."

"If that were the answer, only an expert could have carried out the task of removing every piece of paint."

"Agreed," said Robin. "So I dismissed that as well. My third idea was that the crown on the back"—she turned the icon over and stared at the little piece of silver embedded in the wood—"indicates, as your expert suggested, that this is the original by Rublev and not a copy as you have been led to believe."

"I had already considered that," said Adam, "during my sleepless night, and although it would place a far higher value on the work, it is still not enough to explain why Rosenbaum would kill indiscriminately for it."

"Perhaps someone else needs Saint George every bit as much as Rosenbaum does," said Robin.

"But who and why?"

"Because it's not the icon they're after, but something else. Something hidden in or behind the painting."

"That was the first thing I checked," said Adam smugly. "And I'm convinced that it's a solid piece of wood."

"I don't agree with you," said Robin as she began tapping the wood all over like a doctor examining someone's chest. "I've worked with instruments all my life, watched them being made, played with them, even slept with them, and this icon is not solid right through, though God knows how I can prove it. If something is hidden inside, it was never intended to be discovered by laymen like ourselves."

"Quite an imaginative little thing, aren't you?" said Adam.

"Comes naturally," she said as she reluctantly handed the

icon back to Adam. "Do let me know if you ever discover what is inside," she added.

"When I get five minutes to myself I might even spend some time on one or two of my own theories," said Adam, returning the icon to his trench coat pocket.

"Two more kilometers to Solothurn," said Robin, pointing out of the window at a signpost.

Adam buttoned up his coat. "I'll see you off," she said, and they both made their way up the aisle. When Adam reached the front of the coach he asked the driver if he could drop him off just before they reached the next village.

"Sure thing," said the driver without looking back.

Adam turned and shook hands with the manager.

"Leaving us so soon?" said Stephen.

"Afraid so," said Adam. "But thanks for the lift. And I won't forget the calendar." The driver pulled on to the shoulder and pressed a knob, and the hydraulic doors swung back.

" 'Bye, Robin," said Adam, giving her a brotherly kiss on the cheek.

"Good-bye, baby brother," said Robin. "Give my love to mother if you see her before I do." She smiled and waved at him as the door swung closed and the coach returned to the highway to continue its journey on to Frankfurt.

Adam was on his own again.

CHAPTER FOURTEEN

PROFESSOR BRUNWELD was rarely treated with any respect. It was the fate of academics, he had long ago concluded. "The President" was all they had said and he had wondered if he should believe it. Certainly they had got him out of bed in the middle of the night and escorted him silently to the Pentagon. They wanted Brunweld's expert opinion, they assured him. Could it be possible? After Cuba and Dallas he'd begun to believe anything was possible.

He had once read that the Pentagon had as many floors below the ground as above it. He could now confirm that as an established fact.

Once they had handed him the document they left him alone. He studied the clauses for over an hour, and then called them back. It was authentic, he told them, and if the Russians were still in possession of their copy, also signed in 1867, then his adopted country was—what was that awful American expression? ah, yes—in all sorts of trouble.

He began to realize how serious it was when they told him

he would not be allowed to leave the Pentagon until Monday. That didn't surprise him once he'd seen the date on the bottom of the treaty. So it was to be three days of solitude away from his demanding students and chattering wife. He would never have a better opportunity to settle down and read the collected works of Proust.

Romanov knew he couldn't risk standing by the side of the car for much longer. He was too conspicuously dressed not to be noticed by everyone who came out of the hotel. Three minutes later he threw his gray cap on to the backseat and instructed Valchek to get rid of the car and then return to the consulate.

Valchek nodded. He had already carried out Romanov's orders to kill the two British agents as if he had been asked to fix a burst water pipe. The only thing that hadn't run to plan was when Valchek tried to button up the dead chauffeur's uniform. Romanov thought he detected a smirk on Valchek's face when he realized who would have to be the chauffeur.

Romanov slipped into the shadows and waited for another half hour, by which time he was sure the plan must have been aborted from the London end. He hailed a taxi and asked the driver to take him to the Soviet consulate. He didn't notice the taxi driver's look of disbelief at his passenger's chauffeur-clad vision.

Could he really have lost Scott twice? Had he also underestimated him? Once more, and Zaborski was going to require a very convincing explanation.

On his way back to the consulate an image kept flashing across Romanov's mind, but he couldn't make any sense of it. Something had happened outside the hotel that didn't quite fit. If he could only think clearly for a moment, he felt certain it would become clear to him. He kept playing the last thirty minutes over in his mind, as if rewinding the reel of an old film, but some of the frames still remained blurred.

Once Romanov was back in the consulate, Valchek

handed him a large envelope, which had just arrived in the diplomatic pouch from Moscow.

Romanov read the decoded telex a second time, still unable to fathom its possible significance.

"Information has come to light concerning the late Colonel Gerald Scott, D.S.O., O.B.E., M.C. that may prove useful when you make contact with your quarry. Full documentation will be with you by morning, latest. A.I."

Romanov wondered what headquarters had discovered about Scott's father that could possibly prove of interest to him. It was still his avowed intention that the son would be dispatched to join the father long before any further missive from Moscow had arrived.

Romanov thought of his own father and the escape route he had made possible by leaving such a fortune and how, for the sake of advancement, he had betrayed him to the State. Now for the sake of advancement he had to kill Scott and bring home the icon. If he failed. . . . He dismissed both fathers.

"Either Scott's extremely clever, or he's living on an amateur's luck," Romanov said, moving into the small office that had been made available for his use. Valchek, who followed him, did not comment other than to ask what he should do next.

"Tell me what you saw when we were at the hotel."

"What do you mean?" asked Valchek.

"Don't ask questions," said Romanov, changing back into his own clothes, "answer them. Tell me everything you remember seeing, from the moment we drew up outside the hotel."

"We arrived at the Richmond a few minutes before ten," began Valchek, "parked the Mercedes on the far side of the road and waited for Scott to show up. We stayed put for a few minutes after ten, but Scott never materialized."

"No, no, no. Be more specific. Don't just generalize. For instance, do you remember anything unusual taking place while we were waiting?"

"Nothing in particular," said Valchek. "People continually

entering and leaving the hotel—but I'm sure Scott wasn't among them."

"You are fortunate to be so certain. What happened next?" asked Romanov.

"Next? You instructed me to go back to the consulate and wait for you to return."

"What time was that?"

"It must have been about seven minutes past ten. I remember because I checked my watch when that coach left."

"The coach?" said Romanov.

"Yes, the one that was being loaded up with musical instruments. It left about . . ."

"Instruments, that's it," said Romanov. "Now I remember what was worrying me. Cellos, violins, and a double bass that didn't go into the trunk." Valchek looked puzzled but said nothing. "Ring the hotel immediately and find out who was on that bus and where they are heading." Valchek scurried away.

Romanov checked his watch: ten fifty-five. We are going to have to move, and move quickly. He pressed the intercom by the side of the phone. "I want a fast car, and more important, a superb driver." Valchek returned as Romanov replaced the receiver. "The bus was hired by the Royal Philharmonic Orchestra, which is on a European tour . . ."

"Where are they heading next?" asked Romanov.

"Frankfurt."

Adam strolled away from the village, having checked everything with a professional soldier's eye. The main street was deserted but for a little boy who relentlessly kicked a plastic soccer ball into a gap in the hillside which he was using as a goal. The boy turned when he saw Adam and kicked the ball toward him. Adam kicked it back, and the boy took it in his arms, a wide smile appearing on his face. The smile disappeared as he watched Adam continue quickly up the hill. There were only a few old houses on the main road. On one side was a dangerous ravine with tree-covered hills rising in the distance, while on the other side stretched green fields in which cows, bells round their necks, munched happily away. It made Adam feel hungry.

He went further up the road until he came to a sharp bend down the hill. Standing on the corner, he could see down the hill for about half a mile without being seen. He tested the feasibility of his plan for several minutes and soon be-came-expert at picking out British cars or cars with British license plates as far as two or three hundred yards away. It didn't take long to work out how few foreigners bought Brit-ish.

During the next twenty minutes he thumbed optimisti-cally at seven cars with English license plates heading to-ward Zurich, but they all ignored him. He had forgotten just how easy it had been for him when he was a cadet in uni-form. In those days almost everyone would stop. He checked his watch: he could only risk it for a few more min-utes. Three more cars refused to pull up and when a fourth slowed down it only sped away again as Adam ran toward it.

By eleven-twenty Adam decided he could no longer chance being seen on the road. He stared down the ravine, realizing there was no alternative left open to him now but foot. He shrugged and began to climb down one of the steep trails that led into the valley, in the hope of meeting up with the other road that was marked clearly on the map.

He cursed when he looked at the open ground between him and safety. If only he'd started an hour earlier.

"I fear Antarctic has become expendable."

"Why?"

"Because we now know his father was involved in helping Goering to an easy death."

"I don't understand."

"No reason why you should, although it's quite simple. That patriotic stiff-upper-lipped Englishman of yours is the son of the bastard who smuggled a cyanide capsule into Goering's cell at Nuremberg. His reward for service rendered turned out to be the Czar's icon."

"But all the members of the D4 are convinced that he's our only hope."

"I don't give a damn what your D4 thinks because if his father would side with the Germans during a war, why shouldn't the son side with the Russians in peace?"

"Like father, like son."

"Precisely."

"So what am I expected to do?"

"Just keep us briefed as to what the Foreign Office is up to. Our agents in Switzerland will do the rest."

"Faster!" said Romanov, aware that it was not possible, as the ambassador's driver was proving to be a consummate professional. Not once did Romanov feel that he had missed a gap, a light, a chance to overtake. In fact another five kilometers an hour on the speedometer might well have seen them over the precipice. The moment they were on the highway with full lights blazing and the driver's palm almost lodged on the horn, the indicator rarely fell below 130 kilometers per hour. "We must beat them to the border," he kept repeating as he thumped his fist on the leather dashboard. After they had covered one hundred kilometers in fifty-five minutes, the three men began watching ahead of them for the coach, but it was another thirty kilometers before Valchek was able to point ahead and shout, "That must be them, about a kilometer up the hill."

"Force them off the road," said Romanov, his eyes never leaving the bus. The embassy driver swung out to overtake, and once he was in front immediately cut across, forcing the coach driver to throw on his brakes and swerve to the side. Valchek waved dictatorially at the coach driver to slow down, and the man stopped the vehicle just off the road on the edge of the mountain.

"Don't either of you speak. Just leave everything to me," said Romanov, "and remain near the driver in case there's trouble." Romanov jumped out of the car and ran toward the coach, his eyes already searching for anyone who might be attempting to leave the coach. He banged on the door impatiently until the driver pressed a knob and the big doors swung open. Romanov leaped on, with the other two following only paces behind. He took out his passport from an inside pocket, flashed it in the frightened driver's face, and shouted. "Who's in charge here?"

Stephen Grieg stood up. "I am the manager of the company, and therefore . . ."

"Swiss police," said Romanov. Grieg was about to ask a question when Romanov said, "When you left your hotel in Geneva this morning, did you take on any extra passengers?"

"No," said Grieg. Romanov scowled. "Unless you count Robin Beresford's brother."

"Robin Beresford's brother?" inquired Romanov, his eyebrows raising interrogatively.

"Yes," said the manager. "Adam Beresford. But he only traveled with us as far as Solothurn. Then he got off."

"Which one of you is Robin?" said Romanov, staring round a sea of men's faces.

"I am," piped up a voice from the back. Romanov marched down the bus and saw the double bass case, and then everything fitted into place. It always worried him when something was out of context. Yes, that was what hadn't rung true. Why hadn't she put the double bass in the trunk with all the other large instruments? He stared down at the heavy-framed woman who now sat behind the monstrous instrument.

"Your brother is the one called Adam?"

"Yes," said Robin.

"Quite a coincidence."

"I don't understand what you mean," she said, trying not to sound nervous.

"The man I am looking for just happens to be called Adam as well."

"Common enough name," said Robin. "Perhaps you've never read the first chapter of the Bible."

"Six foot one inch, perhaps two inches, dark hair, dark eyes, slim and fit. Not a convincing brother for you," added Romanov, studying her frame.

Robin pushed back her red hair but didn't rise. Romanov could sense from the nervous expressions on the faces around him that it was Scott who had been on the bus.

"Where was your *brother*," he emphasized the word, "intending to go once he had left the coach?" Romanov asked, tapping his passport against his other hand, like a baton.

"I have no idea," said Robin, still not changing her expression from one of uninterested politeness.

"I will give you one more chance to cooperate with me. Where was your brother heading?"

"And I'll tell you once more, I don't know."

"If you refuse to answer my questions," said Romanov, "I shall have to arrest you."

"On whose authority?" asked Robin calmly.

Romanov considered showing her his passport but realized that this girl was sharper than either the driver or the manager.

"With the authority of the Swiss police," Romanov said confidently.

"Then no doubt you'll be happy to show me proof of your identity."

"Don't be insolent," Romanov said sharply. He towered over her.

"It is you who are insolent," said Robin, standing up. "You drive in front of our coach like a lunatic, nearly sending us down the mountain, then the three of you burst in like a bunch of Chicago mobsters, claiming to be Swiss police. I have no idea who you are or what you are, but I'll let you into two secrets. You touch me, and there are forty men on this coach who will beat you and your two cronies into pulp. And even if you managed to get off this bus alive, we are members of the Royal Philharmonic Orchestra of Great Britain, and as such are guests of the Swiss government. In a few moments when we cross the border, we will become the guests of the West German government, so you're about to get yourself onto every front page in the world. Single-handedly, you will bring a totally new meaning to the words 'diplomatic incident.' " She leaned forward and pointing a finger at him, said, "So I'm telling you, whoever you are, in as ladylike fashion as I can, 'Piss off.' "

Romanov stood staring at her for some moments and then backed away as Robin's eyes remained glued on him. When he reached the front he waved at Valchek and the chauffeur, indicating that they should leave the coach. Reluctantly they obeyed him. The coach driver closed the door the moment Romanov's foot touched the ground, and he quickly moved into first gear and drove back on to the highway.

The entire orchestra turned round and gave Robin the kind of ovation normally reserved for the entrance of the conductor.

It went unappreciated. Robin had collapsed back into her seat, shaking uncontrollably, only too aware that not one of the forty men on that coach would have lifted a finger against Rosenbaum.

Sir Morris Youngfield glanced round the table: everyone was in place despite the few minutes' notice the head of the D4 had given them.

"Let's hear the latest report," said Sir Morris, looking up at his number two, who was once again seated at the far end of the table.

"Not clever, sir, I'm afraid," began Lawrence. "Two of our most experienced agents were selected to pick up Scott at the Richmond Hotel as planned and then take him to the safety of the British consulate."

"So what happened?" asked Sir Morris.

"No one at our Geneva office can be certain. Our men certainly never turned up at the hotel, and they haven't been seen since."

"What are the Swiss police saying?" asked Busch.

"They are not being very helpful," said Lawrence, turning to the American. "They are aware that we are not the only foreign power involved, and as is their custom in such circumstances, they have no intention of being seen to favor either side."

"Bloody Swiss," said Snell with feeling.

"And where do we imagine Scott is now?" asked Matthews.

"We've also drawn a blank on that," said Lawrence. Matthews smiled at Lawrence's embarrassment. "We feel certain he must have boarded the coach with the girl"—he looked down at the sheet of paper on the table in front of him—"Robin Beresford. But he wasn't on it when we were waiting for them at the border. The orchestra is due at their Frankfurt hotel in about one hour, so we will be able to find out more then. The German police are being far more cooperative," Lawrence added.

"Meanwhile what else are *we* doing?" asked Sir Morris.

"Checking all the usual places as well as keeping a close eye on Romanov, who, incidentally, turned up on the French border last night. One of our old hands recognized him despite the fact that he's cut his hair very short; doesn't suit him, evidently."

"So Scott could be anywhere by now?" said Matthews. "Do you think he's still in Switzerland or managed to cross one of the borders?"

Lawrence hesitated. "I have no idea," he said without expression.

Sir Morris stared at him from the far end of the table but didn't comment.

"Do you think he'll contact you again?" asked Snell.

"Almost certainly, if he's still alive."

"If Romanov is still in Geneva, Scott must be alive," said Busch. "Because the moment he gets his hands on the icon he will head east."

"Agreed," said Lawrence, "and we have men stationed at the airport checking every flight out to the east. I therefore suggest we follow up any further leads and assemble again tomorrow at seven A.M. unless Scott contacts me before then."

Sir Morris nodded and rose to leave. Everyone stood.

"Thank you, gentlemen," he said, and walked toward the far end of the room. As he passed Lawrence, he murmured, "Perhaps you could come to my office when you have a moment."

Adam slipped and stumbled the last few yards down the ravine before finally landing with a bump on his backside. His hands were cut and bleeding in several places, his trousers torn and smeared with clay and earth. He sat still for about two minutes trying to get his breath back as he looked back up toward the road. He had taken just under an hour to cover what a stone could have managed in three seconds. Still, there had been one advantage: no one could have seen him from the road. He gazed across the valley ahead. Anyone would be able to see him now, but he had left himself with no alternative.

Judge by eye, check by map. The map wasn't much help, but he estimated the distance to the far ridge to be about two more miles. At least the map had promised him there was a road, hidden from sight on the other side of the ridge. He studied the terrain—rolling green fields, no hedgerows to shield him, and then one wide, shallow river. He reckoned he could cover the ground to the road in about twenty minutes. He checked that the icon was securely in place and then set off at an even pace.

Romanov had hardly uttered a word since the three men had been unceremoniously removed from the coach, and Valchek and the driver certainly hadn't ventured any opinions. Romanov knew the girl had called his bluff, and he couldn't afford a further diplomatic incident which would undoubtedly be reported back to his chairman in Moscow. But Romanov would never forget the girl with the man's name.

Solothurn was about forty kilometers back in the direction they had already traveled, and the driver could have completed the journey in about twenty minutes had Romanov not insisted on slowing down as they passed every vehicle that traveled toward them. They checked the occupants of each vehicle on the other side of the road, just in case Scott had managed to thumb a lift. It was a necessary precaution in Romanov's judgment, but it meant a total time of thirty-one minutes before they arrived back in Solothurn. At least Romanov felt confident Scott wasn't heading for the German border—unless he had been very well disguised or traveled in the trunk of a car.

As soon as they reached Solothurn Romanov instructed the driver to leave the car in the middle of the village while they split up to see if they could discover any clues as to the route Scott might have taken. None of the locals whom they questioned had seen anyone resembling Scott that morning, and Romanov was beginning to wonder which border he should now head for when he turned around and saw the driver kicking a soccer ball back to a little boy. Romanov ran down the hill and was about to remonstrate with him when the boy turned and kicked the ball hard at the Russian. Romanov trapped the ball automatically and kicked it firmly past the boy and into the goal. Romanov turned toward the driver and would not have looked back if the ball had not reappeared at his feet. He picked it up in anger and was just about to throw it back at him when he saw the boy's hopeful smile. Romanov held the ball high above his head. The boy ran up and jumped toward the ball, but however hard he tried, he couldn't reach it.

"Have you seen any strangers this morning?" he asked in slow, deliberate French.

"Yes, yes," said the boy. "But he didn't score a goal."

"Where did he go?" asked Romanov.

"Up the hill," said the boy. To the child's dismay, Romanov dropped the ball and began to run. Valchek and the driver followed after him.

"*Non, non,*" cried the little boy, who followed after them. Romanov looked back to see the boy was standing on the spot where Adam had been thumbing lifts, pointing out over the ravine.

Romanov quickly turned to the driver. "Get the car, I need the glasses and the map." The driver ran back down the hill once again, followed by the boy. A few minutes later the Mercedes drew up by Romanov's side. The driver jumped out and handed the glasses over to Romanov, while Valchek spread a map out on the hood of the car.

Romanov focused the binoculars and began to sweep the hills in the distance. It was several minutes before the glasses stopped and settled upon a brown speck climbing up the farthest hill.

"The rifle," were Romanov's only words.

Valchek ran to the trunk of the car and took out a Dragunov sniper's rifle with telescopic sights. He assembled the long, slim weapon with its distinctive wooden skeleton stock and checked that it was loaded. He then raised it, moved it around until it felt comfortable nestled in his shoulder, and swept the ground in front of him until he too focused on Scott. Romanov followed Adam's relentless stride with the binoculars; Valchek's arm moved with him, keeping the same pace.

"Kill him," said Romanov. Valchek was grateful for the clear windless day as he kept the rifle sight in the middle of the Englishman's back, waited for three more strides, then slowly squeezed the trigger. Adam had almost reached the top of the ridge when the bullet tore through him. He fell to the ground with a thud. Romanov smiled and lowered the binoculars.

Adam knew exactly what had ripped through his shoulder and where the shot must have come from. He instinctively rolled over until he reached the nearest tree. And then the pain began. Although the bullet had lost a lot of its power at such a distance, it still stung like an adder's bite, and blood was already beginning to seep through his trench coat from the torn muscle. He turned his head and gazed back behind him. He could see no one, but he knew Romanov must be standing there waiting to take a second shot.

Turning with difficulty, he looked back up toward the edge of the hill. Only thirty yards to the safety of the ridge, but he would have to run over the top, remaining exposed for several vital seconds. Even if he made it, Romanov would still be able to reach him by car within thirty minutes.

Nevertheless, that was his one chance. Slowly, very slowly, he crawled inch by inch up the ridge, thankful for the tree that he could still use as protection. One arm followed one leg, like a beached crab. Once he had covered ten yards, he knew the angle would be against him and Romanov would have a flat, slow-moving target to aim at. He moved four more lengths of his body and stopped.

You can't hold a rifle up on your shoulder forever, Adam thought. He counted to two hundred slowly.

"He's going to make a run for it," Romanov told Valchek, as he raised his glasses, "which will give you about three seconds. I'll shout the moment he moves." Romanov kept the glasses trained on the tree. Suddenly Adam jumped up and sprinted as though it were the last twenty meters of an Olympic final. Romanov shouted, "Now," and Valchek pulled the rifle up into his shoulder, focused on the moving man, and squeezed the trigger as Adam threw himself over the ridge. The second bullet whistled by the side of Adam's head.

Romanov cursed, as he stared through the binoculars, knowing that Valchek had missed. He turned to the open map. The others joined him around the car as he began to consider the alternatives. "He should reach that road in about ten minutes," he said, putting his finger in the middle of a small red line that ran between Neuchâtel and the French border. "Unless the first bullet hit him, in which case it could take him longer. So how long will it take you to get to that border?" Romanov asked the driver.

The chauffeur studied the map. "About twenty-five, at most thirty minutes, Comrade Major," came back the reply.

Romanov turned and looked back toward the hills. "Thirty minutes, Scott, that's how long you've got to live."

When the car sped away, the little boy ran home as fast as

he could. He quickly told his mother everything he had seen. She smiled understandingly. Only children had such imaginations.

When Adam looked up, he was relieved to see the road was only about a mile away. He jogged toward it at a steady pace, but found that the running caused him even more discomfort. He was anxious to stop and check the wound but waited till he reached the road. The bullet had torn through the outer flesh of his shoulder muscle, leaving him in considerable pain. An inch lower, and he would have been unable to move. He was relieved to see that the blood had only made a small stain on his trench coat. He folded a handkerchief in four and placed it between his shirt and the wound. He knew he daren't risk a hospital. As long as he could get to a pharmacy by nightfall, he felt he could take care of the problem himself.

Adam checked the map. He was now only a few kilometers from the French border and decided, because of the wound, to cross into France as quickly as possible rather than keep to his original plan of going up through Basle and on to Bremerhaven.

Desperately he began to thumb at any car that passed, no longer bothering with the nationality of the license plates. He felt he was safe for about twenty minutes but after that he would have to disappear back into the hills. Unfortunately there were far fewer cars driving toward the French border than there had been on the Basle road, and they all ignored his plea. He feared that the time was fast approaching for him to return to the hills when a yellow Citroen drew to the side of the road a few yards ahead of him.

By the time Adam had reached the car the woman in the passenger seat had already wound down the window.

"Where—are—you—going?" asked Adam, pronouncing each word slowly and carefully.

The driver leaned across, took a lengthy look at Adam,

and said in a broad Yorkshire accent, "We're on our way to Dijon. Any use to you, lad?"

"Yes, please," said Adam, relieved that his scruffy appearance had not put them off.

"Then jump in the back with my daughter."

Adam obeyed. The Citroen moved off as Adam checked out of the back window; he was relieved to see an empty road stretching out behind him.

"Jim Hardcastle's the name," said the man, as he moved the car into third gear. Jim appeared to have a large, warm smile perpetually imprinted on his chubby red face. His dark ginger hair went straight back and was plastered down with Brylcreem. He wore a Harris tweed jacket and an open-necked shirt that revealed a little red triagle of hair. It looked to Adam as if he had given up attempts to do anything about his waistline. "And this is the wife, Betty," he said, gesturing with his elbow toward the woman in the front seat. She turned toward Adam, revealing the same ruddy cheeks and warm smile. Her hair was dyed blonde, but the roots remained an obstinate black. "And sitting next to you is our Linda," Jim Hardcastle added, almost as an afterthought. "Just left school and going to work for the local council, aren't you, Linda?" Linda nodded sulkily. Adam stared at the young girl, whose first experiment with makeup hadn't worked that well. The dark overlined eye shadow and the pink lipstick did not help what Adam considered was an attractive girl probably in her late teens. "And what's your name, lad?"

"Dudley Hulme," said Adam, recalling the name on his new passport. "And are you on holiday?" he asked, trying to keep his mind off the throbbing shoulder.

"Mixing business with pleasure," said Jim. "But this part of the trip is rather special for Betty and myself. We flew to Genoa on Saturday and hired the car to tour Italy. First we traveled up through the Simplon Pass. It's a bit breathtaking after our home town of Hull."

Adam would have asked for details, but Jim didn't reckon on any interruptions. "I'm in mustard, you see. Export director for Colman's, and we're on our way to the annual conference of the IMF. You may have heard of us." Adam nodded knowingly. "International Mustard Federation," Jim added. Adam almost wanted to laugh, but because of the pain in his shoulder, managed to keep a straight face.

"This year they've elected me president of the IMF, the high point of my career in mustard, you might say. And, if I may be so bold as to suggest, an honor for Colman's as well, the finest mustard in the world," he added, as if he said it at least a hundred times a day. "As president I have to preside over the conference meetings and chair the annual dinner. Tonight I shall be making a speech of welcome to delegates from all over the world."

"How fascinating," winced Adam, as the car went over a pothole.

"It certainly is," said Jim. "People have no idea how many makes of mustards there are." He paused for a second and then said, "One hundred and forty-three. There's no doubt the Frogs make one or two good attempts, and even the Krauts don't do too badly, but there's still nothing to beat Colman's. British is best after all, I always say. Probably the same in your line of country," said Jim. "By the way, what is your line of country?"

"I'm in the army," said Adam.

"What's a soldier doing thumbing a lift on the borders of Switzerland?"

"Can I speak to you in confidence?" asked Adam.

"Mum's the word," said Jim. "We Hardcastles know how to keep our traps shut."

In the case of Jim's wife and daughter, Adam had no proof to the contrary. "I'm a captain in the Royal Wessex, at present on a NATO exercise," began Adam. "I was dumped off the coast at Brindisi in Italy last Sunday with a false passport and ten English pounds. I have to be back in barracks at Aldershot by midnight Saturday." When he saw the look of approbation appear on Jim's face, he felt even Robin would have been proud of him. Mrs. Hardcastle turned around to take a more careful look at him.

"I knew you were an officer the moment you opened your mouth," said Jim. "You couldn't have fooled me. I was a sergeant in the Royal Army Service Corps in the last war myself. Doesn't sound much, but I did my bit for the old country." The acronym for the corps—"Rob All Serving Comrades"—flashed through Adam's mind. "Have you seen any action yourself, Dudley?" Jim was asking.

"A little in Malaya," said Adam.

"I missed that one," said Jim. "After the big one was over, I went back into mustard. So where's the problem in getting you back to England?"

"There are about eight of us trying to reach Aldershot, and a thousand Americans trying to stop us."

"Yanks," said Jim with disdain. "They only join wars just as we're about to win them. All medals and glory, that lot. No, I mean is there any real problem?"

"Yes, the border officials have been briefed that eight British officers are attempting to get over into France, and the Swiss love to be the ones to pull us in. Only two officers out of twelve made it back to barracks last year," said Adam, warming to his own theme. "Both were promoted within weeks."

"The Swiss," said Jim. "They're even worse than the Americans. They don't even join in a war—happy to fleece both sides at the same time. They won't pick you up, lad, believe me. I'll see to that."

"If you can get me across the border, Mr. Hardcastle, I'm confident I will be able to make it all the way back to Aldershot."

"Consider it done, lad."

The fuel indicator was flashing red. "How many kilometers left when that happens?" demanded Romanov.

"About twenty, Comrade Major," said the driver.

"Then we should still make the French border?"

"Perhaps it might be safer to stop and fill up," suggested the driver.

"There is no time for safety," said Romanov. "Go faster."

"Yes, Comrade Major," said the driver, who decided it was not the occasion to point out they would run out of petrol even more quickly if he was made to push the car to its limits.

"Why didn't you fill the tank up this morning, you fool?" said Romanov.

"I thought I was only taking the consul to lunch at the town hall today, and I had intended to fill the tank up during my lunch hour."

"Just pray for your sake that we reach the border," said Romanov. "Faster."

The Mercedes touched 140 kilometers per hour, and Romanov relaxed only when he saw a sign saying, *Rappelle Douane Dix Kilomètres*. A few minutes later a smile grew on his face as they passed the five-kilometer sign, and then suddenly the engine spluttered as it tried helplessly to continue turning over at the speed the pressed down accelerator was demanding. The indicator on the speedometer started to drop steadily as the engine continued to chug. The driver turned off the ignition and threw the gear lever into neutral. The sheer momentum of the heavy Mercedes took them another kilometer before the car slowed to a complete stop.

Romanov did not even look at the driver as he jumped out of the car and began running the last three kilometers toward the border.

"I've come up with an idea," said Jim, as they passed a signpost warning drivers that the border was only two kilometers away.

"What's that, sir?" asked Adam, who could now feel his shoulder beating like a steady tune hammered out by a child on a tin drum. "When it comes to the time for us to present our passports, you put your arm round Linda and start cuddling her. Leave the rest to me."

Mrs. Hardcastle turned round and gave Adam a much closer look as Linda went scarlet. Adam looked across at the miniskirted, pink-lipped Linda and felt embarrassed by the predicament her father had placed his daughter in. "Don't argue with me, Dudley," continued Jim confidently. "I promise you what I have in mind will work." Adam made no comment and neither did Linda. When they reached the Swiss border a few moments later, Adam could see that there were two checkpoints about one hundred yards apart. Drivers were avoiding one line of traffic in which a row was going on between a customs official and an irate lorry driver. Jim drove up straight behind the gesticulating Frenchman. "Give me your passport, Dudley," he said. Adam handed over the violinist's passport.

Why did you choose this line? Adam wanted to ask.

"I chose this line," continued Jim, "because by the time it comes for our passports to be inspected I reckon the customs officer will be only too happy to allow us through without much fuss." And as if in reaction to his logic, a long line started to form behind Jim, but still the argument raged in front of them. Adam remained alert, continually looking out of the back window, waiting for the moment when Romanov would appear. When he turned back, he was relieved to find that the lorry in front of them was being told to pull over into the side and wait.

Jim drove quickly up to the customs post. "Get necking, you two," he said.

Up until that point, Adam had kept his hands hidden in his trench coat pockets because they were so scratched and bruised. But he obeyed Jim and took Linda in his arms and kissed her perfunctorily, one eye still watching for Romanov. To his surprise she parted his lips and began exploring inside his mouth with her tongue. Adam thought about protesting but realized there was no way he could make it sound gallant or credible.

"The wife, the daughter, and the future son-in-law," said Jim, handing over the four passports.

The policeman started to check.

"What was all the trouble about, officer?"

"Nothing for you to worry about," said the policeman,

flicking through the passports. "I hope it hasn't inconvenienced you."

"No, no," said Jim. "They didn't even notice," he said, pointing over his shoulder and laughing.

The policeman shrugged, and handing the passports back, he said, "*Allez*," waving them on.

"Sharp-as-Mustard Jim, that's what they call me in Hull." He looked over his shoulder toward Adam. "You can stop that now, Dudley, thank you." Adam felt Linda release him with some reluctance.

She glanced at him shyly, then turned toward her father. "But we still have to go over the French border, don't we?"

"We have already been alerted to look for him and I can assure you he hasn't been through this post," said the senior customs officer. "Otherwise one of my men would have spotted him. But if you want to double-check, be my guest."

Romanov went quickly from officer to officer, showing them the blown-up photograph of Adam, but none of them could recall anyone resembling him. Valchek joined him a few minutes later and confirmed that Scott was not in any of the cars still waiting to be allowed over the border and that the Mercedes was being pushed into the border garage.

"Is it back to the hills, Comrade Major?" asked Valchek.

"Not yet. I want to be absolutely certain he hasn't managed to cross the border."

The senior official emerged from his post in the center of the road. "Any luck?" he asked.

"No," said Romanov glumly. "You seem to be right."

"I thought as much. If any of my men had let the Englishman through, they would have been looking for a new job by now."

Romanov nodded in acknowledgment. "Could I have missed any of your staff?"

"Doubt it—unless there's a couple of them taking a break. If so, you'll find them in the bar about a hundred meters up toward the French border point."

Four customs officers and a French waitress were the only people to be found in the bar. Two of the officers were playing pool while the other two sat at a corner table, drinking coffee. Romanov took the photo out once more and showed it to the two men at the pool table. They both shook their heads in an uninterested fashion and returned to sinking the multicolored balls.

The two Russians made their way to the bar. Valchek passed Romanov a cup of coffee and a sandwich, which he took over to the table where the other two border guards sat. One of them was telling his colleague the trouble he had had with a French truck driver who was trying to smuggle Swiss watches over the border. Romanov pushed the photograph of Scott across the table.

"Have you seen this man today?"

Neither showed any sign of recognition, and the younger one quickly returned to his story. Romanov sipped his coffee and began to consider whether he should make a run for Basle or call for reinforcements to sweep the hills. Then he noticed how the young man's eyes kept returning to the photo. He asked once again if he had seen Scott.

"No, no," said the young officer, a little too quickly. In Moscow Romanov would have had a yes out of him within minutes, but he would have to follow a more gentle approach here.

"How long ago?" Romanov asked quietly.

"What do you mean?" asked the policeman.

"How long ago?" repeated Romanov in a firmer voice.

"It wasn't him," said the officer, sweat now appearing on his forehead.

"If it wasn't him, how long ago wasn't it him?"

The officer hesitated. "Twenty minutes, maybe thirty."

"What make of vehicle?"

The young officer hesitated. "A Citroen, I think."

"Color?"

"Yellow."

"Other passengers?"

"Three. Looked like a family. Mother, father, daughter.

He was in the back with the daughter. The father said they were engaged."

Romanov had no more questions.

Jim Hardcastle managed to keep a one-sided conversation going for over an hour.

"Naturally," he said, "the IMF holds its annual conference in a different city every year. Last year it was Denver in Colorado, and next year it'll be at Perth in Australia, so I manage to get around a bit. But as the export man you have to get used to a lot of travel."

"I'm sure you do," said Adam, trying to concentrate on his benefactor's words while his shoulder throbbed on.

"I'm only president for a year, of course," continued Jim. "But I have plans to ensure that my fellow delegates won't forget 1966 in a hurry."

"I'm sure they won't," said Adam.

"I shall point out to them that Colman's has had another record year on the export side."

"How impressive."

"Yes, but I must admit that most of our profits are left on the side of the plate," he said, laughing.

Adam laughed as well but sensed that Mrs. Hardcastle and Linda might have heard the line before.

"I've been thinking, Dudley, and I'm sure the wife would agree with me, that it would be most acceptable to us if you felt able to join the presidential table for dinner tonight—as my guest, of course." Mrs. Hardcastle nodded, as did Linda, with enthusiasm.

"I can think of nothing that would give me greater pleasure," said Adam. "But I fear my commanding officer might not be quite as delighted to hear I had stopped on the way back to England to take in a party. I do hope you'll understand."

"If he is anything like my old C.O. I certainly do," said Jim. "Still, if you should ever be Hull way, look us up." He took a card out of his top pocket and passed it over his shoulder.

Adam studied the embossed letters and wondered what MIFT stood for. He didn't ask.

"Where in Dijon would you like to be dropped off?" asked Jim as he drove into the outskirts of the town.

"Anywhere near the center that's convenient for you," replied Adam.

"Just holler when it suits you, then," said Jim. "Of course, I always maintain that a meal without mustard . . ."

"Can you drop me on the next corner?" said Adam suddenly.

"Oh," said Jim, sad to be losing such a good listener. And he reluctantly drew the car up alongside the curb.

Adam kissed Linda on the cheek before getting out of the back. He then shook hands with Mr. and Mrs. Hardcastle.

"Nice to have made your acquaintance," said Jim. "If you change your mind, you'll find us at the hotel. . . . Is that blood on your shoulder, lad?"

"Just a graze from a fall—nothing to worry about. Wouldn't want the Americans to think they'd got the better of me."

"No, no, of course not," said Jim. "Well, good luck."

As the car moved off Adam stood on the pavement watching them disappear. He smiled and tried to wave, then, turning, he walked quickly down a side street looking for a shopping center. Within moments he was in the center of town, relieved to find that all the shops were still open. He began to search up and down the street for a green cross above a door. Adam had to walk only fifty yards before he spotted one. He entered the shop tentatively and checked the shelves.

A tall man with short fair hair wearing a long leather coat stood in the corner with his back to the entrance. Adam froze. Then the man turned round, frowning at the packet of tablets he wanted to purchase, while at the same time rubbing his thick Gallic mustache.

Adam walked up to the counter.

"Do you speak English, by any chance?" he asked the druggist, trying to sound confident.

"Passable, I hope," came back the reply.

"I need some iodine, cotton wool, a bandage, and heavy adhesive tape. I fell and bruised my shoulder on a rock," Adam explained.

The druggist quickly put the order together without showing much interest.

"This is what you require. That will be twenty-three francs," said the druggist.

"Will Swiss do?"

"Certainly."

"Is there a hotel anywhere nearby?" asked Adam.

"Around the next corner, on the other side of the square."

Adam thanked him, handed over the Swiss notes, and then left the pharmacy in search of the hotel. The Hotel Frantel was, as promised, only a short distance away. He walked across the square and up the steps into the hotel to find several people were waiting at reception to be checked in. Adam flung his trench coat over his bloodstained shoulder and walked past them as he checked the signs on the wall. He then strode across the entrance hall as though he were a guest of several days' standing. He followed the sign he had been looking for, which took him down a flight of stairs, to come head on with three further signs. The first had the silhouette of a man on the door, the second a woman, the third a wheelchair.

He opened the third tentatively and was surprised to find behind it nothing more than a sizable square room with a high-seated lavatory against the wall. Adam locked himself in and let his trench coat fall to the ground.

He rested for a few minutes before slowly stripping to the waist. He then ran a basinful of warm water.

Adam was thankful for the endless first-aid seminars every officer had to go through, never believing they will serve any purpose. Twenty minutes later the pain had subsided, and he even felt comfortable.

He picked up his coat with his right hand and tried to

throw it back over his shoulder. The very movement caused
the icon to fall out of the map pocket and onto the tiled
floor. As it hit the ground, the sound made Adam fear it must
have broken in half. He stared down anxiously and then fell
to his knees.

The icon had split open like a book.

CHAPTER
FIFTEEN

WHEN ADAM RETURNED to the Hotel Frantel an hour later few guests would have recognized the man who had crept in earlier that afternoon.

He wore a new shirt, trousers, tie, and a double-breasted blazer that wouldn't be fashionable in Britain for at least another year. Even the raincoat had been ditched because the icon fitted snugly into the blazer pocket. He considered the shop had probably given him a poor exchange rate for his traveler's checks, but that was not what had been occupying his mind for the past hour.

He booked himself into a single room in the name of Dudley Hulme and a few minutes later took the lift to the third floor.

Lawrence picked the phone up even before Adam heard the second ring.

"It's me," said Adam.

"Where are you?" were Lawrence's first words.

"I'll ask the questions," said Adam.

"I can understand how you feel," said Lawrence, "but . . ."

"No buts. You must be aware by now that someone on your so-called team has a direct line to the Russians because it was Romanov and his friends who were waiting for me outside the hotel in Geneva, not your lot."

"We realize that now," said Lawrence.

"We?" said Adam. "Who are we? Because I'm finding it rather hard to work out who's on my side."

"You don't believe that . . ."

"When you get your girlfriend murdered, chased across Europe by professional killers, shot at and . . ."

"Shot at?" said Lawrence.

"Yes, your friend Romanov took a shot at me today, hit me in the shoulder. Next time we meet I intend it to be the other way round, and it won't be the shoulder."

"There won't be a next time," said Lawrence, "because we'll get you out safely if you'll only let me know where you are."

The memory of Robin's words, "Just be wary of how much you let him know," stopped Adam from telling Lawrence his exact location.

"Adam, for God's sake, you're on your own. If you don't trust me, who can you trust? I admit it looks as if we let you down. But it won't happen again."

There was another long silence before Adam said, "I'm in Dijon."

"Why Dijon?"

"Because the only person who would give me a lift was going to a mustard conference in Dijon."

Lawrence couldn't stop himself smiling. "Give me your number, and I'll phone you back within an hour."

"No," said Adam, "I'll phone *you* back in one hour."

"Adam, you've got to show some trust in me."

"Not now that I know what it is you're all after, I can't afford to trust anybody."

Adam replaced the phone and stared down at the icon, which lay open on the bed. It wasn't the signature of Gorchakov or Seward that worried him. It was the date—June 20, 1966—that read like a death warrant.

* * *

"Goodnight, sir," said the doorkeeper as the senior civil servant left Century House that evening. "Another late night for you," he added sympathetically. He acknowledged the doorman by raising his rolled umbrella a few inches. It *had* been another late night, but at least they had caught up with Scott again. He was beginning to develop quite a respect for the man. But how they failed to pick him up in Geneva still required a fuller explanation than the one Lawrence Pemberton had supplied the D4 with that afternoon.

He set off at a brisk pace toward Old Kent Road, conspicuous in his black coat and pin-striped trousers. He tapped his umbrella nervously before hailing a passing taxi.

"Dillon's bookshop, Malet Street," he told the driver, before getting in the back. Already seven-thirty, but he still wouldn't be too late, and a few minutes either way wasn't going to make that much difference. Pemberton had agreed to remain at his desk until all the loose ends were tied up and he was sure that nothing could go wrong this time. He allowed himself a wry smile as he thought how they had all accepted his plan. It had the double advantage of ensuring enough time for them to get their best men into position, while keeping Scott well out of sight in a deserted hideaway. He hoped that this was the last time they would expect him to come up with an original proposal.

"Eight shillings, guv'nor," said the taxi driver, as he drew up outside Dillon's. He handed over the money and added a six-penny tip. He stood staring at the window of the university bookshop, watching the reflection of the taxi as it moved off. The moment the taxi had turned the corner onto Gower Street he began walking away. In moments he had reached a side road, onto which he turned. Ridgmount Gardens was one of those streets that even London cabbies had to think about for a few moments. He had walked only a matter of yards before he disappeared down some stone steps to a basement flat. He inserted a Yale key in the front door lock, turned it quickly, stepped inside, and closed the door behind him.

During the next twenty minutes he made two telephone calls, one international, one local, and then had a bath. He emerged back on Ridgmount Gardens less than one hour later dressed in a casual brown suit, pink floral open shirt, and brown brogue shoes. The parting in his hair had changed sides. He returned to Dillon's on foot and hailed another taxi.

"The British Museum," he instructed the driver, as he stepped into the back. He checked his watch: nearly ten past eight. Scott would be fully briefed by now, he thought, although his associates would be already on the way back to Dijon, as his plan had allowed for a two-hour delay.

The taxi drew up outside the British Museum. He paid and walked up the twelve steps in front of the museum, admiring the Byzantine architecture as he regularly did each week, before walking back down again to hail another taxi.

"Middlesex Hospital, please," was all he said. The taxi executed a U-turn and headed west.

Poor bastard. If Scott hadn't opened that envelope in the first place, the icon would have ended up with its rightful owner.

"Shall I drive up to the entrance?" asked the cabbie.

"Yes, please."

A moment later he strolled into the hospital, checked the board on the wall as if he were looking for a certain ward, then walked back out on to the street. From Middlesex Hospital it always took him about three minutes at a steady pace to reach Charlotte Street, where he stopped outside a house and pressed a buzzer attached to a little intercom.

"Are you a member?" inquired a voice suspiciously.

"Yes."

On the hour Adam phoned and listened carefully to all Lawrence had to say.

"I'll take one more risk," said Adam, "but if Romanov turns

up this time, I'll hand over the icon to him personally and with it a piece of property so valuable that no amount of money the Americans could offer would be sufficient to purchase it back."

When Adam put the phone down Lawrence and Sir Morris played the conversation back over again and again.

"I think *property*'s the key word," said Sir Morris.

"Agreed," said Lawrence, "but what piece of property could be that valuable to both the Russians and the Americans?"

Sir Morris began slowly revolving the globe that stood by the side of his desk.

"What does that buzz mean?" asked Romanov. "We are not running out of petrol again, are we?"

"No, sir," said the chauffeur. "It's the new calling device now fixed to all ambassadorial cars. It means they expect me to check in."

"Turn round and go back to that petrol station we passed a couple of miles ago," Romanov said quietly.

Romanov started tapping the dashboard impatiently as he waited for the petrol station to reappear on the horizon. The sun was going down quickly, and he feared it would be dark within the hour. They had traveled about ninety kilometers beyond Dijon, and neither he nor Valchek had even seen a yellow Citroen going either way.

"Fill up again while I phone Geneva," Romanov said the moment he saw the petrol station. He ran to the phone booth while Valchek still kept a watchful eye on the passing traffic.

"I am answering your signal," said Romanov when he was put through to the euphemistically titled second secretary.

"We've had another call from Mentor," said the second secretary. "How far are you from Dijon?"

* * *

The member stumbled about the dimly lit room until he came across an unoccupied table wedged up against a pillar in one corner. He sat down on a little leather stool by its side. He swiveled around nervously, as he always did when waiting for someone to bring him his usual malt whiskey on the rocks. When the drink was placed on the table in front of him he sipped at it, in between trying to discover if there were any new faces spread around the dark room. Not an easy task, as he refused to put on his glasses. His eyes eventually became accustomed to the dim light thrown out by the long red fluorescent bulb that stretched above the bar. All he could make out were the same old faces staring at him hopefully; but he wanted something new.

The proprietor, noticing that a regular customer had remained on his own, came and sat opposite him on the other little stool. The member never could get himself to look the man in the eyes.

"I've got someone who's very keen to meet you," whispered the proprietor.

"Which one?" he asked, looking up once more to check the faces at the bar.

"Leaning on the jukebox in the corner. The tall, slim one. And he's young," added the proprietor. He looked toward the blaring machine. A pleasing new face smiled at him. He smiled nervously back.

"Was I right?" asked the proprietor.

"Is he safe?" was all he asked.

"No trouble with this one. Upper-class lad, right out of a top-drawer public school. Just wants to earn a bit of pocket money on the side."

"Fine." The member took a sip of whiskey.

The proprietor walked over to the jukebox. The member watched him talking to the young man. The boy downed his drink, hesitated for a moment, then strolled across the crowded floor to take the empty stool.

"My name is Piers," the young man said.

"Mine's Jeremy," the member said.

"A gentle name," said Piers. "I've always liked the name Jeremy."

"Would you care for a drink?"

"A dry martini, please," said Piers.

The member ordered a dry martini and another malt whiskey. The waiter hurried away. "I haven't seen you here before."

"No, it's only my second time," said Piers. "I used to work in Soho, but it's got to be so rough lately, you never know who you might end up with."

The drinks arrived and the member took a quick gulp.

"Would you like to dance?" asked Piers.

"It's an emergency," the voice said. "Is the tape on?"

"I'm listening."

"Antarctic is in Dijon, and he's found out what's in the icon."

"And did he give them any clue?"

"No, all he told Pemberton was that he was in possession of a piece of property so valuable that no amount of money we could offer would be sufficient to purchase it back."

"Indeed," said the voice.

"The British think the important word is *property*," said the caller.

"They're wrong," said the voice on the other end of the line. "It's *purchase*."

"How can you be so sure?"

"Because the Russian ambassador in Washington has requested a meeting with the Secretary of State on 20 June, and he's bringing with him a bullion order to the value of 712 million dollars in gold."

"So where does that leave us?"

"On our way to Dijon so that we can be sure to lay our hands on that icon before the British or the Russians. The Russians obviously feel confident that it will soon be in their possession. So my bet is that they must already be on the way."

"But I've already agreed to go along with the British plan."

"Try not to forget which side you're on, Commander."

"Yes, sir. But what are we going to do about Antarctic if we get our hands on the icon?"

"It's only the icon we're after. Once that's in our possession, Antarctic is expendable."

Adam checked his watch: a few minutes after seven.

It was time for him to leave because he had decided not to carry out Lawrence's instructions to the letter. He intended to be waiting for *them*, and not as Lawrence had planned. He locked the bedroom door and returned to reception, where he paid for the use of the room and the telephone calls he had made.

"Thank you," he said to the receptionist, and turned to leave.

"Dudley." Adam froze on the spot.

"Dudley," the voice boomed again. "I almost didn't recognize you. Did you change your mind?" A hand thumped him on the shoulder—at least it wasn't the left shoulder, he thought—as he stared down at Jim Hardcastle.

"No," said Adam, wishing he possessed the guile of Robin's father. "I think I was spotted in town so I had to get a change of clothes and keep out of sight for a few hours."

"Then why don't you come to the Mustard dinner?" said Jim. "No one will see you there."

"Wish I was able to," said Adam, "but I can't afford to lose any more time."

"Anything I can do to help?" said Jim conspiratorially.

"No, I've got to get to . . . I have a rendezvous just outside the town in less than an hour."

"Wish I could take you there myself," said Jim. "Do anything to help an old soldier, but I'm a bit stuck tonight—of all nights."

"Don't give it a second thought, Jim, I'll be all right."

"I could always take him, Dad," said Linda, who had slipped up by her father's side and was listening intently.

They both turned toward Linda, who was wearing a tight-fitting black crêpe dress that started as low and ended as high as it dared. Her freshly washed hair now fell to her shoulders. She looked up hopefully.

"You've only just got your license, lass. Don't be daft."

"You always treat me like a child when there's something worthwhile to do," came back the immediate response.

Jim hesitated. "How far is this rendezvous?" he asked apprehensively.

"About five, maybe six miles," said Adam, "but I'll be fine. I can get a taxi easily."

"The lass is right," said Jim, and taking his car keys out of his pocket, he turned to her and added, "but if you ever let on to your mother, I'll kill you." Jim took Adam by the hand and shook it furiously.

"But I'll be just fine . . ."

"I won't hear of it, lad. Never forget that in the end we're both on the same side. And good luck."

"Thank you, sir," said Adam reluctantly.

Jim beamed. "You'd better be getting along, lass, before your mother shows up."

Linda happily took Adam by the hand and led him away to the parking lot.

"Which direction?" she asked, once they were seated in the car.

"The Auxerre road," said Adam, looking down at the piece of paper on which he had written the directions Lawrence had read over the phone to him.

Linda set off at a slow pace, seeming at first to be unsure of the car, but once they had reached the outskirts of the town, Adam suggested that she might go a little faster.

"I'm very nervous," she said, as she put her hand on Adam's knee.

"Yes, I can tell you are," said Adam, crossing his legs quickly. "Don't miss the turning," he added when he noticed a signpost pointing to the left.

Linda swung down off the A road on to a country lane while Adam kept his eyes peeled for the building Lawrence had described. It was another two miles before it came into sight.

"Draw into the side," said Adam, "and turn the lights off."

"At last," said Linda, sounding more hopeful, as she stopped the car.

"Thank you very much," said Adam, as he touched the door handle.

"Is that all I get for risking life and limb?" asked Linda.

"I wouldn't want you to be late for the dinner."

"That dinner will be about as exciting as a dance at the Young Conservatives."

"But your mother will be worried about you."

"Dudley, you're so uptight."

"I wouldn't be in normal circumstances, but if you stay much longer your life could be in danger," Adam said quietly.

Linda turned ashen. "You're not joking, are you?"

"I wish I was," said Adam. "Now, when I get out of this car you must turn round and go back to the hotel and never mention this conversation to anyone, especially your mother."

"I will," Linda said, sounding nervous for the first time.

"You're a fantastic girl," said Adam, and took her in his arms and gave her the longest, warmest kiss she had ever experienced. Adam then got out of the car and watched her nearly drive into a ditch before she headed off back in the direction of Dijon.

He checked his watch: an hour and a half still to go before they were due, and by then it would be pitch dark. He jogged over to the airfield and studied the burned-out buildings that ran alongside the road. It was exactly as Lawrence had described it. It was like a ghost town, and Adam was confident that no one else could be there yet, as they still wouldn't have had enough time to carry out Lawrence's plan.

Looking across the runway, Adam spotted the ideal place

to hide while he waited to see which of the two plans he had prepared would prove necessary.

Flight Lt. Alan Banks of the British Royal Air Force was thankful that the moon shone so brightly that night. He had landed the little RAF Hawker Typhoon in far worse conditions when a runway had been lit up like the Blackpool seafront.

Banks circled the perimeter of the airfield once and studied the two runways carefully. The airport had been out of action for such a long time that none of the aircraft manuals included a detailed ground plan.

The flight lieutenant was breaking every rule in the book, including piloting an unmarked aircraft and informing the French that they would be landing in Paris; not easy to explain overshooting an airport by over a hundred miles.

"I can make a landing on the north-south runway more easily," Banks said, turning to the SAS captain, who sat crouched in the back with his five men. "How near to that hangar do you want me to go?" he said, pointing out of the window.

"Stay well clear, at least a couple of hundred yards," came back the reply. "We still don't know what to expect."

The six SAS men continued to stare cautiously out of the side windows. They had been briefed to pick up a lone Englishman called Scott who would be waiting for them, and then get out fast. It sounded easy enough, but it couldn't be; otherwise they wouldn't have been called in.

The pilot swung the Hawker around to the south and put the nose down. He smiled when he spotted the burned-out Spitfire that had been left derelict on the corner of the runway. Just like the ones his father used to fly during the Second World War. But this one had obviously never made it home. He descended confidently, and as the little plane touched down it bounced along the runway not because the pilot lacked experience but because the surface was so badly pitted.

Flight Lt. Banks brought the plane to a halt about two hundred yards from the hangar and swung the fuselage round a full circle, ready for that quick getaway the captain seemed so keen to execute. He pressed the button that cut the propellers and turned the lights out. The whirring slowed to an eerie whisper. They were forty-three minutes early.

Adam watched the new arrivals suspiciously from the cockpit of the Spitfire some four hundred yards away. He wasn't going to make a run for it across that open ground while the moon shone so brightly. His eyes never left the little unmarked plane as he waited for some clue as to who the occupants might be. He estimated it would be another fifteen minutes before the moon would be shielded by clouds. A few minutes more passed before Adam watched six men drop out of the blind side of the aircraft and lie flat on the tarmac on their stomachs. They were correctly dressed in SAS battle gear but Adam remained unconvinced while he still recalled Romanov's chauffeur's uniform. The six soldiers made no attempt to move. Neither did Adam, as he was still uncertain which side they were on.

All six men on the ground hated the moon and even more the open space. The captain checked his watch: thirty-six minutes to go. He raised his hand, and they began to crawl toward the hangar where Pemberton had said Scott would be waiting, a journey that took them nearly twenty minutes, and with each movement they made they became more confident that Pemberton's warning of an enemy waiting for them was unjustified.

At last a mass of clouds reached the moon, and a shadow was thrown across the whole airfield. The SAS captain quickly checked his watch. Five minutes to go before the rendezvous was due. He was the first to reach the door of the hangar, and he pushed it open with the palm of his hand. He wriggled in through the gap. The bullet hit him in the forehead even before he had found time to raise his gun.

"Move, laddies," shouted the second in command, and the

other four were up in a flash, firing in an arc in front of them and running for the protection of the building.

As soon as Adam heard the Scottish brogue, he jumped out of the cockpit and sprinted across the tarmac toward the little plane, whose propellers were already beginning to turn. He jumped on the wing and climbed in by the side of the surprised pilot.

"I'm Adam Scott, the man you've come to pick up," he shouted.

"I'm Flight Lieutenant Alan Banks, old chap," said the pilot, thrusting out his hand. Only a British officer could shake hands in such a situation, thought Adam, relieved if still terrified.

They both turned and watched the battle.

"We ought to get going," said the pilot. "My orders are to see you are brought back to England in one piece."

"Not before we are certain none of your men can make it back to the plane."

"Sorry, mate. My instructions are to get you out. Their orders are to take care of themselves."

"Let's at least give them another minute," Adam said.

They waited until the propellers were rotating at full speed. Suddenly the firing stopped, and Adam could hear his heart thumping in his body.

"We ought to get moving," said the pilot.

"I know," replied Adam, "but just keep your eyes skinned. There's something I still need to know."

Years of night marches made it possible for Adam to see him long before the pilot.

"Get going," said Adam.

"What?" said the pilot.

"Get going."

The pilot moved the joystick forward, and the plane started moving slowly down the crumbling runway.

Suddenly a dark figure was running toward them, firing long bursts straight at them. The pilot looked back to see a tall man whose fair hair shone in the moonlight.

"Faster, man, faster," said Adam.

"The throttle's full out," said the pilot, as the firing began again, but this time the bullets were ripping into the fuselage. A third burst came, but by then the plane was going faster than the man, and Adam let out a scream of delight when it left the ground.

He looked back to see that Romanov had turned around and was now firing at someone who was not wearing an SAS uniform.

"They couldn't hope to hit us now unless they've got a bazooka," said Flight Lieutenant Banks.

"Well done, well done," said Adam, turning back to the pilot.

"And to think my wife had wanted me to go to the cinema tonight," said the pilot, laughing.

"And what had you planned to see?" asked Adam.

"*My Fair Lady.*"

"Isn't it time for us to be going home?" asked Piers removing his hand from the member's leg.

"Good idea," he said. "Just let me settle the bill."

"And I'll pick up my coat and scarf," said Piers. "Join you upstairs in a few moments?"

"Fine," he said. Catching the eye of the proprietor the member scribbled his signature in the air. When the "account" arrived—a bare figure written out on a slip of paper without explanation—it was, as always, extortionate. As always, the member paid without comment. He thanked the proprietor as he left and walked up the dusty, creaky stairs to find his companion already waiting for him on the pavement. He hailed a taxi, and while Piers climbed in the back he directed the cabbie to Dillon's bookshop.

"Not in the cab," he said, as Piers's hand began to creep up his leg.

"I can't wait," said Piers. "It's way past my bedtime."

"Way past my bedtime," his companion repeated involuntarily and checked his watch. The die must have been cast.

They would have moved in by now: surely they had caught Scott this time? And more important, the . . .

"Four bob," said the cabbie, flicking back the glass. He handed over five shillings and didn't wait for any change.

"Just around the corner," he said, guiding Piers past the bookshop and into the little side street. They crept down the stone steps, and Piers waited as he unlocked the door, switched on the lights and led the young man in.

"Oh, very cozy," said Piers. "Very cozy indeed."

Flight Lieutenant Alan Banks stared out of his tiny window as the plane climbed steadily.

"Where to now?" said Adam, relief flooding through his body.

"I had hoped England, but I'm afraid the answer is as far I can manage."

"What do you mean?" said Adam anxiously.

"Look at the fuel gauge," said Alan Banks, putting his forefinger on a little white indicator that was pointing halfway between a quarter full and empty. "We had enough to get us back to Northolt in Middlesex until those bullets ripped into my fuel tank."

The little white stick kept moving toward the red patch even as Adam watched it, and within moments the propellers on the left side of the aircraft spun to a halt.

"I am going to have to put her down in a field nearby. I can't risk going on, as there are no other airports anywhere near us. Just be thankful it's a clear moonlit night."

Without warning the plane began to descend sharply. "I shall try for that field over there," said the flight lieutenant, sounding remarkably blasé as he pointed to a large expanse of land to the west of the aircraft. "Hold on tight," he said as the plane spiraled down inevitably. The large expanse of land suddenly looked very small as the plane began to approach it.

Adam found himself gripping the side of his seat and gritting his teeth.

"Relax," said the pilot. "These Hawkers have landed on far worse places than this," he went on, as the wheels touched the brown earth. "Damn, mud. I hadn't anticipated that," he cursed, as the wheels lost their grip in the soft earth and the plane suddenly nosedived. A few seconds passed before Adam realized he was still alive but upside down, swinging from his seat belt.

"What do I do next?" he asked the pilot, but there was no reply.

Adam tried to get his bearings and began to rock his body backward and forward until he could touch the side of the plane with one hand while gripping the joystick with his feet. Once he was able to grab the side of the fuselage he undid the belt and collapsed onto the roof of the plane.

He picked himself up, delighted to find nothing broken. He quickly looked around, but there was still no sign of the pilot. Adam clambered out of the plane, glad to feel the safety of the ground. He searched around for a considerable time before he discovered Alan Banks some thirty yards in front of the aircraft, motionless on his back.

"Are you all right?" asked the pilot, before Adam could ask the same question.

"I'm fine, but how about you, Alan?"

"I'm okay. I must have been thrown clear of the aircraft. Just sorry about the landing, old chap, have to admit it wasn't up to scratch. We must try it again sometime."

Adam burst out laughing as the pilot slowly sat up.

"What next?" Banks asked.

"Can you walk?"

"Yes, I think so," said Alan, gingerly lifting himself up. "Damn," he said, "it's only my ankle, but it's sure going to slow me down. You'd better get going without me. That bunch back there with the arsenal can only be about thirty minutes behind us."

"But what will you do?"

"My father landed in one of these bloody fields during the Second World War and still managed to get himself back to England without being caught by the Germans. I owe you a great debt of gratitude, Adam, because if I get back I'll be able to shut him up once and for all. Which lot are chasing us this time, by the way?"

"The Russians," said Adam, who was beginning to wonder if perhaps there was a second enemy.

"The Russians couldn't be better; anything less and Dad wouldn't have accepted it as a fair comparison."

Adam smiled as he thought of his own father and how much he would have liked Alan Banks. He touched the icon instinctively and was relieved to find it was still in place. The pilot's words had only made him more determined to get back to England.

"Which way?" asked Adam.

The pilot looked up at the Great Bear. "I'll head east, seems appropriate, so you'd better go west, old fellow. Nice to have made your acquaintance," and with that he limped off.

"I'm not sure how much longer I can last, Comrade Major."

"You must try to hold on, Valchek. It's imperative that you try. We cannot afford to stop now," said Romanov. "I know that plane isn't far. I saw it falling out of the sky."

"I believe you, Comrade, but at least let me die a peaceful death on the side of the road, rather than endure the agony of this car."

Romanov glanced across at his colleague, who had been shot in the abdomen. Valchek's hands were covered with blood, and his shirt and trousers were already drenched as he tried helplessly to hold himself in. He continued to clutch on to his stomach like a child about to be sick. The driver had also been shot, but in the back while attempting to run away. If he hadn't died instantly, Romanov would have put the next bullet into the coward himself. But Valchek was a different matter. No one could have questioned his courage. He had first taken on the British flat on their stomachs and then the Americans charging in like the Seventh Cavalry. Romanov had Mentor to thank for ensuring they had been there first. But he must now quickly warn him that someone else was also briefing the Americans. Romanov, however, felt some satisfaction in having tricked the Americans into turning their fire on the British while he and Valchek waited to pick off the survivors. The last survivor was an American who fired at Valchek continually as they were making their getaway.

Romanov reckoned he had a clear hour before the French, British, and Americans would be explaining away several bodies on a disused air field. Romanov's thoughts returned to Valchek when he heard his comrade groan.

"Let's turn off into this forest," he begged. "I cannot hope to last much longer now."

"Hold on, Comrade, hold on," repeated Romanov. "We can't be far from Scott. Think of the Motherland."

"To hell with the Motherland," said Valchek. "Just let me die in peace." Romanov looked across again and realized that he could be stuck with a dead body within a few minutes. Despite Valchek's efforts, the blood was now seeping on to the floor like a faucet that wouldn't stop.

Romanov noticed a gap in the trees ahead of him. He switched his lights full on and swung off the road onto a dirt track and drove as far as he could until the thicket became too dense. He switched off the headlights and ran round the car to open the door.

Valchek could only manage two or three steps before he slumped to the ground, still holding onto his intestines. Romanov bent down and helped him ease himself up against the trunk of a large tree.

"Leave me to die, Comrade Major. Do not waste any more of your time on me."

Romanov frowned.

"How do you wish to die, Comrade?" he asked. "Slowly and in agony, or quickly and peacefully?"

"Leave me, Comrade. Let me die slowly, but you should go while you still have Scott in your sights."

"But if the Americans were to find you, they might force you to talk."

"You know better than that, Comrade." Romanov accepted the rebuke, then rose and after a moment's thought ran back to the car.

Valchek began to pray that once the bastard had left someone might find him. He'd never wanted this assignment in the first place, but Zaborski had needed extra eyes on Romanov, and Zaborski was not a man to cross. Valchek wouldn't talk, but he still wanted to live.

The bullet from the 9mm Makarov went straight through the back of Valchek's temple and blew away one side of his head. Valchek slumped to the ground, and for several seconds his body trembled and spasmed, subsiding into twitches as he emptied his bowels and bladder onto the brown earth.

Romanov stood over him until he was certain he was dead. Valchek would probably not have talked, but this was not a time for taking unnecessary risks.

When he woke the next morning he felt the same familiar guilt. Once again he swore it would be the last time. It was never as good as he had anticipated, and the regret always lingered on for several hours.

The expense of keeping up an extra flat, the taxi fares and the club bills nearly made it prohibitive. But he always returned, like a salmon to its breeding ground. "A queer fish," he murmured out loud, and then groaned at his own pun.

Piers began to wake, and for the next twenty minutes he made his companion forget those regrets. After a moment of lying in exhausted silence the older man slipped out of bed, took ten pounds out of his wallet, and left it on the dresser before going to run himself a bath. He anticipated that by the time he returned the boy and the money would have gone.

He soaked himself in the bath, wondering about Scott. He knew he should feel guilty about his death. A death that, like so many others before him, had been caused by his picking up a young Pole whom he had thought was safe. It was now so many years ago that he couldn't even remember his name.

But Mentor had never been allowed to forget the name of the young aristocratic KGB officer he had found sitting on the end of their bed when he woke the next morning, or the look of disgust he had showed for both of them.

CHAPTER SIXTEEN

ADAM LAY FLAT on his stomach in the bottom of the empty barge. His head propped on one side, he remained alert to the slightest unfamiliar sound.

The boatman stood behind the wheel counting the three hundred Swiss francs for a second time. It was more than he could normally hope to earn in a month. A woman standing on tiptoes was eyeing the notes happily over his shoulder.

The barge progressed at a stately pace down the canal, and Adam could no longer see the crashed plane.

Suddenly, far off in the distance, he heard distinctly what sounded like a gunshot. Even as he listened, the woman turned and scuttled down the hatch like a frightened rat. The barge plowed its course on slowly through the night while Adam listened anxiously for any other unnatural noises, but all he could hear was the gentle splash of the water against the barge's hull. The clouds had moved on, and a full moon once again lit up the bank on both sides of the river. It became abundantly clear to Adam as he watched the towpath that they were not moving very fast. He could have run quicker. But even if it had cost him the remainder of his money, he was grateful to be escaping. He lowered himself again and curled up in the bow of the boat. He touched the icon, something he found himself doing every few minutes since he had discovered its secret. He did not move for another half hour, although he doubted that the barge had covered more than five miles.

Although everything appeared absolutely serene, he still remained alert. The river was far wider now than when he had first leaped on the barge.

The boatman's eyes had never left him for long. He stood gripping the wheel, his oil-covered face not much cleaner than the old dungarees he wore—which looked as if they were never taken off. Occasionally he took a hand from the wheel, but only to remove the smokeless pipe from his mouth, cough, spit, and put it back again.

The man smiled, took both hands off the wheel and placed them by the side of his head to indicate that Adam should sleep. But Adam shook his head. He checked his watch. Midnight had passed, and he wanted to be off the barge and away long before first light.

He stood up, stretched and wobbled a little. His shoulder, although healing slowly, still ached relentlessly. He walked up the center of the barge and took his place next to the wheel.

"*La Seine?*" he asked, pointing at the water.

The boatman shook his head, no. "*Canal de Bourgogne,*" he grunted.

Adam then pointed in the direction they were moving. "*Quelle ville?*"

The boatman removed his pipe. "*Ville? Ce n'est pas une ville, c'est Sombernon,*" he said, and put the stem back between his teeth.

Adam returned to his place in the bow. He tried to find a more comfortable position to relax and, curling up against the side of the boat, rested his head on some old rope and allowed his eyes to close.

* * *

"You know Scott better than any of us," said Sir Morris, "and you still have no feel as to where he might be now, or what he might do next, do you?"

"No, sir," admitted Lawrence. "The only thing we know for certain is that he has an appointment for a medical exam on Monday afternoon, but somehow I don't think he'll make it."

Sir Morris ignored the comment. "But someone was able to get to Scott, even though we didn't call D4," he continued. "That icon must hold a secret that we haven't begun to appreciate."

"And if Scott is still alive," said Lawrence, "nothing is going to convince him now that we're not to blame."

"And if we're not, who is?" asked Sir Morris. "Because someone was so desperate to discover our next move that they must have taken one hell of a risk during the last twenty-four hours. Unless, of course, it was you," said Sir Morris. The Permanent Secretary rose from his desk and turned around to look out of his window on to Horse Guards Parade.

"Even if it was me," said Lawrence, his eyes resting on a picture of the young Queen which stood on the corner of his master's desk, "it doesn't explain how the Americans got there as well."

"Oh, that's simple," said Sir Morris. "Busch has been briefing them direct. I never doubted he would from the moment he joined us. What I hadn't anticipated was how far the Americans would go without keeping us informed."

"So it was you who told Busch," said Lawrence.

"No," said Sir Morris. "You don't end up sitting behind this desk risking your own skin. I told the Prime Minister, and politicians can always be relied on to pass on your information if they consider it will score them a point. To be fair, I knew the Prime Minister would tell the President. Otherwise I wouldn't have told him in the first place. More important: do you think Scott can still be alive?"

"Yes, I do," said Lawrence. "I have every reason to believe that the man who ran across the tarmac to our waiting plane was Scott. The French police, who incidentally have been far more cooperative than the Swiss, have informed us that our plane crashed in a field twelve miles north of Dijon, but neither Scott nor the pilot were to be found at the scene of the crash."

"And if the French reports on what took place at the airport are accurate," said Sir Morris, "Romanov escaped and they must have had a couple of hours' start on us."

"Possibly," said Lawrence.

"And do you think it equally possible," asked Sir Morris, "that they have caught up with Scott and are now in possession of the icon?"

"Yes, sir, I fear that is quite possible," Lawrence said. "But I can't pretend it's conclusive. However, the BBC monitoring service at Caversham Park picked up extra-signals traffic to all Soviet embassies during the night."

"That could mean anything," said Sir Morris, removing his spectacles.

"I agree, sir. But NATO reports that Russian strategic forces have been placed at a state of readiness, and several Soviet ambassadors across Europe have requested formal audiences with their foreign secretaries, ours included."

"That *is* more worrying," said Sir Morris. "They don't do that unless they are hoping for our support."

"Agreed, sir. But most revealing of all is that the Active Measures section of the KGB, First Chief Directorate, has booked pages of advertising space in newspapers right across Europe and, I suspect, America."

"Next you'll be telling me they hired J. Walter Thompson to write the copy," growled Sir Morris.

"They won't need to," said Lawrence. "It's a story that will make every front page."

If it hadn't been for the ceaseless throbbing in his shoulder, Adam might not have woken so quickly. The barge had suddenly swung at ninety degrees and started heading east when Adam woke up with a start. He looked at the boatman and indicated that the river was far wider now and could he ease them nearer to the bank so he could jump off. The old man shrugged his shoulders, pretending not to understand, as the barge drifted aimlessly on.

Adam looked over the side and despite the lateness of the hour could see the bed of the river quite clearly. He tossed a stone over the side and watched it drop quickly to the bottom. It looked almost as if he could reach down and touch it. He looked up helplessly at the boatman but he continued to stare over his head into the distance.

"Damn," said Adam, and, taking the icon out of his blazer pocket, held it high above his head. He stood on the edge of the barge feeling like a soccer manager asking the referee for permission to substitute a player. Permission was granted, and Adam leaped into the water. His feet hit the canal bed with a thud and knocked the breath out of his body despite the fact that the water only came up to his waist.

Adam stood in the canal, the icon still held high above his head as the barge sailed past him. He waded to the nearest bank and clambered up on to the towpath, turning slowly around as he tried to get some feel for direction. He was soon able to distinguish the Plow again and plot a course due west. After an hour of soggy jogging he began to make out a light in the distance that he estimated to be under a mile away. His legs were soaking and cold as he started to squelch his way across a field toward the first rays of the morning sun.

Whenever he came to a hedge or gate he climbed over or under like a Roman centurion determined to hold a straight line with his final destination. He could now see the outline of a house, which, as he got nearer, he realized was no more than a large cottage. He remembered the expression *peasant farmer* from his school geography lessons. A little cobbled path led up to a half-open wooden door that looked as if it didn't need a lock. Adam tapped gently on the knocker and stood directly below the light above the doorway so that whoever answered would see him immediately.

The door was pulled back by a woman of perhaps thirty,

who wore a plain black dress and a spotless white apron. Her rosy cheeks and ample waist confirmed her husband's profession.

When she saw Adam standing under the light she couldn't mask her surprise—she had been expecting the postman—but he didn't often appear in a neat navy blue blazer and soaking gray trousers.

Adam smiled. *"Anglais,"* he told her, and added, "I fell in the canal."

The lady burst out laughing and beckoned Adam into her kitchen. He walked in to find a man, evidently dressed for milking, sitting at a sparse wooden table. The farmer looked up and when he saw Adam he joined in the laughter—a warm, friendly laugh more with Adam than against him. When the woman saw that Adam was dripping all over her spotless floor she quickly pulled down a towel from the rack above the fire and said, *"Enlevez-moi ça,"* pointing to Adam's trousers.

Adam turned toward the farmer for guidance, but his host only nodded his agreement and added a mime of pulling down his own trousers.

"Enlevez-le, enlevez-le," the woman repeated, pointing at him, and handed him the towel.

Adam removed his shoes and socks, but the farmer's wife went on pointing until he took off his trousers, but she didn't budge before he had finally removed his shirt and underclothes and wrapped the towel around his waist. She stared at the large bandage on his shoulder but then quickly picked up everything except his blazer and took them over to the sink while he stood by the fire and dried himself.

Adam hitched up the towel around his waist, as the farmer beckoned him to join him at the table, pouring a large glass of milk for his guest and another for himself. Adam sat down next to the farmer, hanging his fashionable new blazer over the back of the chair near the fire. A delicious aroma arose from the pan where the farmer's wife was frying a thick slice of bacon, which she had cut from the joint hanging in the smoky recess of the chimney.

The farmer raised his glass of milk high in the air.

"Winston Churchill," he toasted. Adam took a long gulp from his own glass and then raised it dramatically.

"Charles de Gaulle," he said, and finished off the warm milk as if it had been his first pint at the local pub.

The farmer picked up the jug once more and refilled their glasses. "*Merci*," said Adam, turning to the farmer's wife as she placed in front of him a large plate sizzling with eggs and bacon. She nodded and handed Adam a knife and fork before saying, "*Mangez*."

"*Merci, merci*," Adam repeated, as she cut him a thick oval slice from the huge loaf in front of him.

Adam began to devour the freshly cooked food, which was the first meal he'd managed since the dinner he'd ordered at Robin's expense.

Without warning the farmer suddenly rose from his place and thrust out his hand. Adam also got up and shook it gratefully, only to be reminded how sore his shoulder still was.

"*Je droix travailler à la laiterie*," he explained.

Adam nodded and remained standing as his host left the room, but the farmer waved him down with a further "*Mangez*."

When Adam had finished the last scrap of food—he did everything except lick the plate—he took it over to the farmer's wife, who was busy removing a pot from the stove in order to pour him a large, steaming cup of hot coffee. He sat back down and began to sip at it.

Adam tapped his jacket pocket almost automatically to make sure the icon was still safely in place. He pulled it out and studied *Saint George and the Dragon*. He turned it over, hesitated, and then pressed the silver crown hard. The icon split in half like a book, revealing two tiny hinges on the inside.

He glanced up at the farmer's wife, who was now wringing out his socks. Adam noticed his pants had already joined the trousers on the rack above the fire. She removed an ironing board from a little alcove by the side of the stove and began to set it up, showing no interest in Adam's discovery.

Once again he stared down at the inside of the open icon, which was now laid flat on the table in front of him. The true irony was that the woman pressing his trousers was able to understand every word on the parchment while at the same time unable to explain its full significance to him. The complete surface of the inside of the icon was covered by a parchment, which was glued to the wood and fell only a centimeter short of the four edges. Adam swiveled it round so that he could study it more clearly. The scrawled signatures in black ink at the bottom and the seals gave it the look of a legal document. On each reading he learned something new. Adam had been surprised originally to discover it was written in French until he came to the date on the bottom—20 June 1867—and then he remembered from his military history lectures at Sandhurst that long after Napoleonic times most international agreements remained conducted in French. Adam began to reread the script again slowly.

His French was not good enough to translate more than a few odd words from the finely handwritten scroll. Under *Etats-Unis* William Seward's bold hand was scrawled across a crest of a two-headed eagle. Next to it was the signature of Alexsander Gorchakov below a crown that mirrored the silver ornament embedded in the back of the icon. Adam double-checked. It had to be some form of agreement executed between the Russians and the Americans in 1867.

He then searched for other words that would help to explain the significance of the document. On one line he identified the words "sept million, deux cent mille dollars en or (7,2 million)" and on another "sept cent douze million, huit cent mille dollars en or (712,8 million), le 20 juin 1966."

His eyes rested on a calendar hanging by a nail from the wall. It was Saturday, June 18, 1966. If the date in the agreement was to be believed, then in only three days the document would no longer have any legal validity. No wonder the two most powerful nations on earth seemed desperate to get their hands on it, thought Adam.

Adam read through the document line by line, searching for any further clues, pondering over each word slowly.

His eyes came to a halt on the one word that would remain the same in both languages and required no translation.

The one word he had not told Lawrence.

Adam wondered how the icon had ever fallen into the hands of Goering in the first place. He must have bequeathed it to his father unknowingly—for had he realized the true importance of what was hidden inside the icon, he would surely have been able to bargain for his own freedom with either side.

"*Voilà, voilà,*" said the farmer's wife, waving her hands as she placed warm socks, pants, and trousers in front of Adam. How long had he spent engrossed in his fateful discovery? She looked across at the upside-down parchment and smiled. Adam quickly snapped the icon closed and then studied the masterpiece carefully. So skillfully had the wood been cut that he could no longer see the join. He thought of the words of the letter left to him in his father's will: "But if you open it only to discover its purpose is to involve you in some dishonorable enterprise, be rid of it without a second thought." He did not need to give a second thought to how his father would have reacted in the same circumstances. The farmer's wife was now standing hands on hips, staring at him with a puzzled look.

Adam quickly replaced the icon in his jacket pocket and pulled his trousers back on.

He could think of no adequate way of thanking her for her hospitality, her lack of suspicion or inquisitiveness, so he simply walked over to her, took her gently by the shoulders, and kissed her on the cheek. She blushed and handed him a small plastic bag. He looked inside to find three apples, some bread, and a large piece of cheese. She removed a crumb from his lip with the edge of her apron and led him to the open door.

Adam smiled at her and then walked outside into his other world.

PART III

THE WHITE HOUSE

WASHINGTON, D.C.

June 18, 1966

CHAPTER
SEVENTEEN

THE WHITE HOUSE
JUNE 18, 1966

"I DON'T WANT to be the first Goddamn President in the history of the United States to hand back an American state rather than found one."

"I appreciate your position, sir," said the Secretary of State. "But . . ."

"Where do we stand on this legally, Dean?"

"We don't, Mr. President. Abraham Brunweld, who was my tutor at St. John's, has confirmed that the terms of the ninety-nine-year lease are binding on both sides. The lease was signed on behalf of the Russians by their foreign minister, Alexsander Gorchakov, and for the Americans by the then Secretary of State, William Seward."

"Can such an agreement still be valid today?" asked the President, turning to his chief legal officer, Nicholas Katzenbach.

"It certainly can, sir," said the Attorney General. "But only if they can produce their original. Both the UN and the International Court at The Hague would be left with no choice but to support the Russian claim. Otherwise no international agreement signed by us in the past or in the future would carry any credibility."

"What you're asking me to do is lie down and wag my tail like a prize Labrador while the Russians shit all over us," said the President.

"I understand how you feel, Mr. President," said the Attorney General, "but it remains my responsibility to make you aware of the legal position."

"God dammit, is there any precedent for such stupidity by a head of state?"

"The British," chipped in Dean Rusk, "will be facing a similar problem with the Chinese in 1999 over the New Territories of Hong Kong. They have already accepted the reality of the situation and indeed have made it clear to the Chinese government that they are willing to come to an agreement with them."

"That's just one example," said the President, "and we all know about the British and their 'fair play' diplomacy."

"Also, in 1898," continued Rusk, "the Russians obtained a ninety-nine-year lease on Port Arthur, in northern China. The port was vital to them because, unlike Vladivostok, it is ice-free all year round."

"I had no idea the Russians had a port in China."

"They don't any longer, Mr. President. They returned it to Mao in 1955 as an act of goodwill between fellow Communists."

"You can be damn sure the Russians won't want to return this piece of land to us as an act of goodwill between fellow capitalists," said the President. "Am I left with any alternative?"

"Short of military action to prevent the Soviets claiming what they will rightfully see as theirs, no, sir," replied the Secretary of State.

"So one Johnson buys the land from the Russians in 1867 while another is forced to sell it back in 1966. Why did Seward and the President ever agree to such a damn cock-amamy idea in the first place?"

"At the time," said the Attorney General, removing his spectacles, "the purchase price of the land in question was seven-point-two million dollars, and inflation was then virtually unheard of. Andrew Johnson could never have envisaged the Russians wanting to purchase it back at ninety-nine times its original value, or in real terms, seven hundred and twelve-point-eight million dollars in gold bullion. In reality, years of inflation have made the asking price cheap. And the Russians have already lodged the full amount in a New York bank to prove it."

"So we can't even hope that they won't pay up in time," said the President.

"It would seem not, sir."

"But why did Czar Alexander ever want to lease the damn land in the first place? That's what beats me."

"He was having trouble with some of his senior ministers at the time over the selling off of land belonging to Russia in eastern Asia. The Czar thought this transaction would be more palatable to his inner circle if he presented it as nothing more than a long lease, with a buy-back clause rather than an outright sale."

"Then why didn't Congress object to his little plan?"

"After Congress had ratified the main treaty, the amendment was not strictly subject to approval by the House, as no further expenditure by the United States government was involved," explained Rusk. "Ironically, Seward was proud of the fact he had demanded such a high premium in the repayment clause, which at the time he had every reason to believe would be impossible to repay."

"Now it's worth that in annual oil revenue alone," said the President, looking out of the Oval Office window toward the Washington Monument. "Not to mention the military chaos it's going to create in this country if they've got their hands on the original copy of the treaty. Don't ever forget that I was the President who asked Congress to spend billions putting a tracking station right across that border so the American people could sleep easy in the knowledge that we possessed an early warning system second to none."

Neither adviser felt able to contradict their elected leader.

"So what are the British doing about all this?"

"Playing it close to the vest, as usual, Mr. President. It's an English national who is thought to be in possession of the treaty at the moment, and they still seem quietly confident that they will get their hands on him and the icon before the Russians, so they may yet turn out to be our saviors."

"Nice to have the British coming to *our* rescue for a change," said the President. "But have we meanwhile been sitting on our backsides while the British try to solve our problems for us?"

"No, sir. The CIA has been on it for over a month."

"Then it's only surprising that the Russians haven't got their hands on the icon already."

Nobody laughed.

'So what am I expected to do next? Sit and wait for the Soviets to move seven hundred and twelve million dollars of gold from their New York bank to the U.S. Treasury before midnight on Monday?"

"They must also deliver their original copy of the agreement to me at the same time," said Rusk. "And they have only sixty hours left to do that."

"Where's our copy at this moment?" asked the President.

"Somewhere deep in the vaults of the Pentagon. Only two people know the exact location. Since the Yalta conference, our copy of the treaty has never seen the light of day."

"Why have I never been told about it before today?" asked the President. "At least I could have put a stop to so much expenditure."

"For over fifty years, we've believed the Russians' copy was destroyed at the time of the Revolution. As the years passed it became clear that the Soviets accepted this as a fait accompli, with the final acknowledgment of this fact coming from Stalin at Yalta. Brezhnev must have come across something within the last month that convinced him their copy had only been mislaid."

"Christ, another month, and we would have been clear."

"That is correct, sir," said the Secretary of State.

"Do you realize, Dean, that if the Russians turn up at your office before midnight on the twentieth with their copy, it would make all of Kennedy's efforts over Cuba look like so much piss in a thunderstorm?"

CHAPTER EIGHTEEN

WHEN THE COTTAGE door closed behind Adam, all he could make out was the outskirts of a small town. While it was still so early he felt safe to jog toward *centre ville*, but as soon as the early morning workers began to appear on the streets, he slowed to a walk. Adam opted not to go straight into the center of the town but to look for somewhere to hide while he considered his next move. He came to a halt outside a multistory parking lot and decided he was unlikely to find a better place to formulate a plan.

Adam walked through an exit door at ground level and came to a lift that indicated that the parking lot was on four floors. He ran down the steps to the lowest level, tentatively pulled back the door to the basement and found it was badly lit and almost empty. Adam had chosen the basement as he assumed that it would be the last floor to fill up with customers. He walked around the perimeter of the floor and studied the layout. Two cars were parked in the far corner, and a thick layer of dust suggested that they had been there for some time. He crouched down behind one of them and found that he was safely out of sight to all but the most inquisitive.

He began to fantasize that someone might park a car on that floor and leave the keys in the ignition. He checked the doors of the two cars already parked, but both were securely locked. He settled back to work out a more serious plan of how he could reach the coast by nightfall.

He was deep in thought when he heard a scraping noise that made him jump. He peered round the gloomy basement, and out of the darkness a man appeared, pulling behind him a plastic dustbin half full of rubbish. Adam could barely see the old man dressed in a dirty brown coat that stretched nearly to the ground and left little doubt about the height of the previous employee. He wasn't sure what he would do if the man continued to walk toward him. But as he came nearer Adam could see that he was stooped and old; the stub of a cigarette protruded from his lips. The cleaner stopped in front of him, spotted a cigarette pack, picked it up, and checked to be sure it was empty before dropping it in the dustbin. After that, a candy wrapper, a Pepsi-Cola can, and an old copy of *Le Figaro* all found their way into the dustbin. His eyes searched slowly round the room for more rubbish, but still he didn't notice Adam tucked away behind the farthest car. Satisfied that his task was completed, he dragged the dustbin across the floor and pushed it outside the door. Adam began to relax again, but after about two minutes, the old man returned, walked over to a wall and pulled open a door that Adam hadn't previously noticed. He took off the long brown coat and replaced it with a gray one that didn't look in a much better state but at least it made a more convincing fit. He then disappeared through the exit. Moments later Adam heard a door close with a bang.

The cleaner had ended his day.

Adam waited for some time before he stood up and stretched. He crept around the edge of the wall until he reached the little door. He pulled it open quietly and removed the long brown coat from its nail, then headed back to his place in the corner. He ducked down as the first of the morning cars arrived. The driver swung into the far corner in such a fluent circle that Adam felt sure it must have been a daily routine. A short dapper man with a pencil mustache, dressed in a smart pin-stripe suit, jumped out of the car carrying a briefcase. Once he had locked the car door he proceeded with fast mincing strides toward the exit. Adam waited until the heavy door swung back into place before he stood up and tried on the brown coat over his blazer. It was tight on the shoulders and a little short in the arm, but at least it made him look as if he might have worked there.

For the next hour he watched the cars as they continued to arrive at irregular intervals. Tiresomely, all the owners carefully locked their doors and checked them before disappearing through the exit with their keys.

When he heard ten o'clock strike in the distance Adam decided that there was nothing to be gained by hanging around any longer. He had crept out from behind the car that was shielding him and begun to make his way across the floor toward the exit when a Rover with English registration plates swung round the corner and nearly blinded him. He jumped to one side to let the car pass, but it screeched to a halt beside him and the driver wound down his window.

"All—right—park—here?" the driver asked, emphasizing each word in an English accent.

"*Oui, monsieur,*" said Adam.

"Other—floors—marked—*privé,*" the man continued, as if addressing a complete moron. "Anywhere?" His arm swept round the floor.

"*Oui,*" repeated Adam, "bert ay merst paak you," he added, fearing he sounded too much like Peter Sellers.

Balls, was what Adam expected to hear him reply. "Fine," was what the man actually said. He got out of the car, and handed Adam his keys and a ten-franc note.

"*Merci,*" said Adam, pocketing the note and touching his forehead with his hand. "*Quelle—heure—vous—retournez?*" he asked, playing the man at his own game.

"One hour at most," said the man as he reached the door.

Adam waited by the car for a few minutes, but the man did not come back. He opened the passenger door and dropped the food bag on the front seat. He then walked round to the other side and climbed in the driver's seat, switched on the ignition, and checked the fuel gauge: a little over half full. He revved the engine and drove the car up the ramp until he reached street level, where he came to a halt, unable to escape. He needed a two-franc piece to make the arm swing up and let him out. The lady in the car behind him reluctantly changed his ten-franc note once she realized there was no other way of getting out.

Adam drove quickly out on to the road looking for the sign *Toutes Directions*. Once he had found one, it was only minutes before he was clear of the town and traveling up the N6 to Paris.

Adam estimated that he had two hours at best. By then the police would surely have been informed of the theft of the car. He felt confident he had enough petrol to reach Paris; but he certainly couldn't hope to make Calais.

He remained in the center lane of the N6 for most of the journey, always keeping the speedometer five kilometers below the limit. By the end of the first hour Adam had covered nearly ninety kilometers. He opened the bag the farmer's wife had given him and took out an apple and a piece of cheese. His mind began to drift to Heidi, as it had so often in the past two days.

If only he had never opened the letter.

Another hour passed before he spotted him limping up a hill only a few hundred yards from the main road. A broad smile came over Romanov's face when he realized he could get to Scott long before Scott could hope to reach the road. When Romanov was within a few yards of him the flight lieutenant turned round and smiled at the stranger.

When Romanov left Banks thirty minutes later hidden behind a tree with a broken neck he reluctantly admitted that the young pilot officer had been as brave as Valchek—but he couldn't waste any more time trying to discover in which direction Scott was heading.

Romanov headed west.

The moment Adam heard the siren he came out of his reverie. He checked the little clock on the dashboard. He had only been driving for about an hour and a half. Could the French police be that efficient? The police car was now approaching him fast on his left, but Adam maintained the same speed—except for his heartbeat, which climbed well above the approved limit—until the police car shot past him.

As the kilometers sped by, he began to wonder if it might be wiser to turn off onto a quieter road, but decided, on balance, to risk pushing on to Paris as quickly as possible.

He remained alert for further sirens as he continued to follow the signs to Paris. When he finally reached the outskirts of the city, he proceeded to the boulevard de l'Hôpital and even felt relaxed enough to bite into another apple. In normal circumstances he would have appreciated the magnificent architecture along the banks of the Seine, but today his eyes kept returning to the rearview mirror.

Adam decided he would abandon the vehicle in a large public parking lot; with any luck it could be days before anyone came across it.

He turned down the rue de Rivoli and took in at once the long colorful banners looming up in front of him. He could hardly have picked a better place, as he felt sure it would be packed with foreign cars.

Adam backed the Rover in the farthest corner of the square. He then wolfed down the last piece of cheese and locked the car. He started walking toward the exit but had only gone a few yards when he realized that the strolling holidaymakers were amused by his ill-fitting brown jacket, which he had completely forgotten. He decided to turn back and throw the coat in the trunk. He quickly took it off and folded it in a small square.

He was only a few yards away from the car when he saw

the young policeman. He was checking the Rover's license plate and repeating the letters and numbers into an intercom. Adam inched slowly back, never taking his eyes from the officer. He only needed to manage another six or seven paces before he would be lost in the throng of the crowd.

Five, four, three, two more paces backward, he estimated, as the man continued speaking into the intercom. Just one more pace . . . "*Alors!*" hollered the lady on whose foot Adam had stepped.

"I'm so sorry," said Adam, instinctively in his native language. The policeman immediately looked up and stared at Adam, then shouted something into the intercom and began running toward him.

Adam dropped the brown coat and swung round quickly, nearly knocking the stooping lady over before sprinting off toward the exit. The lot was full of tourists who had come to enjoy the pleasures of the Louvre, and Adam found it hard to pick up any real speed through the dense crowd. By the time he reached the entrance to the car park, he could hear the policeman's whistle a few paces behind him. He ran across the rue de Rivoli, through an archway and into a large square.

By then another policeman was coming from his right, leaving him with no choice but to run up the steps in front of him. When he reached the top he turned to see at least three other policemen in close pursuit. He threw himself through the swinging door and past a group of Japanese tourists who were surrounding the Rodin statue that stood in the hallway. He charged on past a startled ticket collector and on up the long marble staircase. "*Monsieur, monsieur, votre billet?*" he heard shouted in his wake.

At the top of the staircase he turned right and ran through the Special "66" Centuries Exhibition: modern—Pollock, Bacon, Hockney—into the impressionist room—Monet, Manet, Courbet—desperately looking for any way out. On into the eighteenth century—Fragonard, Goya, Watteau— but still no sign of an exit. Through the great arch into the seventeenth century—Murillo, Van Dyck, Poussin—as people stopped looking at the pictures and turned their attention to what was causing such a commotion. Adam ran on into the sixteenth century—Raphael, Caravaggio, Michelangelo—suddenly aware that there were only two centuries of paintings to go.

Right or left? He chose right and entered a huge square room. There were three exits. He slowed momentarily to decide which would be his best bet when he became aware that the room was full of Russian icons. He came to a halt at an empty display case: *Nous regrettons que ce tableau soit soumis á la restauration.*

The first policeman had already entered the large room and was only a few paces behind as Adam dashed on toward the farthest exit. There were now only two exits left open for him from which to choose. He swung right, only to see another policeman bearing straight down on him. Left, two more. Ahead, yet another.

Adam came to a halt in the middle of the icon room at the Louvre, his hands raised above his head. He was surrounded by policemen, their guns drawn.

CHAPTER NINETEEN

SIR MORRIS PICKED up the phone on his desk.

"An urgent call from Paris, sir," said his secretary.

"Thank you, Tessa." He listened carefully as his brain quickly translated the exciting news.

"*Merci, merci,*" said Sir Morris to his opposite number at the French Foreign Ministry. "We will be back in touch with you as soon as we have made all the necessary arrangements to collect him. But for now, please don't let him out of your sight." Sir Morris listened for a few moments. "And if he has any possessions on him, please keep them guarded under lock and key. Thank you once again," he said before putting the phone down. His secretary took down every word of the conversation in shorthand as she had done for the past fourteen years.

Once the police had snapped the handcuffs on Adam and marched him off to a waiting car, he was surprised how relaxed, almost friendly, they became. He was yanked into the back of the car by the policeman to whom he was attached. He noticed that there was a police car in front of him and yet another behind. Two motorcycle outriders led the little motorcade away. Adam felt more like visiting royalty than a criminal who was wanted for questioning for two murders, two car thefts, and traveling under false identification. Was it possible at last that someone had worked out he was innocent?

When Adam arrived at the Ministry of the Interior, he was immediately ordered to empty all his pockets. One wristwatch, one apple, twenty pounds in travelers' checks, eight francs, and one British passport in the name of Dudley Hulme. The station inspector asked him politely to strip to his underclothes. It was the second time that day. Once Adam had done so, the inspector carefully checked every pocket of the blazer, even the lining. His expression left Adam in no doubt he hadn't found what he was looking for.

"Do you have anything else in your possession?" the officer asked in slow, precise English.

Damn silly question, thought Adam. You can see for yourself. "No," was all he replied. The inspector checked the blazer once again but came across nothing new. "You must get dressed," he said abruptly.

Adam put back on his shirt, jacket, and trousers, but the inspector kept his tie and shoelaces.

"All your things will be returned to you when you leave," the inspector explained. Adam nodded as he slipped on his shoes, which flapped uncomfortably when he walked. He was then accompanied to a small cell on the same floor, locked in, and left alone. He looked around the sparsely furnished room. A small wooden table was placed in its center, with two wooden chairs on either side. His eyes checked over a single bed in the corner, which had on it an ancient horsehair mattress. He could not have described the room properly as a cell because there were no bars, even across the one small window. He took off his jacket, hung it over the chair, and lay down on the bed. At least it was an improvement over anything he had slept on for the past two nights, he reflected. Could it have only been two nights since he had slept on the floor of Robin's hotel room in Geneva?

As the minutes ticked by, he made only one decision. That when the inspector returned, he would demand to see a lawyer. "What the hell's the French for lawyer?" he asked out loud.

When an officer eventually appeared, in what Adam estimated must have been about half an hour, he was carrying a tray laden with hot soup, a roll, and what looked to Adam like a steak with all the trimmings and a plastic cup filled to the brim with red wine. He wondered if they had got the wrong man, or if this was simply his last meal before the guillotine. He followed the officer to the door.

"I demand to speak to a lawyer," he said emphatically, but the policeman only shrugged.

"*Je ne comprends pas l'anglais,*" he said, and slammed the door behind him.

Adam settled down to eat the meal that had been set before him, thankful that the French assumed good food should be served whatever the circumstances.

Sir Morris told them his news an hour later and then studied each of them round that table carefully. He would never have called the D4 if he hadn't felt sure that Adam was at last secure. Matthews continued to show no emotion. Busch was unusually silent while Snell looked almost relaxed for a change. Lawrence was the only one who seemed genuinely pleased.

"Scott is locked up in the Ministry of the Interior off the Place Beauvais," continued Sir Morris, "and I have already contacted our military attaché at the embassy. . . ."

"Colonel Pollard," interrupted Lawrence.

"Colonel Pollard indeed," said Sir Morris, "who has been sent over in the ambassador's car and will bring Scott back to be debriefed at our embassy in Faubourg Saint-Honoré. Sureté rang a few moments ago to confirm that Colonel Pollard had arrived." Sir Morris turned toward his number two.

"You will fly over to Paris tonight and conduct the debriefing yourself."

"Yes sir," said Lawrence, looking up at his boss, a smile appearing on his face.

Sir Morris nodded. A cool lot, he considered, as he stared round that table, but the next half hour would surely find out which one of them it was who served two masters.

"Good," said Lawrence. "Any queries?"

"May we know the full details?" asked Matthews.

Lawrence looked toward his chief who nodded his approval.

After Lawrence had gone over his proposed plan and answered any queries the meeting broke up.

Mentor smiled as Sir Morris left the room; his task had already been completed. So simple when you can read upside-down shorthand.

A black Jaguar bearing diplomatic plates had arrived at police headquarters a few minutes earlier than expected. The traffic had not been as heavy as the colonel had anticipated. The inspector was standing on the steps as Pollard jumped out of the car. The policeman looked at the flapping Union Jack on the hood, and considered the whole exercise was becoming rather melodramatic.

Pollard, a short, thickset man dressed in a dark suit, regimental tie, and carrying a rolled umbrella, looked like so many Englishmen who refuse to acknowledge they could possibly be abroad.

The inspector took Pollard directly through to the little room where Adam had been incarcerated.

"Pollard's the name, Colonel Pollard. British military attaché stationed here in Paris. Sorry you've been put through this ordeal, old fellow, but a lot of paperwork had to be completed to get you out. Bloody red tape."

"I understand," said Adam, jumping off the bed and shaking the colonel by the hand. "I was in the army myself."

"I know. Royal Wessex, wasn't it?"

Adam nodded, feeling a little more confident.

"Still, the problem's been sorted out now," continued the colonel. "The French police have been most cooperative and have agreed to let you accompany me to our embassy."

Adam looked at the colonel's tie. "Duke of York's?"

"What? Certainly not," said Pollard, his hand fingering his shirt front. "Green Jackets."

"Yes, of course," said Adam, pleased to have his mistake picked up.

"Now I think we ought to be cutting along, old fellow. I know you'll be relieved to hear that they won't be laying any charges."

The colonel didn't know just how relieved Adam did feel.

The inspector led them both back out into the hall where Adam had only to identify and sign for his personal belongings. He put them all in his pocket, except for the watch, which he slipped over his wrist, and his shoelaces, which he quickly inserted and tied. He wasn't surprised they didn't return Dudley Hulme's passport.

"Don't let's hang around too long, old fellow," said the colonel, beginning to sound a little anxious.

"I won't be a moment," said Adam. "I'm just as keen to get out of this place as you are." He checked his laces before following Colonel Pollard and the inspector out to the waiting Jaguar. He noticed for the first time that the colonel had a slight limp. A chauffeur held the door open for him; Adam laughed.

"Something funny, old fellow?" asked the colonel.

"No. It's just that the last chauffeur who offered to do that for me didn't look quite as friendly."

Adam climbed into the back of the Jaguar, and the colonel slipped in beside him.

"Back to the embassy," said Pollard, and the car moved off briskly.

Adam stared in horror at the flapping Union Jack.

CHAPTER TWENTY

WHEN ADAM AWOKE he was naked.

He tried to look around the room, but he was unable to see what was behind him; his arms, legs, and body were bound tightly by a nylon cord to a chair that had been placed in the middle of the room and that made him all but immobile.

When he looked up from the chair all he could see was Colonel Pollard standing over him. The moment the colonel was satisfied that Adam had regained consciousness he quickly left the room.

Adam turned his head to see all his clothes laid out neatly on a bed at the far side of the cell. He tried to maneuver the chair, but he could barely manage to make it wobble from side to side and after several minutes had advanced only a few inches toward the door. He switched his energies to loosening the cords around his wrists, rubbing them up and down against the wood of the slats, but his arms were bound so tightly that he could only manage the slightest friction.

After struggling ineffectively for several minutes he was

interrupted by the sound of the door swinging open. Adam looked up as Romanov strode through. He decided he was no less terrifying at close quarters. He was followed by another man, whom Adam didn't recognize. The second man was clutching what looked like a cigar box as he took his place somewhere behind Adam. Pollard followed him, carrying a large plastic sheet.

Romanov looked at Adam's naked body and smiled; enjoying his humiliation, he came to a halt directly in front of the chair.

"My name is Alexander Petrovich Romanov," he announced with only a slight accent.

"Or Emmanuel Rosenbaum," said Adam, staring at his adversary closely.

"I am only sorry that we are unable to shake hands," he added, as he began circling the chair. "But I felt in the circumstances certain precautions were necessary. First I should like to congratulate you on having eluded me for so long, but as you will now realize my source in London can place a call every bit as quickly as yours."

"Your source?" said Adam.

"Don't be naive, Captain. You must be painfully aware by now that you're in no position to be asking questions, only answering them."

Adam fixed his gaze on a brick in the wall in front of him, making no attempt to follow Romanov's circumnavigations.

"Pollard," said Romanov sharply, "put Captain Scott back in the center of the room. He seems to have managed to move at least a foot in his getaway attempt."

Pollard did as he was bid, first spreading the plastic sheet on the floor, then maneuvering Adam till the chair was on the center of the sheet.

"Thank you," said Romanov. "I think you have already met our Colonel Pollard," he continued. "That's not his real name, of course, and indeed he's not a real colonel either, but that's what he always wanted to be in life, so when the opportunity arose, we happily obliged.

"In fact the good colonel did serve in the British Army, but

I fear he entered the service of king and country as a private soldier and eighteen years later left, still as a private soldier. And despite an injury to his leg—unfortunately not received from any known enemy of the crown—he was unable to claim a disability pension. Which left him fairly destitute. But as I explained, he always wanted to be a colonel," continued Romanov. "It was a good attempt of yours, 'The Duke of York's?' but as the colonel had genuinely served with the Green Jackets, it was the one tie he felt safe wearing."

Adam's eyes remained fixed on the wall. "Now I confess, our mistake over the Union Jack was lax, but as it is impossible to fly the Russian flag upside down without everyone noticing, it was perhaps understandable. Although in truth Pollard should have spotted it immediately, we must be thankful that you did not until the car doors were safely locked."

Romanov stopped his endless circling and stared down at the nude body.

"Now I think the time has come for you to be introduced to our Dr. Stravinsky, who has so been looking forward to making your acquaintance because he hasn't had a lot of work to do lately, and he fears he might be becoming a little rusty."

Romanov took a pace backward, allowing Stravinsky to come and take his place immediately in front of Adam. The cigar box was still tucked under his arm. Adam stared at the diminutive figure, who seemed to be sizing him up. Stravinsky must have been no taller than five feet and wore an open-necked gray shirt and a badly creased gray suit that made him resemble a junior clerk in a not very successful solicitor's office. A one-day bristle covered his face, leaving the impression that he hadn't expected to be working that day. His thin lips suddenly parted in a grin as if he had come to some conclusion.

"It is a pleasure to make your acquaintance, Captain Scott," began Stravinsky. "Although you are an unexpected guest of the embassy, you are most welcome. You could of course make our association very short by simply letting me have one piece of information. In truth"—he let out a small sigh—"I only require to know the whereabouts of the Czar's icon." He paused. "Although I have a feeling it's not going to be that easy. Am I correct?"

Adam didn't reply.

"It doesn't come as a great surprise. I warned Comrade Romanov after his laudatory description of you that a simple series of questions and answers would be unlikely to suffice. However, I must follow the normal procedure in such circumstances. As you will find, the Russians go by the book every bit as much as the British. Now you may have wondered," added Stravinsky, as if it were an afterthought, "why a man who never smokes should be seen carrying a Cuban cigar box."

Stravinsky waited for Adam's reply but none was forthcoming.

"Ah, no attempt at conversation, I see you have been through such an experience before. Well, then I must continue talking to myself for the moment. When I was a student at the University of Moscow my subject was chemistry, but I specialized in one particular aspect of the science."

Adam feigned no interest as he tried not to recall his worst days in the hands of the Chinese.

"What few people in the West realize is that we Russians were the first to pioneer, at university level, a department of scientific interrogation with a full professorial chair and several research assistants. They are still without one at either Oxford or Cambridge, I am told. But then the West continues to preserve a quixotic view of the value of life and the rights of the individual. Now, as you can imagine, only certain members of the university were aware of the existence of such a department, let alone able to enroll as a student—especially as it was not in the curriculum. But as I had already been a member of the Perviy Otdel it was common sense that I should add the craft of torture to my trade. Now I am basically a simple man," continued Stravinsky, "who had previously shown little interest in research, but once I had been introduced to the 'cigar box' I became, overnight, an enthralled and retentive pupil. I could not wait to be let loose to experiment." He paused to see what effect he was having on Scott and was disappointed to be met by the same impassive stare.

"Torture, of course, is an old and honorable profession," continued Stravinsky. "The Chinese have been at it for nearly three thousand years, as I think you have already experienced, Captain Scott, and even you British have come a long way since the rack. But that particular instrument has proved to be rather cumbersome for carrying around in a modern world. With this in mind, my tutor at Moscow, Professor Metz, has developed something small and simple that even a man of average intelligence can master after a few lessons."

Adam was desperate to know what was in the box, but his look remained impassive.

"With torture, as with making love, Captain Scott, foreplay is the all-important factor. Are you following me, Captain?" asked Stravinsky.

Adam tried to remain relaxed and calm.

"Still no response, I see, but as I explained I am in no hurry. Especially, as I suspect in your case, the whole operation may take a little longer than usual, which I confess will only add to my enjoyment. And although we are not yet in possession of the Czar's icon I *am* at least in control of the one person who knows where it is."

Adam still made no comment.

"So I will ask you once and once only before I open the box. Where is the Czar's icon?"

Adam spat at Stravinsky.

"Not only ill-mannered," remarked Stravinsky, "but also stupid. Because in a very short time you will be desperate for any liquid we might be kind enough to allow you. But, to be fair, you had no way of knowing that."

Stravinsky placed the box on the floor and opened it slowly.

"First, I offer you," he said, like a conjurer in front of a child, "a six-volt nickel-cadmium battery, made by Eveready." He paused. "I thought you would appreciate that touch. Second," he continued, putting his hand back in the box, "a small pulse generator." He placed the rectangular metal box next to the battery. "Third, two lengths of wire with electrodes attached to their ends. Fourth, two syringes; fifth, a tube of collodion glue, and finally, a vial, of which more later. When I say 'finally,' there are still two items left in the box which I shall not require unless it becomes necessary for us to progress to Stage Two in our little experiment, or even Stage Three."

Stravinsky placed everything in a straight line on the floor in front of Adam.

"Doesn't look like a lot, I confess," said Stravinsky. "But with a little imagination I'm sure you will be able to work out its potential. Now: in order that Comrade Romanov and the colonel can enjoy the spectacle I am about to offer it is necessary to add a few details about the nervous system itself. I do hope you are following my every word, Captain Scott, because it is the victim's knowledge which allows him to appreciate the true genius of what is about to follow."

It didn't please Adam that Stravinsky spoke English so well. He could still vividly remember how the Chinese had told him what they were going to do to him in a language that he couldn't understand. With them he had found it easier to allow his mind to drift during their diatribe, but he still ended up in a refrigerator for four hours.

"Now to the practical," continued the gray figure. "By sending a small electrical impulse to the end of the synapse, it is possible to pass on a larger electric message to thousands of other nerves within a fraction of a second. This causes a nasty sensation not unlike touching a live wire when the electrical power has been left on in one's home, more commonly known as an electric shock. Not deadly, but distinctly unpleasant. In the Moscow school this is known as Stage One, and there is no necessity for you to experience this if you are now willing to tell me where I can find the Czar's icon."

Adam remained impassive.

"I see you have not paid attention during my little lecture, so I fear we will have to move from the theoretical to the practical."

Adam began reciting to himself the thirty-seven plays of Shakespeare. How his old English master would have been delighted to know that after all those years of drumming the complete Shakespearean canon into a reluctant student, Adam could still recall them at a moment's notice.

Henry VI, Part One, Henry VI, Part Two, Henry VI, Part Three, Richard II . . .

Stravinsky picked up the tube of collodion glue, removed the cap, and smeared two lumps of it on Adam's chest.

. . . *Comedy of Errors, Titus Andronicus, The Taming of the Shrew* . . .

The Russian attached the two electrodes to the glue, taking the wires back and screwing them to the six-volt battery, which in turn was connected to the tiny pulse generator.

. . . *The Two Gentlemen of Verona, Love's Labour's Lost, Romeo and Juliet* . . .

Without warning, Stravinsky pressed down the handle of the generator for two seconds, during which time Adam received a two-hundred-volt shock. Adam screamed as he experienced excruciating pain while the volts forced their way to every part of his body. But the sensation was over in a moment.

"Do feel free to let us know exactly how you feel. You are in a soundproof room, and therefore you won't be disturbing anyone else in the building."

Adam ignored the comment and, gripping the side of the chair, mumbled to himself *Richard III, A Midsummer Night's Dream, King John* . . .

Stravinsky pressed the plunger down for another two seconds. Adam felt the pain instantly the second time. The moment it was over he felt violently nauseated, but managed to remain conscious.

Stravinsky waited for some time before he volunteered an opinion. "Impressive; you have definitely qualified to enter Stage Two, from which you can be released immediately by answering one simple question. Where is the Czar's icon?"

Adam's mouth had become so dry that he couldn't speak, let alone spit.

"I did try to warn you, Captain Scott." Stravinsky turned toward the door. "Do go and fetch the captain some water, Colonel."

. . . *The Merchant of Venice, Henry IV, Part One, Henry IV, Part Two* . . .

A moment later Pollard was back, and a bottle was thrust into Adam's mouth. He gulped half the contents down until it was pulled away.

"Mustn't overdo it. You might need some more later. But that won't be necessary if you let me know where the icon is."

Adam spat what was left of the water toward where his adversary was standing.

Stravinsky leapt forward and slapped Adam hard across the face with the back of his hand. His head slumped.

"You give me no choice but to advance to Stage Two," said Stravinsky. He looked toward Romanov, who nodded. Stravinsky's thin lips parted in another smile. "You may have wondered," he continued, "how much more harm I can do with a simple six-volt battery, and indeed having seen in numerous American gangster movies an execution by the electric chair, you will know a large generator is needed to kill a man. But first it is important to remember that I don't want to kill you. Second, my science lessons didn't end at Stage One. Professor Metz's mind was also exercised by the feebleness of this stage, and after a lifetime of dedicated research he came up with an ingenious solution known as 'M,' which the Academy of Science named after him in his honor. If you inject 'M' into the nervous system, messages will be transmitted to all your nerves many times more efficiently, thus allowing the pain to multiply without actually proving fatal.

"I only need to multiply a few milliamps by a suitable factor to create a far more interesting effect—so I must ask you once again, where is the Czar's icon?"

. . . *Much Ado About Nothing, Henry V, Julius Caesar* . . .

"I see you are determined that I should proceed," said Stravinsky, removing a syringe from the floor and jabbing the long thin needle into a vial before withdrawing the plunger until the barrel of the syringe was half full. Stravinsky held the needle in the air, pressed the knob, and watched a little spray flow out like a tiny fountain. He moved behind Adam.

"I am now going to give you a lumbar puncture, which, if you attempt to move, will paralyze you from the neck down for life. By nature I am not an honest man, but on this occasion I must recommend you to trust me. I assure you that the injection will not kill you because, as you already know, that is not in our best interest."

Adam didn't move a muscle as he felt the syringe go into his back. *As You Like* . . . he began. Then excruciating pain swept his body, and suddenly, blessedly, he felt nothing.

When he came round there was no way of telling how much time had passed. His eyes slowly focused on his tormentor pacing up and down the room impatiently. Seeing Adam's eyes open, the unshaven man stopped pacing, smiled, walked over to the chair, and ran his fingers slowly over the large bandage that covered Adam's two-day-old shoulder wound. The touch appeared gentle, but to Adam it felt like a hot iron being forced across his shoulder.

"As I promised," said Stravinsky. "A far more interesting sensation is awaiting you. And now I think I'll rip the bandage off." He waited for a moment while Adam pursed his lips. Then, in one movement, he tore the bandage back. Adam screamed as if the bullet had hit him again. Romanov came forward, leaned over and studied the wound.

"I'm relieved to see my colleague didn't miss you completely," Romanov said before adding, "can you imagine what it will be like when I allow Dr. Stravinsky to wire you up again and then press the little generator?"

. . . *Twelfth Night, Hamlet, The Merry Wives of Windsor* . . ." Adam said aloud for the first time.

"I see you wish to leave nothing to the imagination," said Romanov and disappeared behind him. Stravinsky checked that the wires were attached to the collodion glue on Adam's chest, and then he returned to the generator. "I shall press

down the handle in three seconds' time. You know what you
have to do to stop me."

". . . *Troilus and Cressida, All's Well That Ends Well* . . ."

As the handle plunged down, the volts seemed to find
their way to every nerve ending in his body. Adam let out
such a scream that if they had not been in a soundproofed
room anyone within a mile would have heard him. When the
initial effect was over he was left shaking and retching uncontrollably. Stravinsky and Pollard rushed forward to the
chair and quickly undid the nylon cords. Adam fell on his
hands and knees, still vomiting.

"Couldn't afford to let you choke to death, could we?" said
Stravinsky. "We lost one or two that way in the early days,
but we know better now."

As soon as the sickness subsided, Stravinsky threw Adam
back up on to the chair, and Pollard tied him up again.

"Where is the Czar's icon?" shouted Stravinsky.

". . . *Measure for Measure, Othello, King Lear* . . ." Adam said, his
voice now trembling.

Pollard picked up another bottle of water and thrust it at
Adam's lips. Adam gulped it down, but it was as a tiny oasis
in a vast desert. Romanov came forward, and Stravinsky took
his place beside the plunger.

"You are a brave man, Scott," said Romanov, "with nothing left to prove, but this is madness. Just tell me where the
icon is, and I will send Stravinsky away and order the colonel
to leave you on the steps of the British embassy."

". . . *Macbeth, Antony and Cleopatra* . . ."

Romanov let out a sigh and nodded. Stravinsky pushed
the plunger down once again. Even the colonel turned white
as he watched Adam's reaction. The pitch of the scream was
even higher, and the muscles contorted visibly as Adam felt
the volts reach the millions of little nerve ends in his body.
When once more he had been released, Adam lay on the
floor on his hands and knees. Was there anything left in his
stomach that could still possibly come up? He raised his
head, only to be hurled back on to the chair and bound up
again. Stravinsky stared down at him.

"Most impressive, Captain Scott, you have qualified for Stage Three."

Adam passed out.

When Lawrence arrived at Orly Airport that evening he was looking forward to a quiet dinner with his old friend at the ambassador's residence. He was met by Colonel Pollard.

"How is he?" were Lawrence's first words.

"I hoped you were going to tell us," said Pollard, as he took Lawrence's overnight suitcase. Lawrence stopped in his tracks and stared at the tall, thin soldier who was in the full-dress uniform of the Royal Dragon Guards.

"What do you mean?" said Lawrence.

"Simply that," said Pollard. "I followed your instructions to the letter and went to pick up Scott at the Ministry of the Interior, but when I arrived I was informed that he had been taken away twenty minutes earlier by someone using my name. We contacted your office immediately, but as you were already en route to the plane the ambassador ordered me straight to the airport while he phoned Sir Morris."

Lawrence staggered and nearly fell. The colonel came quickly to his side. He didn't understand what Lawrence meant when he said, "He's bound to believe it's me."

When Adam regained consciousness, Romanov stood alone.

"Sometimes," said the Russian, continuing as if Adam had never passed out, "a man is too proud to show lack of resolution in front of the torturer or indeed one of his own countrymen, especially a traitor. That is why I have removed Stravinsky and the colonel from our presence. Now I have no desire to see Stravinsky continue this experiment to Stage Three, but I can stop him only if you will tell me where you have put the icon."

"Why should I?" said Adam belligerently. "It's legally mine."

"Not so, Captain Scott. What you picked up from the bank in Geneva is the priceless original painted by Rublev, which belongs to the Union of Soviet Socialist Republics. And if that icon were to appear in any auction house or gallery in the world, we would immediately claim it as a national treasure stolen by the seller."

"But how could that be . . . ?" began Adam.

"Because," said Romanov, "it is you who are now in possession of the original that the Czar left in the safekeeping of the Grand Duke of Hesse, and for over fifty years the Soviet Union has only had a copy." Adam's eyes opened wide in disbelief as Romanov removed from the inside pocket of his overcoat an icon of Saint George and the dragon. Romanov paused and then turned it over; a smile of satisfaction crossed his face as Adam's eyes registered the significance of the missing crown.

"Like you," continued Romanov, "I only have this one on loan—but you tell me where the original is, and I will release you and exchange the copy for the original. No one will be any the wiser, and you'll still be able to make yourself a worthwhile profit."

"Old lamps for new," said Adam with a sneer.

Romanov's eyes narrowed menacingly. "Surely you realize, Scott, that you are in possession of a priceless masterpiece that belongs to the Soviet Union. Unless you return the icon you are going to cause considerable embarrassment for your country, and you will probably end up in jail. All you have to do is tell me where the icon is and you can go free."

Adam didn't even bother to shake his head.

"Then the time has obviously come to let you into some information you will be more interested in," Romanov said, extracting a single sheet of paper from an envelope he removed from his inside pocket. Adam was genuinely puzzled, quite unable to think what it could be. Romanov opened it slowly and held it up so that Adam could only see the back.

"This single sheet of paper reveals a sentence carried out

in Moscow in 1946 by Judge I. T. Nikitchenko—the death sentence," continued Romanov, "pronounced on a certain Major Vladimir Kosky, the Russian guard in charge of the Soviet watch the night Reichsmarschall Hermann Goering died." He turned the paper around so Adam could see. "As you can see, Major Kosky was found guilty of collaboration with the enemy for financial gain. It was proved he was directly responsible for smuggling cyanide into the Reichsmarschall's cell on the night he died." Adam's eyes widened. "Ah, I see I have dealt the ace of spades," said Romanov. "Now I think you will finally tell me where the icon actually is because you have an expression in England, if I recall correctly: fair exchange is no robbery. Your icon for my icon, plus the legal judgment that will finally vindicate your father's honor."

Adam closed his eyes, painfully aware for the first time that Romanov had no idea what was inside the icon.

Romanov was unable to hide his anger. He walked to the door and flung it open. "He's yours," he said.

Dr. Stravinsky reentered the room and, smiling, continued as if nothing had interrupted him. "Professor Metz was never really satisfied with Stage Two because he found the recovery time even for an extremely brave and fit man like yourself could sometimes hold him up for hours, even days. So during his final years at the university he devoted his time to finding how he could possibly speed the whole process up. As for all geniuses, the final solution was staggering in its simplicity. All he had to produce was a chemical formula that when injected into the nervous system caused an immediate recovery—a rapid analgesic. It took him twelve years and several deaths before he came up with the final solution," said Stravinsky, removing another vial from the cigar box and plunging the needle of a second syringe into the seal on the top of the vial.

"This," Stravinsky said, holding up the little vial in triumph, "when injected into your bloodstream, will aid recovery so quickly that you may even wonder if you ever went through any pain in the first place. For this piece of genius

Metz should have been awarded the Nobel Prize, but it was not something we felt he could share with the rest of the scientific world. But because of him I can repeat the process you have just experienced again and again, never permitting you to die. You see, I can keep this generator pumping up and down every thirty minutes for the next week if that is your desire," said Stravinsky, as he stared down at Adam's white disbelieving face flecked with yellow specks of his vomit.

"Or I can stop immediately after I have administered the antidote the moment you let me know where the Czar's icon is."

Stravinsky stood in front of Adam and half filled the syringe. Adam felt intensely cold, yet the shock of his torture had caused him to sweat profusely. "Sit still, Captain Scott, I have no desire to do you any permanent injury." Adam felt the needle go deep in, and moments later the fluid entered his bloodstream.

He could not believe how quickly he felt himself recovering; in minutes he no longer felt sick or disoriented. The sensation in his arms and legs returned to normal while the wish never to experience Stage Two again became acute.

"Brilliant man, Professor Metz, on that I'm sure we can both agree," said Stravinsky, "and if he were still alive I feel certain he would have written a paper on your case." Slowly and carefully Stravinsky began to smear more lumps of jelly on Adam's chest. When he was satisfied with his handiwork he once again attached the electrodes to the jelly.

"*Coriolanus, Timon of Athens, Pericles.*" Stravinsky thrust his palm down, and Adam hoped that he would die. He found a new level to scream at, as his body shook and shook. Seconds later he felt ice cold and, shivering uncontrollably, he started to retch.

Stravinsky was quickly by his side to release him. Adam fell to the ground and coughed up what was left in his body. When he was only spitting, Pollard placed him back in the chair.

"You must understand I can't let you die, Captain. Now where is the icon?" Stravinsky shouted.

In the Louvre, Adam wanted to holler, but his words barely came out as a whisper, the inside of his mouth feeling like sandpaper. Stravinsky proceeded to fill the second syringe again and injected Adam with the fluid. Once again it was only moments before the agony subsided and he felt completely recovered.

"Ten seconds, we go again. Nine, eight, seven . . ."

"*Cymbeline.*"

". . . six, five, four . . ."

"*The Winter's Tale.*"

". . . three, two, one."

"*The Tempest.* Aahhh," he screamed and immediately fainted. The next thing Adam remembered was the cold water being poured over him by the colonel before he began to retch again. Once tied back in the chair Stravinsky thrust the syringe into him once more, but Adam couldn't believe he would ever recover again. He must surely die, because he wanted to die. He felt the syringe jab into his flesh again.

Romanov stepped forward and looking straight at Adam said, "I feel Dr. Stravinsky and I have earned a little supper. We did consider inviting you but felt your stomach wouldn't be up to it, but when we return fully refreshed Dr. Stravinsky will repeat the entire exercise again and again until you let me know where you have hidden the icon."

Romanov and Stravinsky left as Colonel Pollard came back in. Romanov and the colonel exchanged a few sentences, which Adam could not make out. Then Romanov left the room, closing the door quietly behind him.

Pollard came over to Adam and offered him the water bottle. Adam gulped it down and was genuinely surprised how quickly he was recovering. Yet although his senses were returning to normal, Adam still doubted he could survive one more time.

"I'm going to throw up again," said Adam and suddenly thrust his head forward. Pollard quickly undid the knots and watched Adam slump to his hands and knees. He threw up some spit and rested before the colonel helped him gently back into the chair. As he sat down Adam gripped both sides of the chair legs firmly; then, with all the strength he could muster jackknifed forward, swung the chair over his head, and brought it crashing down on top of the unsuspecting colonel. Pollard collapsed in a heap, unconscious, on the floor in front of Adam and never heard him utter the words, "*Henry VIII*, and *Two Noble Kinsmen*—I'll bet that's one you've never heard of, Colonel. Mind you, to be fair, not everyone thinks Shakespeare wrote it."

Adam remained on his hands and knees over the colonel's body, wondering what his next move should be. He was grateful that the soundproofed room was now working in his favor. He waited for a few more seconds as he tried to measure what was left of his strength. He picked up the water bottle that had been knocked over and drained it of its last drops. He then crawled across to the bed and pulled on his underwear and socks, his not-so-white shirt, followed by the trousers and shoes. He was about to put on the blazer but found the lining had been ripped to shreds. He changed his mind and stumbled like an old man back toward the colonel, removed his Harris tweed coat and slipped it on. It was large round the shoulders but short at the hips.

Adam made his way to the door, feeling almost exhilarated. He turned the handle and pulled. The door came open an inch—nothing happened—two inches—still nothing. He stared through the crack, but all he could see was a dark corridor. As he pulled the door wide open, the hinges sounded to Adam like racing tires screeching. Once he was certain that no one was going to return, he ventured into the corridor.

Standing against the wall, he stared up and down the thin windowless passage, waiting for his eyes to adjust to the dark. He could make out a light shining through a pebbled pane in a door at the far end of the corridor and began to take short steps toward it. He continued on, as if he were a blind man, creeping slowly forward until he saw another beam of light coming from under a door to his right about ten yards away from the one he needed to reach. He edged cautiously on and was only a pace away from the first door when it opened abruptly, and out stepped a small man in a white tunic and blue kitchen overalls. Adam froze against the wall as the kitchen hand removed a pack of cigarettes and a box of matches from his pocket and headed away in the opposite direction. When the man reached the glazed door he opened it and walked out. Adam watched the silhouette outlined against the pebbled window, a match being struck, a cigarette being lit, the first puff of smoke; he even heard a sigh.

Adam crept past what he now assumed was a kitchen and on toward the outer door. He turned the knob slowly, waiting for the silhouette to move. The outer door also possessed hinges that no one had bothered to oil for months. The smoker turned round and smiled as Adam's left hand landed firmly in his stomach. As the smoker bent over, Adam's right fist came up to the man's chin with all the force he could muster. The smoker sank in a heap on the ground, and Adam stood over him, thankful that he didn't move.

He dragged the limp body across the grass, dumped it behind a bush, and remained kneeling by it while he tried to work out his bearings. Adam could just make out a high wall ahead of him with a graveled courtyard in front of it. The wall threw out a long shadow from the moon across the tiny stones. About twenty yards. . . . Summoning up every ounce of energy, he ran to the wall and then clung to it like a limpet, remaining motionless in its shadow. Slowly and silently he moved round the wall, yard by yard, until he reached the front of what he now felt sure was the Russian embassy. The great green wooden gates at the front entrance were open, and every few seconds limousines swept past him. Adam looked back up toward the front door of the embassy, and at the top of the steps he saw a massive man, medals stretching across his formal dress jacket, shaking hands with each of his departing guests. Adam assumed he was the ambassador.

One or two of the guests were leaving on foot. There were

two armed gendarmes at the gate who stood rigidly to attention and saluted as each car or guest passed by.

Adam waited until a vast BMW, the West German flag fluttering on its hood, slowed as it passed through the gates. Using the car to shield him, Adam walked out into the center of the drive, then, following closely behind, walked straight between the guards toward the road.

"*Bonsoir,*" he said lightly to the guards as the car moved forward; he was only a yard from the road. "Walk," he told himself, "don't run. Walk, walk until you are out of their sight." They saluted deferentially. "Don't look back." Another car followed him out, but he kept his eyes firmly to the front.

"*Tu cherches une femme?*" a voice repeated from the shadows of a recessed doorway. Adam had ended up in a badly lit one-way street. Several men of indeterminate age seemed to be walking aimlessly up and down the curbside. He eyed them with suspicion as he moved on through the darkness.

"Wha—?" said Adam, stepping sharply into the road, his senses heightened by the unexpected sound.

"From Britain, eh? Do you search for a girl?" The voice held an unmistakable French accent.

"You speak English," said Adam, still unable to see the woman clearly.

"You have to know a lot of languages in my profession, *chéri,* or you'd starve."

Adam tried to think coherently. "How much for the night?"

"*Eh bien,* but it's not yet midnight," said the girl. "So I would have to charge two hundred francs."

Although he had no money, Adam hoped the girl might at least lead him to safety.

"Two hundred is fine."

"*D'accord,*" said the girl, at last stepping out of the shadows. Adam was surprised by how attractive she turned out to be. "Take my arm and if you pass a gendarme say only, '*Ma femme*.'"

Adam stumbled forward.

"Ah, I think you drink too much, *chéri*. Never mind, you can lean on me, yes."

"No, I'm just tired," said Adam, trying hard to keep up with her pace.

"You have been to party at embassy, *n'est-ce pas?*"

Adam was startled.

"Don't be surprised, *chéri*. I find most of my regulars from the embassies. They can't risk to be involved in casual affairs, *tu comprends?*"

"I believe you," said Adam.

"My apartment is just round the corner," she assured him. Adam was confident he could get that far, but he took a deep breath when they arrived at a block of flats and first saw the steps. He just managed to reach the front door.

"I live on the top of the house, *chéri*. Very nice view," she said matter-of-factly, "but I'm afraid no—how do you say— lift."

Adam said nothing, but leaned against the outside wall, breathing deeply.

"You are *fatigué*," she said. By the time they had reached the second floor she almost had to drag Adam up the last few steps.

"I don't see you getting it up tonight, *chéri*," she said, opening her front door and turning on the light. "Still, it's your party." She strode in, turning on other lights as she went.

Adam staggered across the floor toward the only chair in sight and collapsed into it. The girl had by this time disappeared into another room, and he had to make a supreme effort not to fall asleep before she returned.

As she stood in the light of the doorway, Adam was able to see her properly for the first time. Her blonde hair was short and curly, and she wore a red blouse and a knee-length skin-tight black skirt. A wide white plastic belt emphasized her small waist. She wore black mesh stockings, and what he could see of her legs would have normally aroused him had he been in any other condition.

She walked over to Adam with a slight swing of the hips and knelt down in front of him. Her eyes were a surprisingly luminous green.

"Would you please to give me the two hundred now?" she asked, without harshness. She ran her hand along his thigh.

"I don't have any money," said Adam quite simply.

"What?" she said, sounding angry for the first time. Placing her hand in his inside pocket she removed a wallet and asked, "Then what's this? I don't play the games," she said, handing the thick wallet over to Adam. He opened the flap to find it was jammed full of French francs and a few English pounds. Adam concluded that the colonel was obviously paid in cash for his services.

Adam extracted two one-hundred-franc notes and dutifully handed them over. "That's better," she said, and disappeared into the other room.

Adam checked quickly through the wallet to discover a driver's license and a couple of credit cards in the colonel's real name of Albert Tomkins. He quickly looked around. A double bed that was wedged up against the far wall took up most of the floor space. Apart from the chair he was settled in the only other pieces of furniture were a dressing table and a tiny stool with a red velvet cushion on it. A stained blue carpet covered most of the wooden floor.

To his left was a small fireplace with logs stacked neatly in one corner. All Adam wished to do was fall asleep, but with what strength was left in his body, he pushed himself up, wobbled over to the fireplace, and hid the wallet between the logs. He lurched back toward the chair and fell into it as the door reopened.

Again the girl stood in the light of the doorway, but this time she wore only a short pink negligee, which even in his state Adam could see right through whenever she made the slightest movement. She walked slowly across the room and once more knelt down beside him.

"How you like it, *mon chéri?* Straight or the French way?"

"I need to rest," said Adam.

"For two hundred francs you sleep in any 'otel," she said in disbelief.

"I only want to be allowed to rest a few minutes," he assured her.

"*Anglais,*" she said, and began to try to lift Adam out of the chair and toward the bed. He stumbled and fell, landing half on and half off the corner of the mattress. She undressed him as deftly as any nurse could have done before lifting his legs up on to the bed. Adam made no effort to help or hinder her. She hesitated for a moment when she saw the shoulder wound, bewildered over what kind of accident could have caused such a gash. She rolled him over to the far side and pulled back the top sheet and blanket. Then she walked round to the other side of the bed and rolled him back again. Finally she pushed him flat on his back and covered him with the sheet and blankets.

"I could still give you French if you like," she said. But Adam was already asleep.

CHAPTER
TWENTY-ONE

WHEN ADAM EVENTUALLY awoke the sun was already shining through the small window of the bedroom. He blinked as he took in his surroundings and tried to recall what had happened the night before. Then it all came back to him and he suddenly felt sick at the memory. He sat on the edge of the bed, but the moment he tried to stand he felt giddy and weak and fell back down. At least he had escaped. He looked around the room, but the girl was nowhere to be seen or heard. Then he remembered the wallet.

He sat bolt upright, gathering himself for a few moments before standing up again and trying to walk. Although he was still unsteady, it was better than he had expected. It's your recovery that counts, not your speed, he thought ironically. When he reached the fireplace he fell on his knees and searched among the logs, but the colonel's wallet was no longer there. As quickly as he could, he went to the jacket hanging over the back of the chair. He checked in the inside pocket: a pen, a half-toothless comb, a passport, a driver's license, some other papers, but no wallet. He searched the outside pockets: a bunch of keys, a penknife, a few assorted coins, English and French, but that was all that was left. With a string of oaths he collapsed onto the floor. He sat there for some time and didn't move until he heard a key in the lock.

The front door of the flat swung open, and the girl sauntered in carrying a shopping basket. She was dressed in a pretty floral skirt and white blouse that would have been suitable for any churchgoer on a Sunday morning. The basket was crammed with food.

"Woken up, 'ave we, *chéri? Est-ce que tu prends le petit déjeuner?*"

Adam looked a little taken aback.

She returned his stare. "Even working girls need their breakfast, *n'est-ce pas?* Sometimes is the only meal I manage all day."

"Where's my wallet?" asked Adam coldly.

"On the table," said the girl, pointing.

Adam glanced across the room to see that she had left the wallet in the most obvious place.

"It not necessary of you to 'ide it," she reprimanded him. "Because I'm a whore don't think I'm a thief." With this she strode off into the kitchen, leaving the door open.

Adam suddenly felt very small.

"Coffee and croissants?" she shouted.

"Fantastic," said Adam. He paused. "I'm sorry. I was stupid."

"Not to think about it," she said. "*Ça n'est rien.*"

"I still don't know your name," said Adam.

"My working name is Brigitte, but as you 'ave not use my services last night or this morning you can call me by my real name, Jeanne."

"Can I have a bath, Jeanne?"

"The door in the corner, but don't take too long, unless you like croissants cold." Adam made his way to the bathroom and found Jeanne had provided for everything a man might need: a razor, shaving cream, soap, flannel, clean towels—and a giant box of condoms.

After a warm bath and a shave, delights Adam had nearly forgotten, he felt almost back to normal again, if still somewhat fragile. He tucked a pink towel around his waist before joining Jeanne in the kitchen. The table was already laid, and she was removing a warm croissant from the oven.

"Good body," she said, turning round and scrutinizing him carefully. "Much better than I usually 'ave." She put the plate down in front of him.

"You're not so bad yourself," said Adam, grinning, taking the seat opposite her.

"I am 'appy you notice," said Jeanne. "I was beginning to think about you." Adam spread the roll liberally with jam and didn't speak again for several seconds.

"When 'ave you last eat?" asked Jeanne as he devoured the final scrap left on the plate.

"Yesterday lunch. But I emptied my stomach in between."

"Sick, eh? You mustn't drink so much."

"I think 'drained' might be a better word. Tell me, Jeanne," said Adam, looking at her, "are you still available for work?"

She checked her watch. "One of my regulars is at two this afternoon, and I must be back on the streets by five. So it would 'ave to be this morning," she said matter-of-factly.

"No, no, that's not what I meant," said Adam.

"You could quickly give a girl, how do you say in England?—a complex," said Jeanne. "You not one of those weird ones, are you?"

"No, nothing like that," said Adam, laughing. "But I would be willing to pay you another two hundred francs for your services."

"Is it legal?"

"Absolutely."

"*Alors*, that makes a change. 'Ow long you need me?"

"An hour, two at the most."

"It's better than the rate for my present job. What am I expected to do?"

"For one hour I want every man in Paris to fancy you. Only this time you won't be available—at any price."

* * *

"Scott just contacted me only a few minutes ago," said Lawrence to the assembled D4.

"What did he have to say?" asked an anxious Sir Morris.

"Only that he was turning back the clock."

"What do you think he meant by that?" asked Snell, nervously touching his mustache.

"Geneva would be my guess," said Lawrence.

"Why Geneva?" said Matthews.

"I'm not certain," said Lawrence, "but he said it had something to do with the German girl, or the bank, but I can't be sure which."

No one spoke for some time.

"Did you trace the call?" asked Busch.

"Only the area," said Lawrence. "Neuchâtel on the French-Swiss border."

"Good. Then we're in business again," said Sir Morris. "Have you informed Interpol?"

"Yes sir, and I've personally briefed the German, French, and Swiss police," added Lawrence, which were the only true words he had spoken since the meeting had begun.

Jeanne took forty minutes to get herself ready, and when Adam saw the result he let out a long whistle.

"No one is going to give me a second look, even if I were to empty the till in front of them," he told her.

"That is the idea, *n'est-ce pas?*" Jeanne said, grinning.

"Now, are you sure you know exactly what you have to do?" said Adam.

"I know well." Jeanne checked herself once more in the long hall mirror. "We 'ave rehearse like military exercise four times already."

"Good," said Adam. "You sound as if you're ready to face the enemy. So let's begin with what in the army they call 'advance to contact.'"

Jeanne took out a plastic bag from a drawer in the kitchen. The single word "Céline" was printed across it. She handed it over to Adam. He folded the bag in four, and stuffed it into his jacket pocket before walking into the corridor. She locked the flat door behind them, and they walked down the stairs together and out on to the pavement.

Adam hailed a taxi and Jeanne told the driver, "Tuileries garden." Once they had arrived, Adam paid the fare and joined Jeanne on the pavement.

"*Bonne chance,*" said Adam as he remained on the corner, allowing Jeanne to walk twenty yards ahead of him. Although he still felt unsteady, he was able to keep up at her pace. The sun beat down on his face as he watched her walk in and out of the ornate flower beds. Her pink leather skirt and tight white sweater made almost every man she passed turn and take a second look. Some even stopped in their tracks and continued watching until she was out of sight.

The comments she could hear and Adam couldn't, twenty yards behind, ranged from "*Je payerais n'importe quoi,*" which she reluctantly had to pass up, to just plain "*Putain,*" which Adam had told her to ignore. Her part had to be acted out, and for two hundred francs she would just have to suffer the odd insult.

Jeanne reached the Right Bank of the Seine, and she did not look back; she had been instructed not to turn around in any circumstances. Keep going forward, Adam had told her. He was still twenty yards behind her when she reached the quai des Tuileries. She waited for the lights to turn green before she crossed the wide road, keeping in the center of a throng of people.

At the end of the quai she turned sharp right, and for the first time could see the Louvre straight in front of her. She had been too embarrassed to admit to him that she had never been inside the building before.

Jeanne climbed the steps to the entrance hall. By the time she had reached the swinging doors, Adam was approaching the bottom step. She continued on up the marble staircase with Adam still following discreetly behind.

When Jeanne reached the top of the stairs she passed the statue of the Winged Victory of Samothrace. She proceeded into the first of the large crowded rooms and began counting to herself, noting as she passed through each gallery that there was at least one attendant on duty in each, usually standing around aimlessly near one of the exits. A group of schoolchildren were studying *The Last Supper* by Giovanni, but Jeanne ignored the masterpiece and marched straight on. After passing six attendants she arrived in the room Adam had described to her so vividly. She strode purposefully into the center and paused for a few seconds. Some of the men began to lose interest in the paintings. Satisfied by the impact she was causing, she flounced over to the guard, who straightened up his jacket and smiled at her.

"Dans quelle direction se trouve de la peinture du seizième siècle?" Jeanne asked innocently. The guard turned to point in the direction of the relevant room. The moment he turned back, Jeanne slapped him hard across the face and shouted at him at the top of her voice: *"Quelle horreur! Pour qui est-ce que vous me prenez?"*

Only one person in the icon room didn't stop to gaze at the spectacle. *"Je vais parler à la direction,"* she screamed, and flounced off toward the main exit. The entire charade was over in less than thirty seconds. The bemused guard remained transfixed to the spot, staring after his assailant in bewilderment.

Jeanne continued on through three centuries more quickly than H. G. Wells. She took a left turn into the sixteenth-century room as instructed, and then another left brought her back into the long corridor. A few moments later, she joined Adam at the top of the marble staircase leading down to the front entrance.

As they walked back down the steps together, Adam handed her the Céline bag and was about to part again, when two attendants waiting on the bottom step threw out their arms, indicating they should halt.

"Do you wish a run for it?" she whispered.

"Certainly not," said Adam very firmly. "Just don't say anything."

"Madame, excusez moi, mais je dois fouiller dans votre sac."

"Allez-y pour tout ce que vous y trouvez," said Jeanne.

"Certainly you can search her bag," said Adam, returning to her side before Jeanne could say anything more. "It's an icon, quite a good one, I think. I purchased it in a shop near the Champs Elysées only this morning."

"*Vous me permettez, monsieur?*" the senior attendant asked suspiciously.

"Why not?" said Adam. He removed the Czar's icon from the bag and handed it over to the attendant, who seemed surprised by the way things were turning out. Two more attendants rushed over and stood on each side of Adam.

The senior attendant asked in broken English if Adam would mind if one of the gallery's experts were to look at the painting.

"Only too delighted," said Adam. "It would be fascinating to have a second opinion."

The senior attendant was beginning to look unsure of himself. "*Je dois vous demander de me suivre,*" he suggested in a tone that was suddenly less hostile. He ushered them quickly through to a little room at the side of the gallery. The attendant put the Czar's icon in the middle of a table that dominated the room. Adam sat down and Jeanne, still bemused, took the seat beside him.

"I'll only be a moment, sir." The senior attendant almost ran out while the two other attendants remained stationed near the door. Adam still did not attempt to speak to Jeanne although he could see that she was becoming more and more apprehensive. He shot her a little smile as they sat waiting.

When the door eventually opened, an elderly man with a scholarly face preceded the senior attendant.

"*Bonjour, monsieur,*" he began, looking at Adam, the first man who did not show an overt interest in Jeanne. "I understand that you are English," and without giving either of them more than a glance, he picked up the icon.

He studied the painting carefully for some time before he spoke. Adam felt just a moment's apprehension. "Most interesting. Yes, yes." One of the attendants put a hand on his billy club.

"Interesting," he repeated. "I would be so bold as to suggest," he hesitated, "late nineteenth century, eighteen seventy, possibly 'eighty. Fascinating. Not that we have ever had anything quite like it at the Louvre," he added. "You do realize it's an inferior copy," he said as he handed the icon back to Adam. "The original Czar's icon of Saint George and the dragon hangs in the Winter Palace in Leningrad. I've seen it, you know," he added, sounding rather pleased with himself.

"You certainly have," said Adam under his breath as he placed the icon back in its plastic bag. The old man bowed low to Jeanne and said as he shuffled away, "Funnily enough, someone else was making inquiries about the Czar's icon only a few weeks ago." Adam was the only person who didn't seem surprised.

"I was only—" began the senior attendant.

"Doing your duty," completed Adam. "A natural precaution, if I may say so," he added a little pompously. "I can only admire the way you carried out the entire exercise."

Jeanne stared at them both, quite unable to comprehend what was happening.

"You are kind, monsieur," said the attendant, sounding relieved. "Hope you come again," he added, smiling at Jeanne.

The attendant accompanied the two of them to the entrance of the Louvre, and when they pushed through the door he stood smartly to attention and saluted.

Adam and Jeanne walked down the steps and into the Paris sun.

"Well, can I now know what that's all about?" asked Jeanne.

"You were *magnifique*," said Adam, not attempting to explain.

"I know, I know," said Jeanne. "But why you need Oscar-winning show by me when the picture was always yours?"

"True," agreed Adam. "But I had left it in their safe-keeping overnight. And without your bravura performance it might have taken considerably longer to convince the authorities that it belonged to me in the first place."

Adam realized from the look on her face that Jeanne had no idea what he was talking about.

"You know, that my first time in the Louvre?" said Jeanne, linking her arm through Adam's.

"You're priceless," said Adam, laughing.

"That I'm not," she said, turning to face him. "Two hundred francs was our bargain even if it belongs to you or not."

"Correct," said Adam, taking out the colonel's wallet and extracting two hundred francs, to which he added another hundred. "A well-earned bonus," said Adam.

She pocketed the money gratefully. "I think I'll take an evening off," she said.

Adam held her in his arms and kissed her on both cheeks as if she were a French general.

She kissed him on the lips and smiled. "When you next in Paris, *chéri*, look me up. I owe you one—on the house."

"How can you be so sure?"

"Because Antarctic was willing to give Pemberton too many facts?"

"What do you mean?"

"You told me that Pemberton said he would never phone back if you let him down again. Not only did he phone again, but he peppered you with facts. Which way did he say he was going?"

"Back to Geneva. Something to do with the German girl and the bank."

"The girl's dead and the bank's closed today. He must be on his way to England."

"I would like to rent a car, which I will be dropping off at the coast. I haven't decided which port yet," he told the girl behind the counter.

"*Bien sûr, monsieur,*" said the girl. "Would you be kind enough to fill in the form, and we will also need your driver's license." Adam removed all the papers from his inside pocket and passed over the colonel's driver's license. He filled in the forms slowly, copying the signature off the back of the colonel's Playboy Club card. He handed over the full amount required in cash, hoping it would speed up the transaction.

The girl picked up the cash and counted the notes carefully before checking the back of the license against the signature on the form. Adam was relieved that she hadn't spotted the disparity in the dates of birth. He replaced all Albert Tomkins's documents and wallet in his inside jacket pocket as the girl turned round and removed an ignition key from a hook on a board behind her.

"It's a red Citroen, parked on the first floor," she told him. "The registration number is stamped on the key ring."

Adam thanked her and walked quickly up to the first floor where he handed the key over to an attendant, who drove the car out of its parking space for him.

When the attendant returned the key, Adam handed him a ten-franc note. Exactly the same sum as the other man had given him to let him know if an Englishman who fitted Adam's description tried to hire a car. What had he promised? Another hundred francs if he phoned within five minutes of seeing him.

PART IV

THE KREMLIN

MOSCOW
June 19, 1966

CHAPTER
TWENTY-TWO

THE KREMLIN
JUNE 19, 1966

LEONID ILYICH BREZHNEV entered the room, hardly allowing the other four members of the inner quorum of the Defense Council enough time to stand. Their faces were grim, resolute, no different from their public image—unlike Western politicians.

The General Secretary took his place at the head of the table and nodded to his colleagues to sit.

The last time the inner quorum of the Defense Council had been summoned to a meeting at an hour's notice had been at the request of Khrushchev, who was hoping to enlist support for his Cuban adventure. Brezhnev would never forget the moment when his predecessor had uncontrollably burst into tears because they had forced him to order the Soviet ships to return home. From that moment, Brezhnev knew it could only be a matter of time before he would succeed Khrushchev as the leader of the Communist world. On this occasion he had no intention of bursting into tears.

On his right sat Marshal Malinovsky, Minister of Defense; on his left Andrei Gromyko, the young Foreign Minister. Beside him sat the Chief of the General Staff, Marshal Zakharov, and, on his left, Yuri Zaborski. Even the seating plan confirmed Brezhnev's obvious displeasure with the Chairman of the KGB.

He raised his eyes and stared up at the massive oil painting of Lenin reviewing an early military parade in Red Square, a picture no one other than members of the Politburo had seen since it disappeared from the Tretyakov in 1950.

If only Lenin had realized the icon was a fake in the first place, Brezhnev reflected. . . . Yet, despite the traditional Russian pastime of blaming the dead for everything that goes wrong, he knew that Vladimir Ilyich Lenin was beyond criticism. He would have to find a living scapegoat.

His eyes rested on Zaborski. "Your report, Comrade Chairman."

Zaborski fingered a file in front of him although he knew the contents almost by heart. "The plan to locate the Czar's icon was carried out in an exemplary fashion," he began. "When the Englishman, Adam Scott, was caught and later . . . questioned"—they all accepted the euphemism—"by Comrade Dr. Stravinsky in the privacy of our embassy in Paris, the Englishman gave no clue as to where we would find the icon. It became obvious he was a professional agent of the West. After three hours, interrogation was momentarily suspended. It was during this period that the prisoner managed to escape."

"Managed," interjected Brezhnev.

Just as he had taught his subordinates over the years, the Chairman of the KGB made no attempt to reply.

"Don't you realize," continued the General Secretary, "that we had within our grasp the opportunity to turn the very land the Americans use for their early-warning system into a base for our short-range missiles? If it had proved possible to retrieve our icon, it would also have been possible to site those same missiles along a border less than a thousand eight hundred kilometers from Seattle—two thousand eight hundred kilometers from San Francisco—a mere four thousand kilometers from Chicago. Not only could we have made the Americans' early-warning system redundant, we could have greatly improved our ability to detect any enemy missiles while they were still thousands of kilometers from our nearest border."

The General Secretary paused to see if the Chairman of the KGB had any further explanation to offer, but Zaborski kept his eyes fixed on the table in front of him. When Brezhnev began again it was almost in a whisper:

"And for such a prize we would not have had to sacrifice one life, one rocket, one tank, or even one bullet—because all this was ours by right. But if we fail to locate the Czar's icon in the next thirty-six hours, we will never be given such a chance again. We will have lost our one opportunity to remove a star from the American flag."

Foreign Secretary Gromyko waited until he was certain Brezhnev had completed his statement before he inquired: "If I may ask, Comrade Chairman, why was Major Romanov allowed to continue being involved in such a sensitive operation after it was suspected he had killed"—with this he glanced down at the papers in front of him—"Researcher Petrova?"

"Because when that situation was drawn to my attention," replied Zaborski, at last looking up, "I had only seven days left to tomorrow's deadline, and in my judgment there was *no* one who could have taken over Romanov's place at such short notice—"

There was a timid knock on the door. All the faces round the table showed surprise. The Minister of Defense had given specific orders that no one was to interrupt them.

"Come," shouted Brezhnev.

The great door inched open, and a secretary appeared in the gap. The thin piece of paper in his hand shook, betraying his nervousness. The Minister of Defense waved him in, as Brezhnev had no intention of turning around to see who it was. The secretary walked quickly toward them. As soon as he had deposited the telex on the table he turned and almost ran from the room.

Brezhnev slowly unfolded his tortoise-shell glasses before picking up the missive. Once he had read through the cable, he looked up at the expectant faces in front of him. "It seems an Englishman left an icon in the Louvre and picked it back up this morning."

The blood quickly drained from Zaborski's face.

The four ministers around the table all began talking together, until Brezhnev raised the vast palm of his right hand. There was immediate silence. "I intend to continue my plans on the assumption that it will still be us who gets to the Englishman first."

Brezhnev turned toward his foreign minister. "Alert all our Western ambassadors to be prepared to brief the foreign ministers of the country in which they reside on the full implications of honoring the amendment to the treaty. Then instruct Anatoly Dobrynin in Washington to demand an official meeting with the Secretary of State for late Monday. At the same time I want a further meeting arranged between our ambassador at the United Nations and U Thant."

Gromyko nodded as Brezhnev turned his attention to the Chief of the General Staff. "See that our strategic forces in all zones are put at a state of readiness to coincide with the timing of the announcement of our diplomatic initiative." Zakharov smiled. The General Secretary finally turned to the Chairman of the KGB. "Do we still have advertising space booked in every major newspaper in the West?"

"Yes, Comrade General Secretary," replied Zaborski. "But I cannot be certain they will be willing to print the statement as you have prepared it."

"Then pay every one of them in advance," said Brezhnev. "Few Western editors will withdraw a full-page advertisement when they already have the money in the bank."

"But if we then don't find the icon . . ." began the Chairman of the KGB.

"Then your last duty as Chairman of State Security will be to withdraw all the advertisements," said the General Secretary of the Communist Party.

CHAPTER
TWENTY-THREE

ADAM WOUND DOWN the car window and immediately the warm summer air flooded in. He had decided to avoid the main road to Calais in favor of the N1 to Boulogne. He still considered it possible that Romanov would have men watching at every port on the Channel coast although he doubted if Lawrence or the Americans were aware he had escaped.

Once he had cleared the outskirts of the French capital, he was confident that he could average seventy kilometers an hour the rest of the way. But what he hadn't anticipated was running into a hundred or more cyclists, garbed in their various stripes of reds, greens, blues, blacks, and golds, bobbing along ahead of him. As he drifted past them Adam was able to check accurately that they were averaging forty miles an hour.

Having followed the buildup for the forthcoming World Cup in Britain, he was also able to make out the national colors of France, Germany, Italy, and even Portugal. He honked his horn loudly as he passed a group of four men quite near the front, clad in red-white-and-blue T-shirts with the British team van just ahead of them. A few minutes later he had overtaken the leaders and was able to put the car back into fourth gear.

He switched on the car radio and fiddled around for some time before he tuned in to the Home Service of the BBC. He settled back to listen to the news in English for the first time in days. The usual reports of long strikes, high inflation, and of bad weather holding up the second Test Match at Lord's almost made him feel he was already back home. And then he nearly swerved off the road and into a tree.

The news reader reported matter-of-factly that a young RAF pilot had been found dead in a field off the Auxerre/ Dijon road after his plane had crashed in mysterious circumstances. No more details were available at the present time. Adam cursed and slammed his fist on the steering wheel at the thought of Alan Banks becoming another victim of Romanov. He tapped the icon and cursed again.

"It was foolish of you to contact me, young man," said the old banker. "You're not exactly a hero of the Soviet Union at the present time."

"Listen, old man, I don't have to be a hero any longer because I may never come back to the Soviet Union."

"Be warned: Mother Russia has extremely long fingernails."

"And because of my grandfather's foresight, I can afford to cut them off," the caller said, touching the gold medallion he wore beneath his shirt. "I just need to be sure you don't let them know where I keep the scissors."

"Why should I remain silent?" asked Poskonov.

"Because if I haven't got my hands on Saint George within the next twenty-four hours, I'll phone again with the details of how you can hope to collect a larger golden handshake than you could have expected from your present employers." The banker offered no comment.

The ambassador's secretary rushed into the room without

knocking. "I told you no interruptions," shouted Romanov, covering the mouthpiece with his hand.

"But we've located Scott."

Romanov slammed the phone down. In Moscow, the old Russian banker wound the tape back. Poskonov smiled and listened to Romanov's words a second time and came to the conclusion that Romanov had left him with only one choice. He booked a flight to Geneva.

"Robin?"

"Batman. Where have you got to?"

"I'm just outside Paris on my way back home," Adam said. "Are you sticking to the schedule you outlined on the bus?"

"Sure am. Why, are you still desperate to spending the night with me?"

"Sure am," said Adam, mimicking her. "But when do you get back home?"

"The orchestra is taking the ferry from Dunkerque at six-thirty tonight. Can you join us?"

"No," said Adam. "I have to return by another route. But, Robin, when I reach London can you put me up for the night?"

"Sounds like an offer I can't refuse," she said, and then repeated her address to be sure he had time to write it down. "When shall I expect you?" she asked.

"Around midnight tonight."

"Do you always give a girl so much notice?"

The young KGB officer standing in the adjoining booth had caught most of the conversation. He smiled when he recalled Major Romanov's words: "The man who brings me the Czar's icon need have no fear for his future in the KGB."

* * *

Adam jumped back into the car and drove on until he reached the outskirts of Beauvais, where he decided to stop at a wayside *routier* for a quick lunch.

According to the timetable he had picked up from the Hertz counter, the ferry he wanted to catch was due to leave Boulogne at three o'clock, so he felt confident he would still make it with about an hour to spare.

He sat hidden in an alcove by the window enjoying what might have been described in any English pub as a plowman's lunch. With each mouthful he became aware that the French plowmen demanded far higher standards of their innkeepers than any English farmworker was happy to settle for.

As he waited for his coffee, he took out Albert Tomkins's papers from his inside pocket and began to scrutinize them carefully. He was interested to discover exactly how many weeks he had been claiming unemployment benefits.

Through the window of the inn he watched as the first of the cyclists pedaled by. In the athletes' determination to remain among the leading group, their muscles strained. As they shot through Beauvais, Adam was amused by the fact that they were all breaking the speed limit. The sight of the competitors reminded Adam that he was expected to attend the final part of his medical for the Foreign Office tomorrow afternoon.

Romanov read the decoded message a second time. "Scott returning Geneva. Check German girl and bank." He looked up at the KGB officer who had handed him the missive.

"Does Mentor think I'm that naive?" said Romanov to his Parisian colleague. "We already know from our agent in Amsterdam that he's now on his way toward the French coast."

"Then why should Mentor want to send you in the opposite direction?"

"Because it must be him who's been briefing the Americans," said Romanov coldly.

Romanov turned to the colonel who was standing by his

side. "We know it can't be Dunkerque, so how many other possibilities are we left with?"

"Cherbourg, Le Havre, Dieppe, Boulogne, or Calais," replied the colonel, looking down at the map laid out on the table in front of him. "My bet would be Calais," he added.

"Unfortunately," said Romanov, "Captain Scott is not quite *that* simple. And as the motorway takes you direct to Calais, the captain will expect us to have that part of his route well covered. I think our friend will try Boulogne or Dieppe first."

He checked the timetable the second secretary had supplied him with. "The first boat he could hope to catch leaves Boulogne for Dover at three, and then there's one from Dieppe to Newhaven at five."

Romanov also checked Calais and Le Havre. "Good. Calais left at twelve this morning, and as he phoned the girl after twelve he had no hope of catching that one. And Le Havre doesn't leave until seven-fifteen tonight, and he won't risk leaving it that late. Assuming we can beat him to the coast, Colonel, I think Captain Scott is once again within our grasp."

Once Adam had left the *relais routier* it was only minutes before he began to catch up with the straggling cyclists as they pedaled on toward Abbeville. His thoughts reverted to Romanov. Adam suspected that his agents would have the airports, stations, autoroute, and ports well covered. But even the KGB could not be in fifty places at once.

Adam took the Boulogne route out of Abbeville but had to remain in third gear as he kept to the center of the road in order to avoid the bobbing cyclists. He even had to slam his brakes on once when an Italian and a British rider collided in front of him. The two men, both traveling at some speed, were thrown unceremoniously to the ground. The British rider remained ominously still on the side of the road.

Adam felt guilty about not stopping to help his fellow countryman but feared that any holdup might prevent him catching his boat. He spotted the British team van ahead of him and speeded up until he was alongside. Adam waved at the driver to pull over.

The man behind the steering wheel looked surprised but stopped and wound down the window. Adam pulled up in front of him, leaped out of his car, and ran to the van.

"One of your chaps has had an accident about a mile back," shouted Adam, pointing toward Paris.

"Thanks, mate," said the driver who turned round and sped quickly back down the road.

Adam continued to drive on at a sedate speed until he had passed all the leaders. Then, once again, he put the car into top gear. A signpost informed him that it was now only thirty-two kilometers to Boulogne: he would still make the three o'clock sailing comfortably. He began to imagine what it might be like if he could survive beyond tomorrow. Would his life ever be routine again? Jogs in the park, Foreign Office interviews, workouts with the PTI and even the acknowledgment of the part he had played in delivering the icon into safe hands. The problem was that he hadn't yet decided who had safe hands.

A helicopter looking like a squat green bullfrog swept over him; now that would be the ideal way to get back to England, Adam thought. With help like that he could even make it to Harley Street in time for his medical for the Foreign Office.

He watched as the helicopter turned and swung back toward him. He assumed that there must be a military airport somewhere nearby, but couldn't remember one from his days in the army. A few moments later he heard the whirl of the blades as the helicopter flew across his path at a considerably lower level. Adam gripped the wheel of the car until his knuckles went white as an impossible thought crossed his mind. As he did so the helicopter swung back again and this time flew straight toward him.

Adam wound the window up and, crouching over the top of the steering wheel, stared into the sky. He could see the silhouette of three figures sitting in the helicopter cockpit.

He banged his fist on the steering wheel in anger as he realized how easy it must have been for them to trace a car signed for in the one name they would immediately recognize. He could sense Romanov's smile of triumph as the chopper hovered over him.

Adam saw a signpost looming up ahead of him and swung off the main road toward a village called Fleureville. He pushed the speedometer well over ninety, causing the little car to skid along the country lanes. The helicopter likewise swung to the right and, doglike, followed his path.

Adam took a hard left and only just avoided colliding with a tractor coming out of a newly plowed field. He took the next right and headed back toward the Boulogne road, desperately trying to think what he could do next. Every time he looked up the helicopter was there above him; he felt like a puppet dancing on the end of Romanov's string.

A road sign depicting a low tunnel ahead flashed past them, and Adam dismissed the melodramatic idea of trying to make them crash; he didn't need reminding that it was he who was proving to be the novice.

When he first saw the tunnel he estimated it to be sixty or seventy yards in length. Although it was quite wide, a double-decker bus could not have entered it without the upstairs passengers ending up walking on the bridge.

For a brief moment Adam actually felt safe. He slammed on the little Citroen's brakes and skidded to a halt about thirty yards from the end of the tunnel. The car ended up almost scraping the side of the wall. He switched on his sidelights, and they flashed brightly in the darkness. For several seconds he watched as approaching cars slowed down before safely overtaking him.

At last he jumped out of the car and ran to the end of the tunnel where he pinned himself against the wall. The helicopter had traveled on some way but was already turning back and heading straight toward the tunnel. Adam watched it fly over his head and moments later heard it turn again. As he waited, two hitchhikers passed by on the other side, chatting away to themselves, oblivious to Adam's predicament.

He looked across desperately at the two young men and shouted, "Were you hoping to thumb a lift?"

"Yes," they called back in unison. Adam staggered across the road to join them.

"Are you all right?" Adam heard one of them ask, but he could hardly make out which one, as his eyes had not yet become accustomed to the darkness.

"No, I'm not," Adam explained simply. "I drank too much wine at lunch, and because of a cycle race the road is just crawling with police. I'm sure to be picked up if I go much further. Can either of you drive?"

"I only have my Canadian license," said the taller of the two youths. "And in any case we are heading for Paris, and your car is facing the opposite direction."

"It's a Hertz Rent-a-Car," Adam explained. "I picked it up on the rue Saint Ferdinand this morning, and I have to return it by seven tonight. I don't think I can make it in my present state."

The two young men looked at him apprehensively. "I will give you both one hundred francs if you will return it safely for me. You see, I can't afford to lose my license, I'm a commercial traveler." Adam explained. Neither of them spoke. "My papers are all in order, I can assure you." Adam handed them over to the taller man, who crossed back over the road and used the car lights to study Albert Tomkins's license and insurance before carrying on a conversation with his friend.

Adam could hear the helicopter blades whirling above the tunnel entrance.

"We don't need the hundred francs," the taller one said eventually. "But we will need a note from you explaining why we are returning the car to Hertz in Paris on your behalf." Adam pulled out the colonel's pen and, feeling remarkably sober, he bent over the hood of the car and scribbled on the back of the Hertz agreement.

"Do you want to come back to Paris with us?"

Adam hesitated. Couldn't they hear the noise too? "No. I have to get to Boulogne."

"We could drive you to Boulogne and still have enough time to take the car to Paris."

"No, no. That's very considerate. I can take care of myself as long as I can feel confident that the car will be delivered back as soon as possible."

The taller one shrugged while his companion opened a rear door and threw their rucksacks on the backseat. Adam remained in the tunnel while they started up the engine. He could hear the purr of the helicopter blades change cadence; it had to be descending to land in a nearby field.

Go, go, for God's sake, go, he wanted to shout as the car shot forward toward Boulogne. He watched them travel down the road for about a hundred yards before turning in at a farm entrance, reversing, and then heading back toward the tunnel. They tooted as they passed him in the dark, disappearing in the direction of Paris. Adam sank down on to his knees with relief and was about to pick himself up and start walking toward Boulogne when he saw two figures silhouetted at the far entrance of the tunnel. Against the clear blue sky he could make out the outline of one tall, thin man. They stood peering into the tunnel. Adam didn't move a muscle, praying they hadn't spotted him.

And then suddenly the thin man started walking toward him, while the other remained motionless. Adam knew he could not hope to escape again. He knelt there cursing his own stupidity. In seconds the man would be able to see him clearly.

"Don't let's waste any more valuable time, Marvin, we already know that the traitor's heading back to Paris."

"I just thought perhaps . . ." began the one called Marvin, in a Southern drawl.

"Leave the thinking to me. Now let's get back to the chopper before we lose him."

When Marvin was only twenty yards away from Adam he suddenly stopped, turned around, and began running back.

Adam remained rooted to the spot for several minutes. A cold, clammy sweat enveloped his body the moment he realized his latest pursuer was not Romanov. If one of them hadn't referred to him as a "traitor," Adam would have happily given himself up. Suddenly he had become painfully aware of the difference between fact and fiction: he had been left with no friends.

Adam did not move again until he heard the helicopter rise above him. Peering out, he could see outlined against the arc of the tunnel the Americans heading in the direction of Paris.

He staggered outside and put a hand across his eyes. The sunlight seemed much fiercer than a few minutes before. What next? He had less than an hour to catch the boat but no longer had any transport. He wasn't sure whether to thumb lifts, search for a bus stop, or simply get as far away from the main road as possible. His eyes were continually looking up into the sky. How long before they reached the car and realized it was not him inside?

Cyclists began to pass him again as he jogged slowly toward Boulogne. He kept on moving and even found enough strength to cheer the British competitors as they pedaled by. The British team van followed close behind, and Adam gave it the thumbs-up sign. To his surprise the van came to a halt in front of him.

The driver wound down the window. "Weren't you the fellow who stopped me back in Abbeville?"

"That's right," said Adam. "Has your man recovered?"

"No, he's resting in the back—pulled ligament. What happened to your car?"

"Broke down about a mile back," said Adam, shrugging philosophically.

"Bad luck. Can I give you a lift?" the man asked. "We're only going as far as Boulogne on this stage, but jump in if it will help."

"Thank you," said Adam, with the relief of a bearded beatnik who has found the one person willing to stop to pick him up. The driver leaned across and pushed open the door for him.

Before climbing in, Adam shielded his eyes and once more looked up into the sky. The helicopter was nowhere to be seen—although he knew it couldn't be long before it returned. They would quickly work out there was only one place where the switch could possibly have been made.

"My name's Bob," said the track-suited driver, thrusting out his free hand. "I'm the British team manager."

"Mine's Adam." He took the other's hand warmly.

"Where are you heading?"

"Boulogne," said Adam, "and with luck I could still make my crossing by three."

"We should be there about two-thirty," said Bob. "We have to be; the afternoon stage starts at three."

"Will your man be able to ride?" asked Adam, pointing over his shoulder.

"No, he won't be competing in this race again," said the team manager. "He's pulled a ligament in the back of his leg, and they always take a couple of weeks to heal properly. I shall have to leave him in Boulogne and complete the last leg myself. You don't ride, by any chance, do you?" Bob asked.

"No," said Adam. "Run a little, but haven't done a lot on wheels since my sister crashed the family tricycle."

"We're still in with a chance for the bronze," Bob said, as they overtook the British riders once more.

Adam gave them the thumbs-up sign and then looked over his shoulder through the back window. He was thankful to see that there was still no sign of the helicopter as they drove into the outskirts of Boulogne. Bob took him all the way up to the dockside. "Hope you get that bronze medal," said Adam as he jumped out of the van. "And thanks again. Good luck with the next stage."

Adam checked his watch: twenty minutes before the boat was due to sail. He wondered if it was too much time. He walked over to the ticket office and waited in a short line before buying a passenger ticket. He kept looking round to check if anyone was watching him, but no one seemed to be showing the slightest interest. Once he had purchased his ticket, he headed toward the ship and had just begun to start whistling a tuneless version of *Yesterday* when a black speck appeared in the distance. There was no mistaking it—the sound was enough.

Adam looked up at the gangway that led to the deck of the ship, now only yards away from him, and then back to the speck as it grew larger and larger in the sky. He checked his watch: the ship was due to leave in twelve minutes—still time enough for his pursuers to land the helicopter and get on board too. If he climbed on and the Americans followed, they were bound to discover him. But if the Americans got on and he stayed off, that would still give him enough time to reach Dieppe before the next sailing . . .

Adam jogged quickly back toward the large crowd that was hanging about waiting for the start of the next stage of the road race. As he did so the helicopter swept overhead and started hovering, like a kestrel that is looking for a mouse.

"I thought you said you were desperate to be on that ship."

Adam swung round, his fist clenched, only to face the British team manager now dressed in riding gear.

"Changed my mind," said Adam.

"Wouldn't care to drive the van for us on the next stage?" said Bob hopefully.

"Where does the next stage go?" Adam asked.

"Dunkerque," said the team manager.

Adam tried to remember what time Robin had said her boat left from Dunkerque.

"Six minutes," a voice said over the loudspeaker.

"Okay," said Adam.

"Good," said the team manager. "Then follow me."

Adam ran behind the team manager as he headed toward the van.

"Quatre minutes," Adam heard clearly as Bob unlocked the van and handed him the keys. He stared toward the ship. The two Americans were emerging from the ticket office.

"Deux minutes."

Adam jumped up into the driver's seat, looked over toward the boat, and watched Marvin and his colleague stride up the gangplank.

"Une minute."

"Just get the van to Dunkerque and leave the keys at the British checkpoint. We'll see you when we get there."

"Good luck," said Adam.

"Thank you," said Bob, and ran to the starting line to join his teammates, who were anxiously holding his bike.

"Trente secondes."

Adam watched the gangplank being hoisted up as the starter raised his gun.

"On your marks, set . . ."

The ship's foghorn belched out a droning note and the two Americans started their journey to Calais.

A second later, the gun went off as Adam put the van into second gear and headed toward Dunkerque.

CHAPTER
TWENTY-FOUR

ADAM SAT IN the little dockside cafe waiting for the coach to appear. The team van had been left at the checkpoint and he was not ready to board the ship but he still needed to be sure Robin was on it. It appeared with only ten minutes to spare and Adam greeted her as she stepped off the coach.

"Just couldn't keep away from me, could you?" said Robin.

Adam burst out laughing and threw his arms around her.

"It's good to see you," he said.

"I thought you were going back to England by some mysterious route—you know, spy rocket or something even more exotic."

"I had hoped to," said Adam, "but the Americans were sitting at the controls just as I decided to climb aboard."

"The Americans?" she said.

"I'll explain everything once we're on board," said Adam. Neither of them noticed the young agent who had trailed Robin from Berlin. He sat in a phone booth on the far side of the dock and dialed an overseas number.

* * *

"I wouldn't have believed a word of it a week ago," she said, "but for two things."

"Namely?"

"First, a senior official of the Foreign Office returned Dudley Hulme's passport to him in Amsterdam. Which reminds me to give you yours back." She rummaged around in her bag for a few moments before taking out a dark-blue passport and handing it to him.

"And what's the second thing?" said Adam, taking the passport gratefully.

"I had the doubtful pleasure of coming face to face with Comrade Romanov, and I have no desire to do so again."

"I intend to meet him again," said Adam.

"Why?" asked Robin.

"Because I'm going to kill him."

Romanov and Tomkins arrived in Dover a few minutes before the ferry was due to dock. They waited expectantly. Romanov stationed himself so that he could look through the customs hall window and watch the ferry as it sailed into Dover harbor. He had found the perfect spot behind a coffee-vending machine from which he could observe everyone who entered or left the customs hall, while at the same time remaining hidden from view.

"Just in case he should act out of character for a change," said Romanov, "and fails to go in a straight line, you will cover the car exit and report back to me if you notice anything unusual."

The colonel left Romanov secreted behind the coffee machine while he selected a place for himself on the dockside where he could watch the cars as they entered the customs area some fifty yards from the exit gate. If Scott did leave the ferry in a car Tomkins would easily have enough time to run back and warn Romanov before Scott could hope to clear customs and reach the main gate. At least this would be the one place Scott couldn't risk hiding in the trunk. Both men waited.

The captain switched on his ship-to-shore radio to channel 9 and spoke clearly into the small microphone. "This is the MV *Chantilly* calling the Dover Harbormaster. Are you receiving me?" He waited for a moment, flicked up the switch in front of him and then heard: "Harbormaster to MV *Chantilly*. Receiving you loud and clear, over."

"This is the captain speaking. We have an emergency. A male passenger has fallen out of a lifeboat onto the deck and suffered multiple injuries to his arms and legs." Adam groaned as the captain continued. "I shall need an ambulance to be standing by at the quayside to take him to the nearest hospital once we have docked. Over."

"Message received and understood, Captain. An ambulance will be waiting for you when the ship docks. Over and out."

"Everything will be all right, my dear," said Robin in a gentle voice that Adam had not heard before. "As soon as we arrive, they are going to see you are taken straight to a hospital."

"I must get back to the bridge," said the captain gruffly. "I shall instruct two stewards to bring a stretcher down for your brother."

"Thank you, Captain," said Robin. "You have been most helpful."

"It's quite all right, miss. You did say your brother?"

"Yes, Captain," said Robin.

"Well, you might advise him in future that it's in his best interests to drink less before he comes on board."

"I've tried," said Robin, sighing. "You couldn't believe how many times I've tried, Captain, but I'm afraid he takes after my father." Adam held on to his leg and groaned again.

"Um," said the captain, looking down at the gash across Adam's shoulder. "Let's hope it turns out not to be serious. Good luck," he added.

"Thank you again, Captain," said Robin as she watched the cabin door close behind him.

"So far, so good," said Robin. "Now let's hope the second part of the plan works. By the way, your breath smells foul."

"What do you expect after making me swirl whiskey round in my mouth for twenty minutes and then forcing me to spit it out all over my own clothes?"

Adam was lifted carefully onto the stretcher, then carried out on to the deck by two stewards. They waited at the head of the gangplank and placed Adam gently on the deck while a customs officer, accompanied by an immigration officer, ran up to join them. Robin handed over his passport. The immigration officer flicked through the pages and checked the photograph.

"Quite a good likeness for a change," said Robin, "but I'm afraid they may have to include this under 'unusual scars' in the next edition." She threw back the blanket dramatically and revealed the deep gash on Adam's shoulder. Adam looked suitably crestfallen.

"Is he bringing anything in with him that needs to be declared?" asked the customs official. Adam couldn't stop himself from touching the icon.

"No, I wouldn't let him buy any more booze on this trip. And I'll be responsible for checking his personal belongings through with mine when I leave the ship."

"Right. Thank you, miss. Better see he gets off to the hospital then," said the officer, suddenly aware that a restless mob of people was waiting at the top of the gangplank to disembark.

The two stewards carried Adam down the gangplank. An attendant was on hand to check his wound. Adam waved gamely at Robin as they placed him in the ambulance.

Romanov spotted her as she came through customs. "Now I know exactly how Captain Scott hopes to get off the ship, and we will be waiting for him when he least expects it. Go and hire a car to take us to London," he barked at the colonel.

The ambulance shot out through the customs gates with its lights full on and bells ringing. By the time they had arrived at The Royal Victoria Hospital the attendant had watched his patient's remarkable recovery en route with disbelief. He was beginning to feel that the captain might have exaggerated the scale of the emergency.

Romanov stood by the gate and smiled as he watched the coach carrying the musicians emerge from the deep black hole of the ship and take its turn in the line for customs.

As Romanov's eyes ranged up and down the coach he quickly picked out Robin Beresford. Just as he had anticipated, the double bass was propped up by her side, making it impossible to see who was seated next to her.

"You won't pull that one on me a second time," Romanov muttered, just as the colonel appeared by his side, red in the face.

"Where's the car?" the Russian demanded, not taking his eyes from the coach.

"I've booked one provisionally," said the colonel, "but they'll need your international license. I forgot Scott has got mine, along with all my other papers."

"You stay put," said Romanov, "and make sure Scott doesn't try to get off that coach." Romanov ran to the Avis desk at the same time as Adam was being wheeled into a little cubicle to be examined by the duty registrar.

The young doctor leaned over his patient for several minutes. He had never seen a wound quite like it before. He examined him carefully, before making any comment. "Nasty lacerations," he said finally, cleaning Adam's shoulder wound. "Can you circle your arm?" Adam turned the arm in a full circle and straightened it out again. "Good. No break, at least." He continued to clean the wound.

"I'm going to put some iodine on the open cut, and it may sting a little," said the doctor. He cleaned up both elbows before placing a plaster on them.

"That didn't happen today, did it?" he asked, staring at Adam's half-healed shoulder.

"No," said Adam, without offering any explanations.

"You have been in the wars lately. I'm going to give you an antitetanus injection." Adam turned white. "Funny how many grown men don't care for the sight of a needle," said the doctor. Adam groaned.

"Now that wasn't so bad, was it?" he suggested as he placed a large bandage over the top of the shoulder. "Do you have someone to collect you?" the doctor asked finally.

"Yes, thank you," said Adam. "My wife is waiting for me."

"Good, then you can go now, but please report to your GP the moment you get back home."

Romanov sat in the driver's seat and watched the coach clear customs. He followed it out of the main gate and on to the A2 in the direction of London.

"Are we going to intercept them on the way?" asked Tomkins nervously.

"Not this time," said Romanov without explanation. He never once allowed the coach out of his sight all the way into the capital.

Adam walked out of the hospital and checked to see that no one was following him. The only people in sight were a man in a blue duffle coat walking in the opposite direction and a nurse scurrying past him, looking anxiously at her watch. Satisfied, he took a taxi to Dover Priory station and purchased a single ticket to London.

"When's the next train?" he asked.

"Should be in any moment," said the ticket collector, checking his watch. "The ship docked about forty minutes ago, but it always takes a bit of time to unload all the passengers." Adam walked on to the platform, keeping a wary eye out for anyone acting suspiciously. He didn't notice the dark-haired man in a blue duffle coat leaning against the shutters of the W. H. Smith's stall reading the *Evening Standard*.

Adam's thoughts returned to Robin getting safely home. The London train drew in, packed with passengers who had been on the boat. Adam moved out of the shadows and jumped on, selecting a carriage full of young hoods who were apparently returning from a day at the seaside. He thought it would be unlikely anyone else would wish to join them. He took the only seat left, in the far corner, and sat silently looking out of the window.

By the time the train had pulled into Canterbury no one had entered the carriage other than the ticket collector, who discreetly ignored the fact that one of the youths only presented him with a platform ticket for his inspection. Adam felt strangely safe in the corner of that particular compartment even when he noticed a dark-haired man in a blue duffle coat pass by the compartment door and look carefully in.

Adam was jolted out of his thoughts by a noisy claim made by one of the gang, who, during the journey, had given every appearance of being its leader.

"There's a foul smell in this compartment," he declared, sniffing loudly.

"I agree, Terry," said his mate who was sitting next to Adam and also began imitating the sniff. "And I think it's quite close to me." Adam glanced toward the young man, whose black leather jacket was covered in small shiny studs. The words *"Heil Hitler"* were printed right across his back. He got up and pulled open the window. "Perhaps some fresh air will help," he said as he sat back down. In moments all four of them were sniffing. Sniff, sniff, sniff, sniff. "I think the smell's getting worse," their leader concluded.

"It must be me," said Adam.

The sniffing stopped, and the youths stared toward the corner in disbelief—momentarily silenced by Adam's offensive.

"I didn't have time to take a shower after my judo lesson," Adam added before any of them had found time to recover their speech.

"Any good at judo, are you?" asked the one sitting next to him.

"Passable," said Adam.

"What belt are you?" demanded Terry belligerently. "Go on, tell me, a black belt, I knew it," he added, sniggering.

"I haven't been a black belt for nearly eight years," said Adam casually, "but I've been recently awarded my second Dan."

A look of apprehension came over three of the four faces.

"I was thinkin' about taking up judo myself," continued the leader, straightening his arm. "How long does it take to get any good at it?"

"I've been working at it three hours a day for nearly twelve years, and I'm still not up to Olympic standard," replied Adam as he watched the dark-haired man in the duffle coat pass by the compartment again. This time he stared directly at Adam before quickly moving on.

"Of course," continued Adam, "the only quality you really need if you are thinking of taking up judo seriously is nerve, and no one can teach you that. You've either got it or you haven't."

"I've got nerve," said Terry belligerently. "I'm not frightened of nothin'. Or nobody," he added, staring straight at Adam.

"Good," said Adam. "Because you may be given the chance to prove your claim before this journey is over."

"What're you getting at?" said the *"Heil Hitler"*-clad youth. "You trying to pick a fight or somethin'?"

"No," said Adam calmly. "It's just that at this moment I'm being followed by a private detective who is hoping to catch me spending the night with his client's wife."

The four of them sat still for the first time during the journey and stared at Adam with something approaching respect.

"And are you?" asked the leader.

Adam nodded conspiratorially.

"Nice bit of skirt when you've got it in the hay?" Terry asked, leering.

"Not bad," said Adam, "not bad at all."

"Then just point out this detective git and we'll sew him up for the night," said the leader, thrusting his left hand on his right bicep while pulling up his clenched fist with gusto.

"That might turn out to be unnecessary," said Adam. "But if you could delay him for a little when I get off at Waterloo East, that should at least give me enough time to warn the lady."

"Say no more, squire," said the leader. "Your friend the Peeping Tom will be delivered to Charing Cross all trussed up like a British Rail parcel."

The other three youths burst out laughing, and Adam was beginning to realize that it had taken Romanov only one week to turn him into a storyteller almost in the class of Robin's late father.

"That's him," whispered Adam as the duffle-coated man passed by a third time. They all looked out into the corridor but only saw his retreating back.

"The train is due to arrive at Waterloo East in eleven minutes' time," said Adam, checking his watch. "So what I suggest we do is . . . if you still think you're up to it." All four of his newfound team leaned forward in eager anticipation.

A few minutes later Adam slipped out of the compartment, leaving the door wide open. He started to walk slowly in the direction opposite to that in which the man in the blue duffle coat had last been seen going. When Adam reached the end of the carriage, he turned to find the man was now following quickly behind. As he passed the open compartment the man smiled and raised a hand to attract Adam's attention, but two leather-clad arms shot out, and the man disappeared inside the compartment with a muffled cry. The door was slammed and the blinds pulled quickly down.

The train drew slowly into Waterloo East station.

Robin remained tense as the bus drew into Wigmore Street and came to a halt outside the RPO headquarters. A dark green Ford had been following them for at least thirty miles, and once she had become aware of it she had not dared to move from her seat.

As she dragged her double bass off the bus she looked back to see that the Ford had stopped about fifty yards down the road and turned off its headlights. Romanov was standing on the pavement looking like a caged animal that wanted to spring. Another man that Robin did not recognize remained seated behind the wheel. Adam had warned her not to turn around at any time but to walk straight into the RPO headquarters without stopping. Even so, she couldn't resist looking Romanov in the eye and shaking her head. Romanov continued to stare impassively ahead of him.

When the last musician had left the bus Romanov and the colonel searched up and down the inside of the vehicle and then finally the trunk, despite noisy protests from the driver. Robin eyed them nervously from an upstairs window, as the two jumped back into the green Ford and drove off. She continued watching the car until the back lights had faded away in the darkness.

The colonel swung out of Wigmore Street toward Baker Street, bringing the car to a halt opposite Baker Street Station. Romanov jumped out, walked into a vacant telephone booth, and started thumbing through the A-D directory. Only one Robin Beresford was listed, and it was the same address as the young officer had read to him. He dialed the number and after ten unanswered rings smiled at the realization that she lived alone. He was not surprised.

"What now?" asked the colonel, once Romanov was back in the car.

"Where's Argyle Crescent, NW3?"

"Must be out toward Hampstead," said the colonel. "But I'll just check in the London A to Z road map. What's the plan?"

"Rather than waiting for Miss Beresford to come out we will be waiting for her to come in," said Romanov.

* * *

Robin slipped out of the back of the RPO headquarters about thirty minutes later. She zigzagged around Portman Square, then walked as quickly as she knew how up to the corner. She kept telling herself that Romanov was not coming back, but she found it impossible to stop herself from shaking all the same. She hailed a taxi and was relieved to see one draw up to her side almost immediately. She checked the driver and the backseat, as Adam had advised her, then climbed in.

Romanov arrived at Robin's front door a few moments after she had hailed the taxi. The nameplates on the side wall indicated that Miss Beresford resided on the fourth floor.

The door itself would have proved no problem to any self-respecting petty thief [in Moscow] and Romanov had secured entry within moments. The colonel quickly joined him before they proceeded silently up the dark staircase to the fourth floor.

Romanov slipped the Yale lock faster than Robin could have opened it with her key. Once inside he checked the layout of the room. The colonel stood around fidgeting. "Settle down," said Romanov. "I don't expect the lady will keep us waiting too long." The colonel laughed nervously.

The taxi drew up outside the house as directed. Robin jumped out and tipped the cabbie extra because the witching hour had long passed and she at last felt safe. It seemed ages since she had been home. All she was looking forward to now was a hot bath and a good night's sleep.

Adam stepped off the train at Waterloo East a little after midnight and was pleased to find the underground was still running. He had avoided going on to Charing Cross, as he couldn't be sure which side would have a reception committee waiting for him. He showed the season ticket to the West Indian on the ticket barrier and waited around on the underground platform for some time before the train drew slowly in.

There were several stations between Waterloo and his destination, and even at this time of night there seemed to be a prolonged stop at every one. Several late-night revelers got in at the Embankment, more still at Leicester Square. Adam waited nervously at each station, now aware that he must have caught the last train. He only hoped Robin had carried out his instructions faithfully. He looked around the carriage he was sitting in. It was full of night people, waiters, nurses, party returners, drunks—even a traffic warden. The train eventually pulled into his station at twelve-forty.

The ticket collector was able to give him the directions he needed. It was a relief to reach his final destination so quickly because there was no one else around to ask the way at that time of night. He moved slowly toward number twenty-three. There were no lights on in the house. He opened the swinging gate and walked straight up the path, removed the bunch of keys from his pocket, putting the Chubb one in the lock, pushed open the door quietly, and closed it noiselessly behind him.

At a little after twelve-ten the last train from Dover pulled into Charing Cross station. As Adam was nowhere to be seen, Lawrence instructed his driver to take him back to his flat on Cheyne Walk. He couldn't understand why the agent whom he had handpicked hadn't reported in. When Lawrence arrived home he put the key in his lock, hoping that he would find Adam already waiting for him.

CHAPTER
TWENTY-FIVE

HE PUSHED OPEN the swinging gate and made his way slowly up the path in the pitch-darkness. Once he reached the corner of the house he searched for the third stone on the left. When he located the correct stone, he pulled it up and felt around in the dirt with his fingers. To his relief the spare key was still in place. Like a burglar he pushed it into the lock quietly.

He crept into the hall and closed the door behind him, switched on the light, and began to climb the stairs. Once he had reached the landing he switched off the hall light and pushed open his bedroom door.

As he stepped in and flicked on the light switch, an arm circled his throat like a whiplash, and he was thrown to the floor with tremendous force. He felt a knee pressed hard against his spine, and his arm was jerked up behind his back into a half nelson. He lay on the floor, flat on his face, hardly able to move or even breathe. The first thing he saw was Adam.

"Don't kill me, Captain Scott, sir, don't kill me," he implored.

"I have no intention of doing so, Mr. Tomkins," said Adam calmly. "But first, where is your esteemed employer at this moment?"

Adam kept his knee firmly in the middle of the colonel's back and pressed his arm a few inches higher before the colonel bleated out, "He went back to the embassy once he realized the girl wasn't going to return to the flat."

"Just as I planned," said Adam, but he didn't lessen the pressure on the colonel's arm as he described in vivid detail everything that would now be expected of him.

The colonel's face showed disbelief. "But that will be impossible," he said. "I mean, he's bound to noti—ahhh."

The colonel felt his arm forced higher up on his back. "You could carry out the whole exercise in less than ten minutes, and he need never be any the wiser," said Adam. "However, I feel that it's only fair that you should be rewarded for your efforts."

"Thank you, sir," said the fawning colonel.

"If you succeed in delivering the one item I require and carry out my instructions to the letter, you will be given in exchange your passport, driver's license, papers, wallet, and a guarantee of no prosecution for your past treachery. But if, on the other hand, you fail to turn up by nine-thirty tomorrow morning with the object of my desire," said Adam, "all those documents will be placed thirty minutes later on the desk of a Mr. Lawrence Pemberton of the F.O., along with my report on your other sources of income, which you seem to have failed to declare on your tax return."

"You wouldn't do that to me, would you, Captain Scott?"

"As ten o'clock chimes," said Adam.

"But think what would happen to me, Captain Scott, sir, if you carried out such a threat," moaned the colonel.

"I have already considered that," said Adam, "and I have come to two conclusions."

"And what are they, Captain Scott?"

"Spies," continued Adam, not loosening his grip, "at the

present time seem to be getting anything from eighteen to forty-two years at Her Majesty's pleasure, so you might, with good behavior, be out before the turn of the century, just in time to collect your telegram from the Queen."

The colonel looked visibly impressed. "And the other conclusion?" he blurted out.

"Oh, simply that you could inform Romanov of my nocturnal visit, and he in return would arrange for you to spend the rest of your days in a very small dacha in a suitably undesirable suburb of Moscow. Because, you see, my dear Colonel, you are a very small spy. I personally am not sure when left with such an alternative which I would view with more horror."

"I'll get it for you, Captain Scott, you can rely on me."

"I'm sure I can, Colonel. Because if you were to let Romanov into our little secret, you would be arrested within minutes. So at best, you could try to escape on the Aeroflot plane to Moscow. And I've checked, there isn't one until the early evening."

"I'll bring it to you by nine-thirty on the dot, sir. You can be sure of that. But for God's sake, have yours ready to exchange."

"I will," said Adam, "as well as all your documents, Colonel."

Adam lifted the colonel slowly off the ground and then shoved him toward the landing. He switched on the hall light and then pushed the colonel on down the stairs until they reached the front door.

"The keys," said Adam.

"But you've already got my keys, Captain Scott, sir."

"The car keys, you fool."

"But it's a hire car, sir," said the colonel.

"And I'm about to hire it," said Adam.

"But how will I get myself back to London in time, sir?"

"I have no idea, Colonel, but you still have the rest of the night to come up with something. You could even walk it by then. The keys," Adam repeated, jerking the colonel's arm to shoulder-blade level.

"In my left-hand pocket," said the colonel, almost an octave higher.

Adam put his hand into the colonel's new jacket and pulled out the car keys.

He opened the front door, shoved the colonel on to the path, then escorted him to the pavement.

"You will go and stand on the far side of the road," said Adam, "and you will not return to the house until I have reached the end of the road. Do I make myself clear, Colonel?"

"Abundantly clear, Captain Scott, sir."

"Good," said Adam releasing him for the first time, "and just one more thing, Colonel. In case you think of double-crossing me, I have already instructed the Foreign Office to place Romanov under surveillance and put two extra lookouts near the Soviet embassy with instructions to report the moment anyone suspicious turns up or leaves before nine tomorrow morning." Adam hoped he sounded convincing.

"Thought of everything, haven't you, sir?" said the colonel mournfully.

"Yes, I think so," said Adam. "I even found time to disconnect your phone while I was waiting for you to return." Adam pushed the colonel across the road before getting into the hire car. He wound the window down. "See you at nine-thirty tomorrow morning, Colonel. Prompt," he added, as he put the Ford into first gear.

The colonel stood shivering on the far pavement, nursing his right shoulder, as Adam drove to the end of the road. He was still standing there when Adam took a left turn back toward the center of London.

For the first time since Heidi's death, Adam felt it was Romanov who was on the run.

"What a great honor for our little establishment," said Herr Bischoff, delighted to see the most important banker in the East sitting in his boardroom sharing afternoon tea.

"Not at all, my dear Bischoff," said Poskonov. "After all these years the honor is entirely mine. But now to business. Did you manage to get Romanov to sign the release form?"

"Oh, yes," said Bischoff, matter-of-factly, "he did it without even reading the standard clauses, let alone the extra three you asked us to put in."

"So his inheritance automatically returns to the Russian people?"

"That is so, Mr. Poskonov, and we in return . . ."

". . . Will represent us in all the currency exchange transactions we carry out in the West."

"Thank you," said Herr Bischoff. "And we shall be delighted to assist you in your slightest requirement, but what happens when Romanov returns to the bank and demands to know what has become of his inheritance?" asked Herr Bischoff anxiously.

"I don't think that problem will arise," the Russian banker promised. "Now, I would like to see what is in those boxes."

"Yes, of course," said Herr Bischoff. "Will you please accompany me?"

The two banking chairmen took the private lift to the basement, and Herr Bischoff accompanied his guest to the underground vault.

"I will unlock the five boxes now in your name with the bank's key, but only you can open them with your key."

"Thank you," said Poskonov, and left Herr Bischoff to open the five locks and return to the entrance of the vault.

"Do take as long as you like," said Herr Bischoff, "but at five o'clock the great door is automatically locked until nine o'clock tomorrow morning, and nothing less than a nuclear weapon would prize it open. At four forty-five an alarm goes off to warn you that you only have fifteen minutes left."

"Excellent," said a man who through his entire banking career had never been given a fifteen-minute warning of anything.

Herr Bischoff handed Comrade Poskonov the envelope with Romanov's key in it.

As soon as the massive steel door had been swung closed behind him, the Russian checked the clock on the wall. They had left him with over two hours to sort out what could be transported to Brazil and what would have to be left behind.

A state pension and the Order of Lenin (second class) hadn't seemed much of an alternative to Poskonov.

He turned the key and opened the first of the small boxes and found the deeds to lands the State had owned for decades. He growled. The second box contained the shares of companies once brilliantly successful, now shells in every sense of the word. And to Poskonov's disappointment the third of the small boxes only held a will proving everything belonged to Romanov's father and his immediate heirs. Had he waited all these years to discover the stories the old man had told him of gold, jewels, and pearls were nothing but a fantasy? Or had Romanov already removed them?

Poskonov opened the first of the large boxes and stared down at the twelve little compartments. He removed the lid of the first one tentatively, and when he saw the array of gems and stones that shone in front of him his legs felt weak. He put both hands into the box and let the gems slip through his fingers like a child playing with pebbles on a beach.

The second box produced pearls, and the third gold coins and medallions that could make even an old man's eyes sparkle. He hadn't realized how long it had taken him to go through the remaining boxes, but when the alarm went off he was five thousand miles away already enjoying his newfound wealth. He glanced up at the clock. He had easily enough time to get everything back into the compartments, and then he would return the following day and remove once and for all what he had earned from fifty years of serving the State.

When the last lid had been placed back on he checked the clock on the wall: six minutes to five. Just enough time to glance in the other box and see if he could expect the same again.

He turned the key and licked his lips in anticipation as he pulled the large box out. Just a quick look, he promised himself, as he lifted the lid. When he saw the decaying body with its gray skin and eyes hanging in their sockets he reeled backward from the sight and, falling to the floor, clutched his heart.

Both bodies were discovered at nine the next morning.

The phone rang, and Adam grabbed at it before the shrill tone could deafen him a second time.

"Your alarm call, sir," said a girl's voice gently. "It's eight o'clock."

"Thank you," Adam replied and replaced the receiver. The call had proved unnecessary because he had been sitting up in bed considering the implications of his plan for nearly an hour. Adam had finally worked out exactly how he was going to kill Romanov.

He jumped out of bed, threw back the curtains, and stared down at the Soviet embassy. He wondered how long the Russian had been awake.

He returned to the side of the bed and picked up the phone to dial the number Robin had given him. The phone rang several times before it was answered by an elderly voice saying, "Mrs. Beresford."

"Good morning, Mrs. Beresford, my name is Adam Scott, I'm a friend of Robin's. I was just phoning to check that she reached home safely last night."

"Oh, yes, thank you," said Robin's mother. "It was a pleasant surprise to see her before the weekend. She usually spends the night in the flat when she gets back that late. I'm afraid she's still asleep. Would you like me to wake her?"

"No, no, don't disturb her," said Adam. "I only rang to fix up a lunch date. Can you tell her I'll call back later."

"I certainly will," she replied. "Thank you for phoning, Mr. Scott."

Adam replaced the receiver and smiled. Each piece of the jigsaw was fitting neatly into place, but without the colonel's help he still lacked the vital cornerpiece. Adam began to put everything Tomkins needed, including his passport, personal papers, and wallet, into a large envelope. He removed the icon from his jacket pocket, turned it over, and carefully examined the little silver crest of the Czar. He then flicked open the colonel's penknife and began the slow and delicate task of removing the crown.

Thirty minutes later, Adam was in the lift on the way to the hotel basement. When he stepped out, he walked across to the space where he had parked the green Ford earlier that morning. He unlocked the door and threw the colonel's old jacket onto the seat, then locked the car, checking all the doors before taking the lift back up to the ground floor.

The manager of the men's shop in the arcade had just flicked over the Closed sign, and Adam took his time selecting a white shirt, gray flannels, and a blue blazer, trying them on in their little changing room.

At nine twenty-three he settled his bill with the Royal Garden Hotel and asked the doorman to bring the green Ford up from the parking lot. He waited by the hotel entrance.

As the minutes passed, he began to fear that the colonel wouldn't turn up. If he failed to, Adam knew that the next call would have to be to Lawrence and not Romanov.

His reverie was disturbed by a honk on a car horn; the colonel's rented car had been left by the entrance.

"Your car is waiting on the ramp," said the doorman, as he returned the keys to Adam.

"Thank you," said Adam and handed over the last of the colonel's pound notes. He dropped the wallet into the large envelope, which he sealed, before checking his watch again.

He stood waiting anxiously for another two minutes before he spotted the colonel puffing up the slope leading to the hotel entrance.

He was clinging onto a small carrier bag.

"I've done it, Captain Scott, sir, I've done it," said the colonel, before he had reached Adam's side. "But I must return immediately or he's bound to notice it's gone."

He passed the carrier bag quickly to Adam, who opened the top and stared down at the object inside.

"You're a man of your word," said Adam, "and as promised you'll find everything you need in there." He passed over his own package along with the car keys without speaking. He pointed to the hire car.

The colonel ran to it, jumped in, and drove quickly down the ramp of the Royal Garden Hotel before turning left into Kensington Palace Gardens.

Adam checked his watch: nine thirty-five.

"Could you call me a taxi?" he asked the doorman.

The driver pulled the window down and gave Adam an inquiring look.

"The Wood Workshop, Kings Road."

Adam spent twenty minutes looking around the shop while the craftsman carried out his unusual request. Adam studied the result with satisfaction, paid him two half crowns, and then walked back on to Kings Road to hail another taxi.

"Where to, guv'nor?"

"The Tower of London."

Everyone was in his place for the D4 meeting at nine-thirty, and Busch had gone on the attack even before Lawrence had had the chance to sit down.

"How in hell did you manage to lose him this time?"

"I must take the blame myself," said Lawrence. "We had every port from Newhaven to Harwich covered, but the moment my man saw Romanov and his henchman leave the quayside at Dover and chase off down the motorway after the coach he assumed he must have seen Scott. I had already instructed the senior immigration officer at the port," he continued, "to allow Scott to disembark without a fuss. It had been my intention to take over once he passed through customs. There seemed no reason to change that plan while we had Romanov under close surveillance. Scott then proceeded to fool both Romanov and our man at Dover."

"But we were given a second chance when Scott got on the train," persisted Busch. Lawrence stared at the American waiting to see if he would admit that his two CIA agents had also lost Scott at Dover.

"My man was on the train," said Lawrence emphatically, "but had only the one opportunity to make contact with Scott while he was on his own, and at just that moment he was grabbed and badly beaten up by a bunch of drunken louts—teenagers, apparently—who were on their way back from a day trip to the seaside."

"Perhaps we're recruiting our agents from the wrong class of person," said Matthews, staring down at his briefing papers.

Lawrence made no attempt to reply.

"So, as far as we can tell, Scott, the Czar's icon, and Romanov are still holed up somewhere in London?" said Snell.

"It looks that way," admitted Lawrence.

"Perhaps all is not lost then," suggested Snell. "Scott may still try to get in touch with you again."

"I think not," said Lawrence quietly.

"How can you be so sure?" asked Busch.

"Because Scott knows that one of us in this room is a traitor and he thinks it's me."

"Good morning. Soviet embassy."

"My name is Adam Scott, and I need to get in contact with a Major Romanov."

"Good morning, Mr. Scott. We do not have a Major Romanov working at the embassy," came back the polite reply.

"I'm sure you don't."

"But if you would like to leave your number, I will make further inquiries."

"I'll wait. Wouldn't surprise me if you find him very quickly once he knows who is calling."

There was a long silence at the other end, and Adam only hoped the shilling he had pressed into the phone would prove to be enough. At last there was a click, and then Adam heard a voice.

"Who is this?" said the voice, unable to mask its incredulity.

"You know very well who it is," said Adam curtly. "I want to make a deal."

"A deal?" Romanov repeated, his voice changing from one of disbelief to surprise.

"I'll swap you my icon—which, as you so vividly pointed out, is worthless to me—in exchange for your copy, which is not. But I also require the papers that prove my father's innocence."

"How do I know you're not setting me up?"

"You don't," said Adam. "But you're the one with nothing to lose."

The beeps began to sound across the line.

"Tell me your number," said Romanov.

"738-9121," said Adam.

"I'll phone you back," said Romanov as the line went dead.

"How quickly can we find out where 738-9121 is located?" Romanov asked the local KGB operative who sat opposite him.

"About ten minutes," the aide replied. "But it could be a trap."

"True, but with nineteen hours to go before the icon has to be in America I don't have a lot of choice."

Romanov turned back to the KGB agent. "What's the traffic like in London on a Monday morning?"

"One of the busiest times in the week. Why do you ask?"

"Because I'll need a motorbike and a superb driver," was all Romanov said.

Adam could do nothing about the middle-aged lady who was now occupying his phone booth. He had nervously walked out to check the bridge when she slipped in. She must have been puzzled as to why the young man didn't use the empty booth that stood next to it.

He checked his watch anxiously: 10:45. He knew he couldn't risk waiting a minute after eleven but was confident that Romanov would have traced where he'd made the call from long before then.

The talkative woman was another twelve minutes before she eventually put the phone down. When she stepped out of the booth she gave Adam a warm smile.

Three more minutes and he would have to phone Lawrence and abort his original plan. He began to watch the Beefeaters as they patrolled under Traitors' Gate. Traitors' Gate—how appropriate, Adam thought. He had chosen the spot because he could see clearly up and down the path leading to the drawbridge and felt he could not be taken by surprise. And in desperation there was always the moat that surrounded them on all sides.

For the first time in his life, Adam discovered exactly how long five minutes could be. When the phone rang, it sounded like an alarm bell. He picked it up anxiously, his eyes never leaving the main road.

"Scott?"

"Yes."

"I can now see you clearly, as I am less than one minute away. I will be standing at the end of the bridge by the end of that minute. Be sure you're there with the icon. If you're not, I shall burn the papers that prove your father's innocence in front of you."

The phone went dead.

Adam was delighted that another piece of the jigsaw had fallen into place. He stepped out of the phone booth and checked up and down the road. A BMW motorcycle swerved to a halt at the end of the bridge. A rider dressed in a leather jacket sat astride the bike but only seemed interested in watching the flow of traffic as it passed by the Tower. It was the man seated behind him who stared directly at Adam.

Adam began to walk slowly toward the end of the bridge. He put a hand in his pocket to be sure the icon was still in its place.

He was about thirty yards from the end of the bridge when the second figure got off the bike and started walking toward him. When their eyes met, Romanov stopped in his tracks and held up the small, square frame. Adam did not respond in kind, but simply tapped the side of his pocket and continued walking. Both men advanced toward each other like knights of old until they were only a few paces apart. Almost simultaneously they stopped and faced one another.

"Let me see it," said Romanov.

Adam paused, then slowly removed the icon from his pocket and held it to his chest for his adversary to see. Saint George stared at him.

"Turn it over," said Romanov.

Adam obeyed, and the Russian could not hide his delight when he saw the little silver crown of the Czar embedded in the back.

"Now you," said Adam. Romanov held his icon away from his body, as if brandishing a sword. The masterpiece shone in the summer sun.

"And the documents," said Adam, forcing himself to speak calmly.

The Russian pulled out a package from within his jacket and slowly unfolded them. Adam stared at the official court verdict for a second time.

"Go to the wall," said Adam, pointing with his left hand to the side of the bridge, "and leave the icon and the documents on it."

It was Romanov who now obeyed as Adam proceeded to the wall on the other side of the bridge and placed his icon in the middle of it.

"Cross slowly," called Adam. The two men moved sideways back across the bridge, never getting closer than a couple of yards from each other until they had come to a halt at each other's icon. The moment the painting was within his reach, Romanov grabbed it, ran, and jumped onto the motorcycle without looking back. Within seconds the BMW had disappeared into the dense traffic.

Adam did not move. Although it had only been out of his sight for just over an hour, he was relieved to have the original back. Adam checked the papers that would establish his father's innocence and placed them in his inside pocket. Ignoring the tourists, some of whom had stopped to stare at him, Adam began to relax when suddenly he felt a sharp prod in the middle of his back. He jumped round in fright.

A little girl was staring up at him.

"Will you and your friend be performing again this morning?"

When the BMW motorcycle drew up outside the Soviet embassy in Kensington Palace Gardens, Romanov leaped off and ran up the stairs and straight into the ambassador's office without knocking. The ambassador didn't need to ask if he had been successful.

"It worked out just as I planned. He was taken completely by surprise," said Romanov, as he handed the icon over to the ambassador.

The ambassador turned the painting over and was relieved to see the little silver crown of the Czar. Any doubts he might have had were also dispelled.

"I have orders to send the icon to Washington in the diplomatic pouch immediately. There is no time to be lost."

"I wish I could deliver it in person," said Romanov.

"Be satisfied, Comrade Major, that you have carried out your part of the operation in an exemplary fashion."

The ambassador pressed a button on the side of his desk. Two men appeared immediately. One held open the diplomatic pouch while the other stood motionless by his side. The ambassador handed over the icon and watched it being placed into the pouch. The two couriers looked as if they would have had no trouble in carrying out the ambassador's desk as well, thought Romanov.

"There is a plane standing by at Heathrow to take you both direct to Washington," said the ambassador. "All the necessary documentation for customs has already been dealt with. You should touch down at National Airport around five o'clock Washington time, easily giving our comrades in America enough time to fulfill their part of the contract."

The two men nodded, sealed the diplomatic pouch in the ambassador's presence, and left. Romanov walked over to the window and watched the official car drive the two men out onto Kensington High Street and off in the direction of Heathrow.

"Vodka, Comrade Major?"

"Thank you," Romanov replied, not moving from the window until the car was out of sight.

The ambassador went over to a side cabinet and took out two glasses and a bottle from the refrigerator before pouring Romanov a large vodka.

"It would not be exaggerating to say that you have played your part in establishing the Soviet Union as the most powerful nation on earth," he said as he handed over the drink. "Let us therefore drink to the repatriation of the Aleuts as full citizens of the Union of Soviet Socialist Republics."

"How is that possible?" asked Romanov.

"I think the time has come to let you know," said the ambassador, "the significance of your achievement." He then went on to tell Romanov of the briefing he had received from Moscow that morning.

Romanov was thankful he had never known how much was at stake.

"I have made an appointment to see the Foreign Secretary at three-thirty this afternoon, in order to brief him," the ambassador continued. "We can be sure the British will only be interested in fair play. I am told he is not at all pleased as he had hoped to be in his constituency to open some fête; the British have a strange system for keeping their party system going."

Romanov laughed. "To Aleuts," he said, raising his glass. "But what is happening in Washington at this moment?"

"Our ambassador has already requested a meeting with the American Secretary of State to be scheduled for eight this evening. He is also setting up a press conference at the embassy to follow that meeting. It may amuse you to know that President Johnson had to cancel his visit to Texas this weekend and has requested that the networks should allow him to address 'his fellow Americans' at peak time on Monday on a matter of national importance."

"And we achieved it with only hours to spare," said Romanov, pouring himself another vodka.

"Touch and go, as the English would say. Let us also be thankful for the time difference between here and the United States, because without that we would never have been able to beat the deadline."

Romanov shuddered at the thought of how close it had been and downed his second vodka in one gulp.

"You must join me for lunch, Comrade. Although your orders are to return to Moscow immediately my secretary assures me that the first plane leaving Heathrow for Moscow does not depart until eight this evening. I envy you the reception you will receive when you arrive back at the Kremlin tomorrow."

"I still need the one thousand pounds for . . ."

"Ah yes," said the ambassador, "I have it ready for you." He unlocked the little drawer of his desk and passed over a slim wad of notes in a small cellophane wrapper.

Romanov slipped the tiny packet into his pocket and joined the ambassador for lunch.

Busch barged into Lawrence's office.

"Romanov's got the icon," he shouted.

Lawrence's jaw dropped. A look of desperation appeared on his face. "How can you be so sure?" he demanded.

"I've just had a message from Washington. The Russians have requested an official meeting with the Secretary of State to be arranged for eight this evening."

"I don't believe it," said Lawrence.

"I do," said Busch. "We've always known that God-damned friend of yours, like his father, was a lousy traitor. There's no other explanation."

"He could be dead," said Lawrence quietly.

"I hope he is, for his sake," said Busch.

The phone on Lawrence's desk rang. He grabbed it as if it were a lifeline. "A Dr. John Vance wants a word with you, sir," said his secretary. "He said you had asked him to call."

Vance? Vance? Lawrence recalled the name but couldn't quite place it. "Put him on," he said.

"Good morning, Mr. Pemberton," said a voice.

"Good morning, Dr. Vance. What can I do for you?"

"You asked me to call you after I had examined Scott."

"Scott?" repeated Lawrence, not believing what he was hearing.

"Yes, Adam Scott. Surely you remember? You wanted him to complete a medical for your department."

Lawrence was speechless.

"I've given him a clean bill of health," continued the doctor. "Some cuts and a nasty wound, but nothing that won't heal in a few days."

"Cuts and wounds?" said Lawrence.

"That's what I said, old chap. But don't worry about Scott. He's fit enough to start work whenever you want him. That's if you still want him."

"If I still want him," repeated Lawrence. "Mr. Scott isn't there with you at this moment, by any chance?"

"No," said Vance. "Left my surgery about ten minutes ago."

"He didn't happen to tell you where he was going?" asked Lawrence.

"No, he wasn't specific. Just said something about having to see a friend off at the airport."

Once the coffee had been cleared away, Romanov checked his watch. He had left easily enough time to keep the appointment and still catch the plane. He thanked the ambassador, ran down the embassy steps, and climbed into the back of the anonymous black car.

The driver moved off without speaking as he had already been briefed as to where the major wanted to go.

Neither of them spoke on the short journey, and when the driver drew into Charlotte Street he parked the car in a lay-by. Romanov stepped out and walked quickly across the road. He pressed the bell.

"Are you a member?" said a voice through the intercom.

"Yes," said Romanov, who heard a metallic click as he pushed the door open and walked down the dark staircase. Once he had entered the club it took a few seconds for his eyes to become accustomed to the light. But then he spotted Mentor seated on his own at a little table near a pillar in the far corner of the room.

Romanov nodded and the man, nervously touching his mustache, got up and walked across the dance floor and straight past him. Romanov followed as the member entered the only lavatory. Once inside, Romanov checked whether they were alone. Satisfied, he led them both into a little cubicle and slipped the lock to "engaged." Romanov removed the thousand pounds from his pocket and handed it over to the man who sat down on the lavatory seat. Mentor greedily ripped open the packet, leaned forward, and began to count. He never even saw Romanov straighten his fingers; and when the hand came down with a crushing blow on the back of Mentor's neck he slumped forward and fell to the floor in a heap.

Romanov yanked him up; it took several seconds to gather the ten-pound notes that had fallen to the floor. Once he had them all, he stuffed them into the member's pocket. Romanov then undid the member's fly buttons one by one and pulled down his trousers until they fell around his ankles. He lifted the lid and placed the man on the lavatory seat. The final touch was to pull his legs as wide open as the fallen trousers would allow, the feet splayed apart. Romanov then slipped under the large gap at the bottom of the door, leaving the cubicle locked from the inside. He quickly checked his handiwork. All that could be seen from the outside was the splayed legs and fallen trousers.

Sixty seconds later, Romanov was back in the car on his way to Heathrow.

Adam arrived at Heathrow two hours before the Aeroflot flight was due to depart. He stationed himself with a perfect

view of the forty-yard stretch Romanov would have to walk
to board the Russian aircraft. He felt confident he would
never reach the Aeroflot steps.

Romanov checked in at the BEA desk a little after six. He
couldn't resist taking the BEA flight rather than Aeroflot
even though he knew Zaborski would frown at such arro-
gance; he doubted if anyone would comment on this of all
days.

Once he had been given his boarding card, he took the
escalator to the executive lounge and sat around waiting to
be called. It was always the same—the moment any operation had been completed, all he wanted to do was get home.
He left his seat to pour himself some coffee and, passing a
table in the center of the room, caught the headline on the
London *Evening Standard*. Exclusive. "Johnson Texas Weekend Canceled—Mystery." Romanov grabbed the paper from
the table and read the first paragraph but it contained no information he couldn't have already told them. None of the
speculation in the paragraphs that followed even began to
get near the truth.

Romanov couldn't wait to see the front page of *Pravda* the
next day in which he knew the true story would be embla-
zoned. By Western standards it would be an exclusive.

"BEA announce the departure of their flight 117 to Moscow. Would all first-class passengers now board through
gate number twenty-three." Romanov left the lounge and
walked the half-mile-long corridor to the plane. He strolled
across the tarmac to the waiting plane a few minutes after
six-fifty. The plane carrying the icon would be touching
down in Washington in about two hours. Romanov would
arrive back in Moscow well in time to see Dynamo play
Spartak at the Lenin Stadium on Tuesday. He wondered if
they would announce his arrival to the crowd over the loud-
speakers as they always did when a member of the Politburo
attended a match. Romanov walked up the steps and on

board, stepping over the feet of the passenger next to him, thankful that he had been given the window seat.

"Would you care for a drink before take-off?" the stewardess asked.

"Just a black coffee for me," said his neighbor. Romanov nodded his agreement.

The stewardess arrived back a few moments later with the two coffees and helped the man next to Romanov pull out his table from the armrest. Romanov flicked his over as the stewardess passed him his coffee.

He took a sip but it was too hot so he placed it on the table in front of him. He watched his neighbor take a packet of saccharine from his pocket and flick two pellets into the steaming coffee.

Why did he bother, thought Romanov. Life was too short.

Romanov stared out of the window and watched the Aeroflot plane start to taxi out on to the runway. He smiled at the thought of how much more comfortable his own flight would be.

He tried his coffee a second time: just as he liked it. He took a long gulp and began to feel a little drowsy which he didn't find strange since he had hardly slept for the last week.

He leaned back in his seat and closed his eyes. He would now take every honor the State could offer him. With Valchek conveniently out of the way, he could even position himself to take over from Zaborski. If that failed, his grandfather had left him another alternative.

He was leaving London with only one regret: he had failed to kill Scott. But then he suspected that the Americans would take care of that. For the first time in a week he didn't have to stop himself falling asleep. . . .

Ten minutes later the passenger seated next to Romanov picked up the Russian's coffee cup and put it next to his own. He then flicked Romanov's table back into the armrest and placed a woollen blanket over Romanov's legs. He quickly slipped the BEA eye-shades over the Russian's open eyes. He looked up to find that the stewardess was standing by his side.

"Can I help?" she asked, smiling.

"No, thank you. All he said was that he did not want to be disturbed during the flight as he has had a very hard week."

"Of course, sir," said the stewardess. "We'll be taking off in a few minutes," she added, and picked up the two coffee cups and whisked them away.

The man tapped his fingers impatiently on the little table. At last the chief steward appeared at his side.

"There's been an urgent call from your office, sir. You're to return to Whitehall immediately."

"I had been half expecting it," he admitted.

Adam stared up at the Russian plane as it climbed steeply and swung in a semi-circle toward the east. He couldn't understand why Romanov hadn't boarded it. Surely he wouldn't have taken the BEA flight. Adam slipped back into the shadows the moment he saw him. He stared in disbelief. Lawrence was striding back across the tarmac, a smile of satisfaction on his face.

EPILOGUE

SOTHEBY'S
BOND STREET

LONDON W.1
October 18, 1966

"SOLD FOR FIVE thousand pounds to the gentleman in the center of the room. We now move on to number thirty-two," said the auctioneer, looking down from the raised platform at the front of the crowded room. "An icon of Saint George and the dragon," he declared, as an attendant placed a little painting on the easel next to him. The auctioneer stared down at the faces of experts, amateurs, and curious onlookers. "What am I bid for this magnificent example of Russian art?" he asked expectantly.

Robin gripped Adam's hand. "I haven't felt this nervous since I came face to face with Romanov."

"Don't remind me," said Adam.

"It is, of course, not the original that hangs in the Winter Palace," continued the auctioneer, "but it is nevertheless a fine copy, probably executed by a court painter circa 1890," he added, giving the little painting an approving smile. "Do I have an opening bid? Shall I say eight thousand pounds?"

The next few seconds seemed interminable to Robin and Adam.

"Thank you, sir," said the auctioneer, eventually looking toward an anonymous sign that had been given somewhere at the front of the room.

Neither Adam nor Robin were able to make out where the bid had come from. They had spent the last hour seated at the back of the room watching the previous items coming under the hammer and had rarely been able to work out whose hands they had ended up in.

"How much did the experts say it might go for?" Robin asked again.

"Anywhere between ten and twenty thousand," Adam reminded her.

"Nine thousand," said the auctioneer, his eyes moving to a bid that appeared to come from the right-hand side of the room.

"I still think it's amazing," said Robin, "that the Russians ever agreed to the exchange in the first place."

"Why?" asked Adam. "They got their original back, the Americans extracted the treaty, and I ended up with a copy. As an example of diplomatic ingenuity, it was Lawrence at his most brilliant."

"Ten thousand from the front of the room. Thank you, sir," said the auctioneer.

"What are you going to do with all that money?"

"Buy you a new double bass, get a wedding present for my sister, and hand the rest over to my mother."

"Eleven thousand. A new bidder on the center aisle," said the auctioneer. "Thank you, madam."

"No amount of money can bring back Heidi," said Robin quietly.

Adam nodded thoughtfully.

"How did the meeting with Heidi's parents turn out?"

"The Foreign Secretary saw them personally last week. It couldn't help, but at least he was able to confirm that I had only been telling the truth."

"Twelve thousand." The auctioneer's eyes returned to the front of the room.

"Did you see the Foreign Secretary yourself?"

"Good heavens, no. I'm far too junior for that," said Adam. "I'm lucky if I get to see Lawrence, let alone the Foreign Secretary."

Robin laughed. "I consider you were *lucky* to have been offered a place at the Foreign Office at all."

"Agreed," said Adam, chuckling to himself. "But a vacancy arose unexpectedly."

"What do you mean, unexpectedly?" asked Robin, frustrated by how few of her questions had been answered directly in the last half hour.

"All I can tell you is that one of Lawrence's old team was 'retired early,'" said Adam.

"Was that true of Romanov also?" asked Robin, still desperately trying to discover all that had taken place since they had last met.

"Thirteen thousand," said the auctioneer, his eyes returning to the lady on the center aisle.

"After all, he can't have survived for long once they discovered you had done a switch that gave the Russians back the copy while Romanov ended up presenting you with the original," said Robin.

"He's never been heard of since," admitted Adam innocently. "All our information leads us to believe his boss, Zaborski, is to be replaced by someone called Yuri Andropov."

"Fourteen thousand," said the auctioneer, his eyes settling on the gentleman at the front once again.

"What happened when you produced those court papers proving that it was not your father who had smuggled the poison into Goering's cell?"

"Once that had been authenticated by the Russians," Adam said, "Lawrence paid an official visit to the colonel of the regiment and furnished him with the Foreign Office's conclusions."

"Any reaction?" probed Robin.

"They're going to hold a memorial service in Pa's memory and they have commissioned some fellow called Wood to paint his portrait for the regimental mess. Mother has been invited to unveil it in the presence of all those officers who served with my father."

"Fourteen thousand for the first time then," said the auctioneer, raising the little gavel a few inches in the air.

"She must have been over the moon," said Robin.

"Burst into tears," said Adam. "All she could say was 'I wish Pa could have lived to see it.' Ironic really. If only he had opened that letter."

"Fourteen thousand for the second time," said the auctioneer, the gavel now hovering.

"How do you fancy a celebration lunch at the Ritz?" said Adam, delighted with how well the sale was turning out.

"No, thank you," said Robin.

Adam looked at his companion in surprise.

"It won't be much fun if every time I ask you a question I only get the official Foreign Office briefing."

Adam looked sheepish. "I'm sorry," he said.

"No, that wasn't fair," said Robin. "Now you're on the inside it can't be easy, so I suppose I will have to go to my grave wondering what treaty was inside that icon."

Adam looked away from the girl who had saved his life.

"Destined to remain the Foreign Office's best kept secret," she added.

He turned back slowly to face her.

"Alas . . ." he began, but just at that moment the auctioneer's hammer came down with a thud. They both looked up.

"Sold to the gentleman at the front for fourteen thousand pounds."

"Not a bad price," said Adam, smiling.

"A bargain in my opinion," said Robin.

Adam turned back to her. "After all," he said in a whisper, "imagine what the forty-ninth state would have fetched if it had come up for auction."

A New York Times bestselling novelist
faces the harsh reality of prison life.

A PRISON DIARY
Volume 1

JEFFREY ARCHER

NEW YORK TIMES BESTSELLING
AUTHOR OF *SONS OF FORTUNE*

On July 19, 2001, Jeffrey Archer—international bestselling
author, now known as Prisoner FF8282—was sentenced to four
years in prison and spent the first 22 days in HMP Belmarsh, a
high-security prison that houses some of Britain's most violent
criminals.

During those three weeks, Archer contemplates suicide; he's
moved to the lifer's wing because it's the only place with enough
security to protect him; his cellmate sells a story to the tabloids,
prompting Archer's move to solitary; and prisoners and guards
routinely line up outside his cell to ask him to sign books.

A Prison Diary, Volume 1, is his fascinating account of these events.

"A tale that is not only important but true."
—*The Washington Post*

"Compelling reading. . . . Archer knows how to tell a story."
—*Houston Chronicle*

ISBN: 0-312-32186-4

AVAILABLE WHEREVER BOOKS ARE SOLD
FROM ST. MARTIN'S GRIFFIN

PD1 12/03

Bestselling novelist Jeffrey Archer shares his
experiences of prison life, critiquing the British penal system.

PURGATORY

A Prison Diary: Volume 2

JEFFREY ARCHER

NEW YORK TIMES BESTSELLING
AUTHOR OF *SONS OF FORTUNE*

On August 9, 2001, 22 days after Archer—now known as
Prisoner FF8282—was sentenced to four years in prison for
perjury, he was transferred from a maximum security prison
in London to HMP Wayland, a medium security prison in
Norfolk. For the next 67 days, as he waited to be reclassified
for an "open," minimum security prison, he encountered not
only the daily degradations of a dangerously overstretched
prison system but also the spirit and courage of his fellow
inmates.

Purgatory: A Prison Diary, Volume 2 is Archer's frank,
shocking, sometimes humorous, sometimes horrifying,
account of those 67 days.

"His dialogue sparkles, his narrative is taut and compelling
while his cast of criminal characters stays credible."
—*Mail On Sunday*

ISBN: 0-312-33098-7

AVAILABLE WHEREVER BOOKS ARE SOLD
COMING IN JULY IN HARDCOVER FROM ST. MARTIN'S PRESS

PD2 12/03